EXCLUSION ZONE

EXCLUSION ZONE

John Nichol

Hodder & Stoughton

British Library Cataloguing in Publication Data

ISBN 0 340 67185 8

Typeset by Hewer Text Ltd, Edinburgh
Printed and bound in Great Britain by
Clays Ltd, St Ives plc, Bungay, Suffolk

Hodder and Stoughton
A division of Hodder Headline PLC
338 Euston Road
London NW1 3BH

Dedication

In 1982, two hundred and fifty seven British Servicemen gave their lives during the war to re-capture the Falkland Islands. This book is dedicated to their memory and to the hope that history will not repeat itself.

EXCLUSION ZONE

Chapter 1

Even after 4,000 miles of unbroken grey ocean, the first sight of land appearing under the wing of the Tristar was something of an anticlimax. From 5,000 feet the landscape looked as dull and monochrome as the water surrounding it, and the dun-coloured hills as barren as the desert I had just left.

There was a stir among the other passengers as a shape as sleek and predatory as a shark appeared in the sky to the west. It rocketed towards the Tristar, shrinking the gap between us in seconds, pale sunlight flashing from its wings.

The Tempest pulled a hard turn, then took up station on one side of us, the aircrafts' wingtips no more than ten feet apart.

Jane and the aircrew around me adopted poses of studied nonchalance, but there were gasps from the other passengers. Few of them had ever seen a fighter this close and there was a rush to one side of the jet to take photographs.

The pilot's face was invisible behind his dark visor, but he raised a gloved hand in greeting.

Jane laughed. 'Poser.'

I shifted my gaze to the small town nestled around the harbour. It was a curious combination of the strange and the familiar. White houses were laid out in neat rows under a patchwork of red, green and blue tin roofs, but there was not a tree to be seen and the few roads looked to be dirt, not tarmac.

I felt Jane's hand warm against the bare flesh of my arm as she leaned past me to stare out of the window. 'That's the capital? Imagine what the rest must be like. Shit, it looks like New Zealand on a bad day.'

'My God, we must be in Oz.'

She smiled. 'Very funny, Sean.'

The Tristar swept over the hills and banked for its final approach. The main runway and the shorter emergency strip intersecting it formed a grey cross cut into the landscape. Towards the north, there was a white flash on the hillside, then it disappeared behind a line of cloud and a curtain of silver rain.

Jane settled back in her seat. 'Four months – Jesus, what have we done to deserve this?'

I said nothing. I was staring out of the window at the ghosts in the clouds.

Gusts of wind shook the plane on its approach. It yawed and slipped sideways as it hit pockets of turbulence. The red windsock at the end of the runway was taut and streaming parallel to the ground.

Jane nudged me in the ribs. 'It's got to be gusting at least fifty knots. We shouldn't even be trying to land.'

I smiled. 'If you aren't happy, tell the Captain, I'm sure

he'd love to fly us back to Ascension. We can always come back tomorrow and try again.'

She laughed. 'We could give Rio a shot instead.'

I intercepted the anxious looks from an elderly couple across the aisle and gave them my reassuring face. Then I turned back to the wall of cloud and watched the raindrops streak the Perspex.

That one brief glimpse of the hillside had been enough. Surprised at myself – it had been sixteen years after all – I tried to compose my thoughts, concentrating on the changing note of the engine and the rumble of the flaps and landing gear, until we were down with a thud that drew an involuntary yelp from the old woman across the aisle. The engines thundered, then the jet swung off the main runway and slowed to a halt.

The engines wound down and stopped, and there was a moment of silence, broken only by the rustle of clothing as the passengers got to their feet. Then the door of the Tristar swung open and I heard a roar.

'What's that?' Jane asked.

The man across the aisle paused in his struggle with the overhead locker. 'That's the wind, my dear. Better get used to it. Whatever else, you always have the wind here.' His clothes marked him out as a farmer and he addressed Jane as if they were separated by the width of a ten-acre field. I reached up and helped him free his bags, then headed for the exit.

The rain had already stopped and patches of shadow chased each other across the glistening tarmac as clouds raced overhead. Rows of functional buildings clustered on the north side of the runway. The only trace of colour was the blue glass of the control tower.

At the far end of the runway, mounds of earth and rubble, piled up like spoil heaps from a mine, hid the sheds housing the

Tempests we had come almost nine thousand miles to fly. I let my gaze travel on over the surrounding hills, their peaks capped with snow, stark against the umber peat cladding the slopes.

There was a gentle push in the small of my back. 'Like I said, Sean, we've got four months for sightseeing, though four minutes would be plenty, as far as I can see.'

The farmer pushed past, scowling.

'Nice going, Jane. So much for hearts and minds. We've only been here two minutes and you've already pissed off one of the natives.'

'Make that two,' the man's wife said as she passed us. 'We don't like swearing here and if you knew anything about these islands, you'd know that we don't like being called natives either. We aren't; we just happen to have been here longer than anybody else. When our ancestors came here, it was completely uninhabited. We built this place from nothing.'

'Thanks for the history less—' Jane began, but I cut across her.

'So what do we call you?'

'Kelpers is fine, or Falklanders. You could even use our names, if you like.'

I held out my hand. 'Sean Riever and Jane Clark. Pleased to meet you. And I'm sorry we—'

'Riever? That's an unusual name.'

I smiled. 'Not where I come from. There are hundreds of us in the west of Ireland.'

She inclined her head. 'I only know of one. You don't have any connections here, do you?'

'No, not living ones.'

She seemed about to say more, then thought better of it. 'George and Agnes Moore. We live at Clay Hill, a few miles this side of Goose Green. Be sure to call, if you're passing.

And I hope you'll enjoy your time here. You'll find we're very like our islands. Some find us dull and cold—' she glanced reprovingly at Jane – 'but those who can get past the surface impressions find there's no better place to be.' She gave a brief smile, then turned and hurried away after her husband.

I felt the familiar impact of Jane's elbows in my ribs. 'That put you in your place, didn't it?'

'That's funny, I thought she was talking to you.'

'Right,' she said, linking arms. 'That's enough diplomacy for one day. Now let's get out of this wind.'

We came out of the lea of the Tristar and struggled towards the terminal, the gale snatching away the few words we tried to exchange. Even inside, the noise of the wind was like the roar of an idling jet engine. I found myself raising my voice just to make myself heard.

The civilian passengers hurried away towards waiting friends and relatives. The men were all dressed in tweeds and battered Barbours. Their wives wore head scarves and thick quilted jackets, the colours as muted as the surrounding hills.

'They all look like Irish farmers on market day.'

'Except they're not pissed.'

'I said Irish, not Australian.'

Two figures in RAF uniforms were waiting for us. The older man, a Group Captain, gave an uncertain smile as we strolled up to him arm in arm, then held out his hand. 'Welcome to Fortress Falklands. I'm David Prince, Base Commander, but I answer to "Boss".'

'Sean Riever. This is my nav, Jane Clark. She's on exchange from the Australian Air Force.'

He noted my accent. 'A blond-haired, blue-eyed Irishman?'

'We're not all beetle-browed Celts; the Vikings invaded Ireland too.'

He flexed his fingers like a pianist. 'I know Ulster well, it's a beautiful countr—' He flushed, '– province. What part are you from?'

'I'm not. I'm from Kerry. And Jane's ancestors were transported to Australia from County Wicklow . . . but don't worry, we've both been positively vetted.'

He gestured awkwardly to the man alongside him. 'This is Flight Lieutenant Michael Halliday, better known as Shark. He's been here for two months now, which makes him practically a veteran.'

Shark smoothed his sleek black hair. 'I'll probably be taking you on your familiarisation flight tomorrow. I hope you like peat bogs, because there's nothing much else to see around here.' He favoured Jane with the predatory smile that had obviously earned him his nickname. 'Or not until now anyway. This way to the squadron taxi.'

Leaving the Boss to greet the rest of the guys, he led us to a battered Land Rover painted in the red and white squadron colours. As he went round to the driver's side, Jane leaned across and whispered in my ear, 'Jesus, that bloke fancies himself.'

I nodded. 'Someone's got to; it might as well be him.'

'I'll take you over to the accommodation block first,' Shark said. 'We call it the Death Star. You'll see why the first time you fly over it. The layout's so confusing I guarantee you'll get lost at least six times in the first twenty-four hours.

'You'll not have time to do much more than dump your bags in your rooms for the moment though. There's a briefing with the outgoing crews at 1800 hours and they won't want to be kept waiting.' He grinned. 'After four months here, all they want to do is get drunk and hit that homeward-bound Tristar as quick as they can.'

We threw our bags in the back and jumped in as Shark

gunned the engine. He drove straight across the runway towards the south side of the airfield.

The Death Star was a two-storey wooden construction, put together from interlinked, prefabricated sections. Wings jutted out from the central hub like the spokes of a wheel. There were also some single-storey detached blocks around the edge of the domestic site.

'What are they?'

Shark followed my gaze. 'Chalets for senior officers. They're welcome to them, they have to do a twelve-month tour, poor sods.'

The Land Rover screeched to a halt, throwing up a cloud of dust that was instantly whisked away on the wind. He led us into the lobby and waved his hand around. 'See what I mean?'

Eight identical corridors stretched away from us, painted dull red and cream and punctuated at precise intervals by slit windows like the embrasures in a medieval castle.

'Think this is bad?' Shark said. 'It's only half of it. Go upstairs and you'll see exactly the same thing again. Okay, accommodation's on the top floor. Any empty room is up for grabs. Take your pick. After that I'll show you Fighter Town.'

As he led us along one of the corridors, I could still hear the howl of the wind outside and the rhythmic creaking of the wooden building in response. Cold draughts whistled through every chink in the walls. Jane shivered and pulled her coat closer around her. 'Not exactly Bondi Beach, is it?'

Shark led us up a flight of stairs and along another featureless corridor, then waited as we chose our rooms. I took one looking north across the airfield towards the hills. Jane chose the one next door, flushing a little at Shark's knowing smile. We dumped our bags on the beds then followed him back downstairs and along yet another corridor.

The first interruption to the endless red and cream paintwork was a large, laboriously hand-painted sign: FIGHTER TOWN, MOUNT PLEASANT AIRFIELD – HOME OF THE FALCONS.

'They wouldn't let you spoil their paintwork back home.'

Shark shrugged. 'They couldn't really stop you here, there's nothing else to do except get drunk.' He smiled. 'And there's no shortage of opportunities for that. At the last count there were 360 bars – official and unofficial – on the base. Mind you, once the Mess has closed, any room with a fridge qualifies. The Boss keeps trying to shut down a few of them but he knows better than to mess with ours. The Herc, Tempest and Heli crew bars are always open.'

We passed a few open doorways, glimpsing the usual chaos of maps, papers and polystyrene cups. The wall space between the offices was crowded with painted badges of every squadron that had served in the Falklands. Every crew member had signed his name underneath.

I saw a few familiar ones enclosed in a coffin-shaped border – Drew Miller, Steve Alderson, Mark Hunter. Shark nodded. 'They're the dead ones.' He pointed towards another wall black with RAF name badges. 'Everyone pins up their badge before they leave. If people die, we turn them upside down.'

None of us spoke as we walked past the wall. I knew most of the case-histories; for every person who had died in combat, scores had been killed in training accidents, so routine they rated no more than a brief paragraph in *RAF News*.

When we reached the end of the corridor, Shark threw open a door with a flourish. 'This is The Goose, the bar for 1435 Flight.'

The room appeared to have been furnished from a car-boot sale. There were knackered armchairs, sprouting springs and stuffing, two beaten-up cupboards and a chipped table. A small kitchen off to one side housed only a sink and three ceiling-high fridges.

The walls and shelves of the bar were crammed with the usual collection of squadron photographs and plaques, augmented by a sizeable collection of captured Argentine badges of rank, helmets, weapons, and a wing section from a downed Pucara, its metal skin puckered by the blast holes that had brought it down. The effect was completed by a stuffed ginger tom-cat on a wooden plinth, an old ejector seat from a Tempest and an inflatable sheep.

Shark smirked. 'That's just for the guys who get desperate.'

'It seems to recognise you,' Jane said.

I stifled a laugh. 'What's with the cat?'

'That's Rambo. He was the 1435 Flight mascot. He only came back from the taxidermist's a couple of weeks ago. He was the last member of the squadron to die in combat.' He stroked the cat's fur as he waited for one of us to rise to the bait.

'I give in,' Jane said. 'What happened?'

'He lived up to his name. He attacked one of the police dogs and put it in the vet's. The MPs insisted that he had to be destroyed. We gave him a funeral with full military honours, including a fly-past.' He smiled. 'Don't tell the tabloids; it must have cost about ten thousand quid.'

I strode to the window and looked out. 'Why is everything built of concrete or wood? There aren't any trees around here and it must be cheaper to build with local stone than import stuff from halfway around the world.'

'There's nothing here you can build with; it's the wrong sort of stone apparently. The only other indigenous material is peat and that wouldn't last long in this wind. They burn it on their fires; going into some of those settlements is like stepping back in time.'

I glanced at the walls. Among the photographs were a few pictures painted directly on to the plaster: a couple of amateurish depictions of air combat and some cartoons of Falklands life, mostly featuring sheep, and an unfinished landscape, which was a wistful painting of a misty English scene, its colours so faded that it must have been there for years.

'This guy was obviously pretty homesick,' I said. 'Couldn't he bear to finish it?'

'Something like that,' Shark said. 'He died. Apparently he took off on a training sortie and just flew straight and level smack into the side of Mount Wickham. Killed himself and his nav. The painting was left unfinished as a mark of respect.' He saw the question in my eyes and shrugged his shoulders. 'The investigators called it pilot error; the implication was that it was suicide, but I can't imagine anyone deliberately murdering his crewmate however rough things get, can you?'

There was a long silence. He glanced at his watch. 'Anyway, so much for the guided tour, let's get over to the operational site for the briefing.'

The wind knifed through me as we came out of the building. Flecks of sleet stung my cheeks. We scrambled into the Land Rover and I had to drag the door shut with both hands as the wind tried to snatch it away.

Shark glanced down the length of the runway. 'We'll have to wait for Fat Albert.' A Hercules was coming in to land. The Land Rover rocked on its springs in the gusting wind. I watched the black, pregnant belly of the

Hercules judder and yaw. 'Rather him than me. Jesus! Look at that.'

As it crossed the lighting stanchions, one of its massive wings dipped towards the tarmac. Then it swung ponderously back through the vertical as the pilot hauled on the controls.

The opposite wing dipped, then it levelled and dropped like a brick onto the runway, its tyres adding more thick, black streaks to the scarred surface.

Shark shook his head. 'If the Argentinians ever want to stage another invasion they needn't bomb the airfield, they could just send a Herc on a goodwill visit. If one of those went belly-up, it'd close the runway for a fortnight.'

He put the car into gear and drove across the empty tarmac. The Tristar hangar was twice the size of any other building on the site and only the control tower was taller. An old Phantom jet was perched on a pillar nearby. Beyond it were the Fire Section, the Met building and the compound for the civilian helicopters. There was also a boiler house, dwarfed by its cooling tower and smoke stack.

As Shark pulled up outside the Ops Centre he pointed to an ugly grey concrete building next to it. 'If you like gourmet eating, you're in for a treat. That's the Mess. We call it "Chips" because that's about all you can get there.'

The briefing room was nearly full. The ground troops and the other six aircrew who had flown out with us were lounging on the benches. The departing crew sprawled around the room looked as if they had already begun their celebrations.

I nodded to a few familiar faces, friends from other squadrons, and joined in the banter for a few minutes until the Boss strolled to the podium clutching a sheaf of notes.

He glanced briefly around the room. 'Welcome to the last outpost of Empire, a vital part of our defensive commitments.

You may think that there is no threat, but sixteen years after the Falklands War, we're still at Military Vigilance here. Those of you who have not served on a frontline base in a war zone before will find some things a little strange and maybe even alarming at first.' He paused and gave a reassuring smile.

'The defence of the Falklands boils down to the protection of a strip of concrete here at Mount Pleasant. Nothing else matters. The nuclear submarine, HMS *Trident*, patrolling the Exclusion Zone, the guardship, HMS *Sea Wolf*, in Mare Harbour, the Rapier missile sites on the hilltops, and the detachment of four hundred Royal Marines, including this week's new arrivals—' he inclined his head towards the troops on the benches – 'are all here for that purpose and no other.

'Our first line of defence is 1435 Flight, equipped with Tempest GR7s – for the non-aircrew here, that's the latest generation of fighter/ground-attack aircraft – which are on permanent Quick Reaction Alert, at fifteen minutes notice to get airborne and protect the Exclusion Zone. To assist them in that task, they can be armed with Skyflash and Sidewinder air-to-air missiles, Sea Eagle air-to-surface missiles and CRV7 rocket pods. We also have mountains of old-fashioned iron bombs.

'The Rapier sites augment that air defence, while Trident and Sea Wolf are added insurance against seaborne attack, but the runway at Mount Pleasant is where it starts and finishes. Our task is to keep it open at all costs, not merely so that we can fly sorties ourselves but, much more important, so that the Cobra Force reinforcements – two further Tempest squadrons and two thousand ground troops – can be flown in during any fresh crisis.'

He glanced towards the Marines. 'Unless there are any questions, the remainder of the briefing is for the air and ground crews only. I hope you all enjoy your time here.'

He waited as the soldiers filed out, his hand straying upwards to rearrange the few wisps of hair covering his pate. As the door closed behind the last of them, he cleared his throat. 'The Marines are here to defend the perimeter, but in any alert, all base personnel will be issued with weapons.'

He paused, confident that he had everyone's attention. 'At the first hint of any impending trouble, you will be issued with an SA-80 and we expect you to be able to use it effectively. Some of you will not have laid hands on a weapon in earnest since your basic training, but you will all be required to do regular firing practice on the ranges here.

'Any man who does not meet the exacting standards set by our weapons instructor, Jack Stubbs, will find himself returning to the ranges again and again until he does. Mount Pleasant has a small garrison and every man – and woman – must play their full part in the defence of the base. The runway is what keeps the Falklands British. Lose it and we lose the Falklands too.'

There was a murmur of 'Good riddance,' from somewhere at the back of the room.

David ignored the interruption. 'Despite what you may have heard, the Falklands isn't a punishment block – a gulag for dissident aircrew.' He gave a weary smile at the barracking from those departing. 'I admit it's no Cyprus,' he said, raising his voice to be heard above the hubbub, 'but there's just enough activity from the Argentinians to keep us all on our toes and there's some great flying to be had here.

'I must stress one point, however. I know you're nine thousand miles from home, and there are no factories, MPs, or Nimbies to worry about here, but we still stick to the rules. Anyone exceeding permitted speeds or dropping below minimum permitted levels over land will be in trouble. Noel?'

A sandy-haired squadron leader with a corned-beef complexion rose to his feet. 'I'll keep this short. We all have better things to do tonight. The Boss is absolutely right, though I have to tell you that this is the only place in the world where people phone up to complain because they haven't had low-flying jets over their houses.'

He waited for the rumble of laughter to fade. 'Our job is to police the Exclusion Zone, which extends in a one hundred and fifty mile radius from Mount Pleasant Airfield. The radar sites see three hundred miles out and warn us of incoming trade, so there should be plenty of warning, but the motto here is "No surprises".' He smiled. 'Not that we're expecting any. The quality of Intelligence on enemy aircraft movements suggests we may also have men on the ground inside Argentina with eyes on the airfields at Rio Grande and Rio Gallegos.

'There's been no real pattern to Argentine air activity recently. There was a flurry of incidents three weeks ago, but nothing much since then, though they regularly probe the edge of the Exclusion Zone, testing the capability of our radar and our reaction times. They tend to come in at low-level, pop up to have a look, then high-tail it back before we even get them visual.

'We're at Readiness State 15 and you do nine nights on Quick Reaction Alert and five nights off. You've timed your arrival perfectly, because you'll get five days off before beginning your first spell of QRA on Saturday. We fly with live weapons at all times, though the chances of authorisation to use them coming down the chain from London in time to stop an Argentine invasion are pretty slim.' He acknowledged the laughter from his audience. 'Intruders are warned, intercepted, escorted down, and shot down in that order; or that's the theory anyway.

'There are a couple of routines we observe here that you should know about. On take-off every jet will do a Fiery Cross, as we call it – a simulated attack run across the airfield.' He gave an apologetic smile. 'We have a lot of very bored radar, missile and gun crews sitting in Portakabins on hilltops for months on end. The least we can do is to give them some occasional entertainment. The Hercs do the same thing, except we call it a Smoky Cross, since they never get up enough speed to ignite the fires.

'We also stage an intercept on every aircraft coming in to Mount Pleasant, which basically boils down to the twice-weekly Tristar and the charter-flights from Argentina bringing relatives to visit their war graves. Give the Tristar as close a buzz as you wish – they're used to it – but for your own and the Argentinians' safety, give those charter flights plenty of room. They tend to be nervous about flying in here.'

'Intelligence brief.' A dark-haired woman in her early thirties but with the look of a 1950s librarian stood up, smoothing out imaginary creases from her pencil skirt. One or two of the aircrew wolf-whistled mechanically and she flushed a little in response, though I felt sure that the same tired scenario had been played out at every Intelligence briefing since she arrived.

'A very confused picture at the moment, I'm afraid.'

'Louder.'

She paused, cleared her throat and began again. 'You may have seen some slightly alarming news reports from Argentina in the last few days, but we have no reason to believe they are anything other than the traditional macho posturing. However, the Government in Buenos Aires has made a manifesto pledge to regain the Falklands by the year 2000 and the discovery of oil in the northern sector of the Exclusion Zone will certainly do nothing to cool their ardour.

'On the military front, the good news is that Intelligence suggests that their Air Force Mirages and Daggers are wasting assets. They saw long service with France and Israel before being bought by Argentina, and have been in service with them for twenty years now. They're increasingly unreliable and it is questionable how many they could get airborne in a crisis.'

'Unlike our Tempests, of course,' Noel said.

The Intelligence Officer gave him an uncertain smile. 'The bad news – and there's plenty of it – is that Peru has recently bought thirty Mig 29 Fulcrums.' She paused and glanced around the room. 'That is a suspiciously large number, far in excess of Peru's own realistic needs. We have no solid proof of it as yet, but Intelligence suggests that the Peruvians may be warehousing at least a dozen of them for Argentina. There are reports that Argentinian pilots have been training on them in Peru.

'As you know, the Fulcrum is a very fast, agile and capable aircraft. It's an alarming development, particularly in the light of the other bad news: President Clinton's lifting of the arms embargo on South America which has allowed Argentina to significantly upgrade its weapon systems. Coupled with the suspected purchase of the Fulcrums, it has given them a Beyond Visual Range attack capacity for the first time.

'They also have two squadrons of Skyhawk bombers which though elderly, are still viable, and the navy has its Super Etendards. In theory the French have held to the EC embargo and refused to supply them with Exocets; in practice, it would not be a complete surprise if they had some.

'There have been reports of a build-up of troops around Rio Gallegos but nothing of any significance. Their navy's only remaining cruiser, the *Eva Peron*, left Rio Gallegos two days ago with an escorting guardship, the destroyer *La Argentina*, but that appears to be for routine manoeuvres. They're running north parallel to the coast at the moment, near the territorial limit. Obviously we're keeping a close watch on the situation.'

She gave Noel a sideways glance and a nervous smile, then sat down as he stepped back to the podium.

'Just two more vital pieces of business. Familiarisation flights for all incoming aircrew begin tomorrow morning, briefing 0800 hours. The lateness of that briefing is not unconnected to the final piece of information I have to communicate: welcome drinks for the new crews and bon voyage drinks for those lucky sods going home tomorrow will begin as soon as I've finished speaking. Whoever's getting the first round, mine's a pint.'

There was a ragged cheer and a stampede for the door, but I hung back a little as the rest of the crews disappeared in the direction of the Mess. 'What's up?' Jane said. 'It's not like you to hesitate when there's free drink on offer.'

'I know, it's just that ... Listen, I'll get some fresh air and join you in there in a couple of minutes.'

'No need to go outside then, there's plenty whistling through the cracks in the walls.'

I didn't respond to the joke.

'Are you all right?' she asked.

'Fine.' I saw her doubtful look. 'Honestly. I just need a couple of minutes on my own.'

She shrugged, then walked away down the corridor.

I buttoned my jacket and stepped outside. I stood motionless for a few minutes, staring into the gathering dusk, then turned and made my way to the control tower.

I climbed the stairs and nodded to the crew lounging in their chairs, their feet propped on the desks. 'Sean Riever. I'm with 1435 Flight. Mind if I look around?'

'Help yourself,' one said, 'but you'll soon be heartily sick of the view, I can promise you.'

There were no more incoming flights that day and the radar screens were blank save for the clouds of green traces, as faint as dust motes, showing the flocks of sea-birds returning to their roosts.

A fat marmalade cat uncurled itself from the in-tray, where it had been sleeping. It gave me a disdainful look, yawned and stretched, then stalked to the other end of the desk and lay down again in the out-tray.

'Another busy day over Boddington?' one of the crew asked, ruffling its fur. It ignored him and began grooming itself.

I walked to the far side of the tower and pressed my forehead against the blue-tinted glass, blocking out the dim lights inside the control room as I stared out over the airfield. Rough stone sangars were dotted at intervals along the perimeter track and clustered around the low mounds concealing the bomb dumps and fuel stores. Beyond them, the razor wire of the fence glinted red in the low light of the setting sun. There was not a human being in sight, no visible movement and no sound but the steady moan of the wind.

Pleasant Peak's long shadow across the runway blurred and faded into the surrounding darkness as the red rim of the sun sank below the horizon and the brown of the hillside darkened to a velvet black.

Nothing broke the gloom but the gleaming white fuselage of the Tristar by its cavernous hangar and the white quartz boulders of the memorial on the hillside. I kept staring out until the darkness deepened and the fading, ghost-grey outline of the stones became as faint as old memories. Then I turned without speaking, walked back down the stairs and out into the night.

A wall of noise, cigarette smoke and beer fumes greeted me as I pushed open the door of the Mess. In between Falklands horror stories, the departing aircrew were drowning the last taste of their four-month tour in a tide of cold lager.

I caught a glimpse of Jane through the scrum as I pushed my way to the bar and ordered a drink. As I turned to survey the room, I found Shark at my elbow. 'She's a good looking woman, isn't she?'

I smiled to myself, knowing where the conversation was leading. 'She's a good navigator too.'

'And are you . . .?' He hesitated.

I shook my head. 'We work together, that's all.'

A smile began to spread across Shark's face. 'So you wouldn't mind if—'

'I'm not Jane's guardian, she can do whatever she likes. You should be having this conversation with her, not me.' I paused. 'But she is going out with my best mate.'

Shark stared at me for a moment, his mouth frozen like a fish struggling for breath.

I took a long pull on my beer as he walked away.

'What was that about?' I almost spilled my drink. Jane had sidled up to the bar just behind me.

She laughed. 'You'd better have another one, your nerves are obviously playing up.'

I gave a rueful smile. 'It was the shock. I was afraid you might have heard me slagging you off.'

'What were you really talking about?'

'The only thing anyone ever wants to talk to me about these days. Shark was checking out his chances.'

'With you?'

'No, the sheila from Guneela.'

'And what did you tell him?'

'That he'd have to get in the queue with the rest of the Falklands garrison.'

She signalled to the barman. 'That was almost a compliment, Sean, now I'm definitely going to buy you another drink.'

We chatted for a few more minutes, then I stood up, stretched and yawned. 'I'm knackered. I'm going to hit the sack.'

She nodded. 'Me too, I never can get any sleep in an aircraft.'

'Just as well, considering what you do for a living.'

As we headed for the door, there was a burst of beery banter. I exchanged a resigned look with Jane, then acknowledged the shouts and catcalls with a raised hand and a smile. We shook hands with a few of the outgoing aircrew and then walked off down the corridor, more ribald shouts echoing in our ears.

As Shark had predicted, we were soon lost among the maze of identical corridors, but after two false starts we found ours. Jane paused outside my door. As she said goodnight, she held my gaze for a moment and laid a hand on my arm. Then she kissed my cheek and walked slowly down the corridor.

I was still staring after her when she paused on the threshold of her own room and glanced back. She hesitated a moment, a half-smile on her lips, then stepped inside and softly closed her door, leaving a faint trace of her perfume on the air.

Tired though I was, I could not get to sleep for some time. I tossed and turned, then reached up and opened the curtains. I lay back in the darkness.

I awoke bolt upright, streaming with sweat, my heart pounding. Faceless, steel-helmeted figures had been advancing over a black hill towards me. White rock, like bone, jutted from the ground beneath their feet and the stink of decay carried to me on the wind.

I shuddered, got out of bed and rinsed my face with cold water. I put on the light and read for a while before settling down to sleep, but I could not shake off a sense of foreboding. The images from my nightmare stayed in my mind with every creak as the building flexed in the wind.

I shifted my position and lay with my eyes open watching the clouds scudding over the black, huddled mass of the hills, as the sky slowly lightened towards dawn.

Chapter 2

When I knocked on Jane's door at seven-thirty the next morning, there was a muffled reply. I stuck my head round the door. 'Come on, even you can't oversleep the first mor—' I stopped as I heard the shower. 'I'll go on ahead, see you at breakfast.'

'No, wait for me. I'll only be a minute.'

I sat down on the end of the unmade bed and glanced around the room. We had only been there twelve hours but already it looked as if a bomb had been detonated in her suitcase, blowing clothes, papers, books, magazines and tissues all over the room.

On her bedside table was a pyramid-shaped, Japanese talking alarm clock and a photograph in a battered leather frame. I picked it up; three familiar faces, side-lit by the lurid glare of Las Vegas neon. Jane was in the middle, one arm round Geoff's shoulders, the other round mine.

'Hope you haven't been reading my diary too.' Jane emerged from the bathroom, wrapped in a towel.

I gave a guilty start and put the photograph down. 'No, I only read non-fiction.'

'Well, can you get interested in something for a minute while I put my clothes on?'

'Apart from you putting your clothes on, you mean?'

'You're not interested in that.'

'Don't bet on it.'

She paused, still looking at me, and there was a brief, uncomfortable silence. Then she turned her back, shrugged the towel from her shoulders and wriggled into a tee-shirt. She pulled on her flying-suit and fixed the silver chain of a pendant around her neck.

'That's new, isn't it?'

Her hand closed around it. 'Geoff's grandad gave it to his granny the day he went off to fight in the First World War. It has a tiny picture of him inside it. His granny gave it to Geoff's mother and now—' She paused, her expression unreadable. 'Geoff gave it to me on Sunday night.'

She dragged a comb through her tangle of damp, blonde hair, then grabbed her flying jacket and looked at her watch. 'Not bad, eh? Five minutes, start to finish.'

'I know, and that hedge-backwards look is so of the moment, don't you think?'

'Listen, Sean, if I took an extra five minutes to get ready, I'd be so drop-dead gorgeous you wouldn't be able to stand it.'

'I can't stand it already.'

I was moving for the door as she reached behind her. The wet towel slapped harmlessly against the wall where my head had been resting only half a second before.

After breakfast, I checked the pairings for the familiarisation flights that morning. I was less than totally surprised to see that Shark had arranged things so that he was flying with Jane, while I was paired with Noel.

Shark took the briefing himself. 'Now the departing drunks are safely aboard the Tristar, we can get down to some serious work; nothing too heavy this morning though, just a famil flight. We'll be doing a Fiery Cross to keep the gun and missile crews awake, then a quick tour of the Falklands.

'There are two main islands and about seven hundred smaller ones, and you'll be seeing most of them in the next couple of hours. There are radar sites on Mount Kent, Byron Heights and half a dozen other places we'll be pointing out to you.

'Flying conditions here are exactly what you would expect: constant wind predominantly from the west or south-west, and quite serious turbulence, particularly over the cliffs on West Falkland. As you saw for yourselves on the way in, East Falkland is more low-lying, apart from the central ridge of hills.

'The airfield has been cleverly laid out so that any attacking aircraft can hide behind Pleasant Peak before making their attack run. That's it. Jimmy?'

'Weather brief.' Jimmy was a dour-looking Scot with a pinched face and prominent nose. At bases in the UK, the Met-man was invariably a civilian, full-time meteorologist. In the Falklands there were no such luxuries. Jimmy was a navigator, doubling as a Met-man. His air of permanent gloom had earned him the nickname 'Happy', but it was rarely if ever used to his face.

'You can get all four seasons in five minutes down here,' he said. 'The good news is you're only going to get three of them today, the bad news is the one you won't get is summer. Winds south-westerly, forty knots gusting to sixty, and strengthening late in the day, squalls of rain, hail, sleet and snow coming through like the Four Horsemen of the Apocalypse. Visibility moderate, dropping to poor in the squalls.'

'Survival brief.'

Jimmy resumed his seat, replaced at the podium by a tough-looking soldier with iron-grey hair and a lean, wind-burned face. He wore fatigues, with no markings or badges of rank. I guessed he was Special Forces.

'My name's Jack Stubbs. I double as survival instructor and weapons instructor, so you'll be seeing plenty of me on the firing ranges. The rules of survival here are pretty obvious. Your biggest enemy – apart from the Argentinians – is the cold and wet. The South Atlantic is well-equipped in both departments. Stay out of it if you can, but if you do have to ditch, your friendly neighbourhood Sea King will be with you in somewhere between ten minutes and an hour, depending how close you are to the edge of the Exclusion Zone when you hit the drink. Even in the worst case, your survival is assured, providing you're wearing your immersion suit. If you're not, it's been nice knowing you.

'On what's laughingly referred to as dry land, your priority is the same: avoid the cold and wet. The Falklands may technically be in the temperate zone but wind-chill is a definite hazard. Your first priority must be shelter, both from the wind and the rain.

'Your other survival skills are only likely to be tested in the unlikely event of your Tacbe and your back-up communications both failing simultaneously, but there are a couple of hundred uninhabited islands you might be unlucky enough to land on, so don't automatically expect that you'll be found and rescued in the time it takes to powder your nose.'

I could sense Jane's hackles rising, though he hadn't even glanced in her direction.

'If you do have to go into combat survival mode or if you're forced into Escape and Evasion—' he stilled the beginnings of laughter with a glance— 'they were probably laughing at the idea in 1982 as well, until the Argentinians invaded. As I was saying, if you do go into combat survival or E & E, one thing you definitely won't be short of here is water. It's everywhere and providing you sterilise it with Puritabs, it's safe to drink ... unless you collect it from the middle of a minefield. Food shouldn't be a problem either, but be aware that the rabbit snares in your survival packs are a waste of space; there are no rabbits or other small animals worth trapping.

'Inland, you can kill the first sheep you come across – and even some of the uninhabited islands have those – catch fish, the rivers are stuffed full of them, or eat tussac grass. You peel back the outer leaves and eat the soft heart. It's surprisingly palatable, in fact; it tastes a bit like chestnut.'

'No, it doesn't,' Jane breathed. 'It tastes a bit like shit.'

His eyes flickered towards her, but he never broke stride. 'If you can get to the coast – and let's face it, that shouldn't be too much of a problem in the Falklands, even on E & E – the shoreline is literally crawling with food. There are four or five kinds of crabs, half a dozen sorts of mussels and about fifty other edible species. Stay off the albatross, seals and penguins though. They're all protected species.'

'What about sea-bird eggs?' The questioner, Rees, was the junior pilot on the squadron. His fair hair and unnaturally pink skin made him look even younger than his twenty-three years.

'Sound thinking, son. If you can just manage to keep from starving for the next four months until they start laying again, then you'll be able to eat like a king.'

Rees lowered his head, his cheeks crimson.

Jack spread his arms wide. 'In short, gentlemen – and lady – if you can't survive in the Falklands, you couldn't survive in Harrods with a platinum AmEx card.'

The Boss got back on his feet. 'Questions? Okay, one more thing. I know four months in the Falklands may sound like a life sentence just now, but I want no whingeing . . . especially when you're in the company of Falklanders. I will also not tolerate any lowering of standards, either on or off-duty. We're at the far end of nowhere, eight and a half thousand miles from home, and believe me, I know just how dispiriting that can be at times, but we've a job of work to do and we're going to do it professionally. That's all, let's get to it.'

We straggled out of the briefing room and made our way along the echoing corridor. The windows were fogged with condensation and sleet rattled against the panes. Only ten years old, the changing room was a mess of peeling paint and crumbling concrete.

Jane wrinkled her nose. 'Is that you, Shark, or does the place always smell like this?' She took a rubber immersion suit from the row hanging near the counter presided over by a bored-looking corporal from the ground crew. Part of his job was to wash the suits after every use, but despite his best efforts, they invariably smelt as rank as the changing room itself.

I put on two layers of thermal underwear, dragged the top half of my immersion suit over my head and forced my arms down the sleeves. Even with the inside liberally doused with talc or chalk, the suits were near impossible to get into. I paused, sweating from the effort. 'Houdini didn't know he was born.'

Impassive, Jane watched my struggles for a moment then walked over to me. 'It's caught on a fold of your clothing.' She took hold of the back of the suit and jerked it down. It snapped into place with a slapping sound.

'Thanks.'

There were similar struggles going on all round the room. Shark's muffled voice emerged from a cocoon of black rubber. 'The guy that designs an immersion suit that you can get into without feeling like you've just gone ten rounds with Mike Tyson can have my pension.'

'Why should it be a guy?' Jane asked.

There was another convulsive struggle and his flushed face emerged from the suit. 'I don't give a toss what sex they are, just as long as they get a bloody move on.'

'You think you've got a problem,' Noel said, struggling to pull his suit down over his paunch. 'I must be the only person in the entire RAF who actually fills one of these things.'

I sat down on the bench, pulled on my G-pants and secured the clips and zips, then reached for the heavy life-support jacket. As I picked up my helmet, Noel appeared at my elbow. 'Ready?'

'Ready as I'll ever be.' I tapped Jane on the shoulder. 'Watch out for Shark, his other nickname is Octopus.'

I followed Noel outside. The blast of wind that greeted us was almost a relief; I could already feel trickles of sweat running down my spine.

We drove down to the Quick Reaction Area, wedged into the narrow bench seats of the squadron taxi. The curving roofs of four steel and concrete 'shacks' – the bunkers for the jets – stood within fifty yards of the end of the runway. They were open at either end and had the look of railway tunnels. They were separated from each other by the earth mounds I had seen as I looked around the previous day.

Nearby was a heap of white stones about twenty feet high

and forty feet long. A large official notice warned: 'Airfield Damage Repair Stockpile – Do Not Remove.' Not everyone had been deterred: a message from one of the departing aircrew – 'So long, suckers' – was picked out in white stones on the side of one of the earth mounds.

The sleek grey nose of a Tempest protruded from each shack. The underside of the fuselage and wings bristled with missiles, from which red tags dangled, signifying that they were live.

'This is what all that investment in the defence of the Falklands boils down to,' Noel said. 'Four aircraft – Faith, Hope, Charity and Desperation. Not much is it?'

'Not even with the other half-dozen in reserve.'

'Most of which are usually out of commission, cannibalised for spares.'

I stared at the shacks for a moment. 'These aren't even hardened.'

'I know,' Noel said. 'It's the usual story, defence economies. Hardened aircraft shelters are too expensive, apparently.'

I shook my head in disbelief. 'Too expensive? We spend a couple of billion pounds fortifying Fortress Falklands, building a harbour, fifty miles of road, and a base, including a double runway, all in the middle of a peat bog. Then we spend £80 million more every year garrisoning the place. But if the Argentinians try to invade again, the only protection for the aircraft is four tin shacks and a few piles of earth and stones.'

Noel nodded again. 'You're obviously a smart lad. Fancy a job at the Ministry of Defence?'

He pointed to another group of buildings at the other side of the runway. 'Those are the spare Tempest shacks for the Cobra Force reinforcements if things get tense with Argentina. Of course, by the time they actually arrive it might be too late.'

'And what's that building?' I said, pointing to a long wooden shed.

'That's the Q Area Ops building. It's where the reserve forces would be based.'

He led me over to a low, camouflaged building at the side of the QRA area. Eight aircrew wearing flying suits, G-pants and immersion suits looked up from the armchairs where they were slumped, staring at cartoons on a giant TV screen.

'Morning, guys,' Noel said. 'Anyone start a war last night?'

'They tried,' one of them said. 'We told them to go away and come back on Saturday when you're on duty.'

'Well, if they invade in the next forty-five minutes, Sean and I will take them on. We're going up on a famil flight.'

They nodded, their gaze already swivelling back to the TV screen.

'QRAs are the same the world over,' I said, as the door banged shut behind us. 'Boredom and body odour in equal proportions.'

'It's even more true here. Ninety-nine per cent of life in the Falklands is sitting around waiting for something – anything – to happen.' He gave a weary shake of his head. 'Never mind. Only five more months to go and then I'll be home again.'

'Have you got family with you?'

He shook his head. 'My wife's long-suffering but I thought this posting would be too much even for her, and anyway our kids have both got exams this year. My daughter's taking her A levels and my son's doing his GCSEs. We thought it was better if Molly stayed at home.'

'You must really miss them.'

'You can't imagine how much.' He gave a bleak smile. 'This is my last tour, though. I'm getting too old for this game.'

We walked towards the steep concrete ramp leading to

the first Tempest shack. It was flanked by mounds of earth and stones. A tunnel like a concrete sewage pipe branched off halfway up, linking it to the second.

The base of each mound was formed from rectangular wire mesh cages, packed with loose rocks. 'That's how we shore up riverbanks back home.'

Noel nodded. 'It makes more sense than using them to protect Tempest shacks. Can you imagine the amount of steel and rock shrapnel that would go flying if one of those took a direct hit?'

A solitary boulder stood at the foot of the ramp, inset with a brass plate. I stopped to read the inscription. It commemorated two aircrew killed when their Phantom crashed on an exercise. The names were vaguely familiar and I paused for a few moments, trying to conjure up faces to put to the names, then gave up and followed Noel up the ramp.

The wind seemed to redouble in strength as it forced its way through the open-ended Tempest shack, and the ground crew huddled around the aircraft looked thoroughly miserable. It could have been a tyre-fitting bay but for the bombs and missiles lying against the walls.

I nodded to the ground crew and began checking over the jet. I had flown Tempests for seven years and knew them inside out, but even on the firing ranges we rarely carried more than one or two live missiles. The sight of a full load bristling beneath the wings and fuselage was a new experience for me.

The Tempest was at least fifteen years old, and cared for as painstakingly as a classic car. I patted the fat black tyres as I ducked under the fuselage to check the landing-gear bays, then scrawled my signature on the form held out by the chief engineer.

He examined my handwriting. 'Ever thought of becoming a doctor instead of a pilot?'

I smiled. 'Nice to see you again too, Taff.'

Noel was already in the back seat, loading the mission details into the computer as I clambered up the ladder. The familiar sound and smell of a fast-jet greeted me: the whine of electronics and the stench of Avgas.

I checked the ejection gear and lowered myself onto the tiny, rock-hard seat. Taff leaned over the side of the cockpit, helping me to fasten the leg restraints. I tightened my thigh and shoulder straps and locked them into the quick release buckle. As I twisted and turned, connecting the tangle of hoses and cables to my flying suit, I could feel the sweat again prickling my brow.

As I went through the pre-flight ritual of check and counter-check, it was strange to hear a man's voice responding. The first cycle complete, I fired up the engines, and then closed the canopy. The ground crew scattered at the sound of the warning siren, taking refuge under the wings or behind the generator, until the canopy was safely locked into place. The failsafe explosive charges used to destroy the canopy during an emergency ejection had been known to detonate during routine closures.

I glanced through the canopy. The ageing Perspex gave the clouds streaming above the hillsides a yellowish tinge. The cockpit seemed warmer and the outside world more remote as a result.

Noel's voice crackled in my ear, distorted by the intercom, forcing me to concentrate on another series of checks. The panels remained clear of warning captions and all readings and levels were correct.

'No problems with the jet for once,' I said. 'Maybe that's a good omen.'

'I'll reserve judgement on the omens till we're safely back on the ground, if you don't mind.'

'Come on, Noel, a low-level, near-supersonic flight in a fifteen-year-old Tempest cannibalised from spare parts and held together with Sellotape and string; what could possibly go wrong?'

I checked in with the tower, then gave a thumbs-up to Taff and eased the throttles forward a touch. Even inside the canopy the noise redoubled, as oily black smoke belched from the Tempest's engines. I eased us out of the shack, the wingtips clearing the walls by no more than six inches on either side.

We rolled to a stop on the edge of the runway. 'That's the way to do it. No more buggering around on taxiways, just open the doors and step on the gas.'

As I spoke, I pushed the throttles forward, holding the jet on the brakes as tongues of blue-yellow flame flashed out thirty feet behind. The nose dipped as the afterburners kicked in. We rocked and juddered as I ran my eyes over the panels, completing the final checks.

I felt the familiar smack in the back as I released the brakes. The stone sangars guarding the underground fuel and bomb dumps blurred and disappeared from view as the Tempest catapulted forward. The tower swelled in size, then vanished as we rocketed past.

Noel's dry, matter-of-fact voice recorded the ascending speed. As we crossed the reserve runway, my eyes flicked to the warning panel. 'Captions clear, rotating.'

I pulled the stick towards me and the jet responded instantly. The nose rose and a fraction of a second later there was a faint thud as the wheels left the concrete. The runway disappeared beneath us and we were up, punching through the broken cloud as the landing gear retracted. We levelled out at 5,000 feet and swung away in a wide arc to the north.

'Okay, Sean,' Noel said. 'Have you worked with the new datalink system?'

I glanced down at the tactical display. 'I've had all the briefs, but I've not used it yet. Jane's the expert on it.'

'It's a great system. Basically we're interlinked on a secure data system with Fortress Operations, the radar sites and any airborne Tempests. What anyone else sees on radar, we see as well. Even when we're radar-blind at low-level, we still get a picture from everyone else.

'Right. Now let's do the grand tour with a Fiery Cross for starters. Come down to 800 feet, bearing two-zero-zero.'

We dropped behind the wall of the mountains into the valley behind Pleasant Peak. 'See what Shark meant?' Noel said. 'Any Argentinian that gets this far can just tool along the bottom of the valley, pop over the top and blast the shit out of the place.'

'Let's do it.' I rammed the throttles forward and threw the jet into a hard right turn, rolling inverted to leave the Tempest exposed for only a split second against the sky as we cleared the ridge. Then we were barrelling down the other side as I rolled it back upright.

I glimpsed the spiked tips of Rapier missiles on the sites dotting the surrounding hill tops. They swivelled to track us as I pushed down lower, hugging the ground. I flashed over the airfield on a diagonal run across the runway, clearing the tower by a few feet.

'Good work,' Noel said. 'Now let's go and do the tourist bit.'

I hauled back on the stick. The Tempest's nose came up and we climbed back into the southern sky. I eased back on the throttles and the engine note dropped from a bellow to a roar.

'Come right thirty,' Noel said. 'First stop, Goose Green.'

I felt the hairs on the back of my neck rise at the mention of the place.

We followed the course of a long, broad inlet. Thick underwater forests of kelp darkened the sea close to the shores. Further out the grey water was studded with small islands. The low sun behind us cast the hawk shadow of the jet onto the water, and clouds of wildfowl looking as small as gnats fluttered upwards in alarm.

I shifted my gaze ahead. A narrow isthmus, a ribbon of dark green and brown, lay across the grey water. A cluster of white-walled houses and sheds stood at the water's edge, the corrugated roofs painted in weathered shades of red, blue and green. I craned my neck to look down as we flashed over the isthmus, but it was barely a mile in width. We were past in a flash and back over water.

'This inlet leads into Falkland Sound,' Noel said. 'Turn to the south as you reach it and follow the coastline down.'

'Can we have a look at San Carlos first?'

'That's on the way back. Stick to the itinerary.'

I swung the jet around and followed the Sound southwards, skimming over a handful of scattered islands. The broken cloud opened into blue sky. The air was gin clear and I could see the curve of the earth as I gazed far out across the Southern Ocean. The water, so dull and grey only moments before, now shone the colour of jade, and the brown Falkland hills were tinted purple, orange and blue.

I looked to my left. The southern half of East Falkland was a maze of tarns, lakes and inlets. Water and low-lying land seemed to merge. To my right stood rock stacks carved by the wind and scoured by the sea into strange tortured shapes. Stumps of white rock like broken teeth reared out of the ocean. Beyond them, the cliffs of West Falkland rose sheer from the sea, flanking deserted beaches of pure white sand.

'Great place for a swim,' Noel said, 'if the water temperature was about fifty degrees higher. Not that it matters, if you want a suntan, there's a sodding great hole in the ozone layer over here and you can burn in twenty minutes even if it's freezing.'

We tracked the jagged coastline of West Falkland back to the north and I took the jet down to a few hundred feet, just above the cliff-tops. The Tempest bucked and juddered in the turbulence.

Sea lions lumbered from the rocks, splashing into the surf as the jet skimmed over them. Further up the coast, a colony of penguins scattered in alarm from their burrows among the tussac grass.

'Take her up again,' Noel said. 'We'll buzz the boys at Byron Heights. God knows, they need the entertainment. The only way in or out is by helicopter and they're stuck up there for three months at a stretch.'

A rocky crag capped the peninsula at the north-west tip of the island. Near the summit was a radome and a cluster of Portakabins.

'Funny place for a building site.'

'Don't laugh, the poor buggers have to live in those. They even make the Q shed look good.'

'So is that it?'

'No, there's a chain of islands stretching west another fifty miles or so, but no one lives on them, not even sheep. It's a great place to watch albatross apparently ... if you've nothing better to do. Okay, come right fifty. Next stop Pebble Island, that really is worth a look.'

I took the jet down even lower. The beach of Pebble Island shimmered in the sunlight ahead. As it slipped away beneath us, the air sparkled with refracted light. 'Wow, what is that?'

'There's some kind of mineral in the stone,' Noel said. 'Pretty good, isn't it? Right, that's enough sightseeing, we'll take a blast up A-4 Alley, then head for home.'

He directed me south over the mountains, then we doubled back on our tracks into a long, narrow, rift valley.

'As low as you like and as fast as you like,' Noel said.

'I thought we were under normal operating restrictions here.'

'Do you see anyone who's going to complain?'

He was right. A handful of sheep dotted the hillsides and seabirds clouded the shore. There was no other sign of life. I pressed down hard against the valley floor, feeling the walls of the ravine closing in around me.

I pushed the throttles forward close to the limit, plastered in my seat by the G-force as I threw the jet left and right, following the curves of the canyon as the river snaked away towards the north.

'The Argentinians made their attack runs on the ships in Falkland Sound from here,' Noel said between grunts as he was hurled around in his seat. 'They could fly the whole way out of radar sight, then hit the fleet like a fox in a chicken run.'

As we reached the end of the canyon, I hauled back on the stick, pulling the jet over the ridgeline, then eased the throttles towards me. As we turned for home, the tactical display sprang into life, flashing a message alert.

Noel interrogated the system. 'Possible hostile approaching the Exclusion Zone at 250 miles, high-speed, high-level. Bearing two-eight-zero. Investigate.'

As Noel acknowledged the message, I was already pushing

the throttles forward and banking the Tempest into a long turn to the west, to meet the intruder at the edge of the Exclusion Zone.

I could feel the adrenalin jolt and my breathing was noticeably faster. I'd practised a thousand times on exercises, but if the hostile aircraft held its course, this would be the first time I had ever carried out a real intercept.

'It shows what the datalink system can do,' Noel said. 'That jet's way out of our own radar range, but Fortress just feeds us the picture.'

I glanced down at the display and saw the contact marching steadily towards the computer-generated outline of the Exclusion Zone. 'This is a bit different,' I said, trying to hide the tremor in my voice. 'In two four-month tours patrolling the air exclusion zones in Iraq, the only enemy aircraft I ever saw were troop-carrying helicopters, and they were careful to stay well the right side of the Thirty-second Parallel.'

'Don't get your hopes up,' Noel said. 'I'll be very surprised if he doesn't turn and run as soon as he gets a sniff of us.'

I hoped he was right. I'd no wish to go into combat for the first time relying on a nav I'd never flown with.

I scanned the captions in front of me as I continued the climb. 'Fuel should be all right.' We cleared the coast of West Falkland and levelled off at 20,000 feet.

'Got him, eighty miles. High level, descending. Heading one-zero-zero.'

'Combat power.' The engines howled their way up the octaves as I forced the throttles forward. The juddering vibrations of the airframe intensified and the acceleration pinned me against my seat. The two jets were now closing at one mile every three seconds. 'Arming weapons.' I heard the familiar growl of the Sidewinder aiming system, so sensitive that it was even detecting the latent heat of the passing clouds.

'It's coming up as a Mirage. Fifty miles.' Noel's voice remained flat and unemotional.

I thumbed the radio button. 'Fortress, this is Falcon 2-1. Aircraft identified as Mirage. Permission to intercept.'

'Roger Falcon.'

'Locked on.' A T-bar began flashing over the arrow-head shape of the enemy contact on my screen. I imagined the cacophony of warning sirens in the cockpit of the Mirage.

I switched to the international distress frequency. 'Argentine aircraft, you are about to enter prohibited airspace. Change course or you will be intercepted and engaged.'

I repeated the message three times, punctuated by Noel's countdown. "Thirty miles ... Twenty-five miles ... Twenty.'

I began to rake the sky ahead for the first telltale sign – a dark shadow, a glint of light or a vapour-trail as the other jet descended through a condensation layer.

'He's turning away. Steer three-zero-zero. Fifteen miles. Got him visual yet?'

'Nothing yet ... Nothing ... Nothing ...' A flash of sunlight flickered from the wing of the Argentine jet as it banked away from us. 'Visual. I've got him.'

'He's heading for home,' Noel said.

'Let's make sure.'

As the Mirage completed its turn and streaked back towards the safety of the Argentine mainland, the missile seeker heads fastened on to the heat of its exhausts. The growl of the Sidewinder changed to a strident clamour. 'Locked on.'

I broke the lock at once and eased back the throttles. The scream of the engines in combat power faded to a throaty roar and the black speck ahead of me shrank and disappeared.

I released my pent-up breath and touched the transmit button. 'Fortress, bogie exiting stage left. We're breaking off and heading for home, unless you've any more trade for us.'

'Not at the moment, Falcon. Thanks for your help.'

I didn't know whether to feel relieved or disappointed. I'd been close enough to my first taste of combat to feel the adrenalin surge – and the fear. On balance, I was glad it had not come to a fight this time. If I was ever to put my life on the line in air combat, I wanted Jane watching my back, not Noel, no matter how competent he might be.

'Okay,' Noel said. 'Another triumph for truth, justice and democracy. Now let's head for home.'

My senses were still on hyper alert as I surveyed the sky around us, then pulled the jet back on to an eastward course. 'Don't forget San Carlos.'

'I'll give you a course for it, though there's nothing much to see. Any particular reason?'

'I'd just like to see it.'

We circled over San Carlos Water, a deep natural harbour near the northern entrance to Falkland Sound. Its grey-green waters looked still and calm behind the sweep of the peninsula that shielded San Carlos from the current boiling through the Sound, but I knew that the protection it offered was illusory, for it lay open to the skies. I glimpsed a dark rectilinear shape out of the corner of my eye but we had flashed past it before I could be sure if I was seeing a wreck or a submerged rock.

We flew on over the hills to the east. I was seeing them for the first time, but their names – Mount Usborne, Mount Kent, Two Sisters, Tumbledown and Mount Longdon – were as familiar to me as those of the hills back home.

We flew on in silence, following the contours of the land down towards Stanley. A white road, a straight line ruled across the brown moorland, pointed the way. 'Welcome to civilisation,' Noel said. 'That's just about the only road on the island. And there's the big city. There are three-quarters of a million sheep here, but only about two thousand people in the whole of the Falklands, and well over half of them live in Stanley, so it's a great place for a big night out. Actually, it's the only place for any kind of night out. There are a few pubs and a dance about once a month, if you can stand the excitement. The local talent is all tweed skirts, headscarves and cardigans but there are always the sheep if things get desperate.'

'I grew up in the west of Ireland. It's not so different.'

'Nobody's perfect, I come from Bognor. Right, let's get back to base before any more Argentinians decide to play chicken on the edge of the Exclusion Zone.'

He kept up a stream of talk as we flew back to Mount Pleasant, but I replied only in monosyllables, my eyes drawn back again and again to the dark hills to the north.

As we came in on finals, I saw the red airfield windsock jerking and tugging. I lowered the flaps, feeling the straps of my harness biting into my chest as the jet decelerated. I lowered the landing gear, checked for the three green lights on the panel showing it was down and locked, then we swept in over the perimeter fence.

Three times the wind forced the jet off the centre line. Each time I dragged it back, fighting the stick as the gusts threw us around, then I felt the thud as we touched down. The engines thundered under reverse thrust, adding to the vibrations from the brakes. We slowed to a crawl and I swung the Tempest around on the apron in front of the shack, facing back down the runway. I pulled to a halt, but kept the engines rumbling as I pushed the safe-arm pin into my ejector seat.

A tractor approached, locked on to the landing gear and pushed the Tempest backwards into its steel shack. The ground crew dived for cover beneath the wings as the sirens howled and I raised the canopy. Then they scurried out to fix red warning flags to the missile heads.

We ran through the checks, leaving the jet final-armed and ready to go as soon as it had been refuelled. Then I cut the engines.

The silence was broken only by the whine of the electronics and the metallic clicking as the engines cooled.

Taff stood at the bottom of the steps as I clambered out of the cockpit. 'Nice landing, sir,' he said, his face deadpan. 'We like the undercarriage to have a thorough testing every now and again.'

'Always glad to oblige, Taff.'

The debrief of the sortie took almost half an hour. I heaved a sigh of relief when I finally could head for the changing rooms and strip off my sweat-soaked clothes. My T-shirt hit the floor with a slap. I kicked it into the showers, rinsed and wrung it out, then stood under the cascade of hot water.

The near confrontation with the Argentine jet occupied my mind for a few minutes, but then my thoughts returned to San Carlos and Goose Green. I had glimpsed the narrow isthmus separating the two halves of East Falkland for only a fraction of a second, but when I closed my eyes I could clearly see the dark wooden jetty, the cluster of houses and sheds and, a little apart, two patches of ground enclosed by the neat fretwork of white picket fences.

'That's enough excitement for one day,' Noel said as we got dressed. 'And I hope those Argentinians take the day off tomorrow. I'm going up with Rees – he and I are pairing up from now on – and I'd like to get a few routine sorties under our belts.'

'He's a good pilot,' I said. 'You see him before a sortie and he looks so nervous you think he's going to throw up, but once he's in the air he's as cool as anybody. And he certainly doesn't fly like a novice.'

Noel smiled. 'I'll let you know after tomorrow's sortie. Now, I'm going to get a pot of coffee, put my feet up, take my brain out and watch daytime TV. Care to share my sofa?'

'Thanks, but I've a couple of things to do. I'll catch up with you later.'

Jane was lounging around the crew-room. 'You had some thrills and spills on your run then? All I got was the scenery.'

I nodded, taking a swig of the coffee she handed me.

'So what now?'

'I'm going to borrow the squadron taxi. There's a place I want to have a look at, a battle-site.'

'Bit unusual for you, isn't it? I never had you down as a trainspotter.'

'This is different.'

She waited, but I left it at that.

'Do you want some company?'

'If you don't mind, I'd rather do it on my own.'

She shrugged. 'Why would I?'

I checked, surprised at the edge in her voice, but she was already turning away.

I looked around. Noel was sprawled on the sofa, staring at the television screen. Rees was making coffee for him, while Shark and Jimmy were facing each other across a chessboard. Shark's smile as he surveyed the pieces was even more smug than usual, but Jimmy's face was the picture of deep Caledonian gloom.

'Where do you guys keep the keys for the squadron taxi?' I asked.

Shark looked up. 'In the ignition. It's in the rules of Military Vigilance: "All vehicles are to be parked facing outwards with the keys left in at all times."'

He leaned forward, moved his bishop and said 'Check', then turned back to me. 'The last batch of new MPs obviously hadn't read the rules either. On their first night on duty, they spotted that someone had left the keys in, decided it was a security risk and went round the base removing them from every vehicle. There was an alert that night and when we all came piling out of the building, no one could get to the QRA area because the keys were all in the guardhouse. It was lucky the alert was a test, not the real thing.'

I walked outside. The sky was ice-blue and the low sunlight threw the hills into sharp relief. The few clouds scudded swiftly across the sky, driven by the relentless wind.

I sat in the front seat of the Land Rover, studying the map, then drove off diagonally across the runway. A barbed-wire perimeter fence surrounded the airfield and a bored-looking sentry stood guard at the entrance gates, but there were none of the crash barriers or anti-terrorist precautions there would have been at home.

The cattle grids set in the concrete at the edge of the runway nearly shook the teeth from my head. I wound down the window. 'Any chance you could get those fixed?'

'The grids? They're supposed to be like that,' the guard said. 'It's protection against FOD.' He saw my blank look. 'Foreign Object Damage. The perimeter road and the one down to Mare Harbour are the only sealed roads in the whole of the Falklands, the rest are just hardcore. The grids shake the loose stones out of your tyre-treads on the way back in. It keeps them off the runway.'

I drove up the road for a few miles then turned off onto a rough moorland track leading over the hillside. The Land Rover bounced and jolted over the ruts and even in four-wheel drive it skidded and slewed as it hit patches of peat bog. Twice it almost ground to a halt but I kept it going, creeping on at barely above walking pace towards the white enclosure on the hillside.

It took over an hour to reach it. A steep valley opened up to my left, leading down to a sheltered cove. I could see a red-roofed farmhouse and a cluster of shearing sheds grouped around the head of the inlet.

A neat, white picket fence surrounded the graveyard. The graves were laid out in neat rows, like soldiers on parade, each plot marked out by white quartz stones the size of a fist. I entered through the gate and walked slowly along the rows. I found what I was seeking at the furthest corner of the graveyard.

I don't know how long I spent there, but dusk was falling by the time I retraced my steps and jolted my way back down the hillside. As I looked across to Mount Pleasant, I could see how well the base was camouflaged from a distance, the drab colours of the buildings merging into the dull greys, greens and browns of the landscape. Only as the lights began to come on did it reveal itself.

The same sentry was still on duty. He stopped blowing on his hands and stamping his feet long enough to give me a nod of recognition, then shrank back into the shelter of the guard post.

I drove straight to the Death Star and climbed the stairs to my room. My bag lay half unpacked on the table. I threw my socks and T-shirts into a drawer and hung the rest of my clothes in the wardrobe. In the bottom of the bag was a cardboard tube and a small bundle of yellowing papers, bound with a rubber band. As I lifted the papers out, a medal and ribbon slipped from between the leaves. I picked it up and turned it over to read the inscription on the back, though I could have recited every word from memory.

'I never knew you'd been decorated.'

I spun around, closing my hand defensively. 'I haven't.'

Jane waited for me to continue. 'So whose is it? Your father's?'

'My brother's.' I dropped the medal back into my bag.

'I didn't even know you had a brother.' She studied me in silence. 'It's all right, you know.' She touched my arm. 'If you don't want to talk about it, that's fine.'

'This'll sound stupid.' I hesitated. 'I'll tell you about it sometime, just not right now. Okay?'

She searched my face again. 'So what else have you got in the goody bag?'

'Just this.' I took out the cardboard tube, unrolled the poster it contained and pinned it to the wall. Jane peered at it over my shoulder and I could feel her breath warm on my cheek. 'Rolling hills, turf cottages and picturesque curls of peat smoke rising into an azure sky; all that's missing is a donkey cart. It's not really still like that, is it?'

'Not really. The old homestead is slowly crumbling away. But I still like the poster. It reminds me of when I was a kid.'

We both fell silent. 'Speaking of crumbling,' Jane said, 'there was a phone call for you. You remember the Falkland farmer and his wife on the Tristar? She rang to invite "Mr

Riever and his companion" to tea tomorrow. Clay House, five o'clock prompt. They're having a sort of welcome home party and for some bizarre reason they want us to go along – well, you anyway, I don't think she's a big fan of mine.'

I stared at her. 'Why?'

'She was obviously seduced by that troubled, angst-ridden look of yours.' She reached out and ruffled my hair. 'Come on, I'll buy you a drink in the Mess. We need an antidote before we get poisoned by dinner.'

The rest of the guys were already in position at the bar, or watching CNN on satellite TV. A report from Argentina showed crowds milling around the streets, carrying identical banners bearing the legend 'Malvinas Argentinas'.

'Funny how those people have all got the same handwriting, isn't it?' Jane said.

A speech to the crowd by the new President turned into a rabble-rousing rant. Noel watched for a few seconds, then stormed across the room and turned it off.

Shark laughed. 'Don't get so wound up, Noel. You don't even speak Spanish. For all you know that little tirade could have been about the price of corned beef or Diego Maradona's cocaine habit.'

Rees winced, expecting a further outburst from his new nav, but Noel hesitated, peering at Shark, unsure how much he was being wound up. 'You don't need to speak Spanish to know what that load of bollocks was about.'

'It's worrying though, there's no denying it,' Jimmy said, his brow furrowed in its permanent frown. 'Now they've found oil here, it's not just a matter of injured Argentine pride, there's going to be bucket loads of money at stake as well. In my book that's a recipe for trouble.'

'Not really.' The Boss had been listening to the exchange from his stool at the bar. 'If we got excited every time some Argentinian politician started tub-thumping about the Malvinas, we'd be on permanent war alert.'

Chapter 3

Clay House was a modest-sized farmhouse on a small promontory looking out towards Choiseul Sound. The drive, a muddy, rutted track, was flanked by a thin belt of wind-burned conifers, the first trees I'd seen since we arrived.

The once white walls were stained with lichen and damp, and the green paint on the metal roof was faded and peeling. There was a barn and a group of tumbledown sheds to the rear and an ancient Land Rover in the lean-to garage.

The patch of grass in front of the house was speckled with what looked like sun-bleached sticks. Jane took a closer look. 'Shit, those are bones.'

'It's all right, George and Agnes didn't look like serial killers to me. In places where the soil and the farmers are both very poor, they chuck their meat bones out into the yard. They fertilise the soil as they rot away.'

She shook her head in disbelief. 'Your store of totally useless information is a constant source of wonder. But what about rats, for Christ's sake?'

'They'd starve to death inside a week. What did you use back home? Big Ben pie crusts and empty cans of lager?'

'No, sheep dags or £10 Poms; the Poms are better fertiliser.'

'Don't tell me. They're really full of shit, right?'

'You said it.'

Agnes was standing on the doorstep to greet us. Jane and I had our coats buttoned against the wind, but Agnes was wearing a short-sleeved pullover, as if she were taking the air on a mild English spring day.

'Sean, I'm so pleased you could come, and Jane too.' She led us into a room full of ruddy-faced farmers and their wives.

A peat fire smouldered on the hearth. I smiled at Agnes. 'That smell takes me back. If I closed my eyes I could be back in my grandfather's house in Kerry.'

'We all burn it here. It's the only fuel we have. The council allocates every household a section of moor. Have you ever dug peat, Sean?'

I shook my head. 'I've watched though. It's back-breaking work.'

She nodded. 'And the digging's only half the work. Then it has to be stacked to dry — rickling we call it — and then we have to get it back to the farm, though that part's much easier. A dry peat is only about a quarter the weight of a wet one.'

As she half-turned towards Jane, including her in the conversation, I saw the wiry strength in Agnes. She was old and thin, but there was still muscle and sinew beneath the wrinkled, weather-beaten skin.

'Do you still dig peats by hand?'

'There's no other way. We've tried machines; they don't work.'

'They work in Britain.'

There was a momentary spark of anger in her pale blue eyes, but the reproach was gentle. 'This isn't Britain, Sean.'

Inside, a long table was set with the sort of farmhouse tea I remembered from home, enough meat, cakes, pies and pastries to give a nutritionist nightmares, and not a fresh fruit or vegetable in sight, other than a bowl of yellowing green tomatoes.

'The last of the summer's crop,' Agnes said, following my gaze. 'We grow them in our greenhouse, but the season is never long enough to ripen them properly.' There was a wistful note in her voice. 'Now what can I get you to drink? A cup of tea, or there's wine or George's home-brewed beer.'

'I'll have wine,' Jane said with transparent haste. 'Red, if you've got it? Then white, thanks.'

'I'll try the beer,' I said.

'Aren't you the teacher's pet,' Jane murmured as Agnes moved away.

'Some of these home-brews can be surprisingly good.' I watched with a sinking feeling as Agnes approached carrying a glass of opaque, grey-brown liquid.

She moved on to her other guests, but Jane looked on with glee as I took a mouthful. It was sour and yeasty, but as I caught Agnes's eye, I managed to turn my grimace into a smile of approval.

Jane approached her wine with suspicion. 'It's sweet,' she said.

I smiled. 'There's always the beer.'

We surveyed the assembled company, but Agnes didn't leave us alone for long. 'Come along, Jane,' she said, taking a firm grip on her arm. 'We can't have Sean keeping you all to himself, there are lots of handsome farmers dying to meet you.'

I blew her a kiss as she was led away. George waved me over, breaking off a conversation to introduce me to his companion. Bernard looked no more than thirty, but his black hair was already streaked with grey. His chin was stubbled and there was a scar on his cheek which showed up livid against his red, wind-burned face.

He gave me a curt nod, then turned back to George. 'The Argies will be back. Especially when the offshore oil starts to flow. 1982 wasn't the first invasion and it won't be the last.'

'There was another?' I said. 'I didn't know that.'

Bernard ignored the interruption, but George nodded. 'There were two of them, 1966 and 1970.'

Agnes passed with a tray of tea-cups. 'Don't let them fill your head with nonsense, Sean. They were a couple of planeloads of lunatics.'

'They were lunatics armed with guns,' George said. 'And we were worried enough at the time, even you.'

'Tell me about it,' I said.

'There was — and probably still is — an Argentine society called Condor dedicated to reclaiming the Malvinas. Twenty of them hijacked a flight from Buenos Aires to Gallegos in September 1966, took the other passengers hostage and made the pilot fly to the Falklands.' He began to chuckle. 'When they got here, they discovered their first problem. We didn't have an airport — the only contact with the outside world in those days was the monthly mail ship to Montevideo and the wool ships to Britain — but they forced the pilot to try a landing anyway.

'I was in Stanley picking up some supplies and saw it happen. It came in over Ross Road, cleared the top of the cathedral by no more than a couple of feet and then landed on Stanley racecourse. We all thought it was an accident until they planted an Argentine flag and dragged a policeman into the plane at gunpoint. We only had half a dozen police for the whole of the Falklands, but the remaining ones cordoned off the plane and sat back to await developments.

'One of the Argentinians eventually came out brandishing his gun and began a long speech. It was in Spanish of course and no one could understand a word of it. None of the Condor men could speak any English either, so we stood around staring at each other until one of the school teachers arrived to interpret.

'The man spoke for about twenty minutes. "We are here on behalf of twenty-two million countrymen to end the English invasion of Las Islas Malvinas—"'

'They thought we were all Argentinians too,' Agnes said, 'imprisoned in our land by ruthless English imperialists.'

'They weren't so far wrong there,' Bernard muttered.

'Better than Argentinian ones though, eh, Bernard?' George gave me a ghost of a wink as Bernard shrugged and went back to his drink.

'So what happened?' I asked.

'Oh there was a stand-off for twenty-four hours and then they surrendered. We sent them home via Montevideo on the next ship that docked at Stanley. It was the ultimate indignity for them; it was a British ship.'

'They all lined up at the rail of the ship and sang Argentine songs as it sailed away. It was quite touching.' Agnes flushed at the looks that Bernard and George directed at her. 'Well, I thought so anyway.'

'You'd have thought they'd have had enough after that,' George said, 'but four years later they were back again. This time they turned up in a private plane, the Cronica. They still hadn't done their research very well though; we'd blocked the racecourse after the first incident to stop anyone else trying to land there. They circled a couple of times and then crash-landed on the moor above Eliza Cove. This time they at least had some leaflets printed in English with them, and after planting the Argentine flag again they handed them out.'

'I've still got a copy in a drawer somewhere,' Agnes said, gesturing vaguely towards the kitchen. 'Something like: "We don't come as aggressives but as Argentinian citizens to meet you with our country and the men of this country which are our brothers."'

She smiled at the memory. 'Port Stanley was to be renamed Port Rivero, but they assured us that the property rights of "the natives" would be respected. That was another serious tactical error. As I told you at the airport the other day, you can call us almost anything you like, but you must never call us that.'

George swallowed the remnants of a sandwich. 'Anyway, as I was saying, they did a lot more huffing and puffing, and speech making and flag waving, and then they surrendered again as meek as lambs.'

'I felt quite sorry for them really,' Agnes said. 'They looked so baffled and helpless, as if they couldn't understand why we didn't welcome them with open arms, instead of pitchforks and shotguns. It must have been a bit of a shock to discover that the people they had been taught to think of as countrymen were more British than the British themselves.'

This was too much for Bernard. 'No, we're not. We're Falklanders, Agnes, Falklanders.'

She gave him a look of mock severity. 'You'll give yourself an ulcer with all this pent-up anger, Bernard. You can't hold a grudge forever. Whatever Britain should have done before the war, we've no complaints since then, now have we?'

George pounced again in the brief silence that followed. 'That was the last invasion until 1982, but for years afterwards the approach of any unexpected aircraft was a signal for a mass panic in Stanley.'

He broke off as Jane slid into the chair next to mine, having escaped from the circle of farmers by the fireplace.

'Right,' Agnes said firmly. 'That's more than enough about the good — or do I mean bad? — old days, thank you, George. I'm sure these two must be bored rigid.'

'No, really, I'm enjoying it,' I said, trying to ignore the pressure of Jane's elbow in my ribs. 'Tell me more about what it was like before the war. Has it changed so much since then? I've only been here a couple of days, but—' I hesitated, wary of giving offence. 'It's probably because it's all a little new to me, but I'm feeling every inch of the distance from the UK.'

'I've lived here all my life and that's something I'm always very aware of too,' Agnes said. 'There's a table of postal times in Stanley Post Office, dating from 1892. Back then it took a month for a letter to reach the UK. Know how long it takes now? By surface mail, it's still a month. Not much progress in one hundred years, is it? Even air mail takes a week.' She gave a self-deprecating smile. 'Of course there are telephones and satellite television these days, but some things don't change.'

'You must have felt even more remote before the war,' Jane said. 'At least people have heard of the Falklands these days and know where they are.'

Bernard snorted and started to say something, but Agnes cut across him. 'My dear, you simply can't imagine what life was like then.'

'I could make a stab at it,' Jane said. 'I grew up in the

outback of New South Wales, back of Bourke as we call it. The sheep stations there were so big you might not see your next door neighbour more than once or twice a year.'

'Who owns them?' Bernard asked, suddenly interested.

'Mostly families when I was a kid. These days it's all agribusiness and big corporations.'

He shook his head. 'Then you don't know what it was like here. There were big farms here too, with a couple of hundred thousand acres, but all except a handful of tiny holdings were owned by the FIC – the Falkland Islands Company. When you went to work on a settlement, you were owned body and soul by the FIC.'

'Come on, Bernard,' George said. 'It wasn't that bad. You make it sound like slavery.'

'We weren't slaves maybe, but it was a strange kind of freedom. You worked on a settlement full-time, from one year to the next. If you had a day off, you couldn't go anywhere. There were no roads on the islands and the tracks were so rough you couldn't even get a Land Rover over them without bogging down.

'The only way out from most places was on foot or on the ships that used to call at the settlements to drop off supplies and pick up the wool clip. If you wanted to buy anything – soap, tobacco, chocolate or whatever – there was a settlement shop, open one afternoon a week, a company store usually run by the manager's wife.

'Whatever you wanted was debited against your wages. The rest was credited to your bank or post office account in Stanley. There was nothing to spend your money on at the settlements and they didn't like to pay you cash in case you gambled with it. You worked long and hard and you had to keep your nose clean. If you got on the wrong side of the company's manager you could be black-listed throughout the islands ... and if you didn't work for the company you didn't work at all.'

'Sounds pretty much like slavery to me,' Jane said, winning a rare smile from Bernard. 'What did you do on your nights off?'

'Well, we didn't pop down to Stanley for a disco. We usually just sat around the cookhouse or the dormitory. On special occasions like the end of shearing, we might go up to the Big House for dinner.' He paused. 'You can guess what was on the menu.'

'Mutton?'

'Got it in one. Once a year you got a couple of weeks off, but most people saved their holidays and their money until they could afford a trip to England. We all used to call it "home" back then.' He gave a hard-edged smile at the memory. 'Most people still do. There's even a council proposal to provide free trips for everyone to go to the UK every two years. They call it "social ventilation".

'That's where George and Agnes have just been, off to the UK to get socially ventilated. The council think it will bring us back happier citizens, but not everybody comes back, of course.' He shot a look at a dark-haired woman sitting with her back to us.

'What about schools?' Jane said.

Lost in his thoughts, Bernard didn't reply, and George answered for him. 'The bigger settlements had a school but most of them relied on itinerant teachers, like Agnes.'

'I used to go all over the islands,' Agnes said. 'I'd stay at each settlement for three or four days, then leave the children enough work to last them until my next visit and move on to the next one. There are still half a dozen travelling teachers today.'

'Sounds pretty hit and miss to me,' Jane said. 'We had a

bit of a similar system in the outback, but teachers stayed in one place and taught us all at the same time over the radio telephone. I used to sit at the kitchen table listening to this voice coming over the RT and trying to imagine what the teacher looked like.' She shrugged. 'I never found out. We moved to Sydney when I was eight. My first day in a real school I nearly fainted. I never knew there were so many children in the whole world, never mind in one school.'

'What did — what do the kids do when they get older?' I asked. 'They can't be taught at home all the way up to A levels, can they?'

Agnes shook her head. 'They go to the new school in Stanley. Everyone has relatives there so they stay with them and then come back at weekends, or maybe just holidays if they live in a remote settlement.'

'And before the war?'

'The only decent schools were abroad, in Montevideo or England. You should ask Rose about that. She went to school in Monte.' Agnes pointed to the dark-haired woman. 'You should talk to her anyway, she has a few stories about the war that you might be interested to hear.' She gave me a look but offered no further explanation.

Puzzled, I looked over at Rose. She was tall and slim, but her face was turned away from me as she talked animatedly with a group of other women. What I could see made me curious to see the rest.

Bernard stood up. 'We must be going.'

'Five more minutes, Bernard,' Agnes said. 'We don't see you nearly often enough. George, get him another drink.'

George was reluctant to lose any part of his audience. 'You think we're remote now, Sean?' he said, laying a hand on my arm as Agnes tried to lead me away. 'There was nothing here at all before the war. Even Stanley was a different world. It still is. Did you know that when Stanley puts the clocks forward an hour for summer time, the rest of the Falklands stays on winter time? And there are still people in Stanley today who have never visited the camp—' He smiled at my blank expression. 'Sorry, it's what we call the country – the rest of the Falklands outside Stanley.'

'Now, who'd like some more tea or another glass of wine, or a beer?' Agnes said. 'Sean, you've hardly touched yours.'

'Tea would be fine,' Jane said, as I struggled for a reply. 'Let me help you.'

'I wouldn't hear of it, my dear,' Agnes said. 'Tell Bernard and George a bit more about Australia.'

She steered me away from them. 'Rose, come and meet someone.' Rose and I stood in an awkward silence for a moment, studying each other. She looked quite unlike the other women in the room, more angular, more delicate, and far more beautiful. She had a watchful, guarded look, hinting at a secret sadness, and fatigue had left marks like bruises beneath her dark eyes. Her pale, almost translucent skin was accentuated by the colour of her jade-green dress. It had faded a little with age; it could even have been her mother's, carefully preserved and painstakingly altered.

She scanned my face. 'Have we met before?'

'I don't think so. I'm sure I would have remembered.'

A hint of colour touched her cheekbones and her smile made her look even more beautiful. She held my gaze for a second, then looked away.

'Agnes said you had some interesting stories to tell about the war. I only know what I've read and heard about it back in England, and I'd like to know a lot more.'

She did not reply, but as she continued to study my face,

a different look came into her eyes, almost as if she had found the key to a mystery. The colour in her cheeks heightened a little further.

'If you'd rather not talk about it—'

'Oh no, it's not that. I – I just wonder if now is the right moment.'

'Another time then,' I said, not sure what was expected of me.

'That would be better. I'm sorry to be so cryptic, I just feel a bit awkward about it somehow, with all these people around.'

She hesitated and seemed about to say more when Bernard appeared at her elbow. 'Time to go.'

Rose resisted the pressure on her arm for a moment. 'You're in the Falklands for some time yet, Sean?'

'Four months.'

'Then please come and see us.' She gestured towards Jane. 'Both of you.' She looked to Bernard for confirmation.

There was a momentary pause, then he gave a slow nod. 'You'll be welcome.' His eyes conveyed a different message.

'Black Beck House, above Cattle Creek. The telephone number's 102,' Rose said, as he hustled her away. 'But just call in, we're always there.'

I stood watching her all the way to the door.

'Penny for your thoughts,' Jane said. 'Why are men always such suckers for that vulnerable look? And don't bullshit me, I know you too well.'

Agnes's approach spared me from the need to find a reply. 'You didn't have much time to talk to Rose, I'm afraid.'

'No, Bernard was soon on patrol.'

'They had the evening work to do on the farm.' She paused. 'You shouldn't judge Bernard on first impressions. His manner's a little abrupt, I know, but he's a good man at heart and a very hard-working one. Their land is marginal even by Falklands standards and he's sweated blood to improve it. He works all the hours that God gives, but if ever a neighbour were in trouble—' her gaze rested on George for a moment – 'Bernard would be the first there to lend a hand.' She looked up and smiled. 'Anyway, do make the effort to talk to Rose again. George and I saw very little of the war. The Argentinians herded us down to Goose Green with most of the other farmers and penned us in the shearing sheds like our own sheep, but Rose's family were on their farm throughout the worst of the fighting.'

'I'll definitely talk to her,' I said; 'and now I'm afraid we really must be going ourselves.'

The speed with which Jane set off to collect our coats suggested she was in general agreement with the idea.

'Thanks for inviting us, Agnes,' I said. 'I've enjoyed it, I really have, and I'm touched that you should invite two strangers into your home and make us so welcome.'

'There are no strangers here, my dear, just friends we haven't yet met. I hope you'll come and see us again before you leave. And I hope you find what you're seeking.'

I hesitated, uncertain whether it was a traditional Falklands farewell or one directed at me alone, but Jane had returned before I could reply. Our departure seemed to be the signal for a general exodus, and I had no chance to speak to Agnes again.

Several of the farmers directed shy, wistful looks at Jane as we said our goodbyes and a couple of the bolder ones planted wet, smacking kisses on her cheek.

As we drove off down the track she burst out laughing. 'I'll never complain about another boring night in the Mess again.' She shot me a sidelong glance. 'You seemed to be enjoying yourself, though. You should have seen the looks Bernard was shooting at your back before he barged over and reclaimed his blushing bride.'

'You should have run interference for me.'

'With Bernard? I like the strong, silent types, not the psychotic, speechless ones. Anyway, I didn't notice you rushing to rescue me when Agnes dumped me in the middle of the Young Farmers' Club. Most of them were so paralysed with shyness they could barely speak and the ones who did could have bored for Britain. One of them was such a disgusting lech that he kept asking me if I was wearing suspenders and squeezing my thigh to find out. I'd have decked him, but I was on my best behaviour today, so I just asked him to point out his wife to me. He went white – which was quite an achievement for a man with a face like an over-ripe beetroot – and didn't say another word.' She paused. 'So, were Rose's war stories up to much, or were you too busy salivating to notice?'

'She didn't tell me any. She said she didn't want to talk about it in front of lots of people.'

'I knew it. She's trying to get you alone.'

I shook my head. 'I felt that both she and Agnes knew something . . .' My voice petered out. 'I can't really explain.'

She touched my arm. 'Sorry, I'm just being flippant when you want to be serious.'

I drove on in silence for a few minutes, straining my eyes to pick out the line of the road in the darkness. There were no marker posts, white lines, reflectors or cats' eyes to help me and mud and peat washed down from the slopes had stained the surface to almost the same colour as the surrounding land. I braked involuntarily at each slight bend, rise or dip as the road disappeared momentarily and the beam of the headlights dissolved into a void. It was the only light visible in the whole sweep of land and sea.

A painted skull and crossbones flared white in the headlights and I braked: 'DANGER! MINEFIELD! Keep To The Road. Do Not Enter Fenced Area. Special Care Must Also Be Taken On Beaches And Rivers Adjacent To Fenced Areas. All parts of the Falkland Islands may contain dangerous materials and ammunition. Do not touch anything suspicious. Place a marker nearby and report it to the Joint Services OED Operations Centre, manned 24 hours a day. Tel: Civil 229, BFFI 2393.'

Beyond the sign, I could see the dull glint of barbed wire. 'Sixteen years since the war and they still haven't cleared them.'

'They've cleared a lot of them,' Jane said, 'and they'd probably do the rest if they knew where to find them. The Argentinians didn't even map the minefields and it's a bit much to ask some bomb-disposal bloke to risk his life to clear an area just so that one or two people a year can go for a stroll there.'

I stared at the sign for a moment, then turned the engine and lights off and opened the door.

'Where the hell are you going?'

'Not for a walk, that's for sure. I want to look at the stars.'

After a moment I heard Jane's door open and her hesitant footsteps as she groped her way round the car to stand at my side.

There was no moon but the night was clear, crisp and very cold, with only a few small patches of cloud, racing from west to east. My breath fogged in the air before being blown away on the wind.

I had flown jets all over the northern hemisphere and as far south as the Gulf, but until that moment I had never set eyes on a clear, southern night sky before. I had never seen so many stars in my life. The whole sky seemed filled from horizon to horizon. It was veiled with a faint glow of light, pierced by the diamond-hard shine of individual stars.

It was an awesome, but disturbing, sight. The familiar constellations, as fixed and immutable in my mind as the points of the compass, had disappeared. In their place was a profusion of utterly different clusters and constellations, as if the whole earth had been thrown out of its orbit into some far reach of the galaxy.

I thought how terrible it would be to die here, so far from home that even the heavens were unrecognisable. Finally I discovered a couple of familiar constellations, though even they appeared distorted.

Jane slipped her warm hand into mine. 'Makes you realise how far away you are, doesn't it? It's how I felt when I first came to Britain, but this feels like home to me. When it was really hot in Guneela I used to sleep outside on the decking. I'd lie awake listening to the cicadas and watching the sky darken. Moonless nights there were as black as your hat, but I've never seen as many stars as this. Even a hole in the ozone layer's got its good si—' She broke off, staring upwards, entranced. 'Wow! Look at that.'

There was a streak of light towards the northern horizon, then another and another, as a trail of shooting stars blazed its way to oblivion. As the last fragment of the meteor shower flared then faded, I became increasingly conscious of the pressure of Jane's hand on mine.

Faintly illuminated, her face was turned towards me. I hesitated for a second, feeling my heartbeat quicken as I held my breath, then I stepped away from her and released her hand. Her fingers sliding over mine felt like a caress.

'Come on,' I said, 'we'll have to get back.'

I could feel her gaze on my face as we drove in silence down the rutted track towards Mount Pleasant.

'Let's have a beer before we turn in,' Jane said, as I drove in through the main gates.

I hesitated, reluctant at first, then nodded. 'Okay.'

'Not the Mess though,' she said. 'It'll be heaving with people and I'm not really in the mood for that. Why don't we try out the Fighter Town fridge? With luck there won't be anyone else there until the Mess shuts.'

I pulled up outside the Death Star, dutifully parking the Land Rover facing out, with the keys in.

Fighter Town was in darkness, but I flicked on the lights and grabbed a couple of cans from the fridge. We sat facing each other in two of the battered armchairs. Jane watched me for a moment. 'Tell me something about your brother.'

I shrugged. 'He died a long time ago. You'd hear plenty about him if you visited my mum and dad's place though. It's like a shrine, but with Mike in place of the Virgin Mary. They must have about twenty silver-framed photographs of him, including a huge one over the fireplace of him in his dress uniform at his passing-out parade. There are three spotlights trained on it. It's like everything else in the room is in darkness.' I smiled. 'There's only one picture of me in the room, and even that's one of me and Mike together.'

She rested a hand on my arm for a moment. 'That's tactless of them, but it's the way it goes, even among the living. The child who's a long way away – particularly if they're on the other side of the world – always seems more precious to parents than the one in front of them.

'I'm the beneficiary of that in our family, but I do know all about trying to compete on an uneven playing field. Everyone from my headmaster to my dad and my sister told me I was crazy to think about joining the Air Force. The head wanted me to stay on at school and go to university, and my dad and my sister both thought the Air Force was no place for a woman, though for different reasons.

'My dad, bless him, is scared shitless of flying. He's never even been to an airport, let alone got in an aircraft, and he couldn't bear the thought of his precious daughter risking her neck in one. My sister thought I'd be beaten down by a bunch of blinkered sexists. She was half-right, there's no shortage of those, but I haven't let the bastards grind me down yet. I get sick of it sometimes, though. It's always the same. You don't just have to be as good as the men, you have to be better than them. And even then, you still get a few tiresome wankers who think you must have screwed the squadron boss to get there.' She gave a toss of her head, shaking her hair back from her eyes. 'Anyway, stuff them.'

She paused and gave a rueful smile. 'I'm sorry, we were talking about you and, as usual, I managed to steer the conversation straight round to me. Tell me some more about Mike. I can't imagine how hard it must be to have to compete with someone else's memory.'

'You can't. Compete, I mean. How could you? I felt like I almost had to apologise to my parents for surviving, for not being the one who died.'

'Was he killed here?'

I nodded.

There was the sound of voices and unsteady footsteps in the corridor and a moment later the door crashed open. Shark, Rees and Jimmy burst in, their faces flushed with drink. 'Oops,' Shark said. 'Not disturbing anything, are we? If you were just about to have sex, don't let us stop you.'

Jane rolled her eyes. 'I can only think of one thing worse

than having sex with you watching, Shark.' She paused. 'And that's having sex with you.'

He opened the fridge and tossed her another can. 'I love it when you talk dirty.'

I stood up. 'I'll pass on another beer, thanks, Shark. I don't want to cramp your style. See you in the morning.'

Jane opened her mouth to say something, then changed her mind and shook her head. 'Forget it. I'll see you tomorrow.' She ripped off the ring-pull and took a swig of her beer.

That night, my nightmare returned. I awoke, heart pounding, my pillow drenched in cold, clammy sweat. I pitched it onto the floor, threw back the bedclothes and lay naked in the darkness staring at the ceiling, as the sweat grew cold on my body. Then I pulled the covers around me and slipped back into troubled sleep.

Chapter 4

Winter was closing in. Snow had dusted the ground during the night and there was frost on the window when I woke. I banged on Jane's door a couple of times but ignored the sleepy invitation to come in and wait. 'I'm starving, I'll see you in the Mess.' I hurried off down the corridor before she could reply.

As I walked through the lobby, the Tannoy crackled into life. 'All Air Crew, General Briefing, 0700 hours. Repeat, all—' As I pushed the door open, the metallic voice was drowned in a thunder of rotors as three Sea King helicopters rose into the air from their compound and flew off to the west in echelon formation. I watched them fade from sight, then turned up the collar of my coat against the cold and began walking towards the Mess, on the far side of the runway. The morning was clear and bright, with only a few strands of cirrus cloud streaking the pale dawn sky.

I'd almost finished my breakfast by the time Jane appeared, her hair still damp from the shower.

'You're looking rough,' she said, dropping into the chair opposite me and pouring herself a cup of coffee.

'I haven't been sleeping too well.'

'Something on your mind?'

I hesitated, then shook my head. 'Just bad dreams.'

She studied me over the rim of her coffee cup. 'Don't suppose you know what the briefing's about, do you?'

'No idea, though I saw three Sea Kings take off just now, which is a bit unusual.'

She nodded. 'I guess we'll find out soon enough. Once we've got the briefing out of the way, the day's our own. What do you fancy doing?'

'I'm going to take a walk in the hills.'

'Again?'

'I want to try and get a feel for what it was like for the ground troops during the war.'

She studied my face carefully. 'Do you want some company or did the fact that you said "I" rather than "we" mean you'd prefer to be on your own?'

'If you don't mind, I'd—'

She held up a hand. 'I don't mind, just let me know if and when you want to talk about it. But Sean?' A faint smile played around the corners of her mouth. 'If you keep on sloping off without me like this, I'll start to think you're avoiding me.' She held my gaze for a moment, then her smile broadened. 'Anyway, slogging through stinking peat bogs is the last thing on my agenda for today. I'm going to hit the weights, top up my tan on the sunbed and do a few girly things like painting my toenails. Oh, and I'm supposed to be giving Shark a game of squash as well.'

'Is he any good?'

She shrugged. 'He says he is.'

'No surprises there, but maybe you should play him before you hit the weights, just in case he really is good.'

'I couldn't do that, Sean, I've got to give him every chance. The male ego is a very delicate thing.'

The briefing room was packed. We took a seat on a bench towards the back and I felt a small stab of irritation as Shark squeezed into the space next to Jane a few moments later. She nudged me and pointed towards the front of the room, where eight aircrew were sitting in full flying gear. 'It must be something important if they've brought the guys on QRA up for it.'

'Taff's here as well,' I said. 'It must be earth-shattering, never mind important, if they've dragged him away from the shacks. They probably had to surgically separate him from his socket-wrenches.'

Nobody had any idea why the briefing had been called, but that didn't stop the buzz of speculation around the room. The Boss stood at the front, tapping his pen against his teeth as he waited for the last of us to be seated. He banged the podium with his fist and the hubbub of conversation died away.

He allowed a few moments to elapse before he spoke. 'A curious situation has developed. We have no idea if it's innocent or sinister, but until we have definite information to the contrary, we must assume the worst.' He paused and glanced around the room.

'I don't suppose there's any chance of him explaining exactly what the hell he's talking about,' Jane murmured.

He took a deep breath. 'HMS *Trident* has disappeared. It has missed three consecutive check-in slots with Fleet HQ at Northwood, the Navy has been unable to track it or locate it, and all attempts to communicate with it have proved unsuccessful.'

No one needed the implications of the loss of the *Trident* spelled out. If the base at Mount Pleasant was one pillar of the defence of the Falklands, the other was the hunter-killer nuclear submarine patrolling the icy depths of the South Atlantic.

After the fate suffered by the *General Belgrano*, the Argentine navy would never again risk its capital ships in a seaborne attack against the Falklands unless the *Trident* had first been destroyed.

The Boss again banged the podium and raised his voice to be heard above the continuing rumble of conversation. 'Our Sea Kings are continuing to search the *Trident*'s last-known area of operations, in the north-west sector of the Exclusion Zone, so far without success, but it's too early to say for sure that the sub has been lost and, if so, what the cause may be. There are two possibilities. The Commander may have rigged the sub for silent running and be operating at such a depth that he is unable to send or receive signals traffic.'

He paused. 'As I said, it's possible, but it's unlikely. No order had been issued to that effect and the *Trident* should have been on normal patrol. The other possibility is that the sub has been lost, either through accident, sabotage or act of war.'

The silence grew oppressive. Jane sat rigid at my side, staring ahead of her. I felt a bead of sweat trickle down my forehead.

'The one piece of good news is that there's absolutely no sign whatsoever of any unusual military activity from the Argentinians. I'm quite sure that they would only risk the consequences of attacking *Trident* if they were planning an immediate, full-scale invasion. Had that been so, we would already have seen the first danger signs.' He leaned forward, resting his elbows on the podium. 'I know that I don't have to remind you of the absolute secrecy of the information I have given you this morning. No hint of any problems with *Trident* should go beyond this room. I do not even want you discussing it among yourselves. Is that clear?'

There were a couple of dozen people in the room, but he held the gaze of each of us in turn. '*Trident*'s sister ship, *Neptune*, is making speed to replace it here but it will take a minimum of two weeks to reach the Exclusion Zone. In the meantime, we are potentially vulnerable to attack and our own role in the defence of the Falklands assumes even greater importance. Having said all that, we're not convinced there is any real cause for alarm — other than about the fate of the crew of the *Trident*, of course — and for the moment we don't propose to be stampeded into declaring an emergency. It would have little benefit and might only attract the attention of the Argentinians to something we would rather keep concealed. So unless and until Intelligence on Argentinian military activity leads us to conclude that there is a genuine threat, we will remain at our normal state of readiness — RS 15 — and you're free to go about your usual daily routines. The only change is that I'm cancelling all non-essential sorties for the next forty-eight hours to allow the ground crew to bring every jet up to peak fighting condition. That is all.'

'What do you reckon?' Jane asked as we filed out of the briefing room.

'I don't know. It seems pretty weird either way, doesn't it?'

She stood for a moment lost in thought, her lip caught between her teeth. 'You spend years dreaming about being in combat, wondering what it's like and almost wishing it would happen so that you can find out . . .'

'And when it finally seems like you might, you're suddenly not sure you're so keen on the idea any more? Don't worry, I've got exactly the same feeling in the pit of my stomach.'

'Christ, I hope I can hack it, if it comes to it.'

'Of course you can. You're the best nav in the squadron. It's just your bad luck that you'll be flying with the worst pilot.'

She forced a smile, but there was still a haunted look in her eye. 'Are you still going up on the hills today?'

'I don't see why not. The Boss said there was no reason to change our routine.' I paused, trying to read her expression. 'I can stick around . . .'

She took a deep breath. 'No, I'm just being a dork. You get up there, but watch out for minefields.'

'You watch out for Sharks.'

The red and white Bristows civilian helicopters were housed in a compound on the far side of the control tower. The squat, bulbous choppers were nicknamed 'Erics' in honour of the eponymous and similarly shaped darts player. Alongside the fleet of Islander light aircraft, they were the work horses of the civilian economy of the Falklands. They carried mail and supplies between the settlements, and acted as long-range taxis and emergency ambulances.

I was the only paying passenger on the run down to San Carlos but I saw little of the landscape, sharing the cramped cab with stacks of boxes and cartons, and several bulging sacks.

The pilot headed west along the unbroken wall of the central mountain range. I caught a brief glimpse of Goose Green and Darwin in the distance before he banked the chopper and sent it climbing over the steep ridge of the Sussex Mountains. As it cleared the summit, I could see the long arm of San Carlos Water, sheltered by steep, rocky cliffs.

I tried to imagine it on that May morning sixteen years before. At first sight it looked a graveyard for ships, trapped in the tight confines of the bay, but the high ground that screened it on all sides except the narrow outlet to the north leading to the open sea also gave it some protection from air attack. I knew only too well how hard it was – even on exercise – to clear a ridgeline into a narrow valley, and then select and engage a target in the handful of seconds before it had flashed past.

As the helicopter went into the hover and came into land in a field of rough grass, a group of sea lions lumbered off the narrow shingle beach and splashed into the water, and a cloud of geese rose into the air. San Carlos settlement was just to our north, and across the dirty green waters I could see the rusting outline of a long abandoned freezing works at Ajax Bay, and another of the now familiar clusters of tin-roofed, white-walled settlements. On the near shore was another familiar sight: a neat rectangle of grass, punctuated by crosses and enclosed by a white picket fence

The beat of the rotors slowed and stopped as the engines whined down into silence. 'Which way are you heading?' the pilot asked.

I pulled a folded map out of my jacket pocket and studied it for a moment. 'I want to have a look at the beach at Bonners Bay, and then I'm going over the Sussex Mountains.'

He nodded. '5 Para, right?'

'Right. How did you know?'

'We learned it in school. I can tell you every landing-site and battleground from here to Stanley.' He pointed through the side window of the cab. 'There's a cairn on the beach marking the spot where the first troops came ashore.'

I heard the rattle of an approaching tractor and trailer. I thanked the pilot, jumped down from the cab and moved away quickly, anxious to be alone. I followed the curve of the bay beside a dense bank of gorse, then stood in front of the small cemetery. I made myself read each name aloud, as if calling the long-dead men back for that fraction of a second before their names were whipped away on the wind. Then I stood in silence, my head bowed, thinking not just of them, but of all the other men I had known and served with, who now lay dead.

I turned away and cut down to the shore, the shingle crunching under my boots. A rough cairn of sea-worn rocks cast a long shadow across the beach. A brass plate was set into the side facing San Carlos Water. 'At 4.00 am on 21 May 1982 the men of the Fifth Battalion, the Parachute Regiment, made the first landing by the British Task Force on Falklands soil at this place, "Blue Beach One".'

I looked around me, picturing the scene: the Task Force ships riding at anchor in the bay, their guns belching flame into the darkness as they lay down fire on Argentine positions; landing craft beaching in the shallows and men wading ashore through the icy waters; soldiers digging trenches and building sangars with frantic haste, as the chaos of men and equipment spill onto the beaches around them.

Everywhere noise and confusion, the din of the naval bombardment heightened by the crump of mortars, the hacking cough of heavy machine guns, the rattle of small-arms fire and the roar of tracked vehicles grinding the earth into a liquid slurry.

Soon after daybreak, as the tide of men and machines continue to pour ashore, with the Sea Kings shuttling back and forth trailing loads on cables beneath their bellies, the first Argentine jets streak in over the hills, hugging the contours of the ground, flying through a blizzard of ground fire. White water spouts erupt fifty feet into the air, where bombs have struck home and columns of oily black smoke billow up into the sky.

The men of 5 Para can spare no more than a glance as they tab for the ridgeline of the Sussex Mountains, a thousand feet above them, in a desperate race to secure the high ground before the Argentinians counter attack.

I turned away from the beach and began to stride up the hillside, stumbling over the tussocks and squelching through the peat. There were no minefield signs here, proof of how unexpected a British landing at San Carlos had been, but as I moved further up the hillside, the scars of war were obvious, despite the camouflage of nature.

Jagged shards of rusty metal still protruded from the peat and every few yards there were craters pocking the ground, varying in depth from a few inches to several feet, half-filled with black water. The floor of a narrow side-valley was littered with the rotting carcasses of half a dozen Argentine jets shot down during the landings. Several were Daggers – French Mirages, modified by the Israelis, and later sold on to Argentina. The years of wind and rain had weathered the paintwork and beneath the fading Argentine markings the Israeli Star of David was clearly visible.

I forced myself on up the mountainside, my lungs burning with the exertion. I wanted to suffer, to feel at least a little of what those men had felt, even though I knew it was a futile exercise; they had been in a war-zone, carrying loads of more than one hundred pounds on their backs as they trekked up the mountain into enemy fire.

Lost in thought, I had no warning as a hawk got up with a clatter of wings from almost directly under my feet. My heart pounded as I paused and turned to look back down the slopes towards San Carlos. Dark hooded shapes were moving along the shoreline. I tensed, staring at them for several moments before I realised that they were the sea lions disturbed again by the helicopter, which was now rising into the sky.

It passed overhead, the downwash lashing the grass around me, then disappeared beyond the ridgeline, leaving only a dying echo of its rotors. I struggled up the steepening gradient towards the summit, my muscles protesting at each laboured step as I dragged my boots clear of the peat or stumbled over the white quartz rocks littering the mountain. It was brutal, unforgiving ground, devoid of cover.

As I climbed higher, I came out of the shelter of the lower slopes into the full force of the wind. Flurries of sleet stung my cheeks and clouds streaming in from the west shrouded the summit and wrapped me in a cold embrace. The cloud diffused the light, muffling sounds and distorting distance.

I felt a mounting unease as I climbed higher. It was illogical – there was nothing to fear on this cold mountain but long-dead ghosts – but I could not shake the feeling. The bleating of a sheep echoed eerily in the mist and twice I started at movements on the periphery of my vision, birds or animals gone to ground.

Ahead of me I saw harsh silhouettes above the ridgeline and from one a gun-barrel seemed to be outlined against the sky, trailing tendrils of mist. Crumbling sangars built from rocks and slabs of peat stood in line like butts on a grouse moor, but the gun-barrel was nothing more sinister than a piece of rusting angle-iron. Nearby was a rats' nest of tangled wire, its green insulation sun-bleached and cracked with age. It lay half-buried in the peat, all that was left of the command wires of several Milan missiles.

The sangars still offered some protection from the wind and I huddled in the lea of one. The light grew a little stronger and I felt the first warmth of the sun on my face as the cloud thinned and the sky began to show pale blue through the last strands of mist.

I stood up, leaning into the wind, and scanned the wilderness stretching away from me on every side. The slopes dropped away steeply behind me to the long lead of San Carlos Water. At the far end, I could see the narrow opening into Falkland Sound and beyond that, almost at the limit of my vision, the dull green waters of the South Atlantic stretching away unbroken to the north.

One of the oil exploration vessels, toy-sized from this distance, was toiling up the Sound. Beyond it stood the sheer wall of West Falkland and I could see a smudge of smoke from the settlement of Port Howard hidden behind the hills. The mountainous spine of East Falkland stretched away from me in a long sweeping curve to the east, rising to the twin peaks of Mount Usborne.

To the south and south-east the ground fell away steeply to a broad plain where the sun sparkled on the surface on a myriad lakes, ponds and creeks. Due south of me the plain narrowed towards the bottleneck isthmus of Darwin and Goose Green, a wartime killing-ground far more savage than the one I had already traversed.

Even after all this time, the course of the Paras' advance was still clearly delineated by the shell craters, in places so dense and numerous that it seemed impossible that any man could have passed through that avalanche of fire and survived.

I stood looking down for several minutes, then shifted my gaze to the sharp angles of a white-fenced compound, standing out stark against the dark hillside away to my left.

I began to walk towards it, dropping down off the summit plateau and then following the contour round to the east. I stumbled through more peat bogs, over mounds of tussac grass and across long scree slopes, scoured and stripped by the wind and rain.

When I reached the cemetery, I saw the slim figure of a woman weeding between the graves, her face hidden by the upturned collar of her coat. The wind masked the sound of my approach and I stood watching her for a few moments, then coughed and rattled the latch of the gate.

Rose jumped in surprise, then turned to face me, smiling in recognition. 'I'm sorry,' she said. 'You startled me. It's very rare that anyone comes here.'

She had been working in the corner of the graveyard where I'd stood the day before, and a small posy of fresh flowers was now lying on the grave. She followed my gaze. 'They're past their best, I'm afraid.' She spoke a little hurriedly, almost apologetically.

'They're lovely.' I smiled. 'I didn't think you could grow anything here except tussac grass.'

She searched my expression for a moment, as if looking for hidden slights. 'We can't really. I grew these in the porch alongside the house.' I studied her profile as she turned away from me to gesture towards the settlement near the foot of the valley below us.

We stood in silence for a moment. 'Does somebody tend all the different graveyards?'

'Oh, it's not official or anything, I just like to do it. You could call it paying a debt, I suppose.'

'Rose? Those war stories that Agnes was so keen for you to tell me . . .' My voice trailed away into silence

She glanced along the neat rows of white crosses and looked out over the empty hillside around us. Then she took a deep breath. 'That's your brother's grave, isn't it?'

I nodded.

'I knew it, as soon as I saw you yesterday. You must have wondered what on earth was the matter with me, but it was such a shock, such a strange feeling to see you standing there. It was like seeing a ghost.'

I took out a scrunched-up, yellowing letter that I'd read and re-read a thousand times over the years. She took it from me, holding it carefully as the wind rattled the corners of the pages.

When she looked up again there was a tear in the corner of her eye. 'My father wrote that letter. Your brother saved our lives.' She looked down, re-reading the letter, then folded it with care and put it back in the envelope.

As she turned to hand it back to me, she stumbled on the corner of the grave. I put out an arm to steady her and felt the wiry strength in her slim frame. She blushed but made no effort to pull away. 'Do you remember him at all?' I said. 'You must have been very young.'

'I was twelve when – ' She paused. ' – When it happened, but I remember him very clearly, even though I only ever saw him for five minutes at most.'

'Please tell me about it.'

She led me to a wooden bench and we sat facing out over the rows of graves, looking down towards the distant shore. 'A few days before the Task Force landed at San Carlos, the Argentinians went to all the outlying settlements and rounded up everyone. No explanations, they just herded people into trucks at gunpoint and drove them away. They were all taken down to Goose Green and locked in one of the shearing sheds.' She paused. 'I don't know if they were doing it to stop people helping the British troops or to try and deter air raids on Goose Green, but everyone was terrified, not knowing what was going to happen and fearing that they would be shot.

'For some reason they hadn't disabled our radios, though. When George and Agnes saw the trucks coming towards their place they called my father to warn him what was happening. We took all the food and blankets we could carry and ran away—' She paused. 'Well, stumbled anyway. I was so frightened I could barely walk. We went up the moor to Hill Head Shanty. It's an old, long-abandoned settlement in a dip just under that ridge to the west there.'

I peered in the direction she was pointing but could see nothing but the empty skyline.

'The roof had collapsed at the front, but the ground floor rooms at the back of the house were still reasonably dry. We dragged what was left of the furniture – an old table and a dresser – close to the back of one of the rooms and made a sort of den behind it. My father covered it with all the lengths of broken timber, scrap metal and tin roofing sheets he could move and then pulled what was left of the ceiling down on top of it. If anyone had taken it apart or walked right round to the back of it they'd have found us soon enough, but to a casual glance it just looked like a pile of rubble.

'We heard some soldiers searching for us that first afternoon. I just lay on the floor, shaking with fright, with my hand stuffed into my mouth to stop myself from crying out. They poked around a bit, but didn't find us. There was another search the next day and after that they must have given up, because they didn't come back again. My father crept out that night and looked down on the farm. We couldn't go back home. Some of the soldiers had billeted themselves in our house; they killed all our hens and some of our sheep.

'We stayed in that place for five days. We heard a lot of explosions in the distance away towards San Carlos and Goose Green, but then on the fifth night a battle broke out all around us. We lay on the floor of the shanty, under the table, hearing the thunder of the explosions and feeling the walls shake. The noise seemed to go on for hours. I could hear it even when I pressed my fingers into my ears. Eventually the explosions stopped. I lay still, not daring to move, my ears ringing. My father went outside and saw some Argentinian soldiers on the hillside below us. They looked like they were running away. A short while later he heard someone speaking English.

'He told us, "We're safe! The British are here," and led us out of Hill Head. We were walking down the hill towards the British soldiers, waving a white vest above our heads, when the firing broke out again. The Argentinians had a machine-gun on the ridge behind us. I don't know whether they were firing at us or the British, but I could hear bullets smashing into the ground around us, and whining off the stones. The British soldiers were returning fire and we were caught in the open, between the two sides. There was no cover, nowhere to hide at all.'

Her eyes were unfocused, seeing only her memories. 'I can remember pressing my face down into the ground. I was screaming, but I couldn't even hear my own screams for the noise of gunfire. The shooting died down a little and there were short bursts rather than an endless barrage. In one of the lulls I heard a voice shout, "Cease firing. Cease firing!"

'The British stopped shooting and I lifted my head a fraction. I saw a man not more than fifty yards from us. He got to his knees and raised his arms, holding his gun by the barrel. He knelt there in full view of the Argentinians, waving the gun over his head, and after a minute they stopped firing too. Then he stood up, put his gun down on the ground and started to walk towards us. He stood between us and the Argentinians, then told us to stand up and walk slowly towards the British lines.

'In my nervousness, I stumbled and fell. He picked me up

and carried me the rest of the way. He had blond hair and the deepest blue eyes.' She looked into my face. 'Just like yours. He carried me past the British soldiers lying on the ground with their guns trained on the Argentinians. He set me down behind a small mound of rocks, an old sheepfold, a hundred yards behind them.'

As she talked, I had such a vivid picture in my mind that I could almost smell the cordite on the damp air and see my brother's tall, powerful frame, with the dark-haired girl clasped to his chest.

'My parents and my sister sat down next to me. I peered over the rocks and saw him walk back, pick up his rifle by the barrel and then drop from sight. The firing began again at once and I pressed my face back down in to the earth. I never saw him again. The battle moved on further up the hill, and as you know, he was killed later that night.'

She saw the tears tracking down my cheeks and took my hand. 'Anyway, that's why I come up here and look after the graves.'

We sat in silence, then she released my hand with an embarrassed smile. 'You must have been very young yourself when he died. Do you remember much about him?'

'I was twelve, like you, and I remember a lot about him. He was ten years older than me and he was a hero of mine even before he became one for real. When he came back on leave he'd often get home about five or six in the morning. He'd let himself in, wake me up and sit on my bed, telling me about all the things he'd done and all the places he'd been – sometimes the desert, sometimes the Arctic Circle, although even Aldershot sounded glamorous to me then.' I smiled at the memory. 'As soon as the shops were open he'd take me to town and buy me a new toy, a book or a game. I was so proud walking alongside him in his uniform, seeing all the girls smiling at him. I used to dream of wearing the same uniform myself one day.' I shrugged. 'When I grew up, it seemed too much like trying to step into his shoes; I joined the RAF instead.'

'Is that your strongest memory of him?'

'No, the last one is. When the Task Force sailed for the Falklands, my parents took me down to Southampton to see him off. We stood on the quayside and I waved a Union Jack and cheered myself hoarse as the ship cast off and began to ease away from the dock. I saw Mike long before he saw me. I watched him raking the crowd with his eyes, trying to spot us. I yelled and waved my hands like crazy but everybody else was shouting and waving too.

'The ship was picking up speed, and I thought he was going to miss us, but then he caught sight of me. Our eyes locked for a moment. He gave me the saddest smile and raised his hand in farewell. Then the ship was slipping away down the Solent, gathering speed, and I lost him. I hung on to my mother and cried my eyes out.' I swallowed and cleared my throat. 'Looking back now, I sometimes wonder if I haven't imagined it — a look on his face that wasn't there. I don't think so, though.'

She gave a gentle smile. 'I wish I'd known him.'

'You'd have liked him, everybody did. He could turn his hand to anything. He could play guitar, fix a car, play any sport you could name, climb mountains, scuba dive. He spoke three languages — French, German and Russian — and was clever, handsome and very funny as well. Women were always flocking around him. He was the youngest ever officer in the Parachute Regiment. He had everything going for him . . . until that day.'

She was silent for a moment, studying my face. 'It must have been hard for you, growing up in his shadow.'

I looked up, surprised. 'Not many people think of that.'

'I had a similar experience myself.' She paused. 'At a much lesser level, of course. My elder sister went to school in Montevideo and England, and got a first in English at Cambridge. She's now a senior producer with BBC Television.'

I waited. 'And you?'

'I didn't do quite so well.' She gave a soft, distracted smile. 'I came back to the Falklands from Montevideo, fell in love and got married young, against my parents' wishes.' Her face darkened as she spoke. 'Bernard was a seaman then, he'd fallen out with the FIC and couldn't get work on shore, but when my father died we took over the tenancy of the farm.'

'I'm sorry,' I said.

'It was five years ago.'

'And your mother?'

'She's still alive but she lives in England now. She came from there originally and wanted to go back.' She paused. 'And I think she wanted to be near my sister too. I miss her though.' There was a catch in her voice. 'You've no idea how lonely it can be here.'

Her tone was so desolate that I felt an urge to take her in my arms. 'You could go to England too.'

'No, it's not possible.' She was silent for a moment, then forced a brisk smile. 'There are lots of compensations too, of course. You should see it in spring and summer, when the flowers are in bloom. And when the birds are in their spring moult, the feathers drift over the beaches like snow. They're inches deep in places and when the wind picks up, it's like walking through a blizzard.'

'What about your farm?'

Her smile faded. 'It's hard. Perhaps we're just not cut out to be farmers, but everyone has struggled these past few years. The price of wool has been so poor that sometimes it's hardly been worth clipping the sheep.' She squared her shoulders. 'It's been the same struggle for everyone, of course. I'm not making us out to be a special case, but we have a small farm by Falklands standards and we've no capital to tide us over a bad patch.'

Again she smiled and this time the light danced in her eyes. 'Anyway, that's enough self-pity for one day. You must come down to the farm and stay for dinner. Stay the night if you can, I—' She checked. 'We'd love to hear all about you and your family. You can't imagine the number of times I've tried to picture where your brother came from, what his house and his family were like.'

We walked slowly down the hill, following a path as faint as a sheep track. A few hundred yards above the farm, we reached another tiny graveyard. The gravestones were so worn, weathered and lichen encrusted that the inscriptions were almost impossible to read, but again the graves were neatly tended. On one, a glass bell-jar enclosed a bouquet of white porcelain lilies.

'In the UK, that would have been vandalised years ago,' I said. 'Is it very old?'

'Victorian. It's my great grandmother's grave.'

'And your father?'

'We're not allowed to bury our dead here any more. Anyone who dies anywhere on the islands is taken to Stanley and buried in the cemetery there.' She gave a sad smile. 'Even the dead can't wait to get to Stanley these days.'

Chapter 5

As we came over the last rise before the farm, I saw Bernard standing in the corner of the paddock. His high, thin voice carried to us on the wind. He was cursing his dog as a handful of scraggy sheep repeatedly escaped while he tried to pin them in a fold. Exasperated, he gave it a kick as it slinked past him, tail between its legs. It limped as it made another attempt to encircle the sheep.

He turned to stare at us as we walked across the paddock towards him. His eyes flickered over me and came to rest on Rose.

'I met Sean up at the cemetery. He's the brother of that soldier; the one who saved our lives during the war.'

He gave me another, fractionally longer and friendlier glance.

Rose broke the silence. 'I've asked him to stay for supper.'

'We've not much in.'

She raised her hand in a small, nervous gesture. 'We've enough.'

He shrugged. 'I'll see you later then. I've work to do.'

I followed her down towards the farmhouse. The original building was almost hidden by an ugly accumulation of extensions and additions, including a Portakabin jammed against one wall.

I hung back as she opened the door. 'Perhaps I should be getting back.'

'I'd like you to stay. Please. He's—' She paused. 'He's not good with strangers, we don't get much company here. As you've seen for yourself the road stops at Mount Pleasant. The tracks are bad enough at the best of times and impossible after dark.'

I glanced at my watch. 'Then I should be going soon.'

She shook her head. 'Please. Stay the night if you can. I – We'd both like that. We can take you back in the morning. You can use the telephone if you need to speak to someone.'

I thought for a moment, very aware of the plea in her eyes. 'All right,' I said abruptly. 'That would be great, thank you, but I must check in with base first.'

'Help yourself.'

I called Mount Pleasant and was put through to the crew-room. Shark took the call.

'Anything happening?'

He laughed. 'This is the Falklands, remember. Nothing ever happens here.'

'No developments on that lost item?'

'What?'

'The one the Boss was telling us about this morning.'

'Oh that. No, none at all. We're still looking for it.'

'Okay. I'm staying overnight near Goose Green. If anything crops up, the telephone number's 102.'

Shark whistled. 'You're staying the night? I don't believe it. Forty-eight hours and you've scored already. I've been here two months and I haven't even seen a sheep I like.'

'Don't give up hope, there are plenty more out there. Anyway, I'll be back in the morning. Pass the word back up the line, will you?'

'All right. Jane's here, she wants a word with you.'

Her voice sounded both amused and a little nettled. 'Come on, Sean, tell me you haven't fallen in love again?'

'No, that's just Shark's little joke.'

'It is a "she" though.'

'It's both,' I said wearily, 'a man and wife.'

'So where are you?'

'A place called Black Beck House, down towards Goose Green.'

'Great. I'll come and get you in the morning. I could do with another trip out. We've only been here two days and Mount Pleasant's charms are already beginning to pall a little — or perhaps it's the company I'm being forced to keep.'

'That would be great, if you don't mind. Can you find it all right?'

'I'm a navigator, remember. I can find anything.'

'You couldn't find the target on that last exercise.'

She laughed. 'We're even then, because you couldn't hit it on the one before.'

'Okay, see you in the morning. Watch the track, though. It's about three parts mud to one part stone.'

'I come from Guneela, don't forget,' she said. 'If you can drive the roads in the Wet there, you can drive anywhere. Besides, I want to make sure there really is a husband out there.'

'Oh, there's one of those all right. He's called Bernard.' I hung up before she could reply.

Rose had been feeding slabs of peat into the stove, a once-cream Rayburn, smoked to the colour of a kipper by half a century of use. The furniture and the floral-patterned wallpaper had a similar patina of age, and the only modern items in the room were the telephone and the television set, perched on a corner of the dresser. Like the table and chairs, the dresser was solid but rough-hewn, and I could imagine Rose's father or grandfather making them from timber salvaged from shipwrecks, even saving and straightening the bent nails to be used again.

Rose turned up the draught on the stove, then began wiping down the kitchen surfaces.

'Dusty stuff, isn't it?' I said. 'I grew up in Kerry, in the west of Ireland. We used to burn it there.'

'Tell me about it. What's it like?'

'A bit like here, cold and windy. I used to think it was pretty remote as well, but I've changed my mind since I've seen the Falklands.'

Rose smiled. 'Wait till you've seen some of the settlements on West Falkland before you call us remote. They found a body on Mount D'Arcy a few years ago. It was a shepherd who'd gone missing in the 1930s. The body was lying in the open, but no one had ever passed that way in sixty years.'

She opened the back door. There was a meat-safe the size of a coal-shed just outside. She emerged from it carrying the hindquarter of a sheep. 'I hope you like mutton. It's known as 365 in the Falklands. We seem to eat it every day of the year.'

She made some tea and we sat facing each other across the table as the light faded outside. Rose talked eagerly, her eyes

sparkling as she questioned me about life in the UK, the Air
Force and in the different countries I had seen. 'Your parents
must be very proud of you.'

I laughed. 'I'm not sure they'd agree. I'm a bit of a black
sheep. I'm a constant letdown to them, especially compared to
my brother. To be honest, I'm not even a very good pilot.'

'I don't believe that.'

'It's true. I could be a better one, that's for sure, but as
my father would tell you, I never see anything through. That's
what I always got on my school reports: "Could do better." The
only other things they used to write were comments like, "Sean
has a vivid imagination." What they meant was that I spent all
my time staring out of the window and daydreaming.'

I glanced out of the window for a moment, my eye caught
by the wind whipping the spume from the white-capped waves
rolling in to the bay beyond the fields.

She laughed. 'I believe you.'

I gave a sheepish grin. 'It's beautiful here, but I don't think
I could handle the isolation.'

She gave a wan smile. 'You get used to it, but I miss—'
She paused. 'How can you miss what you've never had? But
I do miss the idea of towns and cities, of woods and forests
and deserts, and anything that isn't peat, tussac grass and
rock. I miss cinemas and theatres, and restaurants and dancing,
and bright-coloured clothes and high heels—' She broke off,
embarrassed by her own enthusiasm, her cheeks flushed and her
eyes shining. 'Don't get me wrong, since the war, life's become
a lot easier for all of us here, in some ways at least. We all have
telephones and satellite TV—' She was silent for a moment. 'It
reminds me of a story I once read – I read a lot, my sister sends
me a box of new books from England every month. It was about
the arrival of the first ever tractor in a remote farming village in

the Alps. From that moment on, just knowing that there was an easier way, the work that the farmers had been doing every day of their lives without ever questioning it, suddenly became a little bit harder and the weight that they were carrying felt that bit heavier.'

She had been staring down at her fingers resting on the table. They were long and delicate, but roughened by hard work. She glanced up at me. 'Television's like that. So are the cruise liners docking at Port Stanley, the flights coming in to Mount Pleasant twice a week – even you servicemen. They all remind us that there is somewhere else and another way to live. Children go away to school and college and, like my sister, they don't come back.'

'You could have gone to college too.'

'I know. There are times now when I wish I had, but I was young and impatient to get my nose out of books and see more of life.' She gave a rueful smile. 'Ironic, isn't it? Instead of that, I came home and got married to the first and only man I'd ever dated.'

'Bernard's very lucky. If I'd . . .'

Our eyes met and my words trailed away. Her lips were slightly parted and her look was a mixture of surprise and excitement. The tick of the clock seemed very loud in the stillness of the room.

She looked away. 'When I was young, I used to dress up in some of my mother's clothes and pretend I was a model; I suppose all girls do. And I used to dream about England, imagining what it was like. Before satellite television, all we had were books and glossy magazines. I built a picture of England from them.' She gave a rueful smile. 'It wasn't a very accurate one – all thatched cottages and stately homes, royalty, handsome men, sophisticated and glamorous women – and the

Beatles, of course. I used to dream—' She hesitated. 'It's silly, I know, but I used to dream that your brother was still alive and that I was married to him. We had a house in London, a thatched cottage in the country with roses round the door and two perfect children.' She looked away in embarrassment.

'Do you have children?'

She blushed. 'No, we don't have any, we—'

I heard the stamp of boots across the yard and the door banged open. Bernard came into the kitchen and we both fell silent as if interrupted in a moment of intimacy.

Rose flushed deeper under his stare. I felt the silence growing, but could think of no way to break it.

'The cow's still to milk,' he said.

'I'm sorry, I'd forgotten the time. I was talking ...' She gave me an apologetic smile. 'I'll only be twenty minutes or so, help yourself to some more tea.' She pulled a coat around her and hurried out into the yard behind Bernard.

I wandered around the room for a couple of minutes, then began leafing through the local newspaper I found on the dresser. It was published weekly and boldly headed, 'The Kelper – the independent voice of the Falklands', but it had more the flavour of a parish magazine. There were only two items of international news, a brief paragraph on the disturbances in Argentina and a table of wool prices on world markets. The list of ships due to dock at Stanley – Japanese, Korean, American, Russian, Canadian, Spanish and Norwegian – read like a roll-call of the world's fishing-fleets. The only non-fishing vessels I could see were an exploration ship and a cruise liner.

The front page story, alongside a picture of an elderly woman holding an envelope, was headlined, 'MISSING LETTER TURNS UP!' The copy was equally riveting. 'A letter Mrs Joyce Hunt had given up for lost arrived this week, over three weeks late. Post Office spokesman Neville Rowley explained: "Joyce's letter had been added to the mail for Dunnose Head settlement by mistake. We had to wait for the next supply run before it could be collected and delivered to the right address. We've apologised to Joyce for the delay." "Accidents do happen," quipped Joyce. 'I'm just glad to have got the letter in the end. It had a picture of my granddaughter in it."'

Further down the page, another brief item caught my eye. 'Leonora Patten lost a £10 note in Ross Road after last Wednesday's Council meeting. If anyone has found it, please leave it at the Upland Goose.'

I shook my head, half-amused and half-envious of a place where, instead of a daily diet of rapes and murders, a misdirected letter or a lost £10 note qualified as front-page news.

I heard the engine of a tractor and looked out of the window. Bernard was backing it across the yard to hook it up with a trailer. He stopped and jumped down from the seat, leaving the engine rumbling. He had stopped a couple of feet short of the trailer and I watched him for a moment as he struggled to connect the coupling, trying to drag the loaded trailer over the rutted yard. I went outside. The sheepdog, now chained to its kennel, started to bark.

Bernard glanced round and shot me a suspicious look.

'I'll guide you back, if you like.'

'Thanks, but I can manage.'

'I know you can, but as I'm sitting around doing nothing, I might as well give you a hand.'

He hauled at the trailer once more, then gave an abrupt nod and climbed back on to the tractor. I waved him slowly back, eased the steel bar into the slot and dropped the locking pin through the hole.

He cut the engine and the wind whipped away the stink of

diesel smoke. In the silence I heard the clank of a pail from the cowshed on the far side of the yard.

Bernard walked round to the back of the tractor, checked the coupling and muttered something that might have been thanks. He glanced up at the darkening sky, then turned his head as if he was scenting the wind. 'Snow's coming.'

The cold steel had chilled my fingers to the bone and I blew on my hands to warm them. 'Do you never wear gloves?' I asked.

He looked down at his red, swollen fingers. 'No. You can't work in them.'

'Even when it's this cold?'

'You don't feel it when you're used to it.' There was a touch of pride in his voice.

There was a flurry of snow, and he nodded to himself as he led the way towards the house. The back of his coat was split down the seams and belted with a piece of baler twine. He held the gate open for me and I saw that the hinges were the soles of an old pair of wellington boots, nailed to the wood.

He followed my gaze. 'Nothing's wasted here.' As he spoke, he had the same look, part-proud, part-defensive.

He put the kettle on to boil, then sat down facing me across the table. 'So what brought you to the Falklands? Your brother's grave?' He spoke without looking at me, his hands cupped on the table in front of him.

'I was posted here for the usual four-month tour.'

'One of our blue-eyed protectors from the Argies, eh?'

I took my time about replying, still trying to weigh him up. 'It's just another job, really.'

'Nice work, though. I bet the women are impressed with your uniforms and your tales.'

'Only the shallow ones.' Again I studied him. 'I'm not

going to start apologising for what I do. I love flying, but like any other job, there's plenty of bullshit and boredom as well, and a fair bit of danger too. I've lost more friends than I care to think about in training accidents, never mind war.'

'You wouldn't swap your life for mine, though.'

'I wouldn't swap my life for anything, but I wouldn't know how to begin to do what you do.'

He looked up sharply, scanning my face as carefully as he'd examined the tractor coupling, then relapsed into silence. After a minute, I tried again. 'Do you own the farm?'

'We rent it, but at least we rent it from a Falklander these days. Ninety per cent of the farms used to be absentee-owned; at least that's changed since the war.'

'There've been a few other changes too, haven't there?'

He gave a grudging nod. 'There's been a few, not all of them for the best.'

'But life's better now than it was, surely? And certainly better than being an Argentine colony?'

'Maybe we'd be better off without either of you.'

I was trying to keep the conversation light, but his truculence niggled me. 'You'd soon want us back, though, if Argentina tried to invade again.'

'Maybe. There wouldn't have been a war last time if you hadn't tried to sell us down the river.' He spoke as if it were my personal responsibility.

'Perhaps so, but in the end we saved your necks.'

'You fought to save your Prime Minister's neck, not ours.'

I took a deep breath and made another effort to find some common ground. 'Well, whatever our past differences, at least we're all working together now.'

'Working together? We can't even sell you the milk from

our cows. The EC won't allow it. Our milk's good enough for us but not for you apparently. Every pint you drink on the Falklands has been imported.'

I smiled. 'You won't get an argument from me about the lunacy of the EC, but even if we don't buy your milk, Britain's put some very serious money into the islands in the last fifteen years. £80 million a year is an awful lot for just over 2,000 people. That's about £40,000 per head.'

He waved his hand across the table-top as if brushing the argument aside. 'Falklanders raised enough money to pay for ten Spitfires to defend the UK in the Battle of Britain. Didn't know that, did you? And it wasn't just money we sent. We lost over forty of our menfolk fighting in Britain's wars, one in fifty of the population of these islands. My grandfather was one of them. We've put plenty – in every way – into the UK. And now we're not the poor relations any more. We pleaded for years for the introduction of a 150-mile limit to protect our fishing grounds, but Britain ignored us. It took the Argentine invasion before an exclusion zone was declared.' He paused. 'Know how much we get from the sale of fishing rights now?'

'£20 million.'

'And do you know how much we got before the war?'

I could have hazarded a pretty accurate guess, but I didn't want to steal too much of Bernard's thunder. I shook my head.

He gave a small smile of triumph. 'Nothing. Now we don't rely on British help any more. We do things for ourselves. We grow fresh fruit and vegetables the year round now, using hydroponics; it's the first regular, guaranteed supply we've ever had.'

'But ninety per cent of your food still comes from Chile.'

'Maybe, but we pay for it with our own money, not British government handouts. In fact, we're self-sufficient in everything

now, apart from defence, and when the oil starts flowing, maybe
that will change too. We won't just be talking about tens of
millions then, but hundreds of millions a year. Long after your
North Sea oil has run out, they'll be pumping oil from off
these shores.'

'Then you'll all be rich, but the Falklands will be changed
forever. It'll be one of the most important pieces of real estate in
the southern hemisphere . . . and you'll definitely need us then, to
stop the Argentinians marching in and taking it from you.'

He shrugged. 'We've offered to pay our defence costs
retrospectively, once the oil revenues build up, but there's
talk that we might recruit our own Defence Force, maybe
from the Gurkhas. They're another lot that the British used
when it suited them and then tried to dump when they'd
outlived their usefulness.'

I wasn't too sure I could argue against that. I remained
silent for a moment, then noticed that Bernard's expression
had softened. For the first time he gave me a smile of genuine
warmth. 'I'm sorry,' he said. 'I don't need to talk to you about
debt. Your brother saved Rose's life and that's not a debt
that's lightly discharged. You're welcome here as long as you
want to stay.'

It was now so dark that we could barely see each other
across the table. Bernard stepped outside for a moment and
I heard the sound of a diesel engine starting up. It settled
into a regular thudding beat and a moment later the bare bulb
hanging over the kitchen table flared into light.

He came back inside kicking sleet from the end of his boots.
'You'll need to take a candle when you go to bed. We turn the
generator off at ten. You'll be sleeping in the Portakabin. It's
warmer than the house.'

Rose came back in shortly afterwards, pausing in the doorway as if to test the atmosphere. As she began to prepare the meal Bernard turned on the television. The tail-end of the news bulletin included a brief item on the continuing street demonstrations in Buenos Aires. Again I saw banners carrying slogans about the Malvinas.

'They can march as much as they bloody want,' Bernard said. 'They won't get these islands, not now, not ever.'

Rose and I did most of the talking over dinner as she pressed me for every detail of my home and family, and every memory I had of Mike. Every time I looked up, her eyes were on me. Each time she would meet my gaze for a fraction of a second and then look away, towards Bernard.

When she spoke, she was animated and excited, words pouring out of her. At times I watched her, almost mesmerised. She was as well-read as anyone I'd ever met, informed and witty. She seemed wasted in this setting, though that was not a sentiment I was ever likely to voice around Bernard.

He did his best to look interested, but said little. When she mentioned books she had read, or talked about places she wanted to see, he seemed to stiffen and a frown creased his brow.

I tried to steer the conversation round to him, but he paused after each question, as if examining it for booby-traps, and when they came, his replies were often hesitant.

'So what do you think of the Falklands?' he said at last.

'I haven't really been here long enough to form an opinion. It does feel a long way from home, but the landscape's beautiful and—'

'The people are friendly?' He smiled. 'We know what most of you think about us. We can see it in your eyes.' He held up a hand as I began to protest. 'I've overheard soldiers talking in pubs in Stanley. You think we're a hundred years behind the times. Most of you are polite to our faces, but behind our backs, you're laughing at us. And you'd rather be anywhere else than here.' He paused. 'It's understandable. But one thing above all you should understand. We're not like you; we're not here because we have to be. We're here because we choose to be.'

All the time I'd been talking to him, I'd been aware of Rose's gaze on me. I looked up suddenly. She flushed and looked away.

'What about your own life, Sean?' she said. 'Are you married?'

Bernard laughed as I shook my head. 'Even if he was, I've never met a soldier yet who was married after six at night.'

'Sean's not a soldier.' Her tone was impatient. She turned back to me. 'Is there someone special? Your friend at George and Agnes's party. . .?'

'We're good mates, that's all.'

Bernard was watching me intently. 'So how are you going to fill your time?' The edge was back in his voice.

'I want to visit the battlefields and walk some of the ground that my brother crossed.'

He was silent for a moment. 'You're both the same, you and Rose,' he said. 'You live too much in the past. You're prisoners of it. And memory is a dangerous thing. It tells lies. We look back on something and remember it as we want it to be, not as it was.' He gestured towards the darkened window. 'What's out there now is what's important, not what happened sixteen years ago. You should let it go. Live in the present, not the past, and not in some dream future that'll never happen.' He had not even glanced at Rose, but it was clear that he was talking to her through me.

There was a long silence. He looked at the clock, pushed his glass away and yawned.

I took my cue. 'If you don't mind, I'll turn in. I'm really tired and I have to be away early in the morning.'

'I'll give you a knock then,' he said. 'Six o'clock too soon for you?'

'It's practically a lie-in. That's one thing aircrew and farmers do have in common.'

Rose showed me to my room. One of the old farmhouse windows had been opened out into a short passageway built from scrap timber which connected it to the Portakabin.

She hesitated in the doorway. Over her shoulder I saw Bernard's dark figure staring at us. I called out, 'Goodnight, Bernard.'

She looked back, then gave me a fleeting smile and said 'Goodnight' in a voice so low it was almost lost in the noise of the wind. As she went back down the hall, he turned and walked away. A few moments later the generator stopped, plunging the house into darkness.

The room smelt faintly of damp and the bedding was cold to the touch. I huddled under the blankets and fell asleep listening to the sound of the wind keening over the hillside.

The familiar nightmare was waiting for me. I stood on a windswept hilltop, watching as the same faceless, malevolent figures moved over the black ground towards me. I looked down and saw Mike, Geoff, Rose and Jane, climbing the hillside below me, oblivious of the danger at their backs.

They looked up, smiled and waved. I tried to scream a warning, but my words were carried away on the wind. Then the firing began. Mike pitched forward into the dirt, then Geoff too fell and lay still. Rose looked up towards me, her hands outstretched, pleading with me. I began to run down the hillside.

＊　　＊　　＊

Bernard's knock did not wake me. I'd been lying there, watching the grey dawn light creeping through the window. I got up at once, but by the time I reached the kitchen he had already gone outside. I watched his stocky figure striding up the moor towards his sheep.

Rose's face was pale and the circles underneath her eyes were even darker, as if she too had slept little, but she greeted me warmly and gave me some breakfast. She offered to drive me down to Goose Green or even back to Mount Pleasant, but I shook my head. 'It's all right, my navigator's coming to pick me up.'

I helped her clear away the breakfast things and we talked as she busied herself around the farmyard, feeding a few scrawny chickens and milking their solitary cow. Just after eight I heard the sound of an engine and saw an Air Force Land Rover bucketing up the track towards us. Jane's long blonde hair was clearly visible through the windscreen.

Rose turned to me in surprise. 'She's your navigator?'

I nodded. 'She's a pretty good one too, but don't let on, she's too full of herself already.'

The Land Rover ploughed to a halt, sending the chickens that had been scratching around the yard squawking for cover. Jane jumped out, shook hands with Rose and gave me a kiss on the cheek. I saw Rose's questioning glance.

'Like I told you, we're just good friends,' I said, wondering why I felt the need to explain. 'Jane goes out with my best mate back in England.'

They stood for a moment, looking each other over in a way that would have been insulting from a man. 'You don't look like a farmer's wife,' Jane said, 'and I mean that as a compliment.'

'Thanks. You don't look like a navigator.'

I hid a smile. There was a definite edge to the exchange.

'We'd better go,' Jane said. 'I promised to have the Land Rover back by ten and it took me over an hour to get here.'

My smile broadened.

'And no, I didn't get lost, smart-arse. That track isn't built for either comfort or speed, and a landslip's wiped out part of it. You can drive back if you like. See if you can do any better.'

I took Rose's hand. 'Thanks a lot, for everything. I'm really glad we met.'

'I'm glad you came. You will come back, won't you?'

'I want to do some walking in the hills on Saturday before we get stuck on Quick Reaction Duty. I could call in then, if it's all right.'

'Till Saturday then,' she said. We stood awkwardly under Jane's steady gaze. Rose made as if to shake my hand, then leaned forward and brushed my cheek with her lips.

She ran back to the house, but as I drove off, I turned to look back and saw her watching from the window, her hand pressed against the glass. As I swung back, I saw that Bernard too was watching me from the moor above the farm. I put my hand out of the window and waved. He half-raised an arm in response, then let it fall back to his side and turned away, busying himself with his sheep.

'I'd say you made quite an impression there, Sean.'

I glanced across at her, then stared through the windscreen, trying to steer the Land Rover around the worst of the ruts and potholes in the track.

'She's lonely.'

'You've got to watch out for the married ones; they're danger.' A faint smile was playing around her lips.

'Thanks for the grandmotherly advice, but it's really not necessary.'

'I wouldn't be so sure. I saw the way she looked at you.'

'She's just grateful for some conversation that isn't about sheep.'

'Get off the grass. She's got big eyes for you. It sticks out like the balls on a dingo.'

'Look, she knew my brother, that's all. He helped to rescue her and her family when the Paras were advancing through here.' I related the story that Rose had told me.

'He was a brave man,' Jane said.

I nodded. 'Mike was always helping people. He used to take me down to the playground in the park. I'd be sitting on the swing waiting for him to give me a push, or going down the slide shouting, "Watch me, Mike, watch me," but he'd be off rescuing some little girl who'd got stuck on the climbing frame or comforting a kid who'd fallen over and skinned his knees.'

Jane sat in silence for a moment. 'Was rescuing Rose's family what he won his medal for?'

'No, that was later, when he died.' I changed gear. 'So what's new? Anything happened back at base?'

'Puh-lease. This is the Falklands, you know.'

'You're beginning to sound like Shark.'

'Shark's all right when you get to know him a bit.'

It was my turn to smile. 'You've got to watch out for the unmarried ones; they're danger.'

I drove on in silence, dividing my attention between the rutted track and the clouds of wildfowl and seabirds rising from the sodden plain below us. Their wings sparkled as they climbed from the still-shadowed ground into the low light of the morning sun.

I glanced across at Jane. She was still watching me. 'You're not getting off the hook that easily, Sean, I know you too well. You're a sucker for that waif-in-distress routine. You've got the hots for her, haven't you?'

I snapped back, 'For Christ's sake, Jane, change the record, will you? Even if you were right, which you aren't—' As I spoke, I felt a stab of guilt at the realisation that what she said might well be true. 'Anyway, its none of your business. What the hell does it matter to you?'

'I'm just interested in why you find her so attractive. Is it that she looks like a victim or is it because you can pretend to be your brother when you're around her?'

'Go fuck yourself.'

'You too.'

We both relapsed into silence, staring fixedly ahead through the windscreen. I was shocked and a little ashamed of the way the row had boiled up from nothing, but there was more to it than that. I realised I had no defences with Jane; she could see right into my soul.

I braked to a sudden halt as I rounded the next bend. The landslip had carried away a section of the road, leaving a black scar down the hillside. I put the Land Rover into four-wheel drive, then pulled off the road, following a line of wavering tyre tracks around the head of it.

I gunned the accelerator, sending the vehicle bouncing and jolting up the hill. It leaned at a perilous angle as we rounded the top and as it righted itself the wheels slid sideways and sank into a morass of peat.

We ground to a halt. 'Shit.' I revved the engine angrily but that only dug us in deeper. The wheels spun and sent flurries of mud behind us. I glared at Jane. 'You drive, I'll dig.'

She avoided my gaze, her jaw still set, but she nodded and slid across to the driver's seat as I got out.

It took me forty minutes' hard digging to get us free. I used the steel tracks carried in the back for just such a contingency, but I also needed the rubber mats from the foot-wells and all the small rocks I could scavenge from the surrounding moorland to give the wheels enough grip. I heaved and strained, pushing from the back as Jane inched the Land Rover out of the bog. By the time it was free I was black with peat and soaked to the skin.

We drove most of the rest of the way back to the base in silence, and when either of us did speak the conversation was strained and terse. Jane got out without a word and banged the door shut behind her.

I went back to my room, stripped off my sodden clothes and showered myself clean. Feeling both stupid and sheepish, I went down to the Mess and bought a bottle of wine as a peace offering. I was about to take it up to her room when I saw her sitting at a corner table, staring out of the window. She looked up as I walked over and hid something behind her back.

'I'm—' We both began speaking together, then fell silent, and then began again simultaneously.

She laughed. 'You first then and make it good.'

'I'm sorry. What you said touched a nerve—' I held up a hand as she began to interrupt. 'But that's because it was at least partly true, and even if it wasn't, I shouldn't have reacted like that.' I handed her the bottle. 'A peace offering; I even bought Australian.'

She smiled and produced an identical bottle from behind her back. 'Here. I couldn't find any Irish chardonnay.' She paused. 'And I'm sorry too. You were right, it's none of my business and I shouldn't have said what I did about your brother. Friends?'

'Always.' I leaned over and kissed her cheek.

'It's practically lunchtime,' she said, 'and we're not on duty today. What the hell, we might as well get a corkscrew and seal the deal.'

I opened one of the bottles, poured us both a glass and toasted her. 'Here's to us, more laughs—'

'And fewer bloody stupid rows,' she finished for me. 'I couldn't believe how angry I was with you.' She gave a guilty smile. 'Nor how happy I was when you got the Land Rover stuck. I was practically punching the air with delight.'

'And I was so furious I could have picked it up bodily and thrown it out of that bog.'

She laughed. 'I wish you had. It would have been a bloody sight quicker.' She drank some of her wine, watching me over the rim of the glass. 'I don't know what's up with us, Sean. We can't be stir-crazy already, can we? We've only been here four days, God knows what we'll be like at the end of four months.'

'It's tough living in each other's pockets as well.'

'But we're not. It'll be different when we're on QRA duty, but at the moment I hardly see you. You're off all over the countryside whenever you've got half a chance.' She paused. 'Perhaps that's part of the problem, maybe I'm a bit jealous.' She met my gaze for a second, then looked away.

I was the first to break the silence. 'It's surprised me how much being here has affected me, but I feel I can't stop. I have to try and understand why he did what he did.' I shrugged helplessly.

This time she held my gaze. 'Don't let it become an obsession, will you? It was over sixteen years ago. I know your brother was a hero, but you've nothing to prove or live up to, to me or anyone else. And you don't have to apologise to anyone for being alive when your brother is dead. Okay, he was clever and brave, and witty and wise, and everybody loved him, but to be honest I'm getting a bit sick of him. I don't want to hear about him any more, I just want to hear about you.' She hesitated and looked anxious. 'I've not said the wrong thing again, have I? We're not going to have another row?'

I shook my head. 'No, but I may be forced to buy you another bottle of wine, just in case.'

She smiled, but her expression was still troubled. 'That's it, really. So just do what you feel you have to do, but then put it all behind you and move on.' She worried her lower lip with her teeth. 'Although it's hard to look to the future here, isn't it? The past seems to cast such a long shadow.'

She drank the rest of her glass in one gulp, then gave me an apologetic smile. 'I shouldn't be so maudlin, should I? But everything about this place gets to me. The cold, the damp and that endless bloody wind—' She broke off and stared out of the window.

'It's more than that, though,' I said, 'isn't it? There's something else.'

She turned to face me, trying to read my expression. 'Perhaps I'm just getting disenchanted with the Air Force.'

'Which one? Yours or mine?'

'Both.' She gestured at the worn carpet and the walls lined with near identical squadron photographs and badges. 'It's like the Common Room at my college. The cleaners never moved the chairs from one year to the next, they just vacuumed around them because they knew nobody would notice, and even if they did, no one would care.' She shrugged her shoulders. 'Sometimes I love this life. I love flying and sharing the jet with you, and all the things that go with it, but sometimes I feel like I'm trapped in a perpetual time-warp, re-living my student years over and over, getting off my face drunk nearly every night, playing stupid pranks, insulated from the real world. Wherever you go, every crew-room's the same, all those petty arguments about whose turn it is to make the coffee or do the washing-up.

'Sometimes I get stalled with all the blokeish stuff too – the drinking games, the knob jokes, the fatuous ideas some forty-year-old boss has for improving squadron morale.' She frowned. 'It sounds like I hate all of it, doesn't it? I don't, but—' She looked past me, watching Shark, Jimmy and Rees standing near the bar, playing darts.

'I'm the only woman on this squadron, Sean. To be accepted in a fast-jet crew-room I've got to be more of a bloke than all the others. If I can swear like a trooper, drink all the blokes under the table and join in all the juvenile banter about sex and penis-size, then I get the ultimate accolade: "For a woman, you're okay – just another bloke." But I am a woman, and I want to keep being one.' She sighed. 'I guess I just mean that I'm not sure I want to do this forever, that's all.'

'But you won't. You and Geoff will want to get married one day and—'

'I doubt it. I can't really see myself as an Air Force wife; twin-set and pearls isn't really my style.'

'Come on, Jane, it's not like that any more.'

She fingered the pendant around her neck. 'Maybe I'm not too sure how much of a future Geoff and I have together.'

'Don't say that. You guys are great together. You're not going to toss all that away just because of a touch of the Falklands blues. It'll all seem different when you get back to the UK.'

She gave a sad smile. 'Ironic, isn't it? I start off trying to talk you out of your depression and two minutes later you're trying to rescue me from mine.' She reached for the bottle, refilled our glasses and then took a swig from hers. 'Right, that's enough introspection for one day. Let's get ourselves outside the rest of this wine and then go and play a couple of videos. Anything will do just as long as it's nothing like the view from this window.'

Chapter 6

The briefing next morning was largely routine. There had still been no signal from the *Trident*, and the searching helicopters had found no trace of the sub. The search would continue, but each passing day increased our pessimism about the outcome.

My mind wandered as Noel ran through the orders for the day, but I pricked up my ears at the last item. 'The last cruise ship of the season is docking in Stanley this morning. There's a battlefield tour organised for them; anyone who wants to join it is welcome. There won't be another one till spring, so this is your last chance on this tour.'

'What time does it leave?' I asked.

As Noel riffled through his sheets of paper, searching for the answer, Jane cocked an eyebrow at me. 'Another trip up the mountains?'

'The last one.'

She smiled. 'Apart from tomorrow, you mean. I distinctly

heard you tell Rose you'd be wandering the hills before you call in on her for your heavy date.'

'The next-to-the-last one, then.'

A sceptical look crossed her face.

'Honestly. You were right. I've got to draw a line under it. I'm going to go on this battlefield tour, make one more trip to the cemetery tomorrow, and then that's it.'

'I'll go with you, then. Don't make that face, I don't mean on the tour, but I'll drive you down to Stanley. I'm desperate for a bit of serious excitement and some heavy-duty shopping.'

'You'll have to go a lot further than Stanley for that,' Shark said, leaning round the back of her seat. 'Though I can probably arrange some serious excitement for you right here on the base.'

Jane laughed. 'What, in your room? I doubt it, Shark. Mild amusement maybe. I suspect the only way you could seriously excite me would be to fly in Brad Pitt for the weekend.'

The Stanley Road looped around the southern perimeter of the base, then struck north towards the hills, following the curving line where the foothills met the plain. The road to the capital was punctuated with shacks and rusting shipping containers, as if dumped by some freak wave and beached miles from the ocean. The door to one hung ajar and I could see it filled to the roof with winter fodder for the sheep.

We passed a handful of settlements, most of them invisible from the road and betrayed only by the rough hand-lettered signs pointing the way along narrow tracks winding down towards the sea. In the whole journey we met only one other vehicle, a battered Land Rover heading up towards the hills.

As we dropped down Sapper Hill into Stanley, I could see the cruise ship negotiating the narrows from Port Williams into the inner harbour. We strolled through the streets while we waited for the liner to dock and the passengers to disembark.

Stanley had the air of a genteel English seaside town, permanently out of season. A couple of fishing boats were tied up at the jetty and neat rows of houses ascended the hillside from the harbour. There were small patches of parkland and more trees than I had seen anywhere else in the Falklands, with evergreens forming thick clumps in some of the more sheltered parts of the town.

We parked near the jetty and then began wandering through the streets. A double arch almost as tall as a nearby house stood on the open ground in front of the cathedral. Jane read the brass plate aloud. 'This arch was made from the jawbones of two blue whales and presented to the Government by the Falkland Islands Company to commemorate the Centenary of the Colony as a British Possession, 1833-1933.'

She produced a camera from her bag. 'Okay, Sean, get under the arch and say "Cheese".'

'If you're going to behave like a tourist, I'm going home,' I said, but I obediently stood in place while she took the photograph. She glanced upwards and then burst out laughing. 'You won't believe this, even the cathedral's got a tin roof.'

I followed her gaze. The tower of the cathedral was capped with a squat spire, faced with brown-painted corrugated metal sheets. We went inside. The walls were lined with plaques commemorating the dead in a score of different conflicts, some dating back over a century.

Jane frowned. 'There's no escaping the past here, is there? Or the dead.'

'Or the wind,' I said as we went back outside. A painstakingly hand-lettered sign reading "Open Air Museum" led us up a side-street on the edge of town. Halfway up the street, there was a small shop selling handmade leather goods. The museum faced it across the road, the way barred by a gate set in a wooden fence. A sign on the gate asked us to '"Pay in the shop, price £1. If shut, put money in tin'.

I dropped a couple of pound coins in the tin nailed to the gatepost and opened the gate. The open air museum proved to be nothing more than a field in which an assortment of elderly surplus military equipment was slowly rusting away. It took us about two minutes to exhaust its possibilities.

'I went to a museum like this in Papua New Guinea once,' Jane said. 'In the middle of nowhere, at the side of a road outside Rabaul, there was a sign saying "Museum of the Japanese Occupation". I followed a track through the jungle for about a mile. At the end of it there was a guy sitting on a tree root, next to a tunnel leading into the hillside. I must have been the first person to walk down that track in weeks, but the guy was still there ready to sell me a ticket.

'I paid him one Kina, he gave me a cloakroom ticket from a roll he had on the tree root beside him and I went into the tunnel. It opened into a Japanese bunker from the Second World War. There were no exhibits as such, no labels or glass cases or anything, it was just the bunker as the Japanese had left it. There were some rusty wireless equipment, an anti-aircraft gun poking its barrels out through a slit in the hillside that was smothered in vegetation, some camp beds, a table and some chairs. That was it. It was a bit like an underground *Marie Celeste*.'

We walked up the hill to the next cross-street and then turned back towards the town. Jane pointed down the street, her shoulders shaking with laughter. 'I'd definitely have paid a pound to see this.'

It was an ordinary-looking suburban street, a row of a dozen or so modest, two-storey houses, each with a patch of front garden, perhaps five yards wide by three yards deep. It could have been a street in almost any English town, except that farm animals were grazing in half the gardens. We counted five sheep, two goats and one rough-coated horse as we travelled the length of the street, pausing every few yards for a photograph.

We stopped at the end to watch a few kids kicking a football around in the street. 'If you did that in England, you'd be run over inside five minutes,' I said. 'And there are some other things about this place you can't knock.'

'Like what?'

'No pollution, no crime.'

'You don't know that for sure.'

I pointed to the houses. 'Notice anything about the doors?'

'Apart from the tasteful colours, you mean? Shit, no locks.'

'Exactly. I can't think of anywhere else in the world where you'd see that.'

'You've obviously never been to Guneela.'

'Nor have you since 1980.'

We turned down the hill to the road facing the harbour and followed it back into the town centre. A zebra crossing marked the heart of Stanley's commercial district. 'This must be a status symbol,' I said. 'There can't be more than one car an hour through here.'

'Guneela had a traffic light. In twenty-four hours you wouldn't see more than a dozen utes, six cars and a couple of trucks, but the next town didn't have one and that was reason enough.'

'And don't tell me, when you were stuck for something to do on a Saturday night you could always head down to Main Street and watch the traffic light change colour.'

'Are you sure you're not thinking of Kerry?'

'No, we never had one. We just had a sheepdog chained up at the side of the road. Every time the sheep came down the road off the mountain he'd bare his teeth, bark his head off and send them back up again. It worked on me too, I was scared stiff of him.'

We walked past the handful of shops selling a bizarre mixture of tinned food, wellingtons, outdoor clothing, and tourist souvenirs. There were china penguins made in England, soft toys made in China and plaques and metal ashtrays embossed with the Falklands crest, made in Japan. Jane pointed to a display of sweaters. 'They probably even buy those from Taiwan.'

'Why shouldn't they? Everyone else does. Anyway, don't blame the Taiwanese for those, they have the unmistakable air of hand-knitting about them. My mother used to knit sweaters like that for me when I was a kid. They were always much too large, in horrendous colour combinations, and they itched like hell. I'd wear them once around the house to please her and then hide them at the back of a drawer.'

She pulled a face as we passed yet another window.

'Perhaps Shark's offer wasn't such a bad one after all,' I said.

'Oh, please. I'd rather join the Stanley hand-knitting circle.'

At the bottom of the street was a tall telegraph pole festooned with a jumbled mass of signs pointing in every direction. 'You wouldn't think there were that many places in the Falklands, would you?' Jane said.

'There aren't. They're all pointing the way home for people stuck down here.'

The signs measured the distance to places all over the world. Many were to great cities – London, New York, Sydney, San

Francisco – but the majority counted the miles to much more humble but even more deeply missed destinations. We stood side by side reading them. 'The Garth Inn, Maesteg, Wales, 8,540 miles. The Blue Bell, Kirby Hill, 8,756 miles.' Jane nudged me in the ribs. 'Shit, they've even got The Rose up there.' I followed her gaze. 'The White Rose, Highgate, 8,551 miles.'

It was our local back in London, a low-ceilinged warren of panelled rooms. In winter the three of us – Geoff, Jane and I – often sat talking for hours, warming ourselves in the glow of the huge open fire. In summer we sprawled on the grass outside, listening to the birdsong. It was only a couple of minutes' walk from the centre of Highgate village, but as peaceful as any remote country pub.

Both of us fell silent, our thoughts far away. I felt a lump in my throat. Nothing had brought home to me the vast distance separating me from home like that crudely lettered signpost.

After a few minutes, Jane slipped an arm through mine. 'That's enough sightseeing. Come and buy me a coffee before you go off to refight the war.'

We drank a cup of weak instant coffee in a café. The only other customers were two tables full of Japanese trawlermen. 'Great,' Jane said. 'They get the fish, the Falklands get metal ashtrays.'

'And twenty million quid a year for the fishing rights. You can buy a hell of a lot of ashtrays with that.'

'You'd think they could spare a couple of quid for a few coffee beans then, wouldn't you?' she said, staring at the contents of her cup.

'And you have the nerve to talk about whingeing Poms.'

She kicked my shin under the table. 'Remember that comment when you phone to ask for a lift back this evening.'

'That's what I like about Aussies, they never hold grudges.

Don't buy too many designer outfits, will you?' I stood up and blew her a kiss.

'Wait here a minute.' She hurried out of the door and disappeared into the shop across the street. She was back two minutes later, holding a battered-looking bouquet of white chrysanthemums. 'I won't come with you, but lay those on the war memorial, will you?'

I nodded. 'Of course I will.'

She smiled and kissed me, then, embarrassed, she pushed me towards the door. 'Better get moving or the tour'll leave without you.'

I walked down to the jetty. The liner was tied up next to the huge floating pontoon used by the oil exploration vessels. Convoys of Land Rovers were ferrying the cruise passengers away. Some were driven off to visit sea lion and penguin colonies along the coast, others made the shorter journey to the Falkland shops.

I joined a third group of just half a dozen people, forming a respectful circle around the man leading the tour. He was in civilian clothes and the craggy, wind-burned features below his grey-streaked black hair could have marked him as a farmer, but he had the bearing of a soldier and the manner of a man used to being obeyed. As he turned towards me, I recognised him from the briefing on our first morning.

I shook his hand. 'Jack Stubbs, isn't it? Sean Riever, I'm with 1435 Flight. Hope you don't mind me tagging along with you today.'

His face clouded for a second and there was a faint hesitation before he spoke. 'No, I don't mind at all.' He glanced round the rest of the group and dropped his voice to a murmur. 'And to be honest, you look likely to be the only one fit enough to finish the tour anyway.'

'You fought in the war yourself?'

He nodded. 'I was in the Paras, a Lance-Corporal back then. I'm a Staff-Sergeant now – not exactly a meteoric rise in fifteen or so years, is it? I'm a Forward Air Controller, and a survival and weapons instructor.'

'Which battalion were you with?'

'5 Para.'

'You'd have known my brother, then, Mike Riever?'

He nodded. 'Yes, I knew him. I was in his platoon. You look very like him.'

'Were you with him when—?' He glanced at his watch and I took the hint. 'I'm sorry, you're busy now, I know. Maybe we could have a pint and a chat later.'

'Sure.' He raised his voice. 'I think we're all here who want to be. I've just a couple of points before we set off. We'll be visiting war memorials here in Port Stanley and the cemeteries and memorials at San Carlos, Darwin and Goose Green. We'll also be overflying the main battle-sites and visiting the battlefields at Goose Green and Black Mountain.

'Goose Green is relatively flat, though the going underfoot is rough, but Black Mountain is a stiff climb. It's the last place we shall visit and though I'll be leading a party up there, anyone who feels they would prefer to pass on that section of the tour will be helicoptered straight back to Stanley. The others will be picked up later from the top of Black Mountain.' He glanced around the small circle of faces. 'And one note of caution. The route we're taking today is perfectly safe, but we are crossing battlesites, and where you've had a battle, you always have battlefield debris. That may mean harmless bits of metal but it could also mean unexploded bombs, missiles or mines. Do not pick up anything from the battlefields, no matter how much you might like a souvenir. Do not even touch anything.'

'What about minefields?' The questioner was a crew-cut, middle-aged man with an American accent.

'All minefields and other danger areas are marked and fenced off. Don't enter them. There is also a very slim possibility of finding a mine that has been washed out of a marked minefield on to a beach or riverbank. It's a very remote chance, but it has happened. As before, if in doubt, don't touch.' He reached into an inside pocket and pulled out a few photographs. 'In case you're in any doubt about the reason, these may help you.' He passed them around. An old couple looked at the first one together, shuddered and handed them to me without looking at the rest. They were photographs of the mangled bodies of animals.

'The sheep were blown apart after straying into minefields,' Jack said. 'The sea lion was unlucky enough to flop on top of a mine that had been washed up on the beach.' He glanced around. 'I'm sorry, but I like to make sure the message has got home.'

I passed them on to the American. He studied them for a moment. 'Why don't you just clear the mines?'

Jack's smile became a few degrees less friendly. 'We have removed a lot of them, and we have an ongoing programme to make areas safe, but there are tens of thousands of mines to be cleared. In most cases we don't know where they are, because the Argentinians who laid them either won't or can't tell us. Even for an expert, clearing a minefield is a very dangerous business. There are men out there every day risking their lives to make the place safer. We have a much easier task today; all we have to do is use a bit of common sense.'

The American looked sceptical.

'It wasn't like invading Panama,' Jack said, giving me a ghost of a wink. 'Sometimes you have to do a bit more than stroll up the beach and pose for the TV cameras. The Argentinians here were fighting back with guns, bombs, missiles and mines. It takes a very long time to clear up after a conflict like that ... and even longer to forget.' He resumed his previous brisk tone. 'Right, anyone who wants to change their mind about the trip is very welcome to do so, but I really wouldn't worry. We must have done at least five hundred battlefield tours over the last fifteen years and we've never had a casualty yet.'

The American joined us as we clambered into a long-wheelbase Land Rover and drove east along Ross Road. 'We'll visit the Liberation Monument shortly,' Jack said, 'but before we stop there, I want to show you one other memorial. Nearly three hundred British troops laid down their lives in the Falklands War, but the Falklanders have done their share of fighting for us too.' He stopped on the eastern edge of the town, by a huge stone cross facing out across the harbour. 'This is the Cross of Sacrifice. There are forty-three names inscribed on it, native-born Falklanders who died fighting in two World Wars. Out of a population of just two thousand, that's the equivalent of a million Britons or—' he gave the crew-cut American a sideways glance – 'about five million Americans. The Falklanders don't owe us any favours.'

He turned the Land Rover around in the shadow of the cross and began to drive back into Stanley. A sudden squall blew up, blotting out the harbour behind a curtain of rain. The streets of Stanley had emptied of people. A few dispirited-looking cruise passengers huddled in shop doorways, waiting out the shower, others were dimly visible through the steamy windows of the handful of pubs and cafés.

Liberation Monument stood on the far side of town, a tall column inscribed with the names of every unit that had fought in the war. It was topped by a bronze figure of Britannia triumphant, staring out over the grey waters of the harbour. Her face bore an odd resemblance to Margaret Thatcher, and there was another echo in the nearby road sign, Thatcher Road.

A long, crescent-shaped wall behind the monument carried the names of the war dead, engraved on a row of marble panels. The rain had eased to a faint drizzle, but water still ran down the face of the memorial, sliding from name to name and adding a further lustre to the sheen of the marble.

The high, curving wings of the memorial acted as a windbreak and as I walked towards it, searching the columns of names, I stepped out of the endless buffeting of the wind into an area of silence, stillness and calm.

The names of the dead were ranged alphabetically under their regiments, units or ships. There were long columns of names under HMS *Ardent*, *Coventry*, *Glamorgan* and *Sheffield* and longer ones still for the SAS, Royal Marines and Welsh Guards. The longest of all was for the Parachute Regiment, with almost equal numbers from the Second, Third and Fifth Battalions. Two-thirds of the way down the list for 5 Para was the inscription: 'Lieutenant Michael Riever, MC.'

I laid the bouquet of white chrysanthemums at the foot of the wall, among a score of poppy wreaths, some still crimson, others faded to a dull brick-red.

As I turned away from the wall, I found myself almost face to face with Jack. He must have stood in front of the memorial countless times before, but his face was a grim, expressionless mask as he faced it again. He stared past me, his lips moving slowly as he murmured the familiar names to himself.

The old couple were the last out of the Land Rover. They stood to one side for a few moments, talking quietly to each other, then walked slowly towards the memorial. There was only a stiff breeze blowing by Falklands standards, but she clung to his arm as if she was fighting her way against a gale.

They stopped three-quarters of the way along the wall. They stared at one of the names of the Welsh Guards for several minutes and I saw the woman reach out and touch the letters cut into the cold stone.

She turned and saw me watching them, and I felt like an intruder. She held out a camera. 'Would you take a picture for us, please?' she said. 'It's for our son, his broth—' Her voice cracked.

I took it from her and they stood to either side of the column of names. The old man was at parade-ground attention, staring straight past me, out towards the sea. His wife stood in profile, her eyes brimming with tears, still fixed on her dead son's name.

We got back into the Land Rover in silence. Jack drove us down Ross Road, through the town and out along the peninsula at the easternmost tip of the mainland. Drawn up around the shores of the inner and outer harbours or languishing in the shallows were the mouldering hulks of another score of ancient ships.

'Stanley was one of the busiest ship repair yards in the world at one time,' Jack said. 'Every vessel that took a battering rounding Cape Horn – and there were plenty of them – would put into Stanley for repairs. If the damage was more than the owners could afford, or more than the value of the ship, it would be abandoned here, either scuttled, dragged up onto the beach or simply left to rot at anchor. One or two of them have been rescued since then, like Brunel's ship, the *Great Britain*, which was towed back to the UK and restored, but most of them are still here.

'Falklanders don't like to see such waste, though. The Falklands Islands Company put a tin roof on one hulk, the

Egeria, and has been using it as a store for over a hundred years. The SAS used another one in the middle of the harbour as an observation post during the war. A patrol stayed on it for nearly two months, right under the Argentinians' noses.'

He turned in through the gates of the old Stanley airfield, where a Bristow's helicopter was waiting. We clambered aboard and flew due west, low over the mountainous central ridge, while Jack kept up a running commentary. We passed over each of the famous battlesites – Wireless Ridge, Mount Longdon, Tumbledown, Mount Kent, Two Sisters, Mount Challenger – and the pilot flew even lower, circling the peaks as Jack related a brief outline of the battle.

'I'm telling the story of the war back to front,' he said, 'because the British Task Force marched on Stanley from west to east, but from previous experience on these tours, I'm expecting that most of you will be flying back without me, while I lead a party of one or two up Black Mountain.'

We flew down to San Carlos and landed to visit the cemetery and the memorial cairn on the beach. Then we flew back over the Sussex Mountains towards Darwin and Goose Green, retracing the route I had walked a few days before.

The helicopter landed again near Burnside House at the neck of the isthmus. Jack led us forward on foot through the battlefield, stopping repeatedly to talk us through the battle, stage by stage.

Only the old couple and I stayed with him every step of the way. The biting wind, the cold and damp, soon cooled the enthusiasm of the others. They huddled in whatever shelter they could find – the lea of a tumbledown building, a sheep pen or a bank of gorse – and emerged with increasing reluctance after each halt.

Eventually we reached Goose Green, a settlement and a

number of huge shearing sheds, clustered around a jetty jutting out into the head of Choiseul Sound. On the other side of the isthmus, the shorter, narrower Grantham Sound curled away north, its narrow opening into Falkland Sound hidden by a shoulder of land.

'This is the objective we were fighting to reach,' Jack said. 'Any textbook of military strategy will tell you that five hundred men advancing across open ground to attack an equally strong force of well-equipped troops in prepared defensive positions is a recipe for disaster. Only the finest assault troops – and in my biased opinion, the Paras are the finest in the world – could have succeeded in such an attack. A lot of men died ... on both sides. Many of them are buried here.'

The two graveyards stood in the open, away from the settlement. They were separated from each other by a strip of grass, a no man's land between the opposing forces. Both were surrounded by white picket fences and laid out in geometric lines, with paths of white gravel separating the neat rows of graves.

A large white cross dominated the Argentine cemetery. In its shadow stood scores of smaller crosses. Some bore names, others were simply inscribed, 'An Argentine Soldier'. Fading, wind-battered bunches of carnations and chrysanthemums lay on the graves. Many of the crosses – even the unmarked ones – were hung with rosaries and family photographs, as if, unable to bear not knowing where their sons lay buried, grieving parents had simply adopted one of the unknown soldiers as their own.

Fewer crosses surrounded the memorial to the dead of the Parachute Regiment, a cairn of rough quartz boulders with an inset brass plaque. 'Don't be fooled by the number of graves,' Jack said. 'There's another Para cemetery on Black Mountain, but all the next-of-kin were also given the option of repatriating the bodies of their loved ones. Most people wanted them back in the UK, but a few chose to bury them here.'

He pointed to another monument a few yards away. It was a more traditional memorial, a stone obelisk on a heavy plinth, but at its side a grave was roughly marked with more small white quartz stones. It stood close to the water's edge, at the foot of a long, low hill.

Jack pointed up the hill. 'The officer buried here led a frontal assault over open ground against an Argentine machine-gun position on the top of that hill. It was an act of enormous bravery, even self-sacrifice, for which he paid with his life.'

The American cleared his throat. 'I read that it was also unnecessary.'

Jack's face flushed and I started forward, fearing for a moment that he might hit the man, but when he spoke, his voice was even, though his eyes never left the American's face. 'Then you'll probably also have read that the whole attack on Darwin and Goose Green was unnecessary, a side-show to the advance on Stanley, undertaken only because of the political need in the UK for a victory to distract attention from the ships and men being lost in San Carlos Water.

'Those opinions may be correct, but soldiers in combat do not have the benefit of hindsight, nor the luxury of questioning their orders. We are told to attack an enemy position or take a piece of ground, and we do so. Some men freeze under enemy fire, others find reserves of courage or are driven, for whatever reason, to acts that may afterwards be called either rash or heroic. Good soldiers assess the risks before each action, and take steps to eliminate as many as possible, but whatever the risks, the bottom line is that when the man says "Go," you go.

'There's not much profit in analysing what went on afterwards, except to learn from the mistakes made. Goose

Green may have been a sideshow, but taking it had a huge impact on Task Force morale and a correspondingly damaging effect on the Argentinians.' He paused and fixed the American with an even more unblinking stare. 'And whether the officer was right or wrong to make that frontal attack no longer matters. He gave his life. I'm not about to start chipping away at a dead man's reputation to make debating points.'

He took a deep breath. 'Now, that's the end of the tour of Goose Green.' He spoke into a radio and almost immediately I saw the helicopter, still waiting near Burnside House, begin to rise into the air.

Jack turned back to us. 'As I said at the start of the tour, the last stage up Black Mountain is hard walking over rough ground. You'll get something of the feeling of what it was like for the ground troops advancing over it, but it is tough going and I recommend it only for those who are in good physical condition.'

The old couple debated between themselves before reluctantly shaking their heads, the others could barely conceal their relief as there was a clatter of rotors in the sky and the red and white helicopter landed in a whirlwind of dust and dirt. They were climbing inside almost before the rotors had stopped turning, eager for the return flight to Stanley for china penguins and hot coffee. The American hung back and tried to press a £20 note into Jack's hand. 'I appreciate your time, hope I didn't annoy you with my questions. I'm a former soldier myself, I served in Korea.'

Jack shook his head. 'No offence taken – or given – I hope, but I've already been paid. There's a British Legion collection box by the jetty in Stanley. It'll do a lot more good there.'

The American hesitated, then shook Jack's hand and climbed into the helicopter.

The old couple were the last to board. I caught the woman's eye. 'Has it helped?'

She gave a sad smile. 'A little. Not as much as I'd hoped.'

Jack leaned into the cab of the helicopter, shouting to make himself heard above the din of the rotors, then stepped clear, crouching as he moved away. He raised a hand as the engine note rose, the rotors blurred and it lifted clear of the ground. It passed overhead and thundered away over the plain, the noise fading until there was only the keening of the wind.

The two of us began to stride away from Goose Green. The ground rose slowly at first, and looking ahead I could see the dark peak above us, but as we neared the edge of the plain, banks of cloud rolled in from the west, hiding the summit from view.

The lower slopes were thickly clad with fern and diddle-dee. It looked like a cross between the heather and bilberry that clothed the hills back home, and proved even harder to walk through. It was waist deep in places and the tough, twisted roots and branches tugged at my ankles.

I stumbled my way on up the hillside. On the higher slopes the diddle-dee gave way to vast, cloying peat bogs that sucked at my boots. The wind was keener here and moisture filled the air, a slow but insistent drizzle that soaked us to the skin. Jack was a good dozen years older than me, but he set a relentless pace, his long rhythmic stride eating up the ground. I kept pace with him, but my panting punctuated the conversation.

'What kept you in the Falklands, Jack? You're not a native – I mean a Falklander – are you?'

'No. I went home at the end of the war, served another seven years and then bought myself out. I mooched around Civvy Street for a while doing security work mainly, but something about this place kept pulling me back. I came back on the tenth anniversary of the landings, intending just to stay a few weeks, but then I kept sticking around a while longer. I got a job for a few months, labouring on the facilities site for the oil exploration companies, and rented a house in Stanley.

'I found I liked the people, and the place itself gets under your skin after a while. In the end I re-enlisted and volunteered for permanent duty here.' He gave a rueful smile. 'One of the very few. There wasn't much for me in the UK any more. I'm divorced, my children are both grown up and live abroad, and after so many years soldiering, I didn't have too many friends in the UK.' He glanced behind him towards the cemetery at Goose Green. 'Partly because I left a lot of them here.'

We walked in silence for a few minutes. 'Anyway, it's been six years now since I came back. I live in Stanley and I've remarried, to a Falklander.' He shot a sidelong glance at me. 'But we're not here to talk about me, are we, son?'

'Were you with him? Did you – did you see him die?'

He gave a slow nod. 'I'll show you the place.'

'Can you talk me through the battle? I know a little, but there are so many gaps, so many questions I can't answer.'

He paused and turned to look at me, scrutinising my face. 'It's not something I often do. Those who were there don't need to be reminded of it; many of them prefer to forget. Those who weren't there haven't earned the right to question what went on.' He fixed me with a stare, his eyes almost black in the shadow of the hood of his combat-jacket. 'But I'll tell you what I can.'

It was a curiously enigmatic answer, but he was already turning away, heading up the hillside once more. A hundred yards above us, a ridgeline interrupted the slope, just below the lowering cloud ceiling.

As we clambered over it, we found ourselves on a narrow

plateau. Erosion had stripped away much of the peat, leaving a bare rockscape of sand and gravel, punctuated by quartz boulders that had tumbled down the screes from the upper slopes.

A stream meandered across the plateau and the brown water dropped over the edge of the cliff in a waterfall that bounced from rock to rock before losing itself among the peat and diddle-dee on the lower slopes. The wind caught some of the water as it fell and whipped it upwards again in a fine spray, mingling with the pall of cloud.

Jack pointed towards the stream. 'That was the start line. We crossed it an hour after last light.'

He took a bearing with his compass and then we splashed through the stream and began to climb into the mist, the hillside stretching away ahead of us.

'The night was eerily quiet,' he said. 'The wind that had blown every moment since we landed had died away. The silence was total and the cold intense; I could see my breath fogging in the night air. We'd waded a river to reach the start line. My boots were soaked and my feet numb with cold.'

He walked more slowly now. His voice was low but urgent, and I could sense the intensity of emotion behind his words. As he talked, I peered into the mist ahead of us. There was nothing for my eyes to focus on and I began to have the uneasy feeling that dark figures were moving just beyond the limit of my vision.

The quiet, insistent voice continued, and I began to see that long-ago night through his eyes. I felt the cold, the tension that hurried every breath, and the fear that was always lurking just beyond the threshold of consciousness. I shared his certain knowledge that many of the men advancing up the hillside alongside him would not live to see another dawn.

I could see the heavy-laden platoon making their slow, silent way up the hillside, slipping from cover to cover, some watching as the others moved, then advancing as the others in turn gave them cover. They struggled upwards, stumbling over clumps of tussac grass, and slipping and sliding as they searched for purchase in the glutinous peat.

Jack's eyes remained fixed on their first objective, an outcrop of rock glowing a faint grey in the darkness. They were a hundred yards short of it when a corporal stood on a mine. There was a single thunderous concussion and Jack threw himself flat. Shrapnel shrieked overhead and then there was a patter like rain as smaller, softer fragments fell to earth around him.

There was a pause, a stunned silence, and then the darkness erupted into an inferno of noise and light. Flares burst overhead, bathing the hillside with fierce white light. Soaring lines of tracer – red, white and yellow liquid fire – sliced across the hillside.

There was the crash and whistle of incoming artillery shells and the dull, echoing thud of mortars. They worried him less than the machine-gun fire. The roar of the detonating shells was terrifying but they buried themselves deep in the soft ground, minimising the spread of shrapnel. The rattle of machine-gun fire was far more deadly. A group of soldiers advancing to his left were caught exposed in open ground and cut apart. The remainder regrouped and advanced again, only to be cut down in their turn.

The plans evolved in the calm of the Field Headquarters all but disintegrated in the bedlam of the battlefield. The need to achieve tactical advantages and strategic objectives faded before the individual struggle to fight and to survive. The men moved on, driven only by some primal impulse to climb higher, silence the guns, kill or be killed.

As he wormed his way forwards, up the hillside, Jack had

no sense of time passing. There was just an endless barrage of noise and waves of fear and panic that he struggled to keep at bay.

Almost without realising it, he reached the relative safety of the rocks and lay flat behind a boulder, his chest heaving and a roaring in his ears. He looked back down the hillside and urged on the stragglers. One by one, the surviving members of the platoon, some wounded, all wide-eyed with fear, followed him into the shelter of the rocks, a boulder field, a sterile, alien landscape of rock and grit. It was impossible to move across it at more than snail's pace.

They paused and regrouped, then began to move forward under relentless enemy fire, struggling over the rocks and boulders. They cleared the boulders one by one as gunfire whined and ricocheted around them. Rock fragments splintered and flew and he felt blood trickling down his face.

They paused again, one hundred yards below the ridge. An overhang of peat, roughly halfway to the top, offered some cover, otherwise the slope above and below it was studded only with a few small rocks.

He fought down his own fear once more, then looked at the faces around him, barely recognisable behind the smears of camouflage paint and the splinter cuts. There were perhaps a dozen of them huddled in the shelter of the outcrop, including a young lieutenant. He knew there were other groups to either flank, but they were as good as alone; their only hope lay in their own actions, not those of others.

The lieutenant tried to rally them, his voice cracking with tension. 'We have to do this,' he said. 'Fire and movement. Either we get those machine guns or we'll all be wiped out.'

As Jack described him, I could see my brother, as clearly as if he had just walked out of the mist in front of me. The stress and fear had etched furrows into his brow but his gaze was steady, his deep blue eyes fixed on the hilltop above him.

He paused, staring at each man in turn. No amount of training could ever prove who could be counted on when under hostile fire for the first time. The biggest and hardest men might literally piss themselves with fright, while others grew in stature, finding a calm in the eye of the storm.

'Spread out. We go on three.' The pale face of one young soldier turned towards him. Mike shook his head. 'Don't think about it. We'll be all right. This is what we have to do.'

He watched as they spread out among the rocks, spacing themselves at roughly ten-yard intervals. As soon as the last was in place, he shouted a countdown, his words barely audible above the endless percussion of the machine guns.

'Three, two, one. Go!'

Then he was off, firing a fierce burst from the hip as he sprinted across open ground, dodging and weaving as he ran. He hurled himself flat behind a rock barely bigger than his head, fired another burst, rolled sideways a few yards, sprinted forward once more, then dived into the cover of the peat overhang as a line of tracer burned its way towards him through the night.

The soldier to his left and a couple of paces behind him was caught in the open, frozen for a second like a dancer in a strobe light, his arms thrown high above his head as the tracer punched a jagged line across his chest. Then he toppled backwards.

The adrenalin surge of exertion, fear and danger made Mike's heartbeat sound like thunder in his ears. Every sense was heightened. The distinct smells of cordite and phosphorus mingled with the sweet, sickly smell of his own blood trickling from the cuts on his face, and the stench of scorched fabric and charred flesh from the dead man lying nearby.

As other members of his platoon dived for cover around him, he rolled over and peered up the hillside, half-screened by the peat bank. The flares dimmed as they drifted down into the battle smoke. The machine guns spat and chattered incessantly, the flash of each round so close to the one before that they seemed to emit a constant stream of light.

The hail of fire intensified, ripping and tearing at the ground, eating away the peat bank which shielded him. Mike pressed himself against the face of the cliff, breathing in the smell of peat and mud.

An image flashed into his mind of Passchendaele and the Somme. Soldiers like him rising from a trench into a hail of fire, each yard of ground gained marked by a funeral cross.

The hillside below him was strewn with the dead and the dying. Beneath the crash of shells, the rattle of machine-gun fire and the high-pitched crack of rifles, there were other sounds that none who heard them would ever forget.

A young soldier flattened himself against the ground near Mike, pressing himself into the peat as if, mercifully, it might swallow him whole, while a torrent of fire raked the ground around him. Mike could hear him screaming over and over again, 'Make it stop. Make it stop.'

Mike loosed a burst towards the skyline, drawing the fire back towards his position. He screamed at the soldier: 'Get a grip. You have to follow me up there. The only way to end this is to silence those guns.'

The soldier swung his head to look at him, his camouflage paint streaked by tears. He gulped down a lungful of air, his mouth framing a ragged O. Then he gave a small nod and Mike saw his knuckles tighten around the stock of his gun.

Mike glanced to right and left. The black-streaked faces of his men looked back at him, waiting for the command. He hesitated for a moment, realising how many familiar faces were already missing, then cursed himself and forced the thought away.

He took several deep breaths and yelled, 'Three, two, one. Go!'

Again they rose and scrambled over the top together. Stumbling forward, the young soldier was hit immediately and tumbled back down the slope. But Mike ran forward, darting and jinking to left and right, firing as he ran.

It seemed impossible that anything could survive the avalanche of fire. From the corner of his eye he saw another man fall, and another, then he was thrown flat as a round clipped the side of his helmet. He lay still for a second, vision blurred and head ringing from the impact, then he rolled over onto his back and fumbled at his belt. He pulled a pin from a grenade and lobbed it towards the trench barely twenty feet above him. It clipped the edge of the sangar, hovered there for a moment, and then fell back, gathering speed as it rolled down the slope. Mike buried his face in the earth. There was a flash and an explosion, and he heard the howl of shrapnel skimming his head. He fumbled for another grenade and hurled it upwards. He watched it arch into the air. It seemed to freeze in the flash of another flare bursting overhead, then it plummeted into the trench. Almost immediately there was a blast that rocked the earth beneath him and the machine gun fell silent.

Mike was already on his feet, sprinting the last few yards. He hurdled the low wall of the sangar and raked the bunker with fire. The machine-gun crew already lay dead, but he saw the barrels of two carbines swinging towards him and cut the two enemy riflemen to pieces with short, controlled bursts before either could get off a shot.

He crouched in the trench, surrounded by the four motionless bodies. The remnants of his platoon joined him a moment later, a Lance-Corporal – Jack – blood pouring from a wound in his upper arm, and three privates. All the other men lay somewhere on the slope below them, dead, wounded or still pinned down by fire.

Mike and Jack exchanged a momentary, weary look. Then they prepared to move forward again. They were almost out of ammunition and liberated the guns and ammunition belts from the enemy riflemen before they advanced.

They cleared two more bunkers with grenades and automatic fire. A body lay at the end of the third trench covered by a blanket. Mike stepped over it, his eyes already moving to the next objective. Then he froze. Nobody covers a body with a blanket on a battlefield.

As he began to turn back, swinging his rifle up, the blanket was ripped apart by a burst of automatic fire. The force of the bullets hurled Mike back against the side of the trench.

Jack emptied his magazine into the enemy soldier, continuing to fire even when the man's body and the blanket that had covered him had disintegrated.

Mike slid slowly down the side of the trench and slumped in a sitting position, his head lolling to one side.

Black … A roaring sound drowned the noise of battle in his ears.

He was freezing.

He thought of his family standing on the dock as he sailed away, and saw his kid brother waving a flag, his eyes glistening with excitement.

Black … He felt Jack's cold fingers scrabbling at his neck, searching for a pulse.

Black …

✫   ✫   ✫

'Sean?' A voice shouted at me and a rough hand shook my arm. 'Sean! Are you all right?' Jack's face swam into focus in front of me. 'Bloody hell, you had me worried for a moment there. You're as white as a sheet.'

His big clumsy fingers loosened my collar and felt for my pulse. I shivered and struggled to sit upright. 'I'm – I'm all right, really. What happened?'

'You keeled over. Don't move for a moment, just lie still.'

'Shit, I'm sorry. I feel so stupid.'

'Forget it. Being up here in the mist is very disorientating, it's easy to get a touch of vertigo and lose your balance.'

We both knew he was just being polite, but I gave him a grateful smile.

He fumbled at his belt, unclipped his water-bottle and made me drink. 'Take your time, but when you're ready, we'll move on. We'll have to get down below the cloudline before the chopper can pick us up.'

I sat up and looked around. We were on the ridge of Black Mountain, in the middle of a network of weather-worn sangars and crumbling, water-filled trenches gouged out of the peat. In one of them, as I now knew, Mike had lost his life.

Jack had been walking among the trenches as he waited for me to recover. I saw him stop and pick up something half-buried in the peat. He walked over and tossed it to me. 'I tell the tourists not to pick up anything from the battlefields, but I think we can make an exception for you. It's the casing from a carbine round, if you want a memento. If you don't, just throw it away.'

I slipped it into my pocket. 'I'll keep it. Thanks.' I stood up and took a few paces. 'Okay, I'm fine now.'

'Sure?' He pulled out his radio. 'Bristow control? Jack Stubbs and one passenger. Black Mountain's fog-bound, but the ceiling's fairly high. We'll come off the top heading south-east and I'll confirm RV as soon as we're below it.'

He checked his map and compass again, and then set off down the slope at an oblique angle to the ridge.

I took a last look around the summit. It was a bleak, unlovely place for a life to end. I stood for a moment in silence looking down into the trench, as I fingered the bullet casing in my pocket, but already the image of Mike I'd held in my mind was fading. I turned away and before I'd gone twenty paces, the mist had swallowed the summit.

We came out of the bottom of the cloud half an hour later, but the visibility was little better, the view across the plain to Mount Pleasant masked by the rain driven on the freshening wind. Jack led us down to a flat area of exposed rock on the east bank of a fast-flowing stream.

We sat down in the lee of a large boulder. He checked his map again and then reached for his radio. 'Bristow control, we're ready for collection. We're at 387426, near the head of Spaniard's Creek ... Right.' He broke the connection. 'He's already airborne. Five minutes.'

We sat in silence as we waited for the chopper, lost in our thoughts. 'Jack? When you were telling me about the battle, you never mentioned the civilians.'

'Who told you about that?'

'I met one of them a couple of days ago.' I waited for a few seconds. 'Why didn't you mention them?'

He didn't answer, and after a moment I tried again. 'The woman — she was a young girl when it happened — told me that Mike risked his life to save her and her family. She said he stood up, unarmed, in full view of the Argentinians to get them to stop firing and then led them to safety. Is that not the way it happened?'

'That's the way it happened.' There was weariness in his voice.

'I don't understand.'

The sound of the helicopter's rotors broke the silence. Jack stood up, pulled a strip of light-reflective material from his rucksack and waved it over his head. The helicopter altered course slightly and came in to land less than half a minute later. Well aware of the danger of peat bogs, the pilot kept it in the hover, its wheels barely touching the ground. We ran for the side-door, bending double to keep clear of the rotors.

'Mount Pleasant or Stanley?' Jack said as we settled into our seats.

'Mount Pleasant.'

'I'm going back to Stanley. We'll finish the conversation some other time.' His tone showed it was not open for debate.

As the helicopter rose into the air, I glimpsed the roof of Rose and Bernard's farm in the middle distance, but the upper slopes of Black Mountain, high above it, were still swathed in cloud. The pilot swung the chopper in a wide loop to the south, steering clear of the line of the main runway at Mount Pleasant.

Looking east, I saw the silvery glimmer of the wings of the biweekly Tristar as it came in on its final approach. I felt a pang of homesickness at the thought of how far it had travelled. As I looked away, back towards the coast, I saw movement on the shoreline, dark shapes diving for cover at the approach of the helicopter. 'What was that?'

Jack shrugged. 'Probably only the local wildlife. It takes a while to adjust to it. When we were advancing on Goose Green during the war, one of our patrols spotted what they thought was a group of Argentinians in balaclavas, creeping along the shore. They opened up with everything they had, including a Milan missile and a few grenades from an M203.' He gave a rueful smile. 'The men in balaclavas turned out to be sea lions. There were no survivors.'

The Tristar had already taxied to a halt by the time we came in to land at Mount Pleasant. The helicopter pilot kept the rotors turning as I thanked Jack and shook his hand. 'I won't insult you by offering you money. You've already chewed out one customer for that today, but if there's anything I can do for you here or in the UK, or anything you need that I could send you when I get back there, just let me know.'

His powerful fist closed around my hand. 'Thanks, but there's nothing I need. A pint in the Mess or the Victory Bar in Stanley some night will settle all debts.'

'And maybe we can finish that conversation then?'

'Sure.' He paused and glanced back down the line of hills, still capped with cloud and fading into the dusk. 'And Sean? Your brother did all right up there, plenty did worse. Don't lose any sleep over it.'

I jumped down from the helicopter and by the time I had ducked beneath the arc of the rotors and scrambled clear, it was already rising into the air again. I caught a glimpse of Jack's face framed in the window, then it had wheeled away to the east, speeding downwind, its tail-light blinking bright in the dusk.

The first passengers were beginning to disembark from the Tristar, one or two visibly flinching at the strength of the wind. As I watched them, I became aware of the noise of it for the first time in days.

There was a note pinned to the door of my room. 'Unfinished business with a bottle of chardonnay. Drop round as soon as you get back. J.'

I hesitated, unsure whether I was ready to talk about it before I'd had time to collect my thoughts, but as I stood there, a warm arm slid around my neck.

'You took your time. Another ten minutes and I'd have had to delete the bit about the chardonnay. Your place or mine?'

'Yours.' I followed her down the corridor, took the glass of wine she handed me and sat down on the chair while she sprawled across her bed.

'So, how was your day?'

'So-so. All I managed to persuade myself to buy in Stanley was a pair of tights and a postcard of a penguin. I was back here by lunchtime and spent the rest of the day warding off Shark attacks.' She studied me for a moment. 'You don't look like your day was too much better.'

'It was mixed. The guy leading the tour was that survival instructor, Jack Stubbs. He was in the same platoon as my brother. He told me a lot about the night he died.' I hesitated. 'Although, I felt he could have told me even more. He was definitely holding back something. He never even mentioned Rose and her family until I brought it up.'

'As you do,' she said with a smile. 'Sorry, go on.'

'When I asked him about it, he was quite evasive. In the end he just said we'd have to finish the conversation some other time.'

'It must be painful for him too.'

I bowed my head in acknowledgement of the reproach. 'I know, but I felt there was more to it than that.'

I described the battle to Jane, as Jack had related it to me. When I'd finished, she sat silent for a minute. 'So how do you feel?'

'I'm not sure yet; better for knowing what happened once and for all, I suppose, and better for having seen the places myself and walked the same ground.'

She divided the rest of the bottle between us and sipped her drink, nursing the glass in her cupped hands. 'And are you walking it again tomorrow?'

'No. I'm going out, but I think I'll stick to the shoreline. I'm not going up on the battlefields again. Maybe I've laid that particular ghost now.'

She scrutinised my face before replying. 'But not entirely. No doubt you'll still be calling in at Black Beck House.'

I shrugged. 'I suppose so. I said I would.'

She hid a smile. 'So you did. Just make sure you're back by six. In case you've forgotten, we start QRA duty tomorrow night.'

Chapter 7

The same dreams and nightmares haunted my sleep again that night, and I was awake and out of bed at dawn. I showered and dressed quickly and walked towards the Ops Centre to collect the squadron taxi. The runway lights were on and I could hear the drone of an incoming aircraft. I stopped and waited as it circled and came into land. Then I saw the Argentine markings on the side of the jet as it rumbled past me and taxied back towards the tower.

The door banged behind me and Noel appeared, dragging heavily on his first cigarette of the day. I waited until the coughing had subsided. 'What's the story with the Argentine plane, Noel?'

'Must be some relatives of their war dead. There's a flight every couple of months or so.'

'At dawn?'

'They're only given certain very restricted slots, supposedly to avoid confrontations with the Falklanders.' He shrugged. 'It seems a bit petty to me, but those are the rules.' He coughed and spat. 'Another triumph for some desk-bound, constipated bureaucrat in Whitehall.'

We walked across the runway together as the aircraft halted outside the main building. The Argentinians were just disembarking as we passed the jet. Most were middle-aged or old women, clad in headscarves and cheap-looking coats, and shivering in the cold. There were a handful of old men as well, and a couple of younger ones.

'They don't look much like your average grieving relative,' Noel said.

'Nor do I, but I went to see my brother's grave the other day.'

He nodded, still staring suspiciously at them.

'They only let bona-fide close relatives of the dead come here, don't they?'

'That's the theory, but we have to rely on Argentine documentation. If they say someone is a father, mother, brother or sister of a dead soldier, we pretty much have to take their word for it. Half their war dead were unidentified and are buried in unmarked graves. Anyway, if they're here on a recce, they won't learn much that they don't know already.' He ground out his cigarette under his boot and we walked across to the Mess.

I drank some coffee and grabbed a handful of toast, then went to pick up the keys to the Land Rover. The sky was streaked with red as the sun crept above the horizon, but the dirt road to Goose Green still lay in the dark purple shadows cast by the hills. The shoreline away to my left was bathed in light and alive with movement as seals and penguins dived among the underwater forests of kelp, and armies of sea-birds took flight.

I stopped at the foot of the Wickham Heights, pulling off the track onto a rare patch of firm ground. I leaned against the bonnet for a while, watching the birds wheeling and diving against the brightening sky, their cries filling the air. I took my bearings and set off across the plain, picking my way around the pools and tarns that littered my path, dark, peaty water shining silver as it reflected the sky. The dry, spent stalks of the tussac grass seemed to glow as the pale sunlight struck them. It remained a desolate and empty land, but it also had grandeur and beauty.

I followed a meandering westward path for an hour or so, crossing a dozen creeks and dark streams flowing silently between steep banks towards the sea. My feet were soaked and my leggings black with peat and eventually I turned inland, seeking firmer going on the higher ground.

As I squelched through yet another bog, feeling more icy water seeping through my laceholes, I came across several sets of fresh bootprints. I stopped, surprised that others had chosen to walk in this bleak and lonely place. I looked around, but I appeared to be alone in the whole vast sweep of landscape.

A few hundred yards further on, I saw a movement just at the periphery of my vision. I swung my head to stare at the ridgeline of Black Mountain high above me and saw — or thought I saw — figures outlined for a moment against the sky. Then they were gone.

I paused. There was no official battlefield tour scheduled, but perhaps there were other servicemen out exploring the battle-sites or a couple of the birdwatchers I had seen in Stanley, festooned with binoculars and cameras. I watched the ridge for a couple of minutes, but I was unwilling to venture back onto the boulder-field just to satisfy my curiosity, and eventually I moved on. My eyes kept straying back to the skyline, hoping for confirmation that there really had been people there, but it remained empty.

Half an hour later I climbed a spur of the foothills flanking Black Mountain and as the valley beyond opened up in front of me, I saw Black Beck House. A thin plume of smoke was rising from the chimney and as I neared the farm, a faint whiff of peat-smoke was carried to me on the wind.

There was no sign of Bernard or Rose and no barking dog as I approached the house, only an oppressive silence. I knocked on the door and waited, but there was no reply. I walked around the farmyard, looking in all the outbuildings, and found their Land Rover parked in a shed. As I turned to look back at the house, there was a movement at the window as a curtain dropped back into place.

I walked back and again banged on the door. A couple of minutes later the door opened a crack and I saw Rose's face. She looked even more pale then before and kept half-glancing behind her.

'Hello, I said I'd call in.'

'Yes.' She made no move to open the door wider.

'Is now a bad time?'

'Yes.'

'Is everything all right?'

Again there was the terse reply. 'I'm sorry. I—' Her voice trailed away into silence.

'It's all right. I can't stay anyway. As I told you the other day, we start our spell on Quick Reaction Alert tonight. If I get out this way after that I'll drop by again.' It was more a question than a statement.

She nodded, saying nothing, but her eyes seemed to be pleading with me.

'Are you sure you're all right?'

Once more the half-glance behind her. 'Yes. I'm fine. Really.'

I searched her expression. 'Something's wrong, isn't it? What is it?' I tried to push my way past her, but she held the door shut with surprising strength.

'No. There's nothing the matter, honestly. Please go.' Her voice caught as if she was close to tears, and again I hesitated, but she seized the chance to close the door. A moment later I heard the sound of the heavy bolt sliding home.

I stood staring at the house for a few moments, then walked slowly away down the hill, pausing frequently to look behind me. The door remained closed and there was no further movement to be seen at the windows. I picked up the track at the bottom of the hill and followed it back towards the place where I had left the Land Rover.

I shook my head, angry with myself that I hadn't insisted and pushed my way in. I was sure that Bernard had been bullying her, perhaps even hitting her. Yet even if I had forced my way inside, I was unsure what I could have done. Bernard's powerful frame suggested that he would be more than a match for me in a fist-fight and in any case, unless I was going to carry Rose off on a white charger, my intervention would only have made things worse for her after I'd gone.

I passed below George and Agnes's farm and as I crossed the head of an inlet a few hundred yards further on, I stopped to watch a group of penguins surfing the waves as they returned to shore. There was a sudden flurry in the water, and one disappeared beneath the surface, then reappeared in the mouth of a leopard seal. It thrashed the surface, beating the water into a pink foam.

A black bar, one of the penguin's flippers, spiralled through the air and landed in the water. The seal gave the penguin a final convulsive shake then, bored of its sport, submerged and disappeared. The penguin lay motionless, a thin slick of its oil spreading slowly across the surface of the sea. The first scavenging gulls were already circling above it.

Indifferent to the commotion, a huge bull elephant seal was shepherding a harem of wives along the beach. I glanced at my watch then dropped down from the track and walked towards the shore. As I neared the edge of the shingle beach, the bull seal reared up and roared.

I froze for a moment, but the seal's defiance was not for me. Following its gaze, I saw another, smaller male elephant seal. The two creatures circled each other warily, like boxers looking for an opening, then with another roar the larger bull launched itself at its rival.

The confrontation was brief but conclusive. The mauled bull reeled and ran, blood pouring from a gash in its neck. The older bull pursued it a short way down the beach. It crashed across a bank of shingle, its flippers struggling for grip, and sent pebbles flying in every direction.

It ran on, leaving a smooth, black, rounded shape exposed behind it. When the old bull seal was certain that it had driven off its rival, it threw back its massive head and roared its triumph. I watched its swaggering return to its harem, then walked along the upper edge of the beach to the site of its battle.

A curve of black rubber, like the inner tube of a tractor tyre, protruded from the shingle. I scraped more of the pebbles away with my foot, gradually exposing a rubber Zodiac. There was no outboard motor or paddles in it, no equipment of any sort and the Zodiac itself had no distinguishing markings. There was nothing to say when it had been concealed there. It could have been buried for months, but it might also have been hidden as recently as the previous night.

I walked along the margin of the narrow beach in both directions, digging my feet into any suspicious-looking mounds of shingle and scraping it aside as I searched for anything else hidden there. I could find nothing.

I began to search the banks of peat just inland from the shoreline. There were no footprints, other than my own, impressed in the black glistening surface, but one area of peat was marked with faint striations, as if something had been dragged along the ground or swept across it to obliterate any tracks. It was possible that the marks were just made by the elephant seals hauling themselves to and from the shore, but I had the uneasy feeling that they were man-made.

I returned to the Zodiac and squatted on my haunches alongside it, staring in silence as I tried to piece together a jumble of apparently unconnected events. I got to my feet and scrambled back up the inlet, then set off at a loping run along the track.

As I ran, I kept my eyes moving over the hillside rising to my left and the broad expanse of shoreline to my right. I had been running for a few minutes when I glanced down towards the shore. A low hill rising from the water-filled plain partly obscured my view, but I could see the still, dark water of a tarn, and beyond it, a long bank of shingle, separating it from the open water of Choiseul Sound.

The track climbed to cross a spur of the foothills and as I ran on, a sleek, black shape previously hidden by the shingle bank, came into view. It had to be the prow of a boat or a submarine. I dived forward and hit the dirt.

I worked my way along the ground, crawling off the track and into the cover of some tussac grass. I lay still, drawing air deep into my lungs as I tried to slow my breathing and my heart-rate. Then I parted the tall, bleached stems of grass and peered out towards the shore. The black shape had not moved. Still and sinister, it either lay in the shallows close to shore, or was drawn up onto the beach itself. There was no sign of any movement around it, save for clouds of seabirds, which circled and swooped down on it, fiercely disputing the right to land.

I rubbed my eyes and stared again. I was now almost sure it was not a submarine, but I could still make no sense of it. Then I saw a skua drive off a rival with a slash of its beak and then plunge it down into the massive, rounded prow. A thin filament came free in its beak. It jerked and tugged, heaving backwards and beating its wings as the filament stretched and then snapped. As it took to the air with its trophy, I heaved a sigh of relief. I was looking at the massive carcass of a beached whale.

Feeling both foolish and relieved, I scanned the hills and the skyline, then picked myself up and began to move off again along the track. Another twenty minutes' running brought me to the Land Rover. It was parked as I had left it, apparently untouched, but I approached it cautiously. Unsure if I was being prudent or merely paranoid, I peered inside the bonnet and lay full length in the dirt to examine the underside before I unlocked the door. I worked the Land Rover around, too scared of bogging down to reverse more than a few inches over the edge of the track, then drove back towards Mount Pleasant.

The track dipped and weaved, following the wavering boundary line between the waterlogged plain and the steeply rising slopes. It was rare for more than a one-hundred-yard stretch to be visible, before the next bump, dip or bend hid it from view. Soon even that limited view ahead was lost.

A bank of cloud had already shrouded the summits of the hills. Now mist rolled in over the lower slopes, closing in around the Land Rover, diffusing the daylight and muffling the engine note. The air became cold and clammy, heightening my feelings of unease. Dark shapes — rocks, a minefield warning, a broken wooden signpost pointing a jagged finger at the sky — loomed suddenly out of the mist and then were gone. I peered through the windscreen, trying to focus only on the dark line of the track as it disappeared into the grey tunnel ahead, but ghost images moved constantly at the periphery of my vision.

A black shape flew out of the mist in front of me and I almost cried out in alarm. I glimpsed the talons and sharp, curving beak of a bird of prey as it twisted in the air, beating its powerful wings to lift clear of the Land Rover. My heart was thumping as I drove on.

I was still some way from the base and took risks, accelerating hard and braking late, trying to cut a few minutes from the journey. As I bucketed over the brow of another rise, a khaki-clad figure materialised. He sprang from the side of the track and raised his hand, motioning me to stop. A gun rested in the crook of his other arm.

I started to brake, then stamped on the accelerator, spinning the wheel towards him. As he jumped back, I realised my mistake and stamped on the brakes again. The Land Rover screeched and skidded, sliding to a halt a few yards past him.

'What the hell are you doing?' he shouted. 'You could have killed me.' His clothes were threadbare army surplus gear and his weapon was a single-barrelled shotgun.

'I'm sorry. I— My foot slipped off the brake.'

'You're not in England now. Show some respect for the place. I lose enough sheep and lambs already to joy-riding soldiers.'

'Why were you trying to stop me?'

'To save your neck by telling you to slow down. There's a landslip just around that bend.'

'I, er- I know. I came past here the other day.'

'Then you're an even bigger fool than I thought.' He spat and then turned to whistle for his dog. I put the Land Rover in gear and accelerated away. I could see him staring after me until he was swallowed by the mist.

I reached the base half an hour later. The guard swung up his rifle at my high-speed approach, but lowered it when he recognised me, and waved me through.

I screeched to a halt in a flurry of gravel by the Operations Centre and sprinted inside. 'Get the Base Commander. Tell him I need to see him.'

'But it's the weekend,' the Duty Officer said.

'So if the Argentinians attack today, you'll ask them to come back on Monday, will you?'

He stared at me incredulously for a moment, then reached for the phone.

I had to pace up and down the corridor outside the Boss's office for ten minutes. Finally I heard footsteps and looked up to see him coming down the corridor in his full-dress uniform. 'This had better be important, Sean, I've had to leave a party of Falkland VIPs.'

'It's important, Boss. I've been walking down towards Goose Green. There were some tracks of military boots in the peat and I saw some figures briefly on the skyline.'

'And you've dragged me out to tell me that?'

'There's more. On the way back I went to look at some elephant seals on a beach. One of them disturbed a pile of shingle. There was a Zodiac buried underneath it.'

He gave me a doubtful look. 'That could have been here since the war.'

'It's not been there that long. I couldn't be sure, but I doubt if it's been there sixteen days, let alone sixteen years.'

He chewed his lip for a moment, staring past me out of the window. 'It could be a Marines or Special Forces exercise.'

'Possibly, but we haven't been told of any, have we?'

He shook his head, still staring out of the window.

I waited as the seconds ticked by. 'Boss, I've seen tracks of what could be Argentinian Special Forces, there's an unexplained Zodiac hidden on a beach, and the *Trident* is missing, probably sunk. What—?'

He held up a hand to silence me. 'The *Trident* is now off the missing list. It made contact with Northwood this morning. It appears that the Commander had simply misunderstood his orders. The *Trident* had just completed a week-long tactical readiness evaluation and had been ordered to resume its prescribed patrol – unspecified, but presumably shadowing the Argentine naval manoeuvres involving the *Eva Peron*.

'For some unexplained reason the Commander thought those orders had been countermanded and he put the sub into a state of high alert, rigged it for silent running and dropped it close to the ocean floor. It was at such a depth that it was unable to send or receive signals traffic. He only realised his mistake when he took the sub off alert seven days later, brought it back to periscope depth and signalled a report to Northwood.'

'But how could he misunderstand his orders? There are checks and failsafe systems.'

'Indeed there are, but the Commander apparently failed to carry them out. He may have been radio silent for the past week, but there's been no shortage of signals between Northwood and the *Trident* since this morning.' He smiled. 'I think it's fair to say that the Commander of the *Trident* will be an ex-Commander about ten seconds after it next docks.

Meanwhile, it's back on patrol, with unambiguous orders to remain in constant radio contact.'

I was silent for a moment, marshalling my thoughts, wanting to make certain that I was right, rather than reluctant to admit that I'd overreacted. 'But even if the *Trident* has been found, it doesn't alter the fact that there's an unexplained Zodiac and suspicious signs that could well point to the presence of Argentine Special Forces. If they are here, shouldn't we be requesting Cobra Force?' I hesitated. 'It's your decision of course, but—'

'No, Sean, unfortunately it's not my decision at all. I'll certainly be reporting it to London immediately, but I can tell you now what the answer will be. I'll put in a request for Cobra Force and I'll be told that a deployment will cost a minimum of two million quid and before they agree to it, they want something a bloody sight more significant than two or three figures on the skyline and an empty Zodiac on a beach that might turn out to have been left by a group of our blokes on exercise.' He paused to check my expression. 'I'm sympathetic, believe me, but we're not dealing with military logic, and we're not just up against the usual budget problems. There's also a faith in Whitehall in the value of sigint that borders on the religious. If GCHQ have intercepted an unusual level of Argentine signals traffic, then they might just do something, but if GCHQ says nothing's happening, then nothing's happening. The fact that Argentina might deploy in total radio silence doesn't seem to have occurred to any of the geniuses at the MoD.

'I'll heighten the alert level, report to London and send a party down to recover the Zodiac. And I'll get the Marines to put out some recce patrols in the area where you saw the figures. For the moment that's all I can do. Wait in the

Ops Room,' he said. 'I'll get someone from the Marines to debrief you.'

'I'm due on QRA at six, Boss.'

He checked his watch. 'You should just make it. And, Sean? Thank you.' He hurried away, shouting orders to the Duty Officer.

A Marine sergeant arrived within minutes to debrief me. I watched the flurry of activity as the guard was strengthened. A few minutes later, three hastily assembled patrols headed out of the main gate. I felt a selfish reassurance at the sight. Whether they found anything or not, it was now their responsibility, not mine.

The only vehicle left outside the Ops Centre was the Boss's blue Land Rover Discovery, so I jogged across to the Death Star. I threw together my toothbrush and shaving gear and enough T-shirts, socks and underwear to see me through the next few days.

The transport laid on to take the aircrew down to the Quick Reaction Area had already left. I looked at my watch, swore, and then began to run down the runway. It was over a mile and painfully hard going into a strengthening wind. It reduced my speed almost to walking pace. Chest heaving, I finally reached the QRA area and pushed open the door of the Q shed.

The decor was social security office modern, a collection of ugly furniture and uncomfortable seats in jarring primary colours, augmented by the usual assortment of battered armchairs rescued from skips. Rees looked up from one of the chairs, gave me a nervous smile and returned to his book. Piles of paperbacks and well-thumbed magazines were stacked on every available horizontal surface, competing for space with used polystyrene cups.

The seemingly inevitable inflatable sheep occupied a place

of honour in an old ejector seat. Its modesty was protected by a parachute harness, artfully arranged across its lap. A cardboard sign hung round its neck, 'In emergency, pull rip cord.'

Shark and Jimmy were throwing darts at a board on the wall, surrounded by a corona of pock-marked plaster. From Jimmy's hangdog expression, he was no better at darts than he was at chess. Nearby was a notice board containing the usual mixture of exhortations, commendations and admonishments from the Administrative Officer.

The operations area of the Q shed was nothing more than an alcove opening off the main room. Noel glanced up and nodded to me from the ops desk, a ledge twelve inches wide by three feet long. On it were a few papers, a telephone and a squawk-box connecting the QRA to the Operations Centre and the radar and Rapier missile sites.

There were two clocks on the wall, identical to the ones that had hung in my school classrooms. One was set to Stanley time, the other to Greenwich Mean Time, five hours behind. The most modern item in the room was the large, grey steel safe. A cardboard sign reading, 'OPEN', dangled from the handle. In the event of an alert, the Ops Officer's second duty, after hitting the triple buttons that sounded the alarms and opened the doors of the Tempest shacks, was to lock the safe.

In theory all classified documents and code-books had to be returned to the safe immediately after use. In practice many were kept in the most useful place – on the ops desk. The unexpected arrival of an Ops Officer on an inspection visit usually provoked a desperate holding action in the area near the door, while one of the aircrew scrambled to gather up the incriminating documents and shove them back into the safe.

I walked through to the TV room. Jane glanced round,

already sprawled in one of the rotting armchairs in front of the television. 'You cut that fine, two more minutes and you'd have been in the shit.'

'For once I'd have had a good alibi.'

'Not snogging Farmer Palmer's wife again, then?'

'Don't tell me you're still jealous?'

'Only of Farmer Palmer. He's my kind of man.'

'Surly and pig ignorant? Yes, you're probably right.'

She stuck her tongue out at me. 'So what really happened?'

'I found a Zodiac hidden on the beach further up the coast. I thought it could be Argentine Special Forces. I had all on to convince the Boss though, he thinks it's just some blokes trying out for Henley.'

'So that alert's down to you?' she said. 'Thanks a lot, pal. They've just moved us up to Readiness State 10. That means we've got to sleep in these suits as well as live in them.'

I laughed. 'I don't see why, from what Geoff says you can be in and out of your clothes in ten seconds when the mood takes you.'

I ducked to avoid the cushion thrown at my head.

'You'll never know, Sean, that's for sure.'

'I don't know, you can't keep too much hidden in QRA accommodation. Where is it anyway?'

'I'll show you,' she said. 'This film sucks.'

The QRA rooms were smaller and much more spartan than the Death Star accommodation. Each of the four rooms had a washbasin, two single beds, a small table and two chairs, and a row of hooks on the breeze-block wall. The beds were right up against opposite walls but even so there was barely room to walk between them.

Jane's Walkman and her tapes, books and magazines were

already piled on the table, but there was no sign of the photograph that she usually kept by her bed.

'Where's Geoff?'

She flushed a little, her fingers straying to the pendant around her neck. 'I left him up at the Death Star. QRA quarters are crowded enough with just two people in them. There's no room for three.' She turned away from me and started sorting through her tapes.

'You're right there, this is even cosier than Kuwait.'

'So there's not much chance of keeping any secrets from one another for the next few days.' She paused. 'Speaking of which, how was – what's her name? Rose?'

'Stop pretending, Jane, you know she's called Rose.' I hesitated, afraid that voicing my worries would only add to the scorn she might heap on me. 'I don't know. She was a bit strange. I didn't even get over the threshold.'

'Maybe Bernard's acting up. Perhaps I'd better go with you next time and make it a double date.'

'Not even a Falklands farmer is that desperate.'

I blocked the cuff that she aimed at my ear. She was close enough for me to smell her perfume and feel the warmth of her body. I held her wrist for a moment, then released it. She made no effort to step away.

'I— Look, I've got a call to make.' I eased past her but her smile mocked me.

'Coward. Who are you calling anyway, not Rose again, surely?'

I didn't answer and walked off down the corridor. I picked up the handset, and flicked through the telephone book, no bigger than a pamphlet. No one answered for over a dozen rings. I was just about to hang up when there was a click from the other end of the line and I heard Rose's voice.

'It's Sean. I just wanted to make sure you were all right.'

There was a pause. 'We're fine, all of us.' Her voice sounded tense and strained.

'All of you?'

'Yes. I have to go, give my regards to your brother.' The line went dead.

I stared at the phone without moving. When I looked round, Jane was watching me.

'There's something wrong.'

'I wouldn't worry. She's just playing hard to get.'

'Jane, I'm serious. When I asked her if she was all right, she said, "Yes, all of us are fine."'

'So?'

'There are only two of them. She also said, "Give my regards to your brother." She knows he's dead, she tends his grave every month.'

'But that's still no reason for a drama. Perhaps she was just trying to pretend that somebody else was calling in case Bernard was jealous.'

I nodded doubtfully. 'Maybe.'

She stretched out her hand and tousled my hair. 'Look, don't chew your liver about it. There's nothing you can do for the next few days while we're stuck in here.'

'I suppose not.'

We walked back to the crew-room. The previous QRA crew had finished packing their gear. They shook hands all round, unable to keep the smiles from their faces at the thought of getting out of their flying gear and into some drinks in the Mess.

'Spare a thought for us poor saps down here,' Jane said.

'Jane, we think about you all the time.'

A gust of cold wind stirred the papers on the table as they

opened the door. They let it bang shut behind them and I heard their footsteps receding into the night.

I changed into my flying gear, then made some coffee and handed a cup to Jane who was again sprawled out in front of the video screen. Shark and Jimmy were once more locked in combat over the chessboard, and Rees was still buried in his book. The others sat around flipping through magazines, writing letters or watching the TV, but I couldn't settle.

Finally I walked through to my room, picked up a book and lay down on the bed. I read for a couple of hours, scarcely registering the words, reading and re-reading the same page over again. Jane looked in on me once or twice, then walked away. Privacy was jealously guarded on QRA; there was so little of it.

Around eleven I turned off the light and lay back on the bed. The only illumination was the dim glow filtering in from the corridor. As I lay with my eyes open, staring at the ceiling, Jane came in. A moment later I heard the rustle of clothing. 'I thought you were sleeping in that flying suit.'

She gave a throaty chuckle. 'You were right, I can be in and out of it in seconds.'

I kept my eyes fixed on the ceiling but I could not shut out the sound of her undressing. Every faint noise seemed louder and I could even hear the thump of my heart. There was a metallic click as she laid her pendant – Geoff's pendant – on the bedside table. A moment later she stood looking down at me. She was wearing only a T-shirt. 'You're in my bed.'

I tried to keep it light. 'Well, it's good of you to lend it to me. You can have it back in the morning, when I've finished with it.'

She still did not move. 'Sean?'

I shifted my gaze to look at her for a moment, but neither of us spoke. She reached out a hand and touched my chest. 'Do you ever wonder?'

'I don't let myself.' It was not strictly true, but I was both aroused and scared about where this was leading.

'So you do think about it.'

'Geoff's my mate, Jane.'

'He's mine too,' she said.

'No, he's more than that.'

She stayed where she was a moment longer, then took her hand away. I could still feel the warmth of her touch as she curled up on the other bed.

'Sean, what if—'

Neither of us spoke again but when I turned my head a few minutes later, I could see the glitter of her eyes in the half-light, still staring at me.

I lay awake a long time, then slept fitfully, waking at each noise from the building: the creak of the timbers in the wind, the click of a door and the murmur of voices. Once a bang brought me juddering awake, bolt upright, sweat starting to my brow. Then I heard a muttered curse and the sound of someone picking up a metal tray.

I woke what seemed like seconds later with Jane shaking my shoulder.

'What is it?'

She laughed. 'It's morning, that's all. Briefing in twenty minutes.'

Her hand lingered on my shoulder for a moment. As she turned to go, I caught her wrist. 'Jane...'

She nodded. 'It's all right, don't sweat it. It's history already. I won't put you on the spot again.'

I released her hand but it was a few seconds before she

stepped away from the bedside and moved out of the room. I lay back, staring at the ceiling, trying to blot out the memory of the touch of her skin. I forced myself to think about Geoff and how he would feel if Jane dumped him for anyone, let alone his supposed best friend. I tried to bring his face to mind, but all I could see were Jane's eyes, fixed on me, glittering in the darkness.

I got out of bed, went to the basin and splashed cold water over my face. Then I stood staring at my reflection in the mirror.

'Sorry. I thought you might want some coffee.'

Jane was standing in the doorway, holding out a cup.

I froze for a moment, unsure of what to do, then grabbed for my shorts. 'It's all right,' I said. 'It's nothing you haven't seen before,' but I couldn't raise my eyes to look at her. Everything between us had changed.

She put the cup down on the table, then stood in the doorway, silently watching me. I could feel the tension in the air between us and my heart was thumping in my chest. I finished dressing, my body half-turned away from her, as if shielding myself from her gaze.

'We should—' I gulped and swallowed. My voice sounded like a stranger's. 'We'd better get to the briefing.'

I looked up at last and our eyes locked. She searched my face for a moment and there was the faint trace of a smile as she turned away.

The rest of the QRA crew were already in the TV lounge, which doubled as the briefing room. Noel was sitting to one side, talking quietly to the Boss. They both stood up as we entered. 'Right,' Noel said, 'now we're all here, let's get on with it. As you know, Sean found a hidden Zodiac yesterday. A patrol has been out and recovered it and we've had Marine recce patrols out in the hills throughout the night, but so far nothing else out of the ordinary has been found.

'The base is maintaining Military Vigilance and we're staying at RS 10 until we have some satisfactory explanation for the incident. We've had no other reports of anything unusual, but just the same, keep alert and keep your eyes peeled for ground activity during your sorties today.

'Falcon 1 and Falcon 2 will be flying a sortie at noon. Fat Albert will be out there for those who need a refuel. We also have another charter of Argentinian relatives arriving today and contrary to previous instructions, I want two jets, Falcon 3 and Falcon 4, to intercept and close escort them, just to give them something to tell the folks at home about. That's all. Intelligence brief.'

The Intelligence Officer stood up. 'No major changes to the situation. The *Eva Peron* and its guardship are now steaming west-south-west on a course that would take them back to Rio Gallegos. The exercise, whatever it was, appears to be as good as over, but we're continuing to monitor.

'There's a good deal of helicopter activity in international waters just outside the Exclusion Zone off the coast south of Rio Gallegos. We've intercepted distress calls from an Argentine trawler, but our offers of assistance from our Sea Kings have been politely declined. It appears the trawler may have gone down and a search is going on for survivors.'

Jane nudged me, 'It's getting to be a regular Bermuda Triangle out there.

'There's one major difference from the *Trident* though; if the trawler is operating at the same depth, it definitely won't be making a surprise reappearance.'

We had spoken quietly, almost under our breath, but the Intelligence Officer still paused and gave us a pointed look. 'Not much new from the Argentine mainland.' She gave a thin smile and pushed her spectacles back on to the bridge of her nose. 'Except that they're still marching up and down the streets; a normal day in Buenos Aires, in other words.'

There were a few polite smiles.

'Weather brief.' Jimmy uncoiled himself from a bench at the front of the room and stood up. 'Wind south-west, forty knots, almost a flat calm for round here, broken cloud, a chance of showers, possibly of snow later, cloud ceiling lowering to perhaps 5,000 feet by dusk.'

As Jimmy collected his papers together, the Boss rose to his feet. 'One final point, we may be at the equivalent latitude to southern England here, but if you haven't already noticed, there's no Gulf Stream to warm us. We're in the path of the Antarctic current and as the name suggests, it's coming to us straight from the ice-cap.

'Winter sea surface temperatures are barely above freezing – perhaps five degrees Celsius offshore and dropping as low as two degrees inshore. That's several degrees colder than the winter temperature of the North Sea or North Atlantic around Britain. It's cold enough to kill you within minutes if you're unlucky enough to have to ditch in it. For that reason it's even more important than usual that you check your immersion suits regularly for any signs of wear and tear. Replace them immediately from stores if there's the slightest blemish.

'I know how you all hate to waste the government's money unnecessarily, but it could make a life-and-death difference. If you have to eject, we'll have a rescue chopper in the air before you even hit the water, but if you're unprotected in these waters – and that's effectively what you'll be if your suit leaks – your survival time is measured in minutes. You'll almost certainly die before we can reach you. Be safe and stay alert. That's all.'

We filed out and walked down the corridor to the changing room. Hard though we both tried to keep the normal banter flowing as we got ready for our sortie, I could still feel the tension between myself and Jane. I cursed myself, wishing I had seen the events of the previous night coming a little sooner and taken quicker steps to head them off. Now it was too late.

Even if we never referred to it directly again, I had the uneasy feeling that it would always be there in the background, a shared knowledge that would make it hard, if not impossible, to rediscover the easy friendship we had shared before. The more I thought about it, the more certain I was that I would lose one, and perhaps both, of my best friends – Jane and Geoff – as a result.

I dug my nails into my palms, telling myself I was being stupid, creating all the necessary conditions for a self-fulfilling prophecy, and I made a huge effort to get us back to normal. As we went through the pre-flight checks, I tried to drown my worries in a stream of banter. Jane still sounded distracted at first, but then she too responded and before long the wisecracks were snapping backwards and forwards almost as fast as usual. There was still an undercurrent, however, and my anxieties were only suppressed, not resolved.

I fired up the Tempest as Jane loaded the mission computers and established the datalink to Shark and Fortress. Then we rolled out onto the runway. Shark lined up his jet alongside us and we blasted off down the runway together. As he broke formation to swing away to the south-east, towards our rendezvous with the tanker, I kept the jet steady on a westerly course.

Jane's faintly mocking voice immediately crackled in my headphones. 'Taking a bit of a circuitous route to Fat Albert this morning, aren't we, Skipper? You wouldn't be planning a pass over a certain farmhouse, would you?'

'Am I that transparent?'

She laughed. 'Only to a professional. Take it down low then, so we can both have a good look.'

We followed the curve of the hills round to the north-west, then dropped down to low level and throttled back. The white walls and red roof of the farm loomed in the canopy and were gone beneath us. There had been no sign of any movement around the building.

'Do you want to go around again?' Jane asked.

'No, once is enough. Let's get to work.' I banked the jet in a broad turn, watching patches of cloud chase each other across the tarns and inlets of the deserted land. Then we were out across the shoreline and skimming over the sea as we began to gain height towards the rendezvous with the Hercules.

'Look down to the right!'

I heard the excitement in Jane's voice and caught a glimpse of a glistening black back arching below us. As the whale vented, a burst of spray shot upwards, making a rainbow in the sky. Then the tail flukes towered out of the water, thrashed once and the monster disappeared from sight.

'Shit,' Jane said. 'That was bigger than the Herc, which by the way is now fifteen miles, ten degrees right, of your nose.'

I corrected course, straining my eyes ahead until I caught sight of a black speck in the sky. I throttled back as the speck swelled rapidly in size, the black bulk of the Hercules dwarfing the Tempest.

A drogue trailed behind it and Shark's jet was already connected, its nose embedded in the basket like a humming bird's beak in a flower. As he dropped away, I eased forward towards the drogue, coaxing the needle of the Tempest's probe into the basket. I heard it lock home and fuel began to pulse down the hose into the jet.

'First time, every time,' Jane said. 'You'd make one hell of a darts player if you could hold your drink better.'

After we'd finished refuelling, I pulled up alongside the Herc to exchange some banter with the crew. 'Everything okay in there? Can we get you something?'

The captain grinned and held up a mug of tea. 'I've got all I need, thanks. It's like a five-star hotel in here. Shame they don't treat you jet-jockeys better.' He waved us away.

Chapter 8

We were making a leisurely circuit of West Falkland to burn up the fuel before landing when the radio crackled into life. 'Fortress to Falcon 2. Radar's showing some Argentine helicopter activity on the edge of the Exclusion Zone. It's probably connected to that air-sea search, but take a look will you?'

Although the helicopters were well outside our radar range, Fortress fed us the information over the datalink. As the contacts appeared on the screen, I pushed the throttles forward and pointed the nose of the jet into the west. We climbed to 3,000 feet to clear Byron Heights, then dropped back to low-level over the sea, racing across the endless procession of steep, rolling waves driven on the wind from the ice-cap far to the south.

I set the radalt to fifty feet. If we flew any lower, a warning would sound and the image in the Head-up Display would begin to flash.

'Painting them now,' Jane said. 'Two contacts eleven o'clock, twenty miles, slow-moving, must be helis.'

Glancing back, I could see the top of her helmet as she leaned over her radar screens.

'Any other hostiles?'

'I've got nothing, but Fortress is seeing another contact, two o'clock at thirty miles.' She paused. 'No sweat, it's too slow for a fast-jet. Must be another heli or a light aircraft.'

I eased back on the stick, raising the jet a couple of hundred feet above the grey, leaden surface of the sea.

'Twenty miles . . . fifteen miles, come left a fraction. Locking them up. Ten miles, on your nose . . . Got them yet?'

I peered through the green haze of the Head-up Display, into the grey murk ahead. Sea and sky seemed to merge into each other. 'Nothing yet, nothing yet. Now. Got them visual.'

Two helicopters hovered over the sea ahead of us, cables trailing below them in the water.

'Fortress, Falcon 2 visual with two helicopters.'

'Any ID on them yet?'

'Standby. Yes. Two SA-332 Super Pumas, trailing cables.'

'What are they up to?' Jane said.

'I don't know. The only helicopter stuff I've ever done was in the work-up to Bosnia.' I peered through the canopy at the outlines of the two choppers. The black holes of the twin engine intakes on top of the canopy looked like eye-sockets. They were carrying missiles, but it was impossible to see what type they were.

'They're no threat to us,' I said, 'but the pattern they're flying is like no air-sea rescue I've ever seen.'

'I'll check the Intelligence Guide.' There was a pause as she flipped through the pages. 'Here we are. "SA-332 Super Pumas. In use with all three services and capable of offensive operations." That's it. Doesn't help us much, does it?'

'Not a lot. I'm not sure about this at all. Something's not right.'

We circled them as I called them up on the distress frequency. 'Argentine helicopters, this is British aircraft Falcon 2. You are infringing the Falkland Islands Exclusion Zone and territorial waters. We are carrying live weapons. Acknowledge or you will be intercepted.'

I repeated the warning twice before there was an acknowledgement in a thick Spanish accent. 'Roger, Falcon 2. This is Argentine helicopter, Bravo 2-2. We are searching for survivors of a sinking. We apologise for the infringement of Malvinas waters, but we shall be moving no further east and where there is hope of finding men alive, we must search.'

'Roger, Bravo 2-2. We are aware of your lost ship.'

'What now?' Jane said.

'Call it in.'

She contacted Fortress on the voice datalink and updated them. The system was so secure that we did not even need to use codes. There were a few moments' silence before the reply came in, the Controller's voice slightly distorted by the encryption. 'Falcon 2, remain in the area and monitor.'

'Let's go and see what the other contact's up to. We'll come back to these two in a minute. By then base might have decided what to do about them.'

As we flew on over the sea towards the site of the other radar trace, something kept nagging at my mind, something I had heard or read, or been told in a lecture. I gave it up for the moment, concentrating on the search for the other contact.

We flew north, parallel with the coast of Argentina for a few more minutes, and found the other aircraft. It was prop-driven and had the markings of the Argentine navy. Its short, fat body and broad tail marked it as a Grumman Tracker. 'Maritime patrol, or anti-submarine warfare,' Jane said, reading from the Intelligence Guide on her lap.

It was just inside Argentine territorial limits and heading further north-west towards the coast as we approached.

'Whatever he was up to, we can't chase him there.' I scanned the instruments. 'Anyway, fuel's getting low, we'd better find out what Fortress wants us to do.'

'Okay,' Jane said. 'It looks like the others have either found what they were looking for or given up anyway.'

As their radar traces began to move back towards the mainland, Fortress came up on the voice link. 'Falcon 2, we see contacts leaving the area. You're clear RTB.'

'That solves our problem then. Give us a course for home, Jane.' I pulled the Tempest back into a turn towards the south-west, easing back a little more on the throttles to conserve fuel. We flew at three hundred feet, over the long South Atlantic swell, which looked even more grey and greasy under the heavy overcast.

'Shit!' she said. 'I don't think there's too much left of that ship they were looking for.'

I cranked my head around. Away to our right, in the area where we had seen the helicopters, the sea seemed strangely flattened, as if a giant hand was pressing down on it. I saw the beginnings of a thick, viscous oil slick, stretching towards the horizon.

'I can't think how we missed it on the way out, we can't have been more than a couple of miles from this position.' I pulled the Tempest into a long sweeping right-hand turn over the area.

Nearer to the centre of the slick, the surface was stubbled

with debris. Anonymous shapes smothered in oil bobbed slowly in the flattened sea.

I shook my head wearily as I looked down, then thumbed the radio to give details of the position of the wreckage to base. 'Come back on an easterly course,' Jane said. 'We're too close to the edge of the Exclusion Zone here.'

We turned back towards the Falklands in silence. I thought of the fate of those sailors. Even those not sucked down into the vortex of their sinking ship would perish within minutes in the icy waters.

As I set the Tempest climbing for base, the nagging thought about the helicopters returned. We flew on in silence. I was still lost in thought as we began descending towards the Falklands coastline and Jane began calling the descent checks. 'Sorry,' I said. 'I was miles away. I'm still not—'

'Look out! Birds!'

A speck in the sky directly ahead of us swelled in a fraction of a second into a flock of seabirds.

Almost without thinking, I had whipped the stick back and hard right, and yanked on the throttles. I caught a glimpse of wings flailing in the pressure wave ahead of the jet and instinctively I ducked. Then there was a crash like a bomb going off, a blizzard of white feathers and a red mist sprayed over the canopy. A bird's severed foot was hurled against the canopy for a micro-second, then torn away by the slipstream, leaving a bloody smear across the Perspex. There was a scream of grinding metal from the right engine. The warning sirens began to howl and the panel lit up like Bonfire Night.

'Right-hand engine failure, shutting it down.' I was shouting through the intercom to make myself heard above the death rattle of the failing engine. My hand flew to the controls, shutting off the fuel to the stricken engine. The Tempest lurched drunkenly from side to side and I had to fight to hold it straight and level.

I darted a hand to the remaining throttle to kill some of our speed, but even that momentary easing of the pressure on the stick was enough to set the jet yawing further to the right. The nose dipped and slid downwards and sideways in the beginnings of a spin. Cockpit lights and flickering captions began to blur and revolve before my eyes. The white-capped waves on the ocean swam into sudden alarming focus, as they accelerated towards me.

'There's something wrong with the controls, Jane.' The sour taste of fear filled my mouth. 'I'm not sure I can hold it. Prepare to eject.'

'Mayday. Mayday. Mayday. Falcon 2, birdstrike. Bullseye two-four-zero, at fifty-two. Standby.'

As the sky rolled back above and the sea below, I dragged the stick back and to the left, sweat pouring down my face as the muscles in my forearms trembled with the effort. As I forced it back, inch by inch, the jet's breakneck fall began to slow.

'Stand by, Jane; getting it back under control.' I prayed that I had enough altitude left to recover the jet. The altimeter stopped, then began to crawl upwards. The radalt warning was flashing; we had bottomed out at less than fifty feet above the sea.

The front and right side of the canopy was covered in a mess of blood and entrails from the birds. I could now see almost nothing through the haze of blood, spread ever wider by the force of the slipstream. I glanced to my right, towards the damaged engine, and froze in horror. A crack snaked up the Perspex canopy. I yanked the throttle back again, losing even more of our speed. The crack now extended from the top to the bottom of the canopy. 'Get all your visors down. The canopy might blow at any moment.'

There was a flash of fear in Jane's voice. 'Should we eject?'

I looked down at the cold, grey ocean below us. 'No. Not yet.' The lower edge of the crack was vibrating in the slipstream and I could feel the knife-edge draught of wind across my face, but the canopy was still holding, for the moment at least.

There was a fresh clamour from the sirens and another blaze of lights from the panel. 'Sean! Right-hand engine fire.'

I craned my head around and peered through the haze of blood on the canopy and saw a black stream of smoke snaking back from the engine. As I watched, the smoke thickened, billowing out in dense clouds. Then there was a flash and a bright corona of fire burst from the engine intakes and licked the edge of the wing, dancing in the slipstream.

Her voice betraying no trace of the fear she must have been fighting, Jane began rapping out the bold face drill from the flight emergency card. There was no room for creative interpretation. The cards laid down the correct procedure to be followed in any conceivable emergency. No deviations were permitted. In major emergencies the aircraft could go out of control within a few seconds. The bold face drills – printed in large bold type on the cards – were the only sure means of saving the aircraft.

My fingers stabbed the buttons and switches in the same staccato rhythm.

'High-pressure cock.'

'Is already shut.'

'Low-pressure cock.'

'Is already shut.'

'Fire button.'

I pressed the button, flooding the engine with inert gas, but there was a heart-stopping pause before the fierce white fire faded to yellow, then red, and then died altogether.

'Check outside again.' I peered out at the airframe. A hole had been torn in the wing and I could see the mangled body of a bird embedded in a tangled mess of wires and control rods.

The buckled and smoke-blackened metal of the wing still twitched and flexed alarmingly as the air-flow dragged across its roughened surface, and the jet handled like a flying brick. I was having to apply strong positive pressure to the stick just to keep the nose up and stop the jet turning to starboard, as the air-drag on the damaged wing forced it inexorably that way. Each fresh patch of turbulence sent it juddering back dangerously close to the brink of instability, but I was managing to hold it under some sort of control.

I shook my head from side to side, clearing the sweat from my eyes. 'Damage report?'

Jane had the information at her fingertips, but she had allowed me to focus on the most pressing emergency, keeping silent to avoid distracting me as I fought the jet and regained control. Now she rattled through a report with barely a wasted word.

'Hydraulics functioning at the moment, but pressure's down and there's a leak of fluid. Not serious yet, but it's dropping quite steadily. I'm monitoring it. Captions showing for the flaps, the undercarriage and the thrust buckets. We could be in for a very bumpy landing.'

'If we get that far.' I checked the fuel levels. 'We're short on fuel now, close to critical.'

As we began to coast in, I tried the flaps. There was no metallic rumble in response to the control. I glanced out to either side of the jet. The flaps had stayed locked in position. I tried twice more without success, then hit the radio button. 'Mayday. Falcon 2 fuel critical, hydraulic leak, no flaps and possible gear failure.'

The urbane voice of the air-traffic controller cut through the static. 'Roger, Falcon 2. It never rains but it pours.' I could hear the siren starting to sound in the background as he hit the red crash button. 'Emergency crews on standby. SAR scrambled. Report status of your gear when you've evaluated it.' His quiet, controlled voice was a calm centre to the storm.

Through the blood-smeared canopy, I made out the dim outline of the coast of West Falkland ahead of us. I shot another glance at the fuel gauge. It told a predictable story, reinforced as the amber warning light began to flash. 'Fuel critical. Give me a course.'

Jane's reply was instantaneous. 'Steer zero-two-zero into King George Bay. Follow the north shore of Christmas Harbour, that'll keep us clear of Chartres Settlement and there should be less turbulence, the cliffs are much lower than anywhere else on that coast. Once we're clear of the mountains we're flying over water all the way, apart from the isthmus around Goose Green. After that, we're over Choiseul Sound until we turn in on finals.'

I saw the sun glinting on the radome on Byron Heights as we swung into the vast sweep of King George Bay. Our course bisected the two claw-like arms of land encircling the bay, but as we passed over Gid's Island, Jane called a turn to the east along the deserted northern shore of Christmas Harbour.

After the birdstrike, the clouds of seabirds rising from the dunes fringing the shore gave me momentary pause. They stayed well away from us, but as we reached the head of the inlet, we hit turbulence over the cliffs. My knuckles whitened on the stick as the damaged wing bucked and twisted, and the vibrations in the airframe redoubled. I could hear my teeth rattling and clamped my jaw tight shut as I again fought to hold the aircraft level. My muscles ached from the effort and sweat drenched my flying suit.

As we cleared the summits of the Hornby Mountains, the last high ground between us and the base, I eased the nose of the jet down a fraction, seeking what shelter I could find from the wind. The vibration lessened as we descended and I was able to relax my grip on the stick a fraction.

Any relief I felt was purely temporary. The next minute another warning sounded. 'Hydraulics are looking bad, Sean. The pressure's dropping much quicker now. I don't know if we'll make it.'

There was nothing useful I could say in reply. Without hydraulic fluid I'd lose control of the aircraft in a few seconds. The only option then would be to grab the ejection handle and get out.

'Just in case, prepare to eject.' I went through the prescribed steps before a premeditated ejection, tightening the leg restraints, lap and shoulder straps, locking the seat belts, and lowering both visors on my helmet.

Still descending, we crossed the broad expanse of Falkland Sound and passed over Brenton Lock, the entrance so narrow that there was barely any clear water visible between the kelp banks advancing from either shore. We flew low over the isthmus below Goose Green, stampeding a few grazing sheep. As we crossed the shoreline, I pressed the button to lower the landing gear.

'The moment of truth. Gear coming down.'

This time there was an answering rumble. I felt the straps bite into my chest as the jet decelerated under the drag on the landing gear. Two green lights and one red showed on the warning panel. 'Front and left gear down and locked. Right gear showing red.'

'Recycle the gear once.'

I tried again with the same result.

'Use the emergency undercarriage lowering system,' Jane said, still reading from the emergency card.

I felt my heart begin to thump a little harder as I reached for the black-and-yellow striped handle that flooded the system with nitrogen gas. Once it was used the gear could not be retracted again. It would be locked solid. I jerked the handle. The red light flickered and went out.

'Thank Christ for that.' I glanced at the fuel gauge again and felt the knot in my stomach grow tighter. Another red warning light was showing on the panel. We were now running almost empty, with only a few minutes' fuel remaining. I jabbed the radio button to call the tower again. 'Falcon 2 on finals. We're out of fuel and very low on hydraulics so we only have this one shot at it. We've also no flaps, so we're coming in fast.'

A different voice cut in. 'Sean, this is Noel. Don't take any unnecessary risks. I'd rather have you eject if you have any doubts. Throw the jet away and we'll pick you up in a few minutes.'

'Thanks, but there's no reason why you shouldn't have all three of us back, though at least one of us will be in pretty rat-shit condition by then.'

Noel's only answer was a terse, 'Roger, your decision.'

As I broke the connection I heard Jane's voice, low but urgent, over the intercom. 'Sean? It's your call, but—'

'I know. Don't worry, I'm not trying to be a hero.'

There was a momentary silence. 'Okay. Go for it.'

'Right. Be ready to eject the instant anything goes wrong. Don't wait for the word, just bang out.'

My breathing was now very fast and shallow and I forced myself to take a few slow, deep breaths, holding each one for a couple of seconds. There was no time for any other preparations. We were now skimming over the plain towards the airfield. The handling of the jet seemed even more sluggish and I cast an anxious eye towards the wing, fearing that part of it might be breaking up. There was no sign of any further damage, but as I nudged the rudder again to line the jet up on the runway there was a yell from the back seat.

'Shit. Hydraulics are almost out. We'll have to come out.'

I tried the stick again. It felt as if it was buried in wet concrete, but the nose came round a fraction. 'We should make it, there's still some response.'

Jane said nothing. It was my decision to make, but I was only too well aware that not one, but two lives rested on it. I had perhaps five seconds.

Smears of blood on the canopy had dried fast in the rush of the slipstream. In places flakes of the dried blood had been ripped away by the wind, but my vision ahead was still obscured.

Peering through it, I could make out the emergency crews, ambulances and fire engines lining the runway, and a Sea King idly hovering, ready if we fell short or overshot and had to eject.

There was mercifully little crosswind, it was blowing almost directly down the runway, but it was still a battle to hold the jet level as the faint outline of the perimeter fence began to show. I coaxed one last effort from my tired muscles, forcing the stick over as the smallest gust of wind set the plane juddering and the wing dipping dangerously towards the ground.

The floodlight stanchions at the edge of the airfield loomed large, then disappeared beneath us. I touched the stick to make a minute correction to our course. 'Hold on, Jane, this is it.'

The jet dropped onto the runway with a crash, lurched back into the air and thudded down again. The nose dipped and then jerked violently upwards. The crack in the Perspex canopy opened wide enough for me to glimpse daylight.

With no steering, I could only straighten the jet by using the right and left brakes. As the jet veered to the right I stamped down hard on that brake. It swung back, but too fast, and I had to stomp on the left brake to correct it. We sped on down the runway, lurching from side to side.

I jerked the throttles to the left to deploy the thrust buckets. The only response was a flashing warning light. The lack of flaps had forced me to approach much faster than usual. We were now racing down the runway at high speed with no steering and no thrust buckets to slow us down.

All we had was whatever hydraulic fluid was left in the emergency reservoir. In theory it was enough for twenty uses of the brakes, but I'd already used a few just trying to keep the jet on line.

'Take the cable,' Jane yelled.

'We've got to get to the fucking thing first.'

I stamped on both brakes at once, trying to drive them through the floor. Almost at once, there was the stench of hot metal and burning oil. The carbon brakes grew hotter and burst into flames, and smoke began filtering into the cockpit.

There were a few moments of absolute clarity, as if my senses had accelerated to match the speed of the jet. I had time to notice the fire crew crouched by the runway, the fire chief's mouth opening and closing soundlessly, shouting orders to his men as we flashed past. I saw the emergency-trucks racing us down the runway, but the flash of their blue lights seemed as slow and measured as the beam of a lighthouse. The radar dish on top of the tower mimicked the pale round faces behind the blue glass, tracking us as we hurtled past.

Then the frozen motion dissolved in an avalanche of speed

and noise. I heard a bang and felt the jet take a violent lurch to the left. The blazing, shredded tyre disintegrated, throwing off smouldering fragments of rubber. The wheel dropped and gouged a furrow out of the concrete, sending up a torrent of sparks.

Reacting by instinct, I released the left brake for a second, then jammed it down hard again as the jet swung back onto line. The end of the runway was racing towards us. The jet still veered from side to side, slower now, but too fast to stop in time. The stench of burning oil and rubber was overpowering, the heat from the burning brakes and flaming tyres palpable even inside the cockpit.

There was another bang, and another. The jet lurched again and the nose dipped. The violent deceleration hurled me forward and the straps sliced into my flesh. The grinding din of metal on concrete doubled and trebled in volume, and fountains of sparks showered around us.

The noise reached a terrible crescendo as we slewed across the apron. I saw the black edge of the peat ahead of us and the barbs of fencing wire just beyond. Then the pressure on my chest ceased abruptly and I slumped back in my seat. It took a moment for me to realise that we had come to a halt. I hit the crash switches, killed the remaining fuel flow and electrics, and pressed the remaining fire button for good measure. 'Safe-arm the seats.'

There were a few seconds of near-total silence and then I heard the clamour of sirens and the screech of the fire trucks' brakes as they ground to a halt around us. Thick, oily black smoke was now filling the canopy. I heard Jane's voice. 'The canopy, Sean. The canopy.'

'I can't. We've no hydraulics.' I stared down at my hands, still gripping the useless stick as if my life depended on it.

It was a moment before I could release my grip, my fingers cramped with pain. Through the blood smears, smoke and flames, I saw white, moon-suited figures running towards us. There was the whoosh of foam as the fire crews went to work on the blazing brakes and tyres, and a clang as metal ladders were thrown against the side of the jet.

The face of one of the fire crew peered in at me through the Perspex, even more remote behind his visor. 'I can't raise the canopy,' I yelled.

He nodded and gave a warning shout. The other fire crew backed away, still training their hoses on the flames.

Holding the emergency canopy handle, attached to a length of cable, the fireman jumped down from the ladder. As he began to sprint away from the jet, still holding the cable in his hand, I shouted 'Heads dow—'

There was a deafening bang as the explosive strip embedded in the canopy detonated and the Perspex disintegrated.

I felt strong hands lifting me and carrying me down. I looked around me, dazed and disorientated, trying to make sense of what was happening. Then my head began to clear. As the fire crew hurried away from the jet, staggering a little under their burden, I could hear and see their feet crunching on shards of glittering Perspex as if we were crossing the surface of a frozen lake.

I glanced back towards the Tempest. It looked a wreck, smoke-blackened, battered and covered in dirty grey foam. There was no sign of Jane. I looked around wildly. 'Jane? Where's Jane?'

'Your nav? She's all right. She's just over there.' The fire crewman nodded towards my right.

She was also cradled between two fire crew carrying her towards the waiting ambulance, but she raised her head and looked at me.

An impassive team of medics loaded us into separate ambulances for the run to the medical centre. Apart from fatigue and a residual headache from the blast that had detonated the canopy, I felt okay, but it was a good hour and a half before they could be persuaded to release me. As I came out of the Sick Bay, Jane rushed from the bench where she had been waiting and hugged me so hard she almost lifted me off my feet.

'You beauty. Give me a kiss, you Pommy bastard, you. That was one ballsy landing.'

'For a crap nav, you didn't do too badly yourself.'

She laughed and aimed a cuff at my head, then thought better of it. 'Perhaps not. If your head aches like mine, you won't be too amused.'

We were both still elated by the adrenalin rush of survival, talking, laughing and joking as the ambulance took us back down to the QRA area. At the far end of the airfield a mobile crane was lifting the wreckage of the Tempest from the runway.

'Taff and the ground crew are going to love us for that,' I said. 'I doubt if they'll ever get that heap of scrap airworthy again.'

The battle-damage repair crew were already at work, jack-hammers clattering as they dug out the sections of runway gouged by the wheels of the Tempest and began to replace them.

'Good time for an Argentine invasion,' Jane said.

'It'll be fixed in a couple of hours.'

Noel was waiting to greet us as we headed for the changing rooms. 'Top job,' he said, gripping our hands in turn. 'Both of you. I wouldn't have fancied getting that jet down in one piece. The Boss would have been here to add his congratulations, but he's been knee-deep in signals traffic for the last couple of hours. God knows what's going on.' He paused. 'Anyway, well done. Get cleaned up and I'll treat you to a celebration cup of coffee. Anything stronger'll have to wait until we come off QRA.'

Tired and sweaty, we both risked a quick shower. My exhilaration soon began to fade. My head ached and my arms and shoulders were sore from the strain of battling the crippled jet, but it was the image of Argentine trawlermen drowning somewhere beneath the black scum of oil covering the ocean surface that kept coming back to me.

The light was already fading by the time we headed through to the crew room. We ate the food sent over from the Mess without enthusiasm.

'It's like Britain in the 1950s.'

Jane looked up from her resigned contemplation of her plate. 'The Falklands?'

'The food.' I pushed my plate away and stared out into the darkness.

I could sense Jane watching me. 'Not still thinking about the birdstrike?'

I shook my head. 'Those poor sailors. My grandfather served on a destroyer in the war. He escorted a lot of convoys on the suicide run through the Arctic into Murmansk. He saw a lot of ships sunk and a lot of men drowned, but the thing he most remembered was the sinking of a British cruiser.

'It was deep in the Arctic winter and the superstructure of the ship was smothered in ice. There was a heavy sea running and a stiff wind out of the North. The cruiser was ripped apart by torpedoes. It went down stern first in seconds. The oil slick flattened the sea, just like it did today. He said that all he could see floating in the oil in the middle of the Arctic Ocean were hundreds and hundreds of pith helmets the Marine bandsmen wore on tropical duty. Those hats bobbing silently on the sea moved him more than all the lifeless bodies he'd seen.'

The door banged and the Boss strode in to the room, his face grim. 'Briefing in two minutes, get the others.'

We exchanged a questioning glance, then leapt to our feet. Most of the guys were in the TV room but Noel was dozing on his bed and I had to shake him awake. We hurried into the briefing room where the Boss was staring at a handful of signals spread out on the podium in front of him. As I walked past him I could see the heading: ALPHA EYES ONLY, the highest security level.

He began to speak before we were seated, his voice cold and measured. 'We've received a series of flash signals from London over the past few hours. All contact with the nuclear submarine HMS *Trident* has again been lost. It was operating on the edge of Argentine territorial waters, monitoring and tracking the exercise being conducted there. The last recorded contact was at 1800 hours local time yesterday. Since then it's missed two routine communication slots.'

I had stopped listening. All I could see in my mind were the two Argentine helicopters and the oil slick spreading slowly over the surface of the ocean, studded with the debris of a wreck.

I felt Jane's hand on my arm. 'Sean, what's the matter? You're as white as a sheet!'

'That wreck.'

She stared at me for a moment, then the realisation hit her. 'Oh, shit. The helicopters.'

I nodded. When I looked up, the Boss had fallen silent and was watching us. Slowly, haltingly, I repeated the details of what we had seen. I raised my eyes to meet his. 'I just didn't realise. I knew something wasn't right, but—'

As he hesitated, Noel stood up. 'That's bullshit, Sean. You

had no reason to believe anything was wrong. We intercepted signals apparently coming from a trawler in distress and you then found two helicopters searching the area, an oil slick and the debris from a wreck. It could all be a false alarm. An Argentine trawler really could have gone down there, and the *Trident* may yet resume contact. There are a hundred other reasons why they could have missed their slots.'

I could not keep the scepticism from my face.

'Anyway,' he said, 'what action could you have taken? We can't shoot helicopters down because they're acting suspiciously.'

I shook my head. 'I could have done something.'

The Boss cleared his throat and spread his hands palms down. 'Let's save the post mortems until later, when the situation becomes clearer. For the moment, I'm moving you up to RS5. I want two crews sitting in those jets, ready to go at all times.'

I was the first to break the ensuing silence. 'What about Cobra Force?'

The Boss lowered his head a little, as if ducking the expected response. 'They're on standby.'

'Standby? We need more than that, Boss. We need them here, on the way, now.'

'Sean, you know the position. Don't you think I'd have those troops here if I could? But the MoD simply won't countenance two squadrons and two thousand troops being flown out here just because the *Trident* has missed two call-in slots. After all, it's not the first time it's happened.'

'Which makes it all the more unlikely that it would happen again. Boss, you've got to persuade them. It's our job to defend these islands. The cost to the MoD of an emergency deployment is a couple of million pounds – small change in the defence budget. If it's a false alarm, that's all we'll lose. If it isn't, we could lose the Falklands. The cost of that would be billions.'

He pursed his lips. 'I hear what you say, Sean, and I understand why you are personally so agitated about this.'

I was halfway to my feet when I felt Jane's restraining hand on my arm, her fingers digging in to the flesh. 'Don't, Sean.'

Noel had already stood up again. 'We're here to fight the Argentinians if necessary, not bicker among ourselves.' He paused to glance at each of us. 'But I have to say I share Sean's concerns. If *Trident* is out of action, where are the other nuclear subs?'

The Boss consulted his papers. 'The Barents Sea, the Gulf and the Western Approaches.'

Noel's ruddy face deepened another tone. 'Then if the *Trident* is out of action, we must have that Cobra Force. We're sitting ducks otherwise.'

The Boss's voice showed his exasperation. 'How many times do I have to say this? I've argued the case with all the force I can muster, but you know as well as I do that decisions on deployments of the scale of Cobra Force are not made by Group Captains. Cobra Force has been placed on standby. At the first signs of any unusual Argentine activity, it'll be mobilised immediately.'

'By which time it could be too late,' Noel said.

The Boss ignored him. 'We're now in a state of high alert. We're bringing the standby jets up to readiness. Each of you will go directly to the armoury to be issued with your personal weapons. Make sure you carry them at all times. That is all.'

As we got to our feet, Noel's voice cut through the silence. 'Falcon Two and Three will take the first spell in the jets. As soon as you've collected your weapons, the rest of you get all the kit you need in your aircraft, ready for a rolling take-off, if necessary. One and Four will do the second shift, then Five and Six. I'll sort out the rest of the rota later. Four-hour shifts. Keep alert.'

Chapter 9

The base was in total darkness, but the silence of the night had been ripped apart. Sea Kings clattered overhead, trailing loads on steel cables, as additional Rapier missile batteries were deployed to their pre-set positions. Vehicles, lights extinguished, sped to and fro, disgorging troops who scattered to every part of the perimeter, boots pounding on the concrete. Stripped-down Land Rovers roared along the runway, each manned by a soldier with a loaded GPMG.

'Where the hell did those things come from?' Jane said. 'I've never seen them around the base.'

I could see the faint outline of troops behind the blue glass of the tower, and more fully armed Marines, their faces smeared with cam cream, manned the sangars around the armoury and the bomb and fuel dumps.

We gave the number of the day to the guards manning the gate in the barbed wire surrounding the armoury, and hurried down the ramp into the underground chamber. Two NCOs were issuing weapons. I signed my name on the form thrust in front of me and holstered a pistol.

We collected our kit from the Q shed, then ran up the ramp to the Tempest shack. I heard Taff's voice bellowing orders. He was standing with his back to me, gesticulating to the jet with one hand. In the other he held an SA-80.

'Shit, the last time I saw him he was holding a pint.'

The other ground-crew were working on the new jet, checking and rechecking. One had his head under one of the engine covers, but alongside the spanners laid out in a neat row on the wing was his rifle.

'I'm not sure how much I like this,' Jane said. 'It's all getting a bit serious, isn't it?' She hesitated. 'Sean? What if I can't—' Her voice trailed away.

'I was just thinking the same. Come on. We'll be fine. We've trained for this for years. We won't blow it.'

Her eyes sought mine. She started to say something else, then shook her head and climbed the ladder to the cockpit.

I followed her up, stowed my kit and connected my helmet. I left it lying on the seat, so that all I had to do if there was a call-out was put it on and fire the engines.

We hurried back to the Q shed. For once, the TV screen was blank. The others sat or stood in silence, while Noel paced up and down the Ops Area, talking as much to himself as to the rest of us. 'Keep yourselves topped up with food and fluids. You need to maintain your energy levels in case—'

As he spoke, there was the dull crump of an explosion. A metallic voice echoed from the Tannoy. 'Alert. Falcon call-out. Alert. Falcon call-out.'

For a moment no one moved, then I dived for the alarm. The two red buttons set the sirens wailing all over the base. The amber button opened the doors of the Tempest shacks.

As we sprinted for the door, the rising chorus of the sirens was punctuated by more explosions and the rattle of small-arms fire.

A column of smoke, black even against the night sky, was billowing from one of the Tempest shacks on the far side of the runway. As I stood transfixed, my heart pounding, there was a second blast and another Tempest shack erupted in flames.

There was another explosion in the sky above me and a burst of blinding white light. A flare drifted slowly down. In its harsh glare I saw a score of black-clad figures moving across the ground between the runway and the perimeter fence, firing as they advanced.

Rees sprinted past, then Noel, struggling to keep pace with him. 'Get to the jets,' he said. 'It looks like a Special Forces attack on the QRA aircraft.'

I stood frozen to the spot.

'Get moving,' Noel yelled. 'Now! Get airborne as fast as you can.' He disappeared into the darkness of the tunnel.

Tracer slashed through the darkness as our own ground troops returned fire. There was the rattle of machine guns and the crack of rifles. Rounds tore at the ground around me and ricocheted from the walls of the Q shed. Still I stood frozen.

'Sean, come on!' Jane dragged at my arm, breaking the spell, and I ran with her, stooping and dodging towards the ramp.

Ahead and to the left of the ramp I glimpsed a huddled group of figures. There was a flash and a roar, and the front of the Q shed, where I had been standing barely five seconds before, disintegrated. A giant bubble of flame expanded outward and then burst in a shower of burning fragments. A corner-post and the tall steel safe stood semi-upright in the wreckage, all that was left of the front half of the building. The rest had disappeared.

I saw figures writhing among the debris and heard terrible, unearthly screams. Then there were fresh bursts of automatic fire and I saw small, dark shapes lobbed through the air.

'Down!' I threw myself forward, flattening Jane beneath me as the grenades detonated and I heard the vicious whine of shrapnel shredding everything in its path above me. I took a ragged breath, shouted 'Up and move!' and ran for the ramp.

Only the terror of what lay behind us drove me into the dark entrance, not knowing what was waiting there. I threw myself flat again and rolled sideways to the wall, but there was no answering gunfire. Scrambling to my feet, I sprinted up the slope, the breath tearing from my lungs. I paused for a second in the shadows at the top of the ramp and Jane flattened herself against the wall beside me.

The Tempest shack was in darkness, but there was a dull, red glow from the jet's already rumbling engines. Figures were huddled at either side of the entrance. As I watched, they began firing at the unseen enemy. Fire ripped back at them almost at once. The jet's needle nose glinted in the light of the tracer rounds burning through the air. I had to fight the urge to bury my face in Jane's shoulder.

I waited for a lull in the firing. 'Ready? Go!' We burst out of cover together, sprinting across the twenty-yard gap. I saw a gun barrel swing towards us and screamed 'Don't shoot!' then dived for the entrance to the shack as firing erupted again to my left.

A strong hand gripped my arm and pulled me further into cover. 'The jet's ready to roll,' Taff said. Instead of a socket-wrench, he was still gripping a rifle. 'The faster you get airborne the better.'

'The tower?'

He nodded. 'Under attack but still functioning. We're hard-pressed here though.'

As if in confirmation, there was the whine and blast of a mortar shell. We both flinched. 'Get up there and help us out,' he said. 'When you're ready, give me the nod and we'll give you what covering fire we can.'

Jane was already strapping herself in her seat as I scrambled up the ladder. Tension made my fingers clumsy as I tried to strap myself in. I forced myself to go slower, even though the firing seemed to get closer with every passing second.

There was no time for pre-flight checks. We'd just have to chance it. If we waited to complete them, we'd never get airborne at all. The Argentine Special Forces – if that's what they were – had already destroyed two of the Tempest shacks and were closing fast on this one.

'Ready?'

'Hell, yes,' Jane said. 'Let's get out of here.'

I gave a thumbs-up to Taff, pressed the button to lower the canopy and pushed the throttles forward, holding the jet on the brakes.

The engines began to roar. I saw Taff's lips move as he shouted to the other crewmen and ground troops. As the canopy warning siren sounded, they exploded out of cover, pouring fire towards the enemy. I saw Taff raise his rifle to his shoulder and squeeze off two carefully aimed bursts. Then his body was punched backwards by a burst of automatic fire. Fibres blasted from his clothing hung in the air as he slumped and fell directly in front of the jet. He twitched and lay still.

There was no way he could have survived, but it was still the hardest thing I had ever had to do. There was a lump in my throat as I released the brakes. We rolled forward a few yards, then there was a soft thud and the jet stopped. Taff's body was jammed against the wheels.

I rammed the throttles forward. The nose dipped and the engines screamed as the afterburners kicked in, and flame torched out of the back of the jet. The twenty-ton aircraft shuddered, jarred and then shot forward, crushing Taff's body beneath its wheels.

The sound of firing was lost in the din of the engines, but I saw the flashes of tracer — bright holes punched in the darkness — cutting through the night towards us.

There was a sound as brittle as a hammer on glass and a bullet smashed into the fuselage a few inches below the canopy. I heard another, deader sound as a second bullet bit into the aircraft's metal skin behind and below me. I held my breath, praying silently.

I watched the runway blurring as we gathered speed, trying not to look at the jagged white lines of tracer sweeping nearer to us. The tower was blacked out, but in the faint glow from the radar screens I could see that several of its windows had been shattered.

Jane was calling the ascending speeds, her voice cracking with tension. 'Eighty knots ... One hundred ... One-twenty ...'

The beam of tracer was almost upon us.

'One-fifty ...'

'Rotating.' I hauled back on the stick. The micro-second's delay in the aircraft's response seemed endless, but then the nose-wheel lifted and the landing gear came off the ground with a thud. I jabbed the buttons. 'Gear travelling ... and the flaps.'

We shaved the perimeter fence, climbing due east. The enemy fire fell away, then ceased as abruptly as it had begun.

'Fortress, this is Falc—' The words froze on my lips as

the Missile Approach Warner erupted. Directly ahead of us there was a flash of light and the hot, dirty-white streak of a missile. The Argentinians were taking no chances. A patrol was lying up, aligned on the centre line of the runway, ready to shoot down any jets that escaped the ground attack. There was no more vulnerable moment in which to attack an aircraft than in the few seconds immediately after take-off.

'Flares! Flares!'

Jane responded instantly. Flares burst from the wingtip dispensers. I cast a despairing glance at the altimeter and air-speed counter. We had neither the height nor the speed, but I had no choice. I threw the jet into a hard left turn. As the G-force pinned me back in my seat, crushing me with my own weight, I heard Jane's helmet rattling against the side of the canopy. I felt the G-pants inflating, clamping my thighs like a vice to force the blood back up my body.

The jet slipped sideways and down, the wing slicing perilously close to the ground. I tasted bile in my mouth and fought down the wave of nausea. I held the turn even as my vision faded to grey. I knew the danger signals. I ground my teeth and grunted with the effort of forcing the grey-out away. The grey and white world flickered for a moment and then colour flooded back in.

I held the turn another second, then levelled the wings and looked behind, forcing my head round. There was a kink in the trail of the missile as it switched course to track us. I pushed the stick forward, forcing the jet even closer to the ground. We were skimming over the banks of peat, so low that I imagined the stems of tussac grass whipping the underside of the fuselage.

The Tempest's engine intakes had been modified with radar absorbent material to make them less visible, but there was nothing I could do to mask the heat of the jet pipes from an infra-red seeker head. If I throttled back to lose the heat signature that the missile was tracking, we would crash. We were too low even to manoeuvre. If I tried another steep turn, the wingtip would spike the ground and catapult us into oblivion.

I forced the throttles all the way forward, but the missile, still accelerating, was flashing towards us as if we were stationary. 'Flares! Flares! Flares!'

The klaxons were still shrieking their warning and my mouth was already framing the word 'Eject' when I saw an outcrop, a stone run white against the black of the peat.

'Flares!' I nudged the stick right and risked touching the ground with the wing as I threw the jet round the outcrop. The grey of the wingtip and the boulders just beneath me seemed to merge, so close that I could see no space between them. Then a gap opened, widening as we swung round the outcrop.

The missile trace disappeared from sight behind me, lost for an instant in the white-hot glow of the flares. A moment later a massive fireball erupted in our wake. There was no sound, only the blinding flash burning into my retina. The klaxons died back into silence.

I counted to three. Then I let out a long breath. My gloves were already sodden with sweat. 'All right, Jane?'

'Yeah.' Her voice was as shaky as mine.

'Then let's get those bastards.'

I pulled the stick back, climbing to 5,000 feet, then banked the jet and began a shallow dive back towards the airfield. 'Arming weapons.'

The Sidewinders under the wings were heat-seeking air-to-air missiles, useless for ground attack, but the Tempest was also carrying six CRV-7 pods under the fuselage. I had never even fired them on a range, but I had simulated their use enough times, and I still remembered the words of the instructor at the briefing where they were introduced: 'Air-to-surface missiles, gentlemen, with fragmentation warheads optimised for low-level attacks on light armour and soft targets ...'

I aligned the jet on the eastern end of the runway and began raking the ground short of it for the aiming marks I had memorised as the missile was launched. I had to make the first shot count. If I missed, I'd be giving the Argentinians another free shot at us; I wasn't convinced they would miss a second time.

I rammed the throttles forward again into full combat power and increased the angle of the dive. The vibrations from the screaming engines rattled the fuselage and shook my hands on the stick. The Argentine patrol was invisible, somewhere in the wasteland of peat and tussac grass.

I saw my markers, a solitary boulder and a small kidney-shaped pond. The missile had been launched from the midpoint between them. I lined up the sights, staring into the Head-up Display as the Death Dot and the aiming point moved together with agonising slowness.

The Missile Approach Warner clamoured again and a streak of flame and smoke shot upwards. 'Flares!'

Although there was little chance of the SAM homing successfully in a head-on shot, I threw the jet left and right and the missile flashed past.

I held the dive until the last minute, my finger poised on the trigger. As I fired, I hauled the stick back and we bottomed out and began to climb. The missile blasted away underneath us, in a trajectory calculated by the Tempest's computers. It ended in a blinding flash. The ground seemed to dissolve as the fragmentation warhead shredded everything in its path.

'Keep checking down and back,' I said, but there was no warning from the klaxons, no sign of another missile launch. The boulder and the small pond were still there, but between them was a massive smoking crater.

I shifted my gaze forward again, already thumbing the radio as I looked out across the airfield. The blast of explosions and the arcs of tracer still lit up the night, counterpointing the constant glow from burning buildings. 'Falcon 3 to Fortress, do you read?'

'Roger, Falcon 3, we're still on the air. We seem to be holding them, but heavy machine-gun and mortar fire are causing us big problems. Stand by for a Forward Air Controller.'

A moment later a new voice came up. 'Falcon 3, this is Wingback.' I seemed to recognise the voice, but was too preoccupied with the detail of what he was saying to pursue it. 'Enemy heavy machine gun is 400 yards north-west of QRA area. Make your attack run over the top of the tower from the south-east and we'll guide you onto it.' Despite the detonations underpinning the sound of his voice, he could have been discussing a cricket score. 'Marker for our position is red smoke. The target is approximately 120 yards from us.'

I circled wide around the base. There were blazes flaring all around the airfield, among the smaller flashes of continuing ground fire. I glanced out of the other side of the jet towards the mountains. There were specks of fire by the Rapier missiles sites on the nearest peaks. It was an ominous sign. If the Argentinians were planning to launch an aerial assault, the sites were prime prior targets.

I pushed the thought away as I banked the jet around for the attack run. I forced the throttles back into combat power and we rocketed down towards the airfield. 'Weapons armed.'

I aligned the jet on the dark mass of the tower. As we flashed over it, ground fire stabbed at us out of the night. I forced myself to ignore it, concentrating only on the cone of my forward vision, framed by the intersecting lines of the Head-up Display.

The radio crackled. 'We see you, Falcon 3. Smoke on now.'

For a moment I saw nothing, then there was a smudge of red ahead of us. I adjusted course slightly, flying down the tunnel of ground fire.

The Death Dot and the aiming point in the Head-up Display intersected at the base of a column of tracer. I pulled the trigger and a stream of missiles leapt from the pods.

I hauled on the stick, sending the jet soaring up and away to the left. I glanced behind and saw the glint of the reflector strips on the back of Jane's helmet as she looked down and back. There was a fierce double-flash from the ground and the line of tracer abruptly winked out.

'Beauty,' she shouted. 'Right on the money.'

I was already reaching for the radio. 'Wingback, next target?'

'Mortar on the low ridge three-quarters of a mile north-north-west of us. It's maybe ten degrees left of the end Tempest shack — or what's left of it. Come in on that bearing and we'll put down two lines of tracer fire to intersect on the target.

'Okay, Wingback, here we go.'

'Fuel's okay, captions are clear. Go for it, Sean,' Jane said. 'Let's make it three out of three.'

I could feel sweat soaking my flying suit, but the adrenalin was holding exhaustion at bay. I felt hyper-alert, almost omnipotent.

As we flashed in over the base we were again greeted by a blizzard of ground fire from the enemy positions. 'Mark those sites, Jane, we'll go for them when we've seen this mortar off.'

Even the sight of a handful of rounds punching up through the wing didn't faze me. The warning panel stayed clear; there was only superficial damage. As we hurtled towards the still-burning Tempest shack, I saw two dotted green lines stitched across the darkness. They wavered, then held firm, intersecting on the dark outline of a low ridge.

I waited for the lock on the target, holding the jet level despite the temptation to yank the stick as fire slashed towards us from the ridge. The dot on the screen slid on to the aiming point. I jabbed the trigger and hauled the jet into a screaming turn.

Once more there was a grunt from Jane as she fought against the G-force. There was a pause and then we both saw a blinding flash of light below us.

The laconic voice of Wingback came straight through on the radio. 'On target, Falcon 3, enemy troops appear to be falling back from the tower, but they're still holding a line north and west of the QRA area. We're ready to push out, but any fire you can bring to bear on them would be appreciated. We'll give you more smoke to mark our positions.'

The tower cut in. 'Falcon 4 is also available, Falcon 3; co-ordinate with him.'

I had not even seen Rees and Noel get airborne and I scanned the sky anxiously for a sign of them.

'He's four miles out, eleven o'clock,' Jane said, scanning her radar screen. 'Now three miles, turn zero-two-zero. Got him yet?'

'Wait ... yes. Visual.' I spotted the dark shape of the aircraft against the clouds. I swung the jet into a tight turn

that brought us into formation, line astern, and about one mile
– seven seconds – separated.

'Follow me in, Sean. I'll take the left targets, you take
the right.'

We barrelled in towards the airfield again. Ahead I could
see a drifting line of smoke. Beyond it ground fire seared
upwards towards Noel's jet. His guns flashed in response as
he strafed the enemy positions. Then he was past the target,
climbing steeply upwards and banking for another run as we
began our own attack.

I held the jet in its shallow dive, saw the tracer slicing
towards us and then squeezed the firing button. There was a
thunderous rattle as the guns spat out high-explosive shells at
2,000 rounds a minute. The muzzle-flashes lit up the cockpit
as if the aircraft were on fire and the smell of cordite filled
my nostrils. I could feel the jet slowing under the force of the
recoil from the guns.

A line of explosions tore across the ground. I eased the
stick up and left a fraction, walking the line of fire onto the
target. Then I released the button and the sound died, leaving
my ears ringing, as the last of the empty shell cases clattered
into the bay beneath the floor of the cockpit.

Three more times we were called in to strafe targets,
then the enemy lines broke. Most pulled back in an orderly
withdrawal, a few turned and ran, pursued by skirmishing
parties of Marines.

'Falcon 3 to Fortress, we're low on fuel, are we clear
to land?'

'Runway clear, Falcon 3, perimeter secure, you're okay
to land.'

I released the radio button, looking down on the airfield as
we circled for our approach. Flames still flickered from a score

of fires and pillars of grey-black smoke rose into the air, but the surface of the runway appeared to be virtually unmarked. 'I can't understand why they didn't crater the runway while they had the chance. We'd have been in deep shit.'

'They must be planning to use it themselves.' Jane voiced the thought that had been nagging at me. We both fell silent.

'Best we get these jets turned round and ready to go again as fast as maybe,' she said.

Rees' jet went in first as we circled, still alert for ground fire or a missile launch. They touched down and braked under reverse thrust. Before they had reached the end of the runway, we were beginning our own approach.

We landed safely and sped through to the QRA area. As I spun the jet round on the apron, another Tempest blasted down the runway and took off, spewing out flares to decoy any SAMs. It banked away to the north and a couple of minutes later I saw the flash of an explosion lighting up the lower slope of Mount Pleasant.

A tractor pushed our jet back into the shack, its concrete walls pock-marked with bullet holes. As I killed the engines, the ground crew swarmed over the jet, almost unrecognisable under the cam cream still smeared on their faces. Avgas began pumping through the hoses and the armourers hurried to fix new missile pods and re-arm the aircraft.

I had to hold fatigue at bay while we ran through the exhaustive checks to get the jet primed and ready to go again. Finally we were finished. I took off my helmet, leaving it on the seat, still connected to the communications cables, and clambered down.

In the distance I could still see and hear sporadic bursts of fire. The push out by the Marines seemed to have faltered. The lines of tracer etched against the black mass of the mountains suggested that the Argentinians had pulled back only as far as defensive positions on the higher ground. There was every chance that they would regroup and then return to the attack.

The remnants of my adrenalin-fuelled elation faded as my gaze took in the ruins of the Q shed and the bodies laid out in a row on the edge of the apron. I tried not to look down at the ground in front of the Tempest shack, but my eyes were drawn to a pool of congealing blood, still marked by the tracks of the Tempest's tyres. A dark, irregular trail showed where Taff's body had been dragged away across the concrete.

Troops were still clustered in defensive firing positions around each of the remaining shacks. Their commander, a white-faced and very young troop officer, pointed us towards the Reserve Forces building. 'It's only lightly damaged, we're using it as an emergency Q shed.' I could see his fingers trembling as he stretched out his hand.

Shark, Jimmy and a few other aircrew sat, stood or paced around a large wooden table inside the shed. There should have been twenty men there, the eight on QRA, plus the dozen reserve aircrew. Including the two still airborne, I counted only ten. I looked around the circle of faces, noting the absentees. I could only hope they were casualties not fatalities, but I didn't ask what had happened; I didn't want to know the answer.

They glanced up as we came in, but nobody spoke. Their faces were pale, grimy and lined with fatigue, and they flinched at the distant gunshots. Rees sat alone, his head in his hands. He looked to have aged years in the space of one evening, and even Noel's normally florid complexion had a sallow look. 'The Boss is just collating the casualty and battle damage reports. As soon as we have a more complete picture of what jets and shacks are still usable, there'll be a sit-rep and briefing.' The effort of speaking was almost too much for him. 'But we'll keep one jet airborne continuously until first light, or until we get the all-clear.'

The building was a mirror image of the Q shed, but even more sparsely furnished. I slumped on a hard wooden chair by the wall, too tired even to think about washing off some of the sweat and dirt. There were a few murmurs of conversation, but most people sat silent, staring at the walls.

Jane sat down next to me, leaned across and squeezed my arm. 'All right?'

'Not really.'

'You did a good job there.'

I shook my head. 'I shouldn't have had to. It was my fault. What happened to Taff and—'

'Don't be stupid.' A couple of heads turned. She flushed and lowered her voice. 'He was already dead when the jet went over him.'

'I didn't mean that. If I'd had my mind on my job earlier today I'd have realised what those Argentine helicopters were up to. If I'd stopped them sinking the *Trident*, they would never have dared to make the attack tonight.'

'That's bullshit, Sean. Those troops were already here. You saw one of their Zodiacs hidden on the beach. The *Trident* might have kept the Argentine navy at bay, but it didn't stop them infiltrating those troops. Snap out of it, Sean. We did what we were ordered to do. We checked it out. It seemed okay. We flew back. End of story. The *Trident* has' – she paused, – 'had all the counter-measures it needed to evade detection and anti-submarine weaponry. They were doing what they were paid to do, just like we are.'

I shrugged, unconvinced, but before I could reply, the door banged. Jack stood just inside the entrance. He caught sight of me and began walking towards us, his rifle still gripped in his left hand. His face was streaked with cam cream.

He stood over us for a moment, then put his helmet down on the table and sat down, laying his rifle across his knees. He nodded to Jane. 'Jack Stubbs, I was the Forward Air Controller for you guys out there.' He turned to me. 'I recognised your voice over the radio. You two did a great job.'

'Thanks, so did you.'

He shook his head wearily. 'I fought one war here. I never thought I'd be fighting another.'

'Have we driven them off?'

'For the moment.'

'Will they be back?'

'Probably.' He sat in silence for a few moments, his head bowed, then glanced up at Jane. 'Do you mind if I have a few words in private with Sean?'

'It's all right, Jack. I've got no secrets from—'

She was already standing up. 'I don't mind. I'm going to get my feet up for a few minutes. It's going to be a long night.' She walked over to a threadbare sofa against the wall and lay down.

Jack looked back at me. 'You've been under fire now. You know what it's like. I thought you'd earned the right to hear the rest of what happened to your brother.'

'About Ro— About the civilians, you mean?'

He nodded.

'Well . . .' I hesitated. 'What he did for those people sounds like an incredibly brave thing to do. Yet it's not even mentioned on the citation for his MC.'

'Oh, it was brave all right, just like that officer at Goose Green was brave.'

'Meaning what?'

'You've seen the terrain. There was no cover worth the name on the whole of Black Mountain. Our silent attack had been compromised when the corporal stood on the mine. We were making a frontal assault against well-entrenched positions – including a heavy machine gun – on the ridge above us. We were hopelessly exposed and taking casualties.

'The absolute priority was to get across that open ground as fast as possible and silence that machine gun. It was the best, the only way of protecting everyone – soldiers and civilians alike. Yet your brother held up the advance to play the hero and rescue the civilians.' He paused. 'Don't get me wrong, I'm not denying it was a hell of a brave thing to do, but it wasn't the smartest move by a long chalk. It was bad soldiering and it could have got himself and the civilians killed, as well as—'

'But it paid off, didn't it? He rescued the civilians and then took out the machine gun.'

He looked away from me, fixing his eyes on the floor. When he spoke again, his voice was flat. 'As soon as he saw the civilians, he shouted "Hold your fire." With the noise of the guns, it took a while for everyone to hear him, but gradually the firing from our side petered out and stopped. Then he held his rifle by the barrel, waved it above his head and slowly stood up, even though the Argentinians were still firing.

'The platoon sergeant was just behind and to one side of him. He yelled at him to get down and was reaching up to pull him back into cover again when a tracer round went straight through his head. I don't think your brother even knew what had happened to the sergeant. He was still staring towards the Argentine lines, oblivious of what was going on behind him.'

He shook his head wearily. 'He stayed exactly where he was and the Argentinians gradually stopped shooting too. Then he put down his gun, walked forward and led the civilians down the hill into a scrap of cover – a low mound of rocks. I think he carried the girl most of the way.

'I don't know if he realised what had happened or even saw the sergeant as he came back to where he'd left his rifle. He just picked it up, dropped into cover and then fired the first shot, which set the whole firework display rolling again. It was immediately afterwards that he led the frontal attack on the machine-gun position.' He shrugged. 'Maybe he did know what he'd done and that was his way of atoning.'

I sat in silence.

'Don't think he's suddenly turned from a hero to a villain,' Jack said. 'Nothing is ever quite that straightforward in combat or anywhere else. Sure, he's still a hero, but there's a very fine dividing line between a hero and the next bloke, who's just doing his job.'

He glanced down at his powerful hands, examining the cuts and scratches on them. 'The platoon sergeant, Lofty Williams, was a hell of a good soldier. He was also a good friend of mine. He died risking his life to save someone else's.' He paused and fixed me with his gaze. 'Just like your brother. The only difference is that there were no medals for Lofty, not even a Mention in Dispatches. He was just another statistic, another name on the Para monument.'

'I'm sorry,' I said.

He picked up his helmet and his rifle. 'I have to get back to my men. Good luck.'

'You too. I'll buy you that pint when this is over.'

He nodded, then turned away.

Chapter 10

Jane left me alone with my thoughts for a few minutes, then wandered over and sat down again. 'Okay?'

'Yes.'

'Do you want to talk?'

'He told me some more about Mike. Including some things I might have been happier not to know.'

'Such as?'

'He wasn't quite as much of a hero as I'd thought.'

'But Rose—'

'He saved Rose and her family, all right, just as she said, but in doing so he got someone else killed.'

When I'd finished telling her the story, she sat in silence for a moment, then said, 'Good. I'm glad.'

'What?'

'Not that someone died. I'm glad for you. It doesn't lessen your brother in any way, in my book at least, but a hero with feet of clay is both a lot more human and a lot less daunting for his kid brother to live up to.'

'But—'

The sirens started to wail and the Tannoy crackled into life. 'Alert. Falcon call-out. Alert. Falcon call-out.'

The table went flying as the guys jumped up.

I groaned. 'Not again.' My legs felt like lead, but Jane dragged me off my chair and we ran for the door. This time there were no explosions, no displays of tracer lighting up the night. Noel, Shark and the other guys were ahead of us as we sprinted for the ramp. They disappeared into the tunnel leading to the other shacks as Jane and I ran straight up the ramp.

The Tempest shack was bedlam, the ground crew running to close the inspection covers, pull the warning flags from the missiles and yank the chocks from under the wheels.

I barely glanced at the crewman holding the ladder for me. 'Ready to go?'

'I hope so, sir. It's fully fuelled and loaded. We've not had time for even half the other checks.'

I jumped into my seat, jammed the helmet on my head and reached for the radio button. 'Fortress, this is Falcon 3 starting up.'

'Roger, Falcon 3. Intelligence suggests enemy aircraft taking off from Rio Grande.'

'Identification?'

'Probably Mig 29s.' He paused. 'And fully armed.'

'Shit.' These weren't Mirages, one step from the scrapyard. Mig Fulcrums were a frightening exception to the generally poor standard of former Soviet military equipment. They were faster than the Tempests and more agile. I could only hope that their Argentinian pilots had not yet had sufficient training to make full use of their aircraft's competitive edge.

I pressed the transmit button again. 'Numbers?'

'Nothing yet . . . Wait . . . Yes. Eight aircraft. Two four-ships. Confirmed taking off. Stand by.' There was a brief pause. 'Falcon this is Fortress. Scramble all aircraft.'

'Falcon 3 scrambling.'

The ground crewman was leaning over the side of the jet, strapping me in as I was speaking. I fastened my harness and waved him away. As he ran clear, I pulled the lever to close the canopy.

'Falcon, check in.' Noel's voice over the radio showed no trace of weariness.

'Falcon 3.'

'5.'

'8.'

'Negative Falcon 11. We're pissing fuel all over the deck. Switching aircraft.'

'Follow us up, Falcon 11, if you can get airborne.'

There was a moment's silence. Including the jet already airborne, only five were ready. The other seven had either been destroyed by the Argentine Special Forces or were unflyable without further repairs. We were heavily outnumbered – eight to five.

Noel's voice interrupted my thoughts. 'Fortress, this is Falcon. Flight of four scrambling . . . anti-missile take-off.'

I eased the throttles away from me and the jet rolled slowly forward. The crewman guiding me out gave me a good luck sign, then ducked out of the way. As we cleared the building, I saw Noel's jet already nosing onto the edge of the runway and then accelerating as the after-burners flared.

'Datalink coming up,' Jane said.

I wound up the engines, feeling as much as hearing the thunder as they belched out smoke and flames that sent battle debris whirling away into the darkness.

'Starting synchronisation,' Jane said. 'That's good. Everyone's on the link.'

Noel's jet was now clear of the ground, flares popping out as he flew flat and low over the perimeter and across the peatlands beyond.

We were already rolling as I pushed the throttles further forward, up to eighty per cent reheat. My seat slammed into the small of my back in the familiar power surge. The jet howled down the runway and I felt the wheels come clear. 'Gear travelling.'

My heart was in my mouth as we lifted off, but not from fear of the duel to come with the Argentine aircraft. 'Keep your eyes peeled, Jane. This could just be a feint to get us airborne over another patrol loaded with Stingers.'

I felt the hairs rise on my neck. We had already used our share of luck. Instead of the usual steep climb, I held the Tempest fifteen feet above the ground, so close that the wash lashed the grass and I felt I could have reached down and touched the perimeter fence. 'Flares! Flares!'

Jane kept flares tumbling out but I held my breath as we skimmed over the peatlands, approaching the location of the other missile launches. I glanced down and could just make out the crater we had blasted, already filled with water draining from the surrounding peat.

'350 knots.'

'Out of reheat.' I pulled the throttles back to kill the afterburners, but held the acceleration up to 450 knots. Then I stood the jet on its tail and headed skywards. There was still no telltale flash of light, no clamour from the missile warner.

We were safe from hand-held SAMs for the moment, but a greater danger was awaiting us.

We banked to the south and I caught sight of the flares of the other Tempests as they followed us down the runway. We kept in a steep climb to 20,000 feet and then levelled out. I edged a little further upwards until the exhaust gases suddenly began to condense in a thick white plume behind us, a trail visible even in the darkness. I dropped 500 feet and it disappeared again. We were at the perfect height; nothing could come down on us from above without leaving a con-trail as a signature.

The other aircraft joined us and we aligned in a wall formation spread at two-mile intervals across the sky. The night was dry, but a patchy overcast obscured the crescent moon. The ground below us was almost uniformly black. When night-flying in Europe there were always the oranges, yellows and whites of house and street lights, and the dazzling glare of the massed lights of towns and cities.

Here there was not a light to be seen. The base was in darkness and none of the farms or settlements was lit. Lakes and creeks, plains and mountains were all invisible. We were flying blind, relying almost entirely on radar and datalink. Only the instruments glowing a faint green in my cockpit told me which way up we were flying.

As we sped out towards the edge of the Exclusion Zone, information relayed by Fortress began to appear on my screen. Although the targets were still well outside our own radar coverage, I could see two sets of contacts, just crossing the jagged line of the Argentine mainland. Fortress had already designated them as hostile and instead of the usual letters they showed as arrowheads with a line projecting from them to show their vector.

'Keep the channels clear,' Noel said. 'No chat.'

A message indicator flashed on the screen. Jane interrogated the system. 'Contacts hostile, clear engage.'

'No shit,' I said. 'Gate, gate, go!' I shoved the throttles forward to the stops, feeling the instant response as the engine noise redoubled and the air speed began to climb.

The radar on Byron Heights was scanning far out beyond the islands, west towards Argentina. Everything it could see was sent by Fortress over the datalink. The two sets of images on the screen marched inexorably towards each other.

'Update on contacts, Jane?'

'We're getting them now. Seventy miles, on the nose, still high-level.'

As our own radar picked them up, each contact was automatically entered into the Tempest's computers and assigned an identification letter. Jane's fingers worked overtime on the data system. 'Raid resolution shows two formations, four aircraft each, all air defenders. There must be more of them out there somewhere.'

'There are only two possibilities,' I said. 'Either they're trying to wear us down and improve the odds for a dawn attack or—'

I was interrupted as the system flashed up another incoming message. 'Texaco on station at 390123, for refuelling.'

'Shit, that's close,' Jane said. 'I didn't think they'd risk Hercs this far out.'

'They've got no choice. It's shit or bust now. They've got to risk the lot to protect the airfield.'

We flew on in silence. 'So what was the other possibility?' she said.

'That the Migs are either a diversion or top cover for a low-level attack – either bombers or more assault troops.'

'If so, then where the hell are they?'

'I wish I knew.'

The radio crackled again and Noel began the sort, giving each of us our priority targets.

The radar warner chimed. 'Trace,' Jane said. An Argentine jet was painting us with its radar, the prelude to a missile lock. Even as it was doing so, we were completing our own attack sequence.

The missile lock was made simultaneously by all five aircraft. A 'T' was superimposed on each hostile symbol as our jets locked to their designated targets. As the last 'T' appeared, I pulled the trigger. 'Fox One. Fox One.' The calls from the other jets, an echo of mine, came a split-second later.

I imagined the sirens screaming in the Argentine jets as their radar warners picked up the lock. The missile leapt from the rail, its exhaust flaring across the sky. It shrank to a pinpoint and then vanished altogether as it accelerated to four times the speed of sound.

Almost at the same moment, our own radar warner began to shriek. 'Spike, Spike,' Jane yelled.

I had two choices. Our missile was away a few seconds before the Argentine counter-shot. I could hold the lock and maintain my present course. If the Mig was destroyed, the Argentine missile would lose its lock. It would fly on harmlessly until it ran out of propellant and crashed into the sea. But if our missile failed, or if a different Mig had targeted us, we would be dead in a matter of seconds.

I jerked the stick and turned tail in a blaze of afterburners. Even if the enemy missile held its lock, it would run out of fuel before it had closed the distance between us. It looked like running away, but holding the line when a missile was heading towards you was Russian roulette with a two-chamber gun. If the first bullet didn't kill you, the second would.

Both sets of fighters began a *danse macabre*, advancing to fire a missile, then retreating before the counter-punch. Each time the two lines moved a little closer to each other. In daylight we would have moved rapidly from the long-range exchanges of radar-guided missiles to the close-quarter stuff: heat-seeking Sidewinders and guns.

At night that was impossible. Even if we'd been wearing night vision goggles, we couldn't have made out the shapes of enemy — or our own — aircraft fast enough to take evasive action. The most likely consequence of a night dogfight was a mid-air collision.

I swung out in a wide arc to the south and climbed another 5,000 feet through a cloud-bank. As we advanced again, there was nothing from the warner as I sorted and locked my target, then sent another missile tearing across the sky. In the confusion of their own sort, the Argentines had either mis-targeted us or lost the radar picture altogether.

The range was too great to see the missile's ferocious impact. The death of the Argentine jet — and probably its crew — was no more than a flicker on Jane's radar screen. 'Fox One the Fulcrum,' she said. 'One down, seven to go.'

A moment later I heard Shark's voice shouting in triumph over the radio. The odds were now almost even, six against five. Then the Argentinians picked us up at last and the radar warner clamoured again. We were now dangerously close to the Migs; barely ten miles, a few seconds' flying time at our closing speed of 1400 miles an hour.

I threw the jet into another sharp turn, washing off some of our speed in the process. I pointed the nose down, grimacing with the effort of pushing against the G-force, to set us diving back through the cloud-bank to regain speed and put some distance between ourselves and the enemy. At the bottom of the dive, I had to grind my teeth, fighting the grey-out, and heard Jane grunting with the effort of doing the same. As I began to level the wings, the G-force dropped from me like a lead weight and the clamour of the radar warner began to fade.

We turned and advanced to fire another missile. With only one Skyflash remaining, it would be our last shot in the battle before returning to base to reload. I fired, held course for a couple of seconds, then turned as the radar warner began to shriek again.

I banked right to put the missile in my eleven o'clock, then as Jane triggered a fresh burst of chaff, I set the Tempest spiralling downwards in a series of tight, corkscrewing manoeuvres, trying to burn off the enemy missile's energy in a series of course corrections.

Suddenly Jane's voice cut through the clamour. 'New contacts, on the deck, in battle formation. Thirty miles heading zero-eight-zero, slow.'

For the moment, I had no time to think of anything but the track of the missile flaring across the sky. It flashed towards us, swerving violently with repeated changes of course, then it ran out of gas and fell away towards the sea.

There was not even a second's respite. I flicked the intercom switch. 'How slow?'

'About 240 knots. No ID coming up yet, might be bombers.'

'I doubt it. They're way too slow. They must be Hercs. That's why they haven't cratered the runway. They're trying to land on it.' I punched the radio button. 'Fortress, this is Falcon 3. Low-level contacts. Thirty miles, three-zero-zero, intercept?'

'Roger, Falcon 3. They're confirmed hostile. Clear engage.'

The Hercs were at minimum height, trying to lose themselves among the radar clutter of the wave tops. They would be easy targets, as long as we could keep the Migs off our backs and strike before they reached the coastline, where they could disappear into any one of a hundred different valleys. We would then be radar-blind until the moment they popped over the last ridge before the airfield, either rising high enough to drop paratroopers or, more likely, hugging the ground to make a rolling troop-landing on the runway.

There was one other problem: we each had only one radar missile left and there were four Hercs. If even two managed to land, it would be more than enough to overwhelm our small, already depleted garrison.

I shot a look at the fuel gauge, wishing we had time for a mid-air refuel. We had more than enough for a subsonic intercept on the lumbering Hercs, but if the Migs gave chase . . . I pushed the thought away. We had no choice.

I thumbed the radio button. 'Falcon 5?'

Shark replied instantly. 'Go ahead.'

'Let's fake another advance on the Migs, but a couple of miles in trail of the others and down five thousand feet. We can start the turn south, but then bug out right, one-five-zero, low-level. We can get down in the weeds below Mount Adam and follow the valley floor out through Port North. If the Hercs hold their present course they should be in our one o'clock, good odds to get in among them.'

'Sounds good to me. Let's do it.'

The other three jets went back into combat power, streaking away from us as Shark took up loose formation. We began our own run-in towards the enemy, holding the power at eighty per cent.

A couple of miles out of range of the Migs' missiles we began to turn south away from them and the Hercs moving steadily in from the west-north-west. Then I rammed the throttles into full combat power and pulled the stick hard right in a diving turn that pushed me to the edge of blacking out. The altimeter unwound from twenty thousand to two thousand feet as we flashed over the wilds of West Falkland.

The radar warner began to scream. Jane's alert came half a second later. 'Spike. Spike.'

I strained my eyes into the darkness ahead. A black wall loomed in front of me, blotting out the faint starlight. I pulled back the throttles and thumbed the radio. 'Tango, Tango.' I flicked on the autopilot and the Terrain-Following Radar.

The Tempest dropped with a sickening lurch as the autopilot cut in, obeying the commands of the TFR in the nose. The ridge loomed ahead, and I could not stop my right hand twitching towards the stick, though it was now useless in my hands. Then the jet soared upwards, clearing the ridge, and plummeted down the slopes of the valley beyond.

The shriek of the warner ceased as we dropped into the radar shadow of the ridge. The jet jolted and shuddered in the pressure wave close to the ground. By peering into the tiny E-scope I could get a couple of seconds' advance warning of the ground ahead, and brace myself for the next lurch. There were a series of thuds, curses and grunts from the back seat as the jet twisted, climbed and dropped without warning, following the dictates of the TFR.

I knew Shark was somewhere just to the rear of us, invisible in the darkness.

'I've lost the Hercs,' Jane said. 'The link's—' The rest of her sentence was lost as the jet bucked to clear an outcrop then dropped again in a sickening freefall. There was a final burst of turbulence that set the wings flexing like a bird's, then the sharp green contour lines on the E-scope faded into a shimmering mass.

We were clear of the coast, racing out over the ocean. I switched off the TFR and the autopilot, and the stick came alive again in my hand. I eased the nose up a fraction and immediately heard Jane's shout of triumph. 'Got them. Four contacts, box formation, fourteen miles in your two o'clock.'

'Shark, I'll take the left pair. You take the right.'

Our calls were near instantaneous. 'Sorted. Locked. Fox One, Fox One.'

The missiles blasted from the jets in unison, barely five seconds after we had made radar contact with the Hercs. I held altitude to maintain the lock, even though I knew I was exposing us to the Migs. Heart in mouth I watched as the computer counted down the seconds to impact. There was a faint glow on the horizon and a micro-second later, Jane called the strike. 'Two hits.'

There was no time to celebrate. I dropped back towards the sea and began a turn to bring us close to the six o'clock of one of the remaining enemy aircraft.

'They've split and widened,' Jane said. Even though they were out of radar view, our display was being updated by one of the other Tempests, tracking the Hercs from higher level. 'Six miles in your three ... Now seven miles in your two.'

The range had to increase as we made the turn while the Herc kept in straight and level flight, and each extra mile we had to close put the Argentine aircraft a fraction nearer to the cover of the coastline.

'Eight miles, in your two o'clock.' The turn complete, we were overhauling the Herc again, covering three miles for every one it could manage.

'Contact again.'

'Arming weapons.'

I flicked the Sidewinder switch and heard the growl as the seeker head began to search for the heat of a target. I could only stare blind into the night as Jane shouted course corrections to me, sending us twisting and turning after our prey as it ran for the safety of a valley.

'Six miles ... on your nose. Five, come left a fraction ... Four, on your nose again. Locking on.'

'Got him!' The target appeared in my Head-up Display, a jinking dot, framed by the target designator. As the L-shaped walls came together to enclose the target, the Sidewinder's growl changed to a strident beeping as the weapons computer showed we were in range.

I pulled the trigger. 'Fox Two. Fox Two.' The Sidewinder's fiery trail carved a series of sinuous curves through the night, sweeping arcs towards the burning exhaust of the Herc's engines.

Ahead, the coast was a dark line ruled across the faint grey sheen of the sea. The Sidewinder would strike home at any second. Suddenly the radar lost the lock and the target disappeared from the HUD. A fraction of a second later there was an explosion in the darkness ahead of us. I waited for Jane's confirmation, even though I already knew it had missed. The Herc had disappeared behind a screening ridgeline the instant before the Sidewinder could blast it apart.

'Lost the lock. No hit,' she said.

The beeping of the Sidewinder had barely been silenced before the radar warner kicked in again. 'Spike. Spike.'

The hunter was now the hunted. 'Shit!' I shook the Tempest left and right, then we were over the coast and running for the foothills.

I aimed the nose into the mountains and then flicked the TFR and autopilot again. The enemy's radar lock on us held for an agonising three seconds before the jet plunged into black radar darkness. The threat from the Migs had been neutralised for the moment, but somewhere ahead of us in the darkness were still two Hercs. We had less than five minutes to find and destroy them before they swept in on Mount Pleasant airfield.

'You'll need to take it back, Sean.' Jane's teeth rattled in her head as the jet soared and plunged over unseen obstacles. 'There's a Rapier site on Mount Rosalie, we're going to pass right over it on this course.'

In theory, the Rapier system should have identified friendly aircraft by electronically interrogating them. In the confusion of battle, it was not a chance I wanted to take.

As we flipped up over the next ridgeline, I shifted the heading bug on the autopilot. The jet turned on to the corrected heading towards the south-east, away from the danger. Almost before we had cleared the shadow of the ridge, the radar warner was shrieking once more.

I swore and sent us plummeting downwards again, flicking the switches to let the TFR and autopilot take us down to 200 feet. In those few seconds our kit had been updated by Fortress and I could see the two Hercules on the screen, in roughly parallel track separated by the central mountain range of West Falkland. They were almost out over the Sound. I let a beat of silence elapse after the radar warner had faded, then retook control of the jet and climbed to clear the 2,000 foot peaks near the east coast of the island.

I could see Shark's position on my screen. 'Falcon 5.'

His reply was instant, though almost broken up by static. 'Steer zero-two-zero, Shark, we'll try and push them further north of their present heading and give the Rapiers on Bodie and Cantera a shot.'

'Roger, Sean. We'll give it our best shot, but we're fuel critical. This will have to be our last crack before refuelling.'

As I acknowledged, I glanced at my own fuel gauge. We had fuel for around five more minutes.

The Hercs were wave-scraping as they crossed the coast of West Falkland and skimmed the open water of the Sound. As our radar painted them, they jinked to the north, trying to open some distance on us.

I set the Sidewinder growling again, even though we were side-on and stretching the range for a successful shot. The head found a target and began to beep. I fired the missile, more in hope than expectation. It lost the lock almost as soon as it left the rail. I saw it whipping from side to side, searching vainly for a target, before disappearing into the wilderness of ocean due north of us, as the Hercs ploughed on towards the east.

I used up a few seconds of precious fuel trying to close enough for another shot on the nearest Herc, but the two blips crossed the coast of East Falkland, and disappeared back into the valleys before I could get another lock with a Sidewinder.

The indicator of Shark's jet on my screen streaked away towards the south-east to rendezvous with the tanker for refuelling, but I knew that by the time he returned to the fray, the battle would already be over. If the Hercs reached the base unscathed, the troops they were carrying would already have deployed, scattering from the aircraft as they rumbled down the runway.

I pulled away to the south of the mountains. 'We can't follow them in there. We're going to have to fly a track from south-west to north-west of the base and try to intercept them as they clear Pleasant Peak.'

'It's a thin hope,' Jane said, 'unless the Rapiers can do something.'

As I banked and put us into a shallow dive towards the plain I saw a burst of explosions like sparks from a bonfire away to the north. A Rapier missile wrote a question-mark in the sky, rising and then throwing a loop in the air as its guidance locked to the target and it streaked away to the east. A handful of seconds later there was a huge flash. The dark silhouette of a Hercules was highlighted for a moment by a corona of fire, then it disintegrated into burning fragments and the darkness swallowed it up.

There was a second and a third launch a few moments later, but this time the missiles tracked nothing but empty sky and flew harmlessly away, disappearing into the distance. I kept my eyes fixed on the dark peaks of the mountains, hoping for another launch, but in vain.

The Herc's position was no longer being updated on my screen. It was now invisible to all our radar eyes. 'Take your best guess for an intercept, Jane.'

I pushed the jet down closer towards the floor of the plain, skimming over the dark, mottled surface as she wrestled with a lightning calculation. 'At their speed, they'll clear the peaks in around forty seconds. Steer zero-three-zero and we may get a shot.'

I set the Tempest on a diagonal track a few miles west of the end of the runway. There was no trace of the Hercules, no sign of a shape moving across the sky. We were less than half a mile from the black mass of the ridgeline and I was already starting to pull up and round when I sensed as much as saw a huge shape form out of the darkness ahead of us.

I hauled back on the stick and rammed the throttles forward. The Tempest engines screamed, but there was a deeper thunder directly in front of me. As the nose came up, I caught a glimpse of the bulbous body of the Herc, then it was past, sliding below us so close that I could read the markings on its fuselage.

We bounced in its wake, then as the wave of turbulence receded, I hauled the Tempest into the hardest turn I had ever made, coaxing every ounce of performance from the already over-stressed airframe. I grunted and groaned as the grey tide advanced. Then the angle of turn eased, the G-force dropped and colour flooded back in.

My right eye was sore and my vision blurred. The force of the turn had burst a blood vessel. I shook my head, then became aware of the clamour of the radar warner. I realised I had no idea how long it had been sounding.

I scanned the sky frantically for a sight of the Herc. I could see flashes and tracer arcs from around the perimeter of the base. The Argentine Special Forces had obviously regrouped and were returning to the attack.

Then I saw the huge bulk of the transport once more looming ahead of us. The Herc was on its final run-in, dropping unerringly towards the runway.

We were almost on it, too close for a Sidewinder shot. I jabbed the weapon button and selected the guns. The thunder of the Tempest's cannon drowned the shrieking radar warner.

The first bursts, the twin tracks illuminated by the tracer, ripped through the air intersecting harmlessly in front of, and below, the Herc. I eased the stick back a fraction and squeezed the trigger again.

The lines of fire moved closer and closer to the target and then 2,000 rounds a minute punched a jagged, diagonal line through its skin. They slashed through the fuselage below the cockpit and ate their way through the body, sliced across the base of the port inner engine, drilled through the wing and clipped the tail.

For a moment the Herc flew on straight and level. I jerked the stick violently back to avoid a collision, and as we soared upwards I cranked my head round. The Herc's wing and fuselage were ablaze and it was slipping down and left in a slide that turned into a spiralling, plummeting fall.

Out of the corner of my eye, I caught a glimpse of something else, a burning white beacon in the darkness swelling from the size of a matchhead to a blinding, all-consuming inferno.

I stared incredulous, then began to frame the words, 'Eject, eject,' as I reached down for the handle. Jane had already reacted a heartbeat faster. I felt the straps whipping around me, pinioning me to my seat. The canopy blew away with a crack and in the millisecond it took the seat to rise up the ejector rails, there was an even more blinding flash as the Mig's missile detonated.

Chapter 11

My first sensation was of icy cold seeping into my bones. I stirred and opened my eyes, but could see nothing. As I moved my head to one side there was a pounding pain in my temples. My mouth filled with black, stinking water.

Coughing and choking, I hauled myself to my knees. I was in a water-filled bog between steep banks of peat. As I looked up, I could see the faint glow in the sky over Mount Pleasant.

I put a hand to my chest. The parachute had already been released and there was no sign of it. I must have twisted the mechanism before I passed out.

I eased off my flying helmet, then pushed myself out of the water and began crawling up the side of the peat bank, my fingers scrabbling into the soft peat. Centimetre by centimetre I raised my head above the edge of the ridge, the hairs rising on the back of my neck.

There was no movement and no sound but the keening of the wind and desultory bursts of faraway small arms fire from the direction of Mount Pleasant.

I turned my head to look to the west and froze. A crouching figure was visible against the sky not more than fifty yards away. I dropped back into cover, waited until the pounding of my heart had quietened and then slowly raised my head again. As I strained my eyes into the night, I recognised the outline of a flying helmet.

I hissed, 'Jane?' but the wind carried the sound away. I dragged myself out of the ditch and began to crawl towards her, pausing every few minutes to raise my head and whisper. I was within ten yards of her when she gave a barely stifled shriek. 'Sean? Jesus, you scared the shit out of me.'

'I must have passed out.' I began to crawl forward again.

'No!' The note in her voice stopped me in my tracks. 'Stay where you are. Don't move.'

'What is it?'

'We've come down in a minefield.'

I peered around me. There was nothing but empty moorland. 'How do you know?'

'The explosion as we came down. Don't you remember?'

I stared blankly at her, but then the memory of the ejection started to trickle back, my seat falling away below me and then a blast that tore the air from my chute canopy.

Then I remembered seeing Jane floating down, the orange survival box dangling on its cord below her. As it touched the ground, it evaporated in a vivid yellow flash. I'd heard the howl of shrapnel. It ripped through the canopy of my chute and I'd plummeted the last twenty yards to the ground.

'Jesus! Are you all right?'

She nodded. 'A few bruises, nothing serious.'

'But that mine was right underneath you.'

'The survival box must have absorbed most of the blast. I was thrown around a bit, but I wasn't hurt.' She paused, staring at me. 'Sean, what are we going to do?'

I chewed at my lip. 'I don't know yet. Follow me and stay exactly in my track.'

I began crawling back the way I had come. Even though I was moving over a patch of ground I had already crossed, the knowledge that a mine could be lying in wait if I put my hand or foot down just an inch or two to one side of my tracks, almost paralysed me. The photographs of bodies mutilated by mines that Jack had produced before the battlefield tour kept coming back into my mind. It was an effort to lift my hand from its refuge and put it down again a few inches further on. Each time I felt my muscles tense and my hair stand on end.

It took at least ten minutes to cover less than fifty yards. The survival box lay on the edge of the hollow. I slithered down the slope and a moment later Jane followed.

I lifted the rucksack full of rations and survival gear out of the box and we huddled together just above the water, hidden from view. We held hands like children frightened of the dark.

'Right, where are we?'

'Apart from in the shit?' She checked her GPS. 'We're about ten miles north-west of the base, on the Wickham Heights.'

I pulled my map from the pocket of my flying suit and shone the thin beam of my torch on it. The minefield was marked as a long but narrow bar, running north to south, at right angles to the line of the ridge. The GPS position put us near the southern end. 'It doesn't look too bad. If we move any direction but north, we should be out of it within one hundred yards maximum.'

'So which way? There could be patrols anywhere.'

I resisted the temptation to remind her that she was the navigator. 'South. Then we can go three ways – east, west or further south – if we hit trouble.'

'But before that, we still have to get out of the minefield.'

There was a long silence. 'We could follow that stream-bed,' she said, doubt in her voice. 'If there were any mines buried near it, they might have been washed out or exposed.'

I nodded. 'It's better than going straight across the moor, but it's still one hell of a risk; it'll only take one mine to kill us both.'

'Have you got a better plan?'

'We could prod for them with some sort of rod or stick—'

She finished the sentence for me. 'But we haven't got one.' She paused. 'We could wait for daylight.'

'No. It won't help us find buried mines and we'd be easy meat for an Argentinian patrol. We must be safe or in cover by daybreak.'

'Then what?'

I stared at the survival box, cudgelling my brains, but I still felt dazed and groggy, and I could see nothing in the box that would help us. Jane followed my gaze. 'Wait a minute. My survival box saved me. Maybe yours can get both of us out of here.'

'Jane, I'm too shit-scared to play guessing games.'

'No more than I am, I promise you. We'll have to lie flat and push the survival box in front of us. If there are any mines, they'll detonate under the box.'

'About three feet from our faces.'

'Then we need something to extend our reach.' She peered into the darkness. 'There.'

I looked, but could see nothing. 'What?'

She moved forward a yard, then lay down against the far side of the hollow and stretched out her arm. I heard her fingers scrabbling on the peat, then her nails scratched against something solid. When she sat upright again she was holding a three-foot length of broken fence-post.

'It's not much, but it'll have to do.'

'If we hit a mine, it'll rip the survival box apart. What do we do then?'

'I don't know. Let's hope we don't hit any. Ready?' She paused. 'Wait, my immersion suit's leaking. I'll have to take it off. This is such rat-shit kit. Check yours.'

I'd been too preoccupied with the immediate danger to be more than vaguely aware of it before, but a raw chill had been spreading slowly over my waist and legs as icy water seeped into my suit. 'Mine's leaking too.'

Jane tore off her flying gear and began tugging at the bulky suit, cursing as she did so. 'The first time you put it to a real test, the seams split. Imagine if we'd landed in the drink. We'd be dead from hypothermia before the search-and-rescue helicopter got near us.'

I helped her pull off the rubber suit. She was shivering with cold. As I began the struggle with my own suit, I felt Jane's strong hands take hold of the collar and jerk it down and away from my back. The wind knifed through me as my frozen fingers fumbled with the zip.

'Right,' she said. 'It's too cold to hang around. Let's get moving, but smear some peat on your face and hands first, it'll act like cam cream. We'll take it five yards at a time, scanning the ground first, and then pushing the box over it. I'll go first, you're still too groggy. Stick right on my heels.'

'No. I'll lead. I'm feeling lucky. The first mine didn't get us, why should the rest?'

'Wait a minute.' She leaned forward and I felt her lips warm on mine.

'What was that for?'

'Just in case...' Her voice cracked.

I stroked her cheek with the back of my hand.

I put my flying helmet on again, more for psychological comfort than for any real protection, then I lay flat, took a grip on the box and began to push it in front of me.

'Shit. It's not heavy enough. We need enough weight to trigger the mines.'

We scrabbled around us, scooping up stones and handfuls of wet peat, taking them only from the area where we had been sitting and dumping them into the survival box. Then I flattened myself against the ground and began to push it forward with the fence-post. Even holding it at arm's length, the leading edge of the box was less than ten feet from my head. It was a terrifyingly small margin of safety.

I peered intently at the ground ahead, checking each pebble and stone. Then I began inching forward, hardly able to breathe. Each time the box scraped against a rock, I flinched and pushed my head down into the peat. We had covered perhaps twenty yards when there was a sudden ear-splitting, bowel-loosening roar. There was no flash or explosion in front of me. I froze in panic for a second, unable to understand what had happened.

Then I saw the red glow of a jet's exhaust as it skimmed down the other side of the ridge and turned in towards Mount Pleasant. There was another roar, and another, as more Argentine jets blasted up the slope of the mountain and over the ridgeline, to begin their attack runs on the base.

Even in that brief moment I recognised the profile of the

jets. They were not Mirages this time, but Super Etendards and Skyhawks – strike aircraft loaded with bombs and missiles. The plan to land their own troops on the runway had failed, now they were trying to ensure that no British reinforcements could do the same.

'Look!'

Jane was pointing away to our left. I saw a series of black shapes outlined against the sky – a square block, the circular dish of a mobile radar and a tall rounded column like a telephone-box with sharp spikes jutting out of both sides.

There was a frenzy of activity around it. Figures stood upright firing small arms at the marauding jets, as others sprinted to and fro, stumbling under the weight of missiles. The commander stood motionless among the bedlam, his arm raised above his head like a conductor leading an orchestra, his baton a hand-held sight slaved to the missile stack.

He pointed it at the lead jet and as he swung his arm, following its course, the missile stack swivelled in time with him, and a Rapier blasted off the side. It rose almost vertically, then its sensors picked up the jet's heat signature and it flashed away in a long, shallow-angled dive that ended in a blaze of pyrotechnics as the missile blasted the jet apart.

The seeker heads were already swivelling, homing on the next target. The flare of missiles lit up the night. Some struck home, but others careered wide of their targets as the jets roared in, dumping high explosive and napalm on the airfield and strafing it with gunfire.

Even from this distance I could see the ugly, blood-red pillars of fire reaching up into the sky. Argentine jets continued to skim over our heads on their attack runs. Although the Rapiers took their toll, I could see no sign of Tempests in the air.

I put my head down and began to push the survival box

in front of me again. In the flare of another Rapier launch, I saw a series of thin black lines stretching across the moor, twenty yards ahead of us.

'I can see the fence, Jane, we're almost out of the minefield.' I pushed the box forward again. There was a dry scraping sound and then a blast. I felt myself lifted, shaken and dropped back into the soft peat. I lay still for a moment, not even daring to breathe, then raised my head. The front half of the box and its contents had been shredded like a packet of crisps. The stench of explosive hung on the air.

As the ringing in my head subsided, I looked back towards Jane. 'Okay?'

'Yes ... I think. What now?'

'We push what's left of the box the rest of the way to the fence.'

Jane gave me a long look. 'Then I'll go first.'

'No chance. If anyone's getting a medal out of this it's going to be me.' My attempt at sangfroid would have been more impressive without the tremor in my voice.

I forestalled any further argument by rolling over and worming my way forward again. Had I stopped to think I would have been too scared to move at all.

There was precious little left of the survival box and the jagged edges left by the blast from the mine made it dig into the earth like a bulldozer. Every couple of feet, I had to stop, lift it clear of the mound of peat it had pushed up in front of it, and then begin again.

I had no idea how long I had been inching forward. I scarcely registered the continuing thunder of jets, the flash of missiles and the crump of bomb blasts. My world was bounded by the smell and feel of damp peat under my body, the thin scraping sound of the survival box as I pushed it forward over the rough ground, and the pain in the cramping muscles of my arms.

I heard a metallic noise and froze again, then realised that the box had struck not a mine, but the lowest strand of barbed wire. I crawled forward, over the mangled remains of the box, climbed over the fence and dropped to the ground.

I turned to look back. A few inches from my face was a skull and crossbones on a red and white sign: DANGER – MINES. DO NOT ENTER. It was the confirmation I needed. Even though I knew we were still far from safe, I let the feeling of release wash over me.

A moment later Jane landed alongside me. We hugged each other in the shared exultation of just being alive and I felt wet tears on her face.

'We've been there and looked it in the face, Sean. If we get through this—'

'Let's get through it first. If we can make it to the Rapier site we should be okay.'

We began to move away from the minefield, following the contour round towards the hilltop half a mile away. A handful of jets were still sweeping across the sky. We had covered half the distance when Jane tugged my arm. 'Better lie up in cover till they've stopped firing. God knows what's going on up there. Let's wait till it quietens down, we don't want to get ourselves shot.'

We crouched behind a rock, watching and waiting. Another jet blasted overhead and once more the missile stack swivelled and fired. Almost immediately I heard the whoosh of a second rocket. This one was launched from a second hilltop to our right, however, and its trajectory was not upwards but a flat line straight into the heart of the Rapier site.

The radar dish disintegrated in a melee of smoke and flame.

Several figures were hurled into the air by the force of the blast, but I saw the Rapier site commander outlined against the glow. He was still staring up into the sky, unaware among the thunder of jets and the roar of explosions that his attackers were on the ground.

Then another missile struck. The figure crumpled and disappeared inside a ball of fire and the Rapier stack toppled and fell. A hail of automatic fire riddled the site. The isolated flashes of gunfire from the defenders ceased altogether. We pressed ourselves flat to the ground, watching in horror as dark, helmeted figures rose from cover and began a cautious advance. There were no more bursts of fire as they moved through the wreckage, but a series of single shots. No prisoners were being taken.

We watched, impotent, for a few seconds, then without exchanging a word, turned and began to crawl across the hillside, away from the base and its false promise of safety, out into the wilderness of peat and rock.

We skirted the southern edge of the minefield and headed on across the no man's land between the summit plateau and the steep hillsides reaching to the coastal plain far below us. We moved fast, keeping low to the ground, and put a mile between us and the Rapier site before we stopped in the shadow of a large boulder.

'What are we going to do?' Jane said. 'Should we use the Tacbe?'

'We'd be telling the Argentinians as well as the Brits where we are.' I stabbed a finger towards the glow on the skyline. 'And to be honest, if there are any assets left there by now, I'm not sure they'll want to risk them to bring in aircrew. So I guess we either find a place to lie up and await developments—'

Her face swung round to look at me. 'Which we're not going to do?'

I nodded. 'As you say. The alternative is to put all that training to good use at last and try to get back to base.' I pointed down the hillside towards the sea. 'See that stone run there?'

She followed the direction of my pointing finger. A broad ribbon of grey, as faint as the phosphorescence of the surf on the night ocean, cut through the black mass of the peat-covered hillside.

She nodded.

'Follow the line of it down.' Near its end, where it disappeared from sight beyond the cliffs, there was a faint white lozenge. 'There's a farm there. If the Argentinians haven't already got there first, we can try to raise the base on the phone. Come on.'

As I got ready to move off along the hillside, I heard her voice faint and mocking in my ear. 'Would that still have been the best plan if Rose hadn't lived there?'

'Something was going on there. Remember the way Rose acted and the things she said when I phoned? An Argentinian patrol could have taken them prisoner.'

'Isn't that a bloody good reason not to go anywhere near the place?'

I shook my head. 'I've got to go down there, Jane.'

Her face was close to mine, her tanned skin paled to white in the darkness. 'Sean, we're in this together. I'm with you every step of the way.'

I waited. 'But?'

'But I need to know that what we're doing is the right thing, and that we're not doing it either because of guilt about those Argentinian helicopters, or' – she paused – 'or because you're trying to turn into your brother again.'

I didn't reply.

'We're not Paras or Marines or Special Forces, Sean. The most useful thing we can do is also the most selfish one – make sure we get back to Mount Pleasant alive. If we do that, we can get back in the air, if there are any jets left to fly by then.' She studied my face and laid a hand on my arm. 'What you did back there in that minefield was very brave. Let's not get stupid though. Agreed?'

I exhaled slowly. 'Agreed.'

There was a long silence. 'Then let's get on with it.'

Many things I had learned during my flight training and my early years with the squadron had been half-forgotten. But like every other pilot, I never needed reminding of the importance of escape and evasion and combat survival training. Too many jets crashed, too many aircrew had to eject, for it to be ignored.

I ran through every drill I could remember as I led the way to a hollow shielded from the high ground. We sat facing each other, our heads almost touching in the dark. 'Okay, we move separately, one watching and listening while the other moves. No talking, not even whispering, from here. We'll use hand signals, or if you need to attract my attention in a hurry throw a small stone.

'We'll keep on this contour until we've crossed the stone run, but we'll be very conspicuous there against the rocks. If there are Argentinian patrols out they'll be on the high ground overlooking us, but there looks to be a break in the stone run, maybe a small escarpment.'

I pointed to a darker band crossing the pale grey of the dyke. 'We'll cross there and box around to approach the farm from the west. If there are any hostiles there, they're more likely to be concentrating on the east side and the track up from the sea.'

As I spoke, I heard Rose's words in my head, 'All of us are fine, regards to your brother.' I felt my fingers close involuntarily around the butt of my pistol.

I checked my watch, stared, shook it and checked it again. Less than four hours had elapsed since we had been sitting in the Q shed.

We moved away over the hillside, half-crouching, half-crawling between clumps of tussac grass, the soft peat sucking at our feet. I again led the way, pausing to watch and listen every fifty yards as Jane caught up.

I tried to steer a course across the rock and firmer ground where we would leave less sign, but the darkness made it impossible to distinguish between firm ground and wet peat.

An hour's painful progress took us to the edge of the stone run. We lay motionless for a full fifteen minutes, raking the skyline and the surrounding landscape with our eyes, searching for any unfamiliar shape or movement.

There was nothing, only the relentless wind stirring the tussac grass and rattling the dry leaves of the diddle-dee. Finally, I squeezed Jane's hand and sent her forward across the broad expanse of stone.

She inched her way from rock to rock, flattening her body against the steep slope. She was perhaps a third of the way across when I glanced towards the skyline and froze. The quartz pebble in my palm had been clenched so tightly it was warm to the touch. I tossed it after her. There was a faint chink as it clipped a boulder just by her.

She stopped instantly. I peered towards the skyline, between the fronds of tussac grass. The unmistakable outline of a head was looking down in my direction.

I eased my pistol from its holster and slid off the safety-catch. For two or three minutes none of us moved. Then I saw the black-streaked, pale disc of Jane's face as she turned slowly towards me, keeping the back of her head to the ridgeline. I remained motionless, praying that she would do the same.

There was a rustle of movement from the hillside above me. The shape on the skyline grew larger as it moved towards me. I took aim, the pistol an extension of my arm, forced myself to calm my breathing and began to squeeze the trigger.

I stiffened as the figure above me moved again, then let out a sigh and relaxed my grip. The curl of a ram's horn was dimly outlined against the cloud-covered night sky before its owner dropped its head and began to graze once more.

I could feel the sweat cold on my brow. I waved my hand, signalling Jane to move on across the rocks, and a few seconds later she reached the far side and dropped into cover.

I began the same nerve-wracking journey. The quartz boulders were sharp and angular beneath my hands, but also slippery with lichen and moss. The stones seemed held in momentary stasis, like a river suddenly frozen in full spate.

I was almost across when my foot slipped on a boulder. I pitched forward and my head struck the ground. I stifled a groan of pain, then heard the sound of a stone clattering away, bouncing from rock to rock with an almost musical note.

I flattened myself against the boulders and closed my eyes in an involuntary, childlike reaction — what cannot see, cannot be seen. I stayed motionless for several minutes after the stone had ceased its fall, then opened my eyes and put a hand up to my head. My vision swam for a moment, the faint glow of the stone-run shimmering white in the darkness, then my head cleared.

I crossed the last few yards as fast as I could and dropped

into cover beside Jane. When I touched her hand, she was shaking. We began to move away down the hillside.

The lower slopes were thickly carpeted with diddle-dee and as we forced our way through the tangled growth, the dry stems and branches scratched against our flying suits, but the wind hid any trace of the noise.

A few hundred yards above the farmhouse, the slope of the cliff was broken by a small hillock. I waved Jane up alongside me and put my lips close to her ear. 'If there are Argentinians on the farm I'd expect a sentry there, wouldn't you?'

She nodded. 'Remember what I said.'

'We're not going to attack, we're going to go around. You go first and I'll cover you. Head for that dark patch fifty yards right of the shoulder of that hill. And Jane, no more than twenty-yard stages. I couldn't hit a cow's arse at a bigger range than that.'

'Just make sure you don't hit mine.'

We both knew the banter was just another defence mechanism. She flattened herself against the ground and began to worm her way forward. I tried to follow her progress, straining my eyes into the darkness, but darting constant anxious looks towards the mound.

As soon as she stopped moving, I began to inch forward, closing the gap between us. I stopped five yards short of her, outside the range of the first burst of fire (if there was to be one), and she began to move on again.

I knew that a pistol was not much use against an Armalite in a one-on-one contact, but I was confident I could use the split second as a sentry brought his gun to bear on Jane to get off at least one shot.

I kept raking the mound of diddle-dee and tussac grass with my eyes, but I could see no sign of a sentry, no telltale profile, no angular shape, no movement or reflected light.

It took us twenty-five minutes to cover 300 yards. Then we were safely past the hillock and looking down on the roof of the farm. The white walls of the building shone faintly in the starlight.

Once more we waited a full ten minutes, searching every patch of shadow for movement or a standing figure, then we began to move again. This time I led the way, using the dense clumps of gorse and the rough stone wall of a paddock to hide our approach on the farm. We crept forward and flattened ourselves against the wall of the generator shed on the edge of the farmyard.

The generator engine was cold and silent, but there was a faint glow from the living-room window of the farm, dimly reflected in a headlight of the Land Rover which was parked in the gloom of the barn.

I let my gaze travel on around the outbuildings. I could see no movement and there was no sound but the insistent rattling of a piece of metal roofing on the shed.

'We need to get a look through the window.'

A muscle tugged in Jane's cheek as she nodded.

I took a last look around the yard. As I stared into the barn, the faint light reflecting in the Land Rover's headlamp was suddenly extinguished. I whipped my head round to look at the farmhouse. The window was still illuminated.

I placed a warning hand on Jane's arm and peered back into the darkness. Then I saw a movement and heard the faint scrape of a boot on concrete. A soldier in battledress stood just inside the barn door, his face smeared with camouflage paint.

There was the cold glint of a gun barrel as the soldier leaned forward to look towards the house. He pulled back into the shadows again, but I could still see his faint outline. He leaned back against the wall and lowered the barrel of his rifle, resting it on the toecap of his boot.

I pulled Jane back out of the soldier's line of sight and around the corner of the generator shed. I began looking around for a weapon other than my pistol. The wind whistled through a broken pane. On the sill, among a mess of oil cans and greasy rags, I saw a heavy metal wrench. I reached in through the window, moved the debris aside with infinite care and picked up the wrench.

We stood huddled against the wall as we worked out a strategy, our heads close together like two lovers in a doorway. I checked my watch. 'It's 3.14 . . . Now! Make your move at exactly 3.30. If it all goes to rat-shit, hit cover and shoot anything carrying a gun that isn't me.'

She whispered, 'Take care,' and touched my cheek, then disappeared around the back of the shed into the darkness. I went in the opposite direction, in a wide loop that took me out of and around the farmyard to reach the back of the barn.

I inched down the side, picking my way through a tangle of scrap metal, half-buried by weeds. I paused and glanced anxiously at my watch, wishing I had allowed a little longer. Finally I reached the corner, heart pounding and sweat dripping from my brow.

I swallowed a couple of times, wiped my hand on my jacket and took a firm grip on the wrench. Then I eased my way around and stood to the side of the barn doorway. If the soldier had stayed where he was, I was now separated from him by only the width of the wall. If he had moved to the other side . . .

I pushed the thought away and closed my eyes for a second, visualising every movement I would make. I checked my watch again, seeing the seconds tick slowly by. I took a tighter grip on the wrench and tensed myself, my eyes focused on the gap between a shed and a trailer, at the far side of the yard.

Suddenly Jane stepped from cover. At the first, faint stirring of movement from just inside the barn door, I stepped around the corner, swinging the wrench in my outstretched arm with all my strength.

I moved so quickly that the soldier's gun barrel had barely lifted from the toecap of his boot. The wrench smashed into his face and his nose disintegrated in a spray of blood. As he crumpled and began to fall his finger tightened on the trigger.

The rifle fired a single round. It smashed through the soldier's boot. His shriek of pain was silenced by a second blow with the wrench and he fell to the ground with a noise like a wet sandbag.

I was already sprinting for the house, switching the wrench to my left hand as I pulled out my pistol. Jane was there a split second ahead of me, flattening herself against the wall by the door.

I saw the dark outline of a figure cross the lighted window. It had its back to us, but held a gun in one hand. I hurled the wrench through the glass and launched myself through the shower of fragments in a rolling dive that carried me halfway across the room. A split second later Jane burst through the door.

A soldier stood in the middle of the room, panic etched across his face. He fumbled with his rifle, the barrel swinging in a trembling curve towards Jane in the doorway. I had a split second, no more. I raised my arm and squeezed the trigger, firing at point-blank range.

Both shots struck home. The first punched a hole in the centre of the soldier's chest. The impact threw him backwards and the second shot went in just below his chin, and out through the back of his head. The force of it twisted him round and smashed him head first into the wall. As he slid to the floor, he left a trail of blood and brains on the plaster.

I jerked my head from side to side, seeking new targets, but expecting the impact of a bullet at any moment. Another figure moved in the far corner of the room. I swung my pistol round, heard a scream and froze. Rose was tied to a chair, staring in horror at the body slumped in the corner of the room. Otherwise the room was empty.

'Any more?' Jane yelled. 'Are there any more?'

Rose was still staring at the body. 'Not in the house.'

'Where?'

She dragged her eyes away from the stain on the wall. 'They went out last night. Four of them.'

'We've got to move fast,' Jane said. She grabbed a clothes-line from a hook behind the door. 'Check that guy, I'll go and tie the other one up.'

I walked across the room and turned the soldier over, still holding my pistol at the ready. Even though I knew he was dead, I felt for a pulse in his neck. There was none. Then I stared into the soldier's face. He must have been older, but he looked like a boy, no more than eighteen or nineteen years old.

Jane came back inside, tossing the clothes-line onto the table. 'No need for that, he's dead as well. Two out of two; you don't mess around, do you?

I tasted bile in my mouth, ran to the sink and puked. I rinsed my mouth out and then turned back to face the room, wiping the tears from my eyes, my face clammy with sweat. I could not stop myself from looking at the body again. Then I turned, hurried across to Rose and untied her hands. The wire had bitten into her wrists, breaking the skin and leaving livid weals. Her face and arms were also badly bruised.

'Bastards.'

She looked up at me, her eyes frightened and pleading. I touched her face gently. 'It's all right, Rose, you're safe now.' I hoped she was more convinced than I was.

'Sean, come on,' Jane said. 'Let's move it.'

'Where's Bernard?'

'He kept shouting and swearing at them. He's outside, in the peat store, I think.'

'Is he—'

'I don't think so.'

I ran outside and pushed open the door of the peat store. Bernard was lying on one side, his wrists and ankles bound, and a gag stuffed in his mouth. His face was black with peat dust and there was a crust of dried blood around one eye.

I untied him and left him rubbing his wrists as I ran back inside and picked up the phone. The line was dead. I shook my head in answer to Jane's unspoken query and stood for a minute, trying to think what to do. I had planned no further than reaching the farm.

'Sean,' Jane said. 'We've got to move now.'

'Right, let's go. Rose, grab a coat. We'll take you and Bernard down towards Goose Green. You'll be safer there.'

Jane began to protest, but I pointed to the body. 'We can't leave them here.'

'I'm going nowhere.' Bernard stood framed in the doorway.

'Come on, Bernard, don't be stupid. If you're here when that Argentinian patrol comes back and finds two dead bodies they'll kill you as well.'

'*If* they come back,' he said, 'they'll not catch me unawares a second time.'

'These are trained soldiers, you can't fight them off with a twelve-bore and a pitchfork. Think of your wife, if not yourself.'

'Rose will go with you. I'm staying on my farm. Everything I've worked and sweated for is here. I'm not leaving it for those Argie bastards to steal or destroy.'

'They'll kill you if you stay here, you stubborn fuckwit.'

He folded his powerful arms across his chest. 'I'm not leaving.'

'Then you're a fool.'

Rose had been looking from Bernard to me. 'I – I can't leave him here. I'll stay with him.'

'No.' Bernard's voice was as gruff as ever, but there was a tenderness in the look he gave her. He reached out to touch her hand. 'Like he said' – he jerked his head at me – 'you'll be safer with them.'

Still she hesitated, searching his face.

'Sean, we've got to move,' Jane said.

There was a moment's silence, each of us frozen, staring at the others. Then Bernard spoke, his voice hard-edged, his face expressionless. 'Go on, Rose, go now.'

She still did not move and he erupted in anger. 'Go on. Get out. It's what you want, isn't it? Fuck off. I don't want you here.'

She started to speak, then her eyes filled with tears and she turned and stumbled after Jane. As I made to follow them, Bernard's hand clamped around my arm. 'You've got what you wanted. Make sure you look after her.'

He shoved me outside. I glanced back and saw his look of utter desolation, then he slammed and bolted the door.

Rose still hesitated, but she did not resist as I took her arm and led her away. Jane started towards the

Land Rover, but I caught her arm. 'No, they'll be watching the track.'

'Which way then?' she said. 'The hills?'

'No. We'll cut down towards the coast.' I checked my watch. 'We've got two hours of darkness left, let's make the most of it.'

I took Rose's arm. 'Stick by my side and do everything I do. Move when I move, stop when I stop, and don't speak. If you want to attract my attention, squeeze my arm.'

After another glance back at the farmhouse, she gave an abrupt nod.

Chapter 12

We crossed the yard and moved out through the paddock. I covered the first few hundred yards fast, more worried about putting distance between ourselves and the farm than about concealment.

The farm was barely visible in the darkness behind us as we slowed our pace, moving on with more caution. Jane led the way and I covered her, working our way down the hillside in fifty-yard stages, keeping roughly parallel to the track down towards Goose Green.

We reached the neck of the isthmus half an hour before dawn and paused in the shelter of three scrubby wind-blasted pine trees, some farmer's doomed attempt to raise a windbreak.

I rubbed my eyes wearily. 'Do you have friends in Goose Green?'

Rose gave me a wary look. 'There are people we know.'

'Okay. Now we don't know if there are more Argentinian

forces there, so wait here until it's full daylight, then walk across the fields to the settlement. Don't go on the road in case it's mined. Walk in the open and keep your hands on your head. That way, if there are enemy troops there, you won't be shot.'

She heard me out in silence, but then shook her head. 'I can't stay here, Sean.' Her voice was low but firm.

'Well, you can't come with us,' Jane said. I knew she was speaking to me as much as to Rose. 'We're going to try and get back to base through enemy lines. We're trained for this, you're not. If we take you with us, you'll get yourself killed and us with you.'

Rose's voice was flat and unemotional; her eyes never left my face. 'I can't stay here. If you take me with you I can more than pull my weight. I've lived on this land all my life. I know where the ground is firm and where it's boggy. I know where the streams and rivers run. I know where to walk and where to hide. I've been up on those hills in blizzards and white-outs more times than I can count, finding sheep and dragging them off the moor.'

Jane shot me another warning look, then pulled me a couple of yards away from Rose and began speaking in a fierce whisper. 'This is madness, Sean. We've a job to do. We have to reach base somehow and get back into the air. Rose can only put us at risk.' She read my expression and shook her head impatiently. 'Even if we get her back to Mount Pleasant, you can't just bring a civilian into a war zone.'

'The whole of the Falklands is a war zone, Jane. There are two dead Argentinian soldiers in her farmhouse to prove it. Can you imagine what would happen if the rest of that patrol found her? They won't even know we've been there. All they'll know is that Rose has escaped and two of their mates are dead.

They won't be in any mood to ask questions if they find her again.' I paused and gave her a gentle smile. 'It'll be all right, Jane. Trust me. When have I ever let you down?'

She stared back at me, unsmiling. 'Just now.'

We both held the look for a moment, then I turned back to Rose. 'Okay, let's go.' I glanced up at the sky to the east. 'We need a lying-up place for the day, and we need to find it in the next hour at most.'

'Let me think for a minute,' Rose said.

I waited, avoiding Jane's eye, until Rose nodded. 'Okay, this way.'

'I'll lead,' I said. 'You stay on my heels and direct me. Jane will cover us.'

We moved away from the isthmus, heading almost due east into the slowly lightening sky. We walked through a flat, water-filled landscape, the sodden peat quaking gently beneath our feet. It was impossible to avoid leaving footprints.

Countless streams and creeks lay across our path and there was no option but to ford them. I had to grind my teeth to stop from crying out at the shock of the cold water as I plunged into a creek up to my waist. I put my arm around Rose to help her up the bank and felt her slight frame shivering with cold.

The light was growing stronger. We passed a few hundred yards from one isolated settlement and the dogs set up a chorus of barking as the wind carried the scent to them. I waved Jane forward alongside us. 'We haven't time to box around the place, let's just keep moving. All right?'

She glanced at Rose, then back at me. 'Why ask me? You're the one making all the big decisions.'

'Come on, Jane. We're in this together.'

She nodded. 'All three of us.'

As we began to move forward again, I saw movement

ahead and slightly to our left, closer to the settlement. As I looked at it again, I recognised the building. I signalled to the others and crouched down, trying to make sense of the dark hooded shapes.

Rose followed my gaze. 'It's all right. They're birds of prey. We call them turkey buzzards. There must be some carrion there.'

As we drew level I glanced across at them. Separate groups of birds with black bodies and blood-red heads were tearing at two huddled shapes on the ground. There was a feeling of dread in my stomach.

Before I could stop her, Rose was moving towards them. The buzzards hopped a few yards to one side, and formed a hungry half-circle, impatient to return to their feast.

'Oh no.' Rose reeled away. The two bodies were riddled with bullet-holes. One, a man, lay face down, a shotgun still held in his hands. The other, a grey-haired woman, lay on her back. I stepped closer. The buzzards had pecked out her eyes, but I still recognised the face. It was Agnes Moore.

I held Rose for a moment, then released her. 'We can't do anything for them now. We must go on. It's almost light.'

She wiped the tears from her eyes, then turned away. We crossed the track and moved over a sloping plain between two broad tarns. The water was as black as coal. The wind stirring its surface carried the sharp, salt tang of the sea.

I glanced again at the sky. 'How much further?'

Rose pointed ahead, towards a low hill rising from the surface of the plain. 'Just beyond that.'

When we rounded the shoulder of the hill, I saw that it sloped down to the edge of another large tarn. Its narrow, steeply sloping shingle beach was flanked by dunes covered in tussac grass. At intervals along the shore were a handful of conical structures, like small tepees. Boulders and shingle had been roughly piled in a circle, then capped with driftwood and clumps of tussac grass.

'They're hides,' Rose said. 'We use them for duck shooting.'

As she made to move forward, I grabbed her arm and pulled her to the ground. Jane dropped alongside us. 'What's up?'

I pointed across the tarn. It was separated from the open water of Choiseul Sound by another, broader ridge of shingle. Rising from it, partly concealed by the ridge, was a black, rounded shape.

'What is it?' Jane said. 'A sub? A Zodiac?'

Rose eased herself up onto her elbows, her shoulder pressing into me as she leaned across to peer out from behind a clump of grass. 'It's a fin whale. It must have beached itself.'

I looked again. 'Shit. I'm sorry. I should have recognised it. I saw it the other day.'

We crept out of our cover and moved down to the edge of the tarn. We walked along the shingle, leaving no track, then cut up to the entrance of the largest hide, in the middle of the beach. We crawled into it. There was barely room for the three of us to huddle inside. Through the chinks in the rough stonework I could look out over the landscape all around us, though the low hill partly obscured the view to the north.

I could feel Rose's shoulder shaking and heard her teeth chattering. 'You have to take your clothes off and wring as much water out of them as you can. Then put them back on. Jane and I will get on either side of you and we'll share our body warmth. We can't move again until nightfall.'

Rose gave me a doubtful look, but she stripped off her clothes and began wringing them out. I couldn't stop myself from glancing at her body. She was painfully thin, the line of her ribs showing as she stretched to pull her jersey over her head, and her breasts were as small as a girl's. I took her clothes from her and squeezed a little more water from them, but they were still clammy and cold when she struggled back into them.

I slipped the rucksack off my shoulders and pulled out the silver foil blanket. I draped it over her and shared out some water and emergency rations: dried fruit, biscuits and chocolate. Then we huddled down together under the blanket.

'I'll take the first watch. You two try and get some sleep.'

Rose huddled into my armpit and slowly her shivers subsided. I heard her breathing grow slower and more even, and looked down at her, studying her face. The dark semi-circles were even more deeply etched beneath her eyes. She stirred and looked up at me, so close that I could see my face reflected in her dark pupils. I flushed and looked away, and after a moment she closed her eyes again and nestled down even closer to me.

Jane was slumped across her other shoulder, already snoring. I shook my head in disbelief. She could sleep on a clothesline in the middle of an air-raid.

The grey dawn light strengthened and the shoreline came alive with birds. I could see the dark curve of the stranded whale's back. Skuas and gulls fought each other for purchase on its hide, as they ripped and tore at it with their slashing beaks.

A flock of upland geese circled overhead and landed in a clatter of wings, honking mournfully to one another. An endless procession of penguins shuffled down the dunes and across the shingle, splashing out through the water of the tarn towards the Sound. They passed close enough to the hide for me to wrinkle my nose at their fishy stench.

My smile froze as I heard the sound of voices. It was low and indistinct, but seemed to be coming from just beyond the shingle bank on the far side of the tarn.

I eased my pistol out of my holster and fumbled for the spare clip, cursing myself for not having reloaded before. I reached over and was about to shake Rose and Jane awake when the murmuring voices broke off in a bark, like a smoker's cough. A pair of sea lions waddled into view and belly-flopped into the tarn.

I could feel tiredness dragging at me, but forced myself to stay alert. The time crawled by and I felt the cold sinking deep into my bones. Wind penetrated every gap in the walls of the hide and the air was as damp as fog. A sudden hailstorm dusted the ground with white, then was swept away on the wind. A patch of sunshine followed, turning the water to jade, then that too was gone as rain and sleet marched in from the west, stippling the water and painting it grey once more.

Careful not to disturb Rose, I craned my neck to peer out through a chink in the wall, just before the weather closed in around us. At first I saw nothing but a few grazing sheep, but then another movement caught my eye. I glimpsed a group of four figures moving slowly down the hillside. They were too far away to identify, but there was no mistaking the thin black silhouettes of the guns they carried at the ready.

As the squall passed, I saw them again. The lead-scout in the patrol advanced a few yards, paused and dropped to one knee to study the ground, then advanced again. The other three followed him, their heads swivelling from side to side as they scanned the ground around them.

I felt sick. They were following the exact route that we had taken and there was no doubt in my mind that they were tracking the footprints we had left in the wet mud and peat.

A fresh squall blanked out the sight of them again. I leaned over to shake Jane by the shoulder. A strand of Rose's hair brushed against my forehead and her breath was warm on my cheek.

Jane awoke silently, instantly alert. 'What is it?' she whispered, then read the danger in my expression. 'Trouble?'

I nodded. 'A patrol.'

Rose had woken too. Her eyes searched my face, then she pulled herself up and sat with her arms wrapped around her knees, staring out across the tarn.

I sat in silence, thinking furiously. If the patrol had tracked us this far, they would certainly be able to follow our tracks the rest of the way to the tarn. We couldn't stay where we were. If we did, we would inevitably be found. We had left no sign on the shingle, but the hides dotted along the shore were the only hiding places.

Our pistols would be as much use as popguns against four men carrying Armalites. After killing their two comrades, we could expect no mercy.

I raked the shoreline. Apart from the hides there was no cover, no shelter, not even a boulder to hide us. There was nothing, except . . .

I turned and peered through the chink in the back of the hide. The four figures were closer now, moving like ghosts as mist and rain drifted around them. I knew we had just one hope. If the Argentinians were following our tracks, they would shortly pass behind the low hill that had screened the hides from our sight as Rose had led us here at dawn.

If we moved, then, keeping the hill between us, we would have perhaps five minutes when we were out of their sight. It might just be long enough. It would have to be.

Never taking my eye from the crack in the wall of the hide, I told Jane and Rose my plan.

'You're crazy,' Jane said.

'Then tell me a better one.'

She fell silent.

'Rose?'

Her voice was firm. 'Better to try that than be caught by those bastards again.'

'What about the birds?' Jane said. 'There are hundreds of them. They'll take off and give us away.'

'No, they won't,' Rose said. 'Birds here aren't scared of humans; they don't see enough of them to be frightened.'

We jumped as hail rattled on the roof like gunfire and a squall shrieked through, blotting the soldiers from sight. It had passed within a minute, but the patrol had already disappeared from view behind the hillock.

'Let's go. Fast.'

We spilled from the hide and, crouching low to the ground, we ran down the shingle bank and began splashing through the freezing water of the tarn. We could not go round it; that would take too long and whichever side we went, it would bring us back into the soldiers' line of sight.

The cold took my breath away. My feet slipped and slid on the pebbles and though the water was only thigh-deep, it dragged at my aching muscles like quicksand.

I could feel the seconds slipping by. The hairs on my neck were rising, anticipating the shouted challenge, the crack of a rifle and the savage impact of a round.

I glanced to left and right. Rose and Jane were no more than a yard behind me. I could hear Rose's laboured breathing and saw her mouth hanging open as she forced herself through the water, but Jane betrayed no sign of the effort she was making. Her face was set and determined, her eyes fixed on the far shore of the tarn.

My own heart was pounding and my breathing was growing ragged by the time I at last felt the bottom sloping upwards. The water level dropped to my knees, then my calves, then I was splashing through the last few feet of shallows, crossing a narrow band of peat and sprinting over the shingle bank separating the tarn from the open water of the Sound.

All the way across I had been fighting the overwhelming urge to look behind me. Now as we crested the bank and began to race down the shingle towards the dead whale, I swung round, dropped to the ground and peered back. The squalls of rain and hail had passed and the watery sun was struggling to find a way through the racing clouds. For a moment I saw nothing moving in that whole desolate sweep of landscape. Then I caught a glimpse of sunlight on steel.

The four soldiers had split up and were rounding each side of the hillock. The leader of one group raised his hand and motioned the other two down towards the line of hides spread across the shore. Then he and the other soldier began to move forward as well, advancing slowly, their attention fixed on the hides.

I eased myself up a fraction and peered across the belt of shingle we had just crossed. Three scuffed tracks marked our path over the peat at the edge of the tarn, our footprints glistening in the sunlight.

I sank down out of sight and then hurried down the other side of the pebble mound towards the shore. Rose and Jane had already reached the beached carcass of the whale. A few skuas edged warily away from them along the beach and a couple of gulls took flight at their approach, circling lazily above them. The rest of the birds barely paused in their attacks on the whale's tough hide.

The three of us paused in the shadow of the whale, on the

seaward side. I looked up at the creature towering over us. It was fifty, perhaps sixty feet long and around ten feet high. Its hide was brownish-grey, but so dark that it had appeared black from a distance. A paler, greyish white chevron extended from behind its head down along its flanks and a bony ridge ran along its spine, culminating in the sharp blade of its dorsal fin. Long parallel grooves stretched from its chin halfway along the underside of its massive body.

The hide was marked with scars and striations. Many were old, left by past battles or the scraping of rocks and icebergs against its flanks, but the attacks of the skuas and gulls on its bloated corpse had added fresh wounds.

In places the hide hung in tatters like peeling wallpaper in a derelict house. Where it was ripped and torn, the grey-white blubber was exposed and thin streaks of oil trickled down the flanks, coating the pebbles on the beach.

The sickly sweet stench of decay filled my nostrils as I stepped closer. I glanced from Jane to Rose. 'All right?'

Rose nodded. Jane just said, 'Hurry.' She moved round and back up the beach to keep watch from behind the ridge of shingle.

I pulled out my survival knife and took a deep breath. 'Not there,' Rose said. 'You'll be trying to cut your way through the rib cage. They're built just like us. You need to cut into the stomach.'

I moved a few feet towards the tail. The skuas and gulls rearranged themselves around me and then returned to their feast. I took a firm grip on the knife handle, then stooped down and reached in where the whale's distended belly met the shingle. I began to cut at the hide.

Despite the cold, I was soon pouring with sweat. The hide was as tough and unyielding as tyre rubber. As I hacked and cut at it, oil oozed from the blubber beneath the skin, coating the blade and handle of the knife, and making it harder and harder for me to maintain my grip. Several times the knife caught in the leathery hide, twisted out of my hand and fell to the shingle. With painful slowness, I widened the cut running parallel to the ground.

'Not so straight,' Rose said. 'Make it rougher, more natural looking.'

I nodded, unable to spare the breath to speak. She looked at me for a moment, then slipped away out of my sight, returning a few seconds later, holding Jane's knife. She knelt down alongside me, shoulder to shoulder, and began hacking at the hide.

The stench was overpowering, a hideous cocktail of fish oil and rotting flesh. Every breath I took made me want to gag. Rose appeared less disturbed by it, methodically hacking at the hide, extending her end of the jagged cut along the line of the shingle.

I knew that time was running out and worked feverishly, straining my ears for any warning sound from Jane. I shook the sweat from my eyes and slashed at the hide in a frenzy. At last we had a ragged gash just over a yard across. We laid down our knives for a moment and tugged and heaved at the flap, exposing the layer of putrefying blubber.

As I began to hack through it, thick yellow whale oil oozed from the cut, like blood trickling from a wound. Then I heard Jane's voice, low but insistent. 'They're coming round the side of the tarn. We haven't got long.'

We threw ourselves back into our work, ripping at the blubber with our knives and then tearing at it with our bare hands. Lumps of it spattered onto the pebbles. The layer was four inches deep and as thick and glutinous as lard. I could see dark brown whale meat appearing beneath. The stench was stronger now and even the gusting wind did little to dissipate it.

I heard the soft clatter of pebbles as Jane slid round the side of the whale and came hurrying towards us.

'Quick.'

I grabbed the knife again and slashed viciously right and left at the whale. Shreds of meat flew past my face as I kept up the frenzied attack. I dug into the flesh with all my strength, felt it give a little, resist, then there was a rending sound like ripping cloth and my blade plunged hilt-deep into the whale's stomach.

There was the hiss of escaping gas and I retched but forced myself to drag the knife sideways, extending the cut. There was another outrush of gas, a momentary silence and then a slippery, slimy avalanche of entrails cascaded onto the shingle.

I hesitated for no more than a second, then began pushing my way in through the rip in the whale's side. The entrails oozed around me like a cold, clammy tide. Whale oil and blubber like mucus clogged my hair, ears, eyes and mouth. I coughed and choked, fighting down a wave of panic. Then I was through, dragging myself into a dim black hole.

I worked my way around in the confined space, slashing through a tangled mass of guts with my knife. I could see only the faintest glow of light from the rip in the whale's side and that was extinguished as I felt a hand on my arm and Rose began to haul herself inside. She clawed at her face, trying to free her mouth and nostrils of the filth, then I heard her gag and vomit.

Jane came last. Her struggle to get through the hole set a tide of fluids and entrails swirling around us and slapping against the stomach wall. I pulled Rose by the arm and we began to wriggle sideways and back, away from the opening, forcing ourselves feet first, deeper into the chest cavity.

With my other hand, I grabbed Jane's ankle and tugged on it. She understood at once, for I heard the slow movements as she also worked her way back, away from the opening.

I felt the hardness of a rib beneath me, as solid as a tree branch, then a rougher surface. I braced myself against the whale's collapsed lung and pushed myself a little further back until I felt the weight of some unseen organ – perhaps the whale's heart – pressing down on me. I could move no further.

Rose was jammed into the same restricted space, close enough for me to feel her heartbeat. Jane lay on the other side of me, a little further forward.

The stench was strong enough to suffocate us. Each breath tasted thick and viscous. I wondered how long we could survive on the small amount of air that was seeping in through the gash in the whale's side.

I stuck the knife upright near my right hand, then pulled out my pistol and did my best to wipe the oil and filth from it. I had no idea if it would fire or if the barrel was blocked, but if I had to use it, I would.

I tried to ignore the stench and the feel of the slime surrounding us, focusing my mind only on the lozenge of grey half-light in front of me. Almost at once the light increased a fraction, then dimmed again.

I held my breath and felt my heart rate start to climb. There was a squawk as the skuas and gulls fought over the new selection of entrails spread out before them.

The muffled sound of the sea-birds' strident wranglings masked any other noise. There was no way of knowing if the patrol was within inches of us or had already passed by.

Adrenalin kept the cold at bay for a while, but I could

feel it slowly seeping back into my bones, and Rose's shoulder trembled against my side. I reached down, squeezed her hand and felt a faint pressure in return.

The sea-birds fell silent. Straining my ears, I heard the rhythmic crunch of booted feet moving over the shingle. Then it stopped. We lay motionless in the darkness, waiting.

There was no prior warning, no movement, just a sudden eruption of noise as a volley of gunfire ripped through the area around the gash in the whale's side. Bullets smashed through the carcass showering us with gobbets of torn flesh and blubber.

The shooting stopped as abruptly as it had begun. I felt the wild beating of Rose's heart against my arm. Then the gunfire began again. I heard the line of fire move away from us, raking the whale down towards its tail. Then it returned, marching past the gash in its stomach, advancing towards where we lay.

I closed my eyes, steeling myself for the first impact. I thought of my brother and his death on the dark hillside looking down towards this bleak cove.

Like him, I would die here, far from my home, but no one would ever know what had happened to me. There would be no funeral, no memorial. My rotting corpse would simply merge with the putrefying flesh of the whale. My bones would be picked clean by the scavenging birds, stirred and scattered by the wind with the dusty rattle of dead leaves, before being swept away by a winter storm. The icy Antarctic current would carry them off into the depths, where they would lie in the dark, freezing pit of the ocean floor.

I threw my arm around Rose and pulled her closer, half-shielding her body with my own, and stretched a despairing arm towards Jane as more rounds stitched a jagged line along the whale's chest.

I tried to drag myself away from the gunfire, deeper into

the whale's body, but I was caught, pinned between the blade and the whale's rock-hard sternum. I braced myself, flinching at each shot.

A round passed so close to my head that I felt the hot wind of its passage. Another ripped through the pack on my back, jerking me sideways. A third smashed through a whale rib, and splinters of bone needled my thigh. A fourth smashed into my heel. The shock sent the breath whistling from my lungs.

I froze, waiting for the waves of pain to engulf me. The gunfire moved on towards the head, grinding through bone and the baleen of the whale's mouth like a chainsaw through a felled oak.

Then there was silence again. I felt a dull ache from my foot, but not the searing pain I had expected. I reached behind me, straining to touch my foot, but terrified of what I might discover. My probing fingers worked down my boot. The leather stopped abruptly, shredded by the round which had carried away my boot-heel. I winced as I touched torn flesh, but the bone felt intact.

The silence grew. Then as the ringing in my ears from the gunfire began to dull, I heard another noise, faint at first but growing louder. I strained to make sense of it, a dull rasp like a butcher cutting meat.

The silence that followed was broken by a few muffled words of Spanish. Rose's breathing was fast and shallow, but I knew she had not been hurt. The bullets would have had to have passed through my body first.

I moved my head a fraction to look towards Jane. The barely discernible outline of her head in the darkness was suddenly thrown into sharp relief. Frozen in the brief flare of light, I saw a dark shape, small and rounded, tumbling through the opening into the whale's stomach.

Reacting even before my brain had processed what I had seen, I put my hand on the back of Rose's head and forced her down into the entrails, then flattened myself into the same vile mess.

There was a second's silence, then a blast so loud that the sound reverberated through every nerve end. Shrapnel from the grenade screamed over me and I felt the spattering of flesh across my back.

I pulled my face out of the muck and relaxed the pressure on Rose. She came up, gasping for air. Jane lay to one side, utterly motionless. I watched her with mounting terror, my eyes flickering from her to the dim glow from the gash in the whale's side, as I waited for the blaze of light that would signal another grenade.

I could hear nothing but the ringing of my ears from the explosion. I lowered my head and waited for whatever came next.

Rose's shivering brought me back to my senses. I had no idea how much time had passed. I could hear her ragged breathing and my hand was still clasped in hers.

I raised my head again. Jane lay in the same position, unmoving. I strained every sense. There was no sound or movement from outside the whale. I lay there, counting slowly to a thousand in my head.

Still hearing and seeing nothing, I released Rose's hand and stretched out towards Jane, a fraction of an inch at a time. My fingers closed around her calf, through the ripped leg of her flying suit. Her flesh felt as cold as a corpse.

I think it was only then that I realised what she meant to me. I choked back a sob, took a deep breath, then moved my hand up towards the knee, searching for a pulse. As I did so, I felt a faint movement.

Jane slowly raised her head and looked towards me. I almost wept with relief. I stared longingly at the grey oval of her face, then lowered my head onto my arm, my hand still resting on her leg, while my other arm cradled Rose's shoulders.

Chapter 13

When I opened my eyes again the light had faded almost to black. For a moment I was only conscious of the terrible cold.

I found Rose's ear with my mouth and whispered, 'Are you all right?'

I had to strain to hear her reply. 'I'm very cold, that's all. I need to rest some more.'

'No.' I felt her stir at the urgency in my voice. 'We must get out, get the blood moving. It's the only thing that'll keep us alive.'

I reached out in the darkness towards Jane. 'Jane? Were you hit? Are you injured?'

There was a long pause, then I heard her voice, slow and slurred. 'No. I don't think so. I don't know.'

More scared by their deadly lethargy than the chance that the Argentinians might still be lying in wait, I began to drag myself forward. The flesh of the whale resisted at first, then began to give up its cold embrace. I squirmed forward a few inches, reached back and tugged at Rose's arm, my fingers stiff and clumsy. Half-urging, half-dragging her, I got her to move towards me.

I pushed and pulled at Jane too, ignoring her sleepy request for 'Just a little while longer.' Minutes had dragged by before we had moved the few feet back down into the whale's stomach. It must have been night-time and moonless, for I could see not the faintest trace of light. I searched with my fingers for the opening, groping my way along the stomach wall. The opening had to be there somewhere. I did not have the strength to cut through that hide again.

I stopped and sat motionless. Then I felt the faintest breath of cold air on my cheek. I turned my face towards it and reached out with both hands. My fingers sank once more into the bloated flesh. I tried again, a little lower, and this time I felt it give. I pushed harder and the cold air felt stronger on my face.

Keeping my left hand on the opening, scared of losing it again, I reached back and helped the other two up to where I was lying. 'I'll go first, but you must follow me straight away. Keep one hand on my ankle and I'll lead you out. Don't make me crawl back in here again to find you.'

I began to worm my way forward, heaving at the dead weight of the whale's flesh with my head and shoulders, and struggling through the mass of blubber and entrails, inch by inch.

Already exhausted, I lay still for a few seconds, my chest heaving, then pushed forward again. My flailing right hand touched nothing but air. I hauled myself forward, half out of the gash. I wiped the slime from my nostrils and drew in a lungful of air. It was the sweetest smelling breath I had ever taken.

I glanced around me. There was no sound but the waves

breaking on the shore and no sign of movement. Had the enemy been waiting, I would already have been dead. I rolled onto my side, using my hips to force the opening a little wider, and called softly to the others.

There was an agonising pause, then Rose's head appeared. I pulled her by the arm while Jane pushed from behind. They both slithered out and all three of us lay in a heap on the beach for a few minutes, resting and filling our lungs.

Then I eased myself up, crouching in the shelter of the whale as I scanned the surrounding land and searched the skyline for movement. The faint glow of the stars hardly penetrated the overcast, but I could see no sign of immediate danger.

I straightened up and beckoned to the others. 'Get up, move around and get the circulation going. Rub your arms and legs as hard as you can.'

I rubbed at my own body for a few minutes, my hands slipping on the whale oil, then took a few uncertain steps, my legs cramping with the effort. I began to walk down to the shore, where the breaking waves showed as a faint white line in the darkness.

I limped heavily on my shattered boot and the pebbles on the beach ground into my exposed heel, sending waves of pain up my leg. I sat down and peered at my heel. In the faint starlight I could see a livid tear running straight across the flesh, but there were no broken bones.

I limped down the beach, squatted at the waterline and began rinsing my face and hands in the freezing seawater. I had to stifle a shout of pain as salt water burned into the gash on my heel.

Rose and Jane walked unsteadily down the shingle behind me. 'Don't wash too much of the oil and blubber off,' Jane said. 'It'll help to stop us getting any colder.'

There was a biting wind, but we were all reluctant to go back near the whale. Instead we huddled together on the shingle. I reached for the rucksack, but the round that had gone through it had torn ragged holes in the side and back and ripped the ration packs to shreds.

I threw them aside. There was no point in delaying. We moved back up the shingle, past the whale and onto the ridge. The flood plain lay unbroken to our east, and I could see the sheen of numerous stretches of open water. To the north was the dark shadow of L'Antioja Ridge which led directly to Mount Pleasant.

The three of us put our heads together. 'I think we have to risk the Tacbe,' Jane said. 'If they still have a chopper, they could have us out of here in ten minutes.'

'And if they don't, we'll have told the Argentinians exactly where we are.'

She nodded. 'That's the risk.'

'Too big a risk. We're only a few miles from Mount Pleasant. Our chances must be better if we walk in.'

'Even though we might blunder into one of their positions?'

'We might, but I think it's better odds.'

Jane hesitated, then shrugged her shoulders. 'I hope you're right, Sean. I hope you're right.'

I turned to Rose. 'Any ideas on the best route?'

She thought for a few moments. 'We'll come to Swan Inlet a couple of miles east of here. It's too wide to ford there but we could follow it inland towards the ridge and cross near Swan Inlet Ditch. That runs out of the main channel, almost due east. It leads into Mocho Pond. The road from Mare Harbour runs along an embankment just above it, near the junction with the Stanley Road.'

I frowned. 'That's one place the Argentinians really will be watching.'

'Then we could still follow the Ditch,' she said. 'But move north, parallel with the road. There are lots of streams and creeks there, there must be a culvert under the road we could use. That would bring us close to the perimeter of Mount Pleasant.'

'And that's where our troubles will really begin,' Jane said. 'If the Argentinians don't shoot us, there's every chance our guys will' – she paused – 'if there are any of our guys left. What if they've been overrun?'

'Then we're fucked whatever happens.'

We moved off in single file towards the east. We reached the inlet in an hour and turned north along the bank. Every few hundred yards we had to cross a stream feeding into the main channel. Some were tiny, a few were deep, fast-flowing creeks, and we were all soon drenched to the bone again.

Scudding clouds blocked most of the light from the rising moon, but each break in them bathed the land in grey cold light. We flattened ourselves against the sodden land and wormed our way into cover until the cloud returned. Snow flurries blew through on the gusting wind, chilling us to the bone.

At length Rose caught my arm and pointed down the bank. 'This is the place.'

I looked doubtfully at the broad expanse of water that lay between us and the far bank.

'It's the best place,' Rose said. 'A broad arm of the inlet runs a good half-mile west just above here. It'll force us right off track.'

'Do we wade it or swim it?'

'Swim.' There was a catch in her voice. 'It's probably too deep to wade and anyway the bottom is sure to be soft mud.'

I hesitated for a second. 'Okay, let's do it. One at a time. As soon as I reach the other bank, come straight after me.'

I stripped off my clothes, bundled them into what was left of the backpack and held it above my head as I lowered myself into the water. It was an icy, heart-stopping shock. I pushed off and began swimming, trying to make no sound or splash. By the time I was halfway across, I felt drowsy despite the exertion, and a voice in my head kept telling me to stop for a while and rest, just for a few moments.

Then I choked on a mouthful of filthy water. In a panic I struck out for the far bank again, flailing like a drowning man. Even when I reached the far side, I struggled to crawl up the slimy bank, twice slipping back.

At last I reached the refuge of a grassy ledge. I no longer felt cold and the voice still kept telling me to rest, but I knew where that would lead. I forced myself to my feet and gave myself a ferocious rub down with my shirt and then dragged my clothes back on.

I turned and saw the white figure of Rose already halfway across the black water. She reached the bank coughing and spluttering, and clung to me as I hauled her up the bank, racked by shivers that shook her like a dog. I began rubbing her down, forcing circulation back into the skin. Jane slipped from the water a moment later, as sleek and silent as a seal.

As soon as they were dressed again, I leaned over to whisper in Jane's ear. 'We need to move faster for a while, she could die of exposure.'

'We need to stay alive too. If we move too fast, we could blunder straight into a patrol.'

We tracked the shore of the inlet northwards towards the black mass of the ridge. I could see no difference in the terrain, but Rose suddenly caught my arm. 'Go slower, the Ditch is quite close now.' Her teeth were still chattering with cold.

I scanned the flat peaty ground ahead of us, the quartz pebbles glowing faintly. Just at the limit of my vision was a broader band of black, running at right angles to our track.

We reached the edge of it a few minutes later, a dark, rank-smelling ditch with a ribbon of water in the bottom. Clumps of coarse grass clung to the upper banks of the Ditch, while the lower half was slimy with mud.

We moved forward along the bank for forty minutes. Jane was now leading, while Rose and I covered her. I saw her rise to peer past a clump of tussac grass, then flatten herself against the ground. I laid a warning hand on Rose's arm and pressed a finger to my lips, then inched forward to join Jane. 'What is it?'

'Enemy position.'

I slowly parted the strands of tussac grass and peered into the darkness. For a moment I could see nothing, then I picked up the dull sheen of a steel helmet on the ridge ahead of us. As I scanned left and right, I saw three other soldiers, their rifle barrels glinting. At the centre of the arc of figures, shielded by a rough sangar, was a heavy machine gun.

I looked to the north beyond the Ditch, and caught glimpses of a similar huddle of forms, on the ridge above it. 'Move back.' My voice was so low I could scarcely hear my own words.

We crawled backwards for a hundred yards then held a whispered conversation. As I spoke to Jane, I kept shooting anxious glances at Rose. She was tired and listless and seemed to struggle to follow the conversation.

'The only way through is the Ditch.'

'If there's nobody down there,' Jane said.

'Would you be if you didn't have to be?'

'You've got a point.'

'Come on then, I'll go first. Rose in the middle. Jane, you take the rear.'

She glanced at Rose and shook her head. 'I'll be the hero this time, Sean. You might need to keep Rose moving.'

'I'll be all right,' Rose said, her words almost lost in the wind. 'I just need to rest for a while.' Her head drooped towards her chest.

'No!' My voice was low but insistent.

Her head snapped up, startled. 'I'm fine,' she said. 'I'm just terribly tired.'

I felt her skin. She was frozen. 'No, Rose, you must keep going. If you stop you'll die.' I led her a little further back into a hollow and roughly rubbed her arms and legs again.

I moved back to where Jane was waiting, restlessly scanning the ground ahead of us. 'Jane . . .' I groped for the right words. 'Please be careful. I . . .' My voice tailed away.

She turned back towards me, searching my face. Her eyes widened in surprise at what she read there. She leaned towards me for a moment and her fingers brushed against my cheek. Then she slid silently down the bank of the Ditch and began to move away.

I waited a few seconds then helped Rose down the bank. The bottom was slimy, stinking mud. As she began to crawl forward, I held her back for a second. 'Smear some more mud on your face and hands.' She did so mechanically, and I darkened my own face and then followed behind her.

We tried to keep to the muddy bank above the rivulet of water but it made very little difference; we were soon soaked once more. After we had crawled fifty yards I tugged her ankle, then crept forward to whisper in her ear. 'Belly crawl from here until you see Jane do any different.'

I lost all track of time as we inched forward through the mud only yards from the Argentinian soldiers on either bank above us. My flesh crept. There would be no shouted challenge if we were spotted, only high velocity rounds tearing into our flesh. We would not even hear the sound of the shot until after the bullets had hit us.

If there was a patrol in the Ditch, or they had booby-trapped it . . . I forced myself to concentrate only on the next few inches to be covered. My arms ached from the effort of hauling myself forward and twice I saw Rose stop and lower her head to rest it in the mud.

I crawled alongside her and whispered, 'Keep going, Rose. Keep going. Not much further.'

At last we reached a bend. Jane was huddled in its shelter, waiting for us. 'We're past the main danger, I think. All we have to worry about now is our own side.'

I took the lead again as we moved another few hundred yards, then I led them up the opposite bank, on to the north side. The cloud had thickened again and the night was even darker, but I could just see an outline on the low rise ahead of us. It was the size and shape of an upturned dustbin.

I stopped and stared. Jane crawled up beside me. 'What the hell's that?' She frowned, then I saw her shoulders relax. 'It's all right, it's the navigation beacon for Mount Pleasant. We're only a couple of hundred yards from the road.'

We crawled over the rise, flattening ourselves against the ridgeline to avoid giving ourselves away, either to the watching Argentinians behind or the British forces ahead of us.

After more than twenty-four hours out of contact with the base, anything could have happened, but I had been oddly reassured by the sight of the Argentine position. If the base had already been overrun they would have been facing outwards, not inwards.

We inched our way down the far side of the rise. The line of the road showed as a pale ribbon, running due north along an embankment of rock and shingle bulldozed out of the surrounding plain.

We worked our way around the foot of it until I heard a whisper of water. Ahead of us was a circular opening set in the face of the embankment, a concrete storm drain. I worked my fingers slowly around the edge of the opening, feeling for booby-traps, then I crawled through it. The wind whipped around me as it forced its way through the narrow opening.

I inched my head out at the far end of the pipe and looked around. To my left the road curled away in a loop towards the west before swinging back to the main gates of the base. Ahead of me, only 400 yards distant, lay the perimeter fence.

Beyond it I could see the outline of the tower, but the massive block of the Tristar hangar had disappeared. All that was left were two broken pillars jutting into the sky and a twisted section of roof that ended in mid-air as abruptly as a ski jump. The entire base was in darkness.

The other two joined me just outside the mouth of the storm drain. 'Don't relax yet. This is the most dangerous time.' I squeezed Rose's shoulder. 'But we're almost there; hold on.'

She turned her face towards me and tried to smile. 'Now what?'

'Now we wait and watch a little longer.'

We moved away from the embankment and crouched down a hundred yards from the fence, lying in a hollow that gave us some protection from all directions.

We waited for fifteen minutes and then I heard the rumble

of an engine. Two armoured Land Rovers were moving along the perimeter track, separated by about 400 yards. I waited until the lead vehicle was almost level with me, then stood up, my hands held high.

As I did so, the night erupted with gunfire. I dropped like a bag of cement, landing across Rose and crushing the air from her lungs. Bullets thwacked into the peat around us, cutting through the tussac grass like a buzz saw. A blizzard of shredded grass settled on my skin.

Then the firing stopped. There was an eerie silence. I eased the battered pack from my shoulders and searched through it for something white to wave. In the end I dumped the mangled contents and gripped the pack itself.

I started to raise it in my right arm, thought better of it and transferred it to my left. I reached up slowly, waving it above my head.

Nothing happened. I took another deep breath and then with agonising slowness I rose to my knees and then my feet, keeping my arms high and well clear of my body. 'We're British. 1435 Flight.'

There was a brief pause. 'Stand still. Give the number of the day,' a voice shouted.

'I don't know it. We were shot down the night before last. There are three of us, two downed air crew and one civilian.'

'Stand up, come forward, and keep your hands up.'

Jane and Rose stood up alongside me and we began to stumble forward over the rough ground.

'Stop. Move left fifty yards.'

We came to a narrow gate in the fence.

'Down on the ground. Face down, flat out, arms spread.'

We dropped to the ground and I heard a clang as the gate opened, and the sound of boots crunching over the gravel.

Rough hands searched me and took my pistol. Then my hands were jerked up behind my back and I was handcuffed, hauled to my feet and man-handled through the gate and into the back of one of the Land Rovers.

Rose and Jane were dumped alongside me and two Marines clambered in to guard us.

'We're aircrew. Tempests. We were shot down.'

'Shut up.' There was a pause. 'Jesus, what a fucking stink.' They leaned out over the tailboard of the Land Rover, gulping in fresh air as it sped back across the base. As soon as it stopped, we were hustled out and pushed through a doorway. As the steel door clanged shut behind us a light flared.

I bowed my head, trying to shield my eyes.

'Who are you?' The disembodied voice came from somewhere beyond the lights.

'Flight Lieutenant Sean Riever and Captain Jane Clark, 1435 Flight, and Rose Calder, a Falklands civilian.'

'Thanks, Sergeant, I'll vouch for them.'

I almost wept with relief at the Boss's urbane tones. 'Welcome back, Sean and Jane. We'd given you up for lost.'

The blinding light was dimmed and our handcuffs were removed. He stood facing us, among a group of officers and half a dozen Marines. He wrinkled his nose. 'You're a little ripe, to say the least.'

I glanced round at Rose and Jane. Their hair, faces and clothes were slimy with dirty yellow whale oil and streaks of stinking blubber, and I knew I was in no better shape.

Rose stared straight ahead, as if hearing and seeing nothing. 'It's okay, Rose, we're safe now.'

She turned her blank face towards me. Then she swayed, her knees buckled and she collapsed on the floor. I touched her face, her skin was blue-tinged and icy cold to the touch.

A medic pushed me aside. 'She's hypothermic.'

He called for a stretcher. As Rose was carried away, the Boss looked from Jane to me. 'You two don't look too good either. We'll debrief you in the Medical Centre.'

We were led through the doors and down into the basement. Rose was carried into a side-room and I heard the sound of running water as medics scurried to and fro. After we'd been examined, we sat huddled in blankets, drinking hot soup as we talked the Boss through the last thirty-six hours. Two Ground Force Commanders sat on either side of us, occasionally interrupting to ask a question.

When we had finished speaking, he glanced at them. 'All right?'

They nodded and moved away.

'Now I'll bring you up to speed with the situation here. There's good and bad. The Argentinians have lost an awful lot of aircraft: eight Super Etendards – that's two-thirds of their total force – ten, perhaps eleven Mirages and four Hercs.'

'What about our own losses?'

'Severe. We're down to three serviceable jets. Four were destroyed on the ground and two, including your own, were shot down. The other one would fly if we had the spares.' His face was haggard. 'We don't. Not that that matters. We only have crew for two of them anyway – Noel, Rees, Shark and Jimmy.'

I felt sick. 'What about the others?'

'We lost ten aircrew – six dead, four seriously wounded – in the direct hit on the Q shed and the attack on the Operations Building. Two more aircrew were in their jet inside the Tempest shack when it was hit by an anti-tank missile, and another two were shot down over the sea. There's been no trace of them.'

He fell silent, staring at the floor. 'The Rapier sites have taken a pounding but four are still active, and there were no raids at all last night. We think we may have beaten off the air threat.' His tone remained bleak.

'What about their ground forces?' Jane said.

'It's a bit of a stalemate. We think they're too short of men and ammunition to launch another attack, but they're dug in and holding a line extending from the Wickham Heights down to Swan Inlet' – he gave a grim smile – 'as you discovered. The Marines are aggressive patrolling to deter any further incursions, but we don't have the men to push the enemy back any further. We've lost a hell of a lot of ground troops, including our Forward Air Controller.'

'Jack Stubbs? What happened?'

'I don't know. We haven't even been able to retrieve the bodies yet.'

He rubbed his face with his hand. 'Reinforcements are on their way, the Cobra Force of Tempest squadrons and ground troops.' He met my gaze. 'I know, I know, but the time for inquests will be when this mess is over, not now.' He took a deep breath. 'Deploying the tankers from the Gulf to re-fuel them has been a nightmare. They will be here in' – he paused and consulted his watch – 'around fourteen hours.'

'But?'

'The *Eva Peron* has put to sea with its guardship and is less than six hours sailing time from us.'

'What about our own guardship?'

He shook his head. 'Hit by an Exocet. It's crippled, unable even to fire its guns or missiles.' He put the tips of his fingers together and thought for a moment before speaking again. 'As

I said, help is on the way, but unless we can stop or sink that Argentine cruiser, the reinforcements will arrive too late.

'We don't have enough ground forces to hold off a determined assault. Even if we did, the Argentinians could lie-up off shore and destroy the runway with their guns.' Once more he paused, pinching the bridge of his nose between his forefinger and thumb. 'You know the equation: if we lose the runway, we lose the Falklands. There's no Task Force to save us this time. We don't have enough ships in the entire UK fleet to form one. We have one last chance.' He glanced from me to Jane. 'This is asking a lot after what you've both been through already.'

I interrupted him. 'We're both fit and ready to go.'

Jane nodded.

'Good.' He looked at his watch. 'It's nearly three o'clock. Get a hot shower, some food and what rest you can. We're briefing in an hour. Take-off will be at dawn.'

Jane got to her feet and followed him out of the room. I hung back and looked into the bay where Rose was being treated. She was lying back in a bath. A medic was bending over her, taking her temperature, and she did not see me at first.

I stood in the doorway for a moment, looking at her. As the medic moved away she caught sight of me. The faintest hint of colour touched her cheek, and she moved her hands to cover herself, then sank back into the bath with a weary smile.

'Are you okay?'

She gave a slow nod.

'I have to fly a mission, but these guys will take good care of you.'

She saw the shadow cross my face. 'Sean?' Her voice was almost a whisper. 'Is it over? Are we safe now? Both of us?' She held my gaze.

Finally I nodded. 'You're safe now.'

'That's not what I asked.'

I shrugged. 'Like I said, I have to fly a mission.'

She reached out and took my hand. There was another, unspoken question in her eyes.

I couldn't meet her gaze and looked away. I stood helpless before her, unable to say the words she wanted — or thought she wanted — to hear.

After a moment she released my hand and let her arm fall back into the water. A tear trickled down her cheek.

'Bernard loves you, Rose.'

She shook her head. 'He sent me away.'

'You didn't see the look in his eyes after you'd turned away. He sent you away to keep you safe.' There was a long silence. 'You must rest. I'll come and see you as soon as I get back.'

The tears still tracked silently down her cheeks.

'Rose, I'm not my brother. I—' I paused, helpless. 'I'm sorry. I have to go.'

I walked out of the sick bay and along the corridor to the showers. There was still a smell of smoke in the building, and piles of debris in the corridors had been roughly swept to one side, but the only damage I could see — in the basement at least — were a few cracks in the walls and some patches of bare blockwork where the plaster had fallen off.

The changing room was heavy with steam. There were clean flying suits hanging on the hooks and I could see the faint outline of Jane's body through the half-drawn plastic curtain of one of the shower cubicles. I stripped off my stinking clothes and kicked them away across the floor.

I walked towards the showers, but paused, my eyes drawn towards Jane's cubicle. I could see her through the gap in the curtain. She stood with her arms raised, letting hot water cascade over her body. Her eyes were closed and a smile of pure pleasure was playing around her lips. I had always looked away before when she was changing into her flying clothes. Now, feeling like a thief, but unable to stop myself, I let my eyes travel down over her body.

Her long blonde hair, darkened by the water, clung to her neck and shoulders. Her tanned skin seemed to glow with the warmth of the shower and her bikini marks showed a vivid, glistening white. Rivulets of water traced the smooth lines of her body. She soaped herself, arching her back like a cat, her hands moving down over her strong shoulders, her breasts and flat stomach, and over the soft curve of her hips.

I took a step towards the shower, then paused, fighting the urge to step into the shower and slide my arms around her. I hurried away into a cubicle on the opposite side of the room. Shuddering in the unaccustomed warmth, I washed my hair and body over and over again, trying to rid myself of the cloying whale oil. I heard the other shower stop and the slap of Jane's feet across the floor. I shut my eyes as I rinsed the shampoo from my hair and reached for the soap.

My fingers touched warm flesh.

I opened my eyes, shaking my head to clear the water from them. Jane stood there, naked and glistening.

She reached out and took my hands in hers, pressing them into her shoulders. I felt her hands tracing the outline of my body, stroking my neck, my shoulders, working down around my hips. I could not hide how aroused I was. 'Jane, I—'

She silenced me with her lips and I crushed her to me, the touch of her skin one continuous caress of my body. We kissed hungrily, clinging to each other as the shower cascaded around our shoulders. She pulled away a fraction, her eyes unfocused, the pupils dark pools, then pulled me towards her again.

A smile lit up her beautiful face. I opened my mouth to

speak again, but she laid her fingers on my lips. 'We nearly died out there. In less than two hours time we're going to be in another dark place, with people trying to kill us. We may not come back. I don't care about anything else. Only the present, this moment, matters. The future can take care of itself.'

She slid her arms around my neck, her mouth hungrily seeking mine. I kissed her mouth, her neck, her breasts, and as I gave myself up to her, she wrapped her thighs around me, arching her back against the wall. We stared into each other's eyes and our bodies moved together, deep and slow. I felt the climax building within her, and lost myself too, crying her name as I came.

I held her as the waves ebbed away, the shower water as warm and soft on my skin as summer rain. I looked into her eyes, imprinting every detail of her face on my mind.

Then there was the sound of footsteps in the corridor. She kissed me once more, then slid past me, out of the cubicle. There was a knock on the outer door. 'Briefing in twenty minutes.'

I called an acknowledgement and heard Noel's footsteps disappearing down the corridor.

We struggled into our clothes, but just before we left the changing room, I locked her in my arms. 'Jane?'

'I know.' She turned to push the door open, then checked and swung back to face me. 'But the sooner we blow the bastards out of the water, the sooner we can be back here.' She smiled. 'Now let's get some food, while we still have time. I'm starving.'

One wall of the Mess was pock-marked by bullet holes and the windows had all been blown out in the air raid. Rough sheets of plywood filled the empty frames.

We sat facing each other across a table. Her hair was damp and her face still flushed.

'What about Geoff?' I said.

'I've already told him.'

'What?'

'I phoned him the afternoon before we went into QRA. I didn't want to send him a Dear John letter. I wanted to do it face to face really, but it felt like I would be cheating him if I waited till we got back to England.'

'What did you say?'

'I just told him it wasn't working. But you know what he said straight away? "It's Sean, isn't it?" I denied it, but . . .' She shrugged. 'I never was much of a liar.'

We sat in silence, studying each other's faces. I felt strangely at peace, even though I knew that the minutes were ticking away to the briefing. As long as we neither moved nor spoke, I felt that nothing could break the spell.

Finally Jane squeezed my hand and murmured, 'Look out, here comes Shark.'

He stopped by the table, looking uncertainly from Jane to me. His eyes were deep-shadowed and his previous brash assurance had been stripped away. He looked suddenly vulnerable. Jane glanced at me, then slid along the bench to make room for him.

He gave her a brief smile of gratitude, then sat down heavily. 'Are you two all right?'

'As all right as we can be,' Jane said. 'What about you?'

'I'm okay.' He paused, then shook his head. 'No, I'm not. I wish those reinforcements would get here. I wish it would stop.'

'It will – one way or the other.'

He glanced across at me. 'Do you think we can do it?'

'Why not?' I said, faking a confidence I was far from feeling. 'It's a big target.'

He nodded absently, his mind on something else. He turned to look at Jane. 'If ... if anything happens to me, would you go and see my parents, tell them what it was like? I don't want them just to have some anonymous officer turning up on their doorstep, telling them how sorry he is, and then leaving them with nothing more than a brown paper parcel of my personal effects.'

She laid a hand on his arm. 'If you want me to go and see them, of course I will. But it's not going to be necessary, Shark. We've lost a lot of friends, but we've come through the worst now. We're not going to fail now ...'

'You're right,' he said, without conviction. 'Sorry to lay that on you. Thanks.'

He stood up and walked slowly away, his shoulders hunched.

'Poor bastard,' I said.

She nodded, her eyes following him across the room. 'He'll be all right though, once he gets back in the cockpit.'

'Perhaps.'

Even the limited warmth in the Mess had made me feel drowsy and I drank several cups of black coffee. Jane eyed me narrowly. 'Do you want some speed? We've some in the escape kit.'

I shook my head. 'Sheer terror's the only stimulant I need. I'll get through this on adrenalin. And don't worry, I won't fall asleep at the wheel.'

She rewarded the feeble joke with a smile, but there was a long silence. 'What do you really think?' she said finally.

I shrugged. 'We've got them outnumbered, three aircraft to two ships.'

'If only it were that simple.'

Chapter 14

I carried another cup of coffee with me as we moved through to the briefing room, which was undamaged save for a huge jagged crack across one wall, running from floor to ceiling. The four other aircrew were already seated on the benches.

Jimmy sat there in silence, his features cast in perpetual gloom, stoically awaiting his fate. Shark was pouring out a stream of nervous chatter to Rees, who barely seemed to register a word. He stared at the floor as if it might open up and swallow him. Noel sat slightly to one side. He looked to be simmering with suppressed anger, clasping and unclasping his hands, impatient to be airborne, to get it over with, whatever the outcome might be.

The Boss led the briefing, but before he spoke, he looked each of us in the eye. Then he leaned forward, resting his knuckles on the podium. 'You guys have worked miracles already, but now I've got to ask you to dig even deeper. I won't underplay in any way the difficulty of the task that faces you, but you already know how vital it is that you succeed.

'The Argentinians have committed acts of unprovoked aggression against us. They landed forces on the sovereign territory of the Falklands. They attacked this base and killed thirty-seven people, including several good friends of yours and mine, and they murdered Falkland civilians, as Sean and Jane saw for themselves. They also sank the *Trident*, and no death could be more terrible than to be trapped in a steel coffin deep below the ocean. The lucky ones would have died at once, but some men might have survived the initial attack, closing the hatches to seal off their part of the sub as the sea poured into the rest of it.

'They would do it instinctively, without thinking, but it would condemn them to an even more horrible death. As the sub sank to the bottom they would face the choice of slowly suffocating as the oxygen dwindled and ran out, or of opening the hatches and being squashed like worms by the pressure of the ocean floor. That is what the Argentinians have done to your comrades.' He took a deep breath. 'The odds are stacked against you. We're not sure what air cover they'll put up to protect those ships, but we do know they've taken a mauling already and are running scared of us. We can only hope they don't know how few aircraft we have left. Even without air cover, however, those ships are more than able to defend themselves. But whatever they throw at you, you have got to get through.

'If that cruiser is allowed to shell the airfield and get its combat troops ashore, the game's up. The garrison will be overrun and wiped out, and by the time those Tempest squadrons get here, they might as well ditch in the sea. There'll be nowhere to land and neither they nor the tankers will have enough fuel to get back to Ascension.

'In short, we're in the shit and we're looking to you to get us out of it. The fate of all of us here, the whole garrison and two-and-a-half thousand Falklanders, is in your hands.'

He let the silence build, then nodded curtly to the Intelligence Officer. She stood up and took his place at the podium. 'We estimate a force of three thousand crack troops and equipment was embarked on the two ships. A flotilla of lesser craft has been marshalled in the inland waters just off Rio Gallegos ready to convoy a further five thousand troops.

'The Argentinians have learned the lessons of last time. These are not raw conscripts, they are tough, well-trained regular troops. If they're allowed to land, the battle for the Falklands will be over.' Her voice cracked. She paused and pushed her glasses back onto the bridge of her nose, a characteristic gesture.

'The *Eva Peron* is a former Royal Navy cruiser.' She gave a grim smile. 'Just another of life's ironies. It dates from the Second World War, but should not be underrated because of that. It has been recently and expensively overhauled and its engines and armaments are far from antique.

'The guardship is a Meko type 360 destroyer, *La Argentina*, length 125.9 metres, beam 14 metres, range 4,500 miles at its eighteen-knot cruising speed, top speed just over thirty knots. Armament includes eight MM40 Exocets in two quads, eight Aspide SAMs, one five-inch turret forward, four twin 40mm Bofors, six Mark 32 torpedoes – two triples – and two twin ASW rocket launchers.

'Your main worries are obviously the SAMs and the Bofors guns. The cruiser was designed to survive the impact of a single torpedo strike or several hits by bombs. Its most vulnerable areas are the magazine – obviously – and the bridge, but taking out the bridge would not only require great accuracy, it would also not be enough in itself to stop the ship, or destroy its fighting potential.'

She nodded to a member of the ground crew waiting by the door, who dimmed the lights. She switched on an overhead projector and a cross-section of the ship appeared on the screen behind her. 'The magazine is three decks down, in this section' – she tapped the image with her wooden pointer – 'and as you would expect, it's armoured. Six inches of best Sheffield steel.'

She signalled to the crewman who turned the lights back on. She looked around, muttered, 'Good luck,' and almost ran from the room.

'Weather brief.' Jimmy uncoiled himself from the bench and stood up. His normally sallow features were grey with fatigue. 'Its marginal. If this was an exercise, we'd already have called it off. Wind speed sixty-five now and strengthening every minute, westerly, veering south-west and building, showers, sleet, hail, the works. Visibility two to three miles maximum, much less in the squalls.'

As he sat down, Noel strode to the podium. 'We're airborne at 0600 hours, aiming to come out at them out of the sun while it's still low in the sky.' He paused. 'If there is any sun. The guardship is obviously not the prime target, but it will offer a very convincing defence. I'm reluctant to waste time and weapons on it, but if we can take it out in a couple of strikes, our chances of landing the killer punch on the cruiser will be at least trebled.

'I'll be leading us in, Shark, you're number two, Sean, you're number three. We'll take one pop each at the guardship, and whatever the results, we'll then switch to the cruiser. The best hope of achieving the velocity to penetrate through three decks and armour plate is to go for a high-level LGB attack.'

I saw Rees' eyes light up. Using laser-guided bombs from 20,000 feet would almost guarantee success.

'Sadly, we're not going for that option,' Noel said. 'With no air cover, nor any defence suppression aircraft to counter the ship's SAMs, the target marker would be a sitting duck. We just can't afford to lose another jet.'

'What about Sea Eagles, then?' Shark said.

Once more we were offered a glimmer of hope. It had been some time since I'd used the anti-ship missiles, but they could be relied upon to do the job, and their stand-off capability would keep us out of harm's way.

Noel fell silent and glanced towards the Boss. As he stood up, his eyes already told the story. 'I'm sorry, guys. Because of the cost, the MoD would only let us have four Sea Eagles. We lost the lot when one of the bunkers went up.'

I could see Noel's jaw clench and his knuckles whiten. 'I'm sure we'll be taking these matters up in due course ... if we get the chance.' He paused. 'So, in case you haven't guessed, we're back to a lay-down attack – one hundred feet, fast and low, straight into the lion's den.'

I looked around at the faces of the others. They told the same story. It was almost impossible to believe that we were reduced to the tactics used by the Harriers during the Falklands War, sixteen years before.

'You're going with iron bombs. That's two 1,000-pounders per jet, six shots at sinking two ships.' Noel's expression showed that he fully shared our concern. He turned over his hands and stared at his palms. 'We also have no Herc to refuel from and we're at extreme range, so we haven't got much gas to fool around with—'

He broke off as Shark raised a hand. 'What about Argentinian air cover?'

Noel shrugged. 'As you've heard, we've inflicted severe damage on them, but they'll be just as aware as us that this is the last chance. They've had Migs on intermittent patrol and I'm sure they'll put everything they've got in the air as soon as they realise the ships are under attack, but they don't have enough assets left to mount a constant CAP over the ships and they don't have radar or satellite overview. As soon as the guardship makes radar contact with you, they'll scramble everything they have . . . but, with luck, by the time they arrive it should be too late.

'If there is air cover, we'll have to deal with it. And just to make you feel even better, we've only got three Skyflash missiles left – one per jet. It's just like the Sea Eagles, the MoD didn't want to waste money by letting us have too many of them.' I saw a muscle twitch in his cheek. 'But our task is to take out those ships, no matter what the distractions.' He paused and glanced at each of us. 'Nor the risks to ourselves.'

We filed out of the briefing room in silence. I glanced at the faces around me. We all preferred an instant reaction, getting airborne in minutes without time for reflection, rather than a premeditated sortie that left time for nerves to jangle and the consequences of failure to be explored.

Noel strode ahead of us down the corridor trying, not altogether successfully, to mask his anxiety and exude the natural confidence of a commander. Jimmy's expression remained unaltered, the corners of his mouth pulled down. Rees looked as if he would throw up at any moment, but I knew that once he was airborne he would be the calmest of us all. Shark was still jabbering away, but his face was even more pale than usual and his eyes had a haunted look.

'Do you think Shark's going to be okay?' I said. 'I've never seen him act like this before.'

Jane glanced across at him. 'He's speeding,' she said. 'Look at his pupils.'

She began rummaging through her pockets, a troubled expression on her face.

'Are you all right?' I asked.

'Yes. No. I can't find my pendant. The chain must have broken.'

'I'll look in the showers, maybe it fell off in there.'

I pushed open the door and looked around. Our crumpled towels still lay on the bench, like an unmade bed after a night's love-making. There was no sign of the pendant anywhere.

'Do you remember having it when we got back from the E & E run?'

'I don't think so. I don't know. It could be anywhere, in that minefield or inside that whale.' She shuddered at the memory.

'It'll turn up, Jane. You might just have left it in your room at the Death Star.'

She gave a doubtful nod. 'Maybe.' She paused, checking my expression. 'It's not because it's Geoff's. It's like a talisman to him and his whole family. They think nothing can go wrong as long as it's safe. It's stupid, I know, but I half-believe it myself.'

I shrugged. 'We've all got a superstition. Mine's wearing odd socks.' I hitched up the legs of my flying suit to prove it. 'When I was based at Marham, I knew a guy who wouldn't fly a sortie unless he'd stroked the Ops Room cat on his way out. It went missing one day and he refused to fly. They had to threaten him with a court martial to get him airborne.'

'What happened?'

'Nothing. He took off, flew a routine sortie and landed safely. He never even looked at the cat again after that.'

She gave me a doubtful look. 'Is that true or are you just trying to cheer me up?'

'It's true.' I glanced over my shoulder, then kissed her forehead. 'Come on.'

The changing room had a chaotic look. In place of the usual neatly folded and stacked kit and equipment, piles of unwashed flying suits and immersion suits still lay where they had been thrown after the previous missions.

The corporal presiding over the room caught my eye. 'Bit of a mess, I'm afraid, sir. We've had other, more pressing problems to deal with.' As he turned round to reach for something on the shelf behind him, I saw that his left arm was roughly bandaged. 'What happened?'

He looked round. 'This? I took a bullet. I'm okay, though. It hurts like hell but it could have been worse. We're the lucky ones, aren't we?'

He nodded towards the shelves where flying helmets were still stacked, each one stencilled with a name. More than half of them would never be used again. As I glanced back at him, he held my gaze. 'Make the fuckers pay, sir.'

I nodded.

As I turned away, the doctor came in carrying a plastic bag full of small, white capsules. He seemed almost furtive. 'Anyone want any of these?'

Nobody spoke and most of us shook our heads, but I saw Shark catch his eye. The doctor walked over to him. He looked at his eyes, hesitated a second, then handed him two more capsules.

'Much more of that and Shark won't need a jet to get airborne,' I muttered.

Jane put a hand on my arm. 'Go easy on him, Sean. We've all got to get through this the best way we can. If it helps him do his job, then it's fine by me.'

I chose the least worn-looking immersion suit I could find on the rack, then walked over to the benches and began struggling into my gear. I resolved the usual dilemma of discomfort in the cockpit versus survival in the sea, in the usual way. I put on two pairs of thermal underwear and a woollen survival suit, then hauled on the immersion suit, helped by liberal doses of French chalk. It clouded the air around me and some settled on my face, giving my reflection in the mirror the pallor of a ghost.

I dragged on my G-pants and combat jacket, then began a mental checklist of my kit, tapping each pocket with superstitious care. I looked around. The others were all changed, except for Shark who was still fumbling with his G-pants, his movements slow and listless. He met my eye for a second and then looked away, gulping and swallowing like a man about to be sick. Finally he stood up.

I glanced at Jane. Her gaze was rock steady.

'All right?'

'Yes. Let's do it.'

The Boss stood by the table next to the door, ready for the out-brief. 'Okay, guys, the airfield is reasonably secure. We've pushed the attackers back some distance from the perimeter and you should be safe to make a normal take-off, but be on the look-out and keep your heads down. Do you all know the letter and number of the day? Have you removed all surplus items from your kit and all personal effects, other than your dog tags?' His voice cracked. 'Oh, sod this. Look, give it your best shot. Good luck.'

He stepped out from behind the table and shook our hands in turn as we filed past him. Then Noel pushed open the doors. A pool of light spilled out into the pre-dawn darkness. I could hear the keening of the wind across the airfield and as we came out of the lea of the building, I felt its cutting edge, despite my layers of clothing.

The door banged behind us and we clambered onto a battered, camouflaged bus. A row of neat round holes had been punched down the near side. On the opposite side, where the rounds had exited, the bodywork had burst outwards in blooms of broken metal. Several of the seats had been shredded and clumps of blood-stained foam-rubber still lay on the floor.

We sat silent as the bus rattled down towards the Tempest shacks, bumping over patches of repaired runway, near-white against the darker grey of the rubber-streaked concrete. The twisted outlines of bombed and burnt buildings loomed out of the darkness around us.

The doors of the surviving Tempest shacks were open and pools of harsh white light spilled onto the apron. One of the empty shacks had been pressed into use as a temporary morgue. As we passed its open door, I could see black rubber body-bags being manhandled on to the bomb-racks.

Only three of the shacks still housed aircraft. As well as the usual Sidewinders and a single Skyflash missile, two squat iron bombs hung from the pylons beneath the wings of each jet.

Jane noticed my expression. 'What's the matter?'

'Nothing. Just someone walking on my grave.'

'What do you mean?'

'Seeing iron bombs always creeps me out a little. On my first posting, before you and I buddied up, a friend of mine was killed on the bombing range at Finnington. An engineer screwed up. The bombs should have been set to detonate twenty feet above the ground, but with the usual few seconds' delay so that they didn't fully arm until clear of the aircraft. The engineer forgot to set a delay. They were fully armed on release and when the second bomb of the stick came off, it proximity fused on the first one a few feet below it. My friend was blown apart; just another training accident.'

'What happened to the engineer?'

'He was court-martialled and discharged from the Air Force. I heard he'd committed suicide.'

She squeezed my arm so hard that, even through the immersion suit, I could feel her fingers digging into my flesh. 'Come on, Sean, get a grip on it. It's not going to happen to us.'

We came down the steps and stood in an uncertain circle for a moment at the side of the bus. Noel started to say something, then changed his mind, and with a curt nod he turned and walked towards his jet. Rees trailed behind him. Jimmy walked to his jet like a condemned man approaching the scaffold. Shark winked as he followed him, but the bravado did not conceal the trembling of his lip.

I hesitated for a second before I went into the Tempest shack. The mounds of earth and stone blunted the force of the wind, and the moist, dank smell of peat hung on the breeze, mingling with other, almost indefinable scents, like salt spray and the sour tang of kelp.

I took a deep breath, then glanced across at Jane. 'All right?'

She nodded. 'Just like I was the last time. Stop worrying about me, Sean. We can't let what's happened change the way we work. The best way we can look after each other is to keep one hundred per cent focused on our own jobs.'

'I'm not sure I can.'

'You've got no choice.' She turned away from me, ran across the concrete and began climbing up the ladder to the jet.

I glanced up at the sky. There wasn't even the faintest red glimmer in the east; even the false dawn was still a good half-hour away. The faces of the ground crew were etched with fatigue and the usual barely ordered chaos of the interior of the Tempest shack was even closer to complete disarray. Equipment and weaponry were stacked on every side and pieces of twisted metal cut from damaged jets had simply been dumped outside the shack when replacement panels were bolted on.

I checked over the aircraft, then signed the form one of the ground crewmen held out to me. 'Bring it back in one piece,' he said. 'We're getting short of spares.' He gave a tired smile then turned away to shout to one of his men.

I climbed the ladder to the cockpit. Jane's head was already bowed over her radar screen as she inputted data. I began strapping myself in, helped by the ground crewman.

We completed the first cycle of pre-flight checks. I scanned the dials and captions again, then spoke to the ground crew over the intercom. 'Starting APU.' The auxiliary power unit coughed into life with a roar and a cloud of blue smoke.

'Clear. Starting right engine.' I pushed the button. There was a whine which swelled into a ground-shaking rumble. The ambient temperature, close to zero a few seconds before, climbed to over 400 degrees Celsius. I started the left engine and the thunder redoubled, the vibrations of the engines shaking the fuselage in a steady, pulsing rhythm.

I ran my eyes over the warning panels, frowning as a couple of captions lit up. They were minor faults, but in a routine sortie they would have been enough to send us looking for another jet. On a combat mission, minor problems had to be ignored.

'Closing canopy.' I lowered my visor and closed my eyes as

the warning siren began to howl and the ground crew scattered. The siren wound down as the canopy locked into place, halving the engine noise.

A moment later, I heard Noel's voice over the radio. 'Falcon. Check in.'

'Two.'

'Three.'

'Okay, two minutes to roll-out.'

I glanced at my watch, waiting as the second-hand completed its circuit, then eased the throttles forward. It was exactly five fifty-six. As the Tempest's nose emerged from the shack, I glanced left and right and saw the other two jets in line with us. The sky ahead was now streaked with red.

'Abort brief.' I'd recited it to Jane, with minor variations, on a thousand flights before. 'Gusting wind from the right, dry runway. If there's a major loss of thrust or a warning caption with the wheels on the runway, I'll abort, engage reverse thrust, and use the hook. If you think I need the hook, call it and call the abort. Any problems after rotate, I'll select combat power and we'll deal with it at height. If I can't maintain the climb and we're still in trouble, I'll call eject.'

Rees had taken up station on the left of the runway with Shark on his right wingtip a couple of metres away. I slotted in behind them. There was a brief interchange with the tower, then they began to wind up the power. Their jets rocked and shuddered, straining against the brakes as tongues of blue-yellow flame flashed from the engines, reaching to within a couple of feet of my wingtips. I felt the jet-wash shaking the aircraft, then they released the brakes and rocketed away down the runway. They lifted off, lurching and twisting as the wind struck them.

I pushed the throttles forward through maximum dry power and into reheat. The fuel burn immediately increased tenfold as the after-burners kicked in with a surge of power that forced down the nose.

I made a final check of the warning panel, but then hesitated a moment, motionless in the cockpit. I thought of my parents at home in England, and of my brother preparing for the battle that would bring his death. I remembered the look in Rose's eye as I left her in the Sick Bay, her question still unanswered. And I thought of Jane in the back seat ...

I gritted my teeth and pushed the throttle forward all the way to the stops. The jet sprang forward, unleashed. As the runway blurred and the air-speed shot upwards, Jane and I kept up a constant cross-talk.

'Fifty knots.'

'Engines good, panel clear.'

'One hundred knots. Cable.'

We were past the wire.

'140 knots.'

The last chance to hit the brakes and stop on the runway.

'170 knots. V-rotate.'

'Rotating.' I eased the stick back and felt the jet lift clear of the runway. It seemed to hang for a moment, as it always did, then we were blasting upwards into the cloud layer.

'250 knots.'

'Out of re-heat.' I eased the throttles back a little, but kept accelerating until we punched out of the top of the cloud at 8,000 feet. We levelled off and joined the other two circling aircraft. Shark flew in battle formation, one nautical mile to the right of Rees. I was behind them by the same distance.

We began a long turn to the south-west, crossing the still dark coastline of East Falkland as the first pale light of dawn began to show in the east. Our chosen course was a gamble.

An approach from the south-east would give us the best line of attack on the guardship, but it was also the best angle for its defences — eight Aspide surface-to-air missiles and four twin 40 mm Bofors anti-aircraft guns, antique but still very effective.

We flew on over West Falkland. As we approached the coast, we closed up to within a few metres of each other and I put the throttles to idle for a cruise descent to low-level, conserving precious fuel. As we descended, I took careful note of the height of the cloud tops, the layers of haze and the height at which con-trails became visible.

We dropped steadily lower and the cloud layer reached up for us. Wisps and tendrils of mist touched the wings and licked along the fuselage. We plunged between two towering banks of cumulus, like mountain walls shielding a narrow valley, then a thick dark layer of cloud closed around us, cold and grey. Rain coated the canopy and ran along the Perspex in rivulets, pushed by the slipstream.

I kept my eyes fixed on the wingtip of Shark's jet a couple of metres from my own. Whenever it moved or twitched, my hand pushed the stick the same way. The cloud thinned and petered out just below 2000 feet and I dropped back a mile behind the other two jets.

We flew on clear of the coast, still descending towards the dark waters of the ocean, skimming the scattered islands. Away to the south I could see the lights of a trawler fleet.

Jane's voice dragged me back. 'Okay, contact. Looks like the ship, about 100 miles.'

The light was a little stronger now, the east brightening behind us, though ahead lay only darkness. We flew still lower, dropping below one hundred feet, then fifty. The greasy, dark-grey swell of the ocean seemed to reach for me; I could almost feel it slapping against the underside of the jet.

We flew on, hugging the sea. Jane's voice offered steady reassurance. 'Still got the ship. No hostiles. Screen clear.'

I glanced down at the display. The only players showing were our own three aircraft and the computer-generated blip designating the hostile guardship.

The jet carried electronic counter-measures, a jamming pod that in theory at least could defeat the acquisition radars of the destroyer's missiles, but our best hope was an undetected approach at minimum low-level, rising into radar vision only as we were about to deliver the attack.

We were still some distance from the target when the radio crackled. 'Two contacts, fast, high-level, heading two-seven-zero.'

I looked down and saw the contacts appear on the screen, as data was fed directly to us by Fortress.

'We might be lucky,' Jane said. 'They're heading away from us. It could be two Migs returning to base.'

A moment later, I heard the radar warner chime for the first time. I felt my pulse beginning to beat faster and my mouth was dry.

When Jane spoke again I could hear the tremor in her voice. 'Contacts fifty miles, turning.'

'Have they spotted us?'

'I can't say yet. They may just be flying a racetrack pattern ... Turn complete, now on zero-three-zero, forty-five miles.'

I heard the clatter of Jane's keyboard as she inputted the new data, programming the computer with the course and speed, and fixing the offset position in the weapon system. The new heading she gave me was confirmed by Noel a moment later.

'Ship heading fifteen degrees, at twenty knots,' Jane said. 'Contacts eighteen miles. Still fast, very high-level. I don't think they've seen us yet.'

'They will.' The ships, the Migs and the Tempests were on a collision course, three arrows pointing at the same area of grey ocean, though as yet – as far as we could tell – we were the only ones that knew that.

Noel's voice broke the silence. 'Right, we're not going to get past these guys unseen. Let's see if we can take them out of the equation.'

I flicked the radar into air-to-air mode as I set the Tempest soaring upwards. The attack was a gamble, but one we had to take. If we could kill the Migs, the ships would be far more vulnerable.

'Lock our man up, Jane.'

'Locked up.'

The target designator on the screen changed shape, showing a positive lock. My fingers closed around the trigger and our only Skyflash left the rails in a blaze of flame and smoke.

I could tell from the display that Rees and Shark had also fired their missiles. The enemy obviously knew as well. As I watched the designators on the screen, the two Migs turned tail and began to streak away from us.

Within a few more seconds it was clear that the gamble had failed. The missiles ran out of power in their vain pursuit of the Migs and began to plunge downwards towards the sea.

I could hear Noel breathing hard as he made contact again. 'It's down to iron bombs and good luck now. Let's take it back to low-level.'

'Forty miles to target.'

'Combat power.' I rammed the throttles forward. 'Arming weapons, stick-top live.'

'Falcon 2. Trace left two o'clock. Fifteen miles.'

The enemy Migs were returning to the fight. With no radar missiles, we were at their mercy. Our only tactic now was to try to evade them. 'Kick right twenty degrees.'

The jet lurched as I pulled a hard turn. I held it for twelve seconds – two miles – then came back on track, still moving in towards the Argentinian ships.

'Thirty-five miles.' We were barely four minutes from our target. Then the radar warner began to clamour.

'Spike!' Jane shouted.

'Notch right.' I hurled the jet into another hard G-turn at ninety degrees to our previous course, trying to hide the jet in the radar clutter generated by the sea. Vibrations began at the wingtips and intensified as they travelled through the wings and fuselage, making the whole aircraft judder under the force of the turn. I held it until I heard, 'Screen clear,' from Jane, her voice straining with the effort of speaking under such heavy G.

I stayed on that course for a few more seconds, then swung back onto the intercept course for the enemy ships. There was no point in trying to disguise our target. There was nothing else there.

Every instinct told me to gain height and confront the Argentine jets, not hide among the radar clutter of the ocean surface, but our only targets were the two ships.

I was making frantic mental calculations, trying to work out if we would reach the guardship before the Migs could get visual with us. I thought we would just make it, but I also knew that the ship would already have been alerted. Every gun- and missile-crew would now be on station, raking the sky for a sight of us. Any hopes of a surprise attack had gone.

My thoughts were again interrupted by the radar warner. 'Spike! Spike!'

'Break right. Chaff.'

Jane punched the button and I caught a sparkle of light

from the corner of my eye as clouds of silver foil billowed out in our wake from the dispensers beneath the wingtips.

In air combat I had discovered there was little time for fear, my attention fully occupied by the adrenalin surge of combat and the physical effort of fighting the jet, trying to outwit my opponent, attack him as he was attacking me.

Now I felt helpless, pinned to the surface of the ocean, trying to hold my concentration on the attack against the guardship and ignore the threat from the jets above us.

'Missile! Ten o'clock.'

I swung my gaze frantically left and caught a glimpse of a white trail in the sky. 'Chaff! Chaff!' I pushed the nose down even further until the wind whipping the caps of the waves caused the canopy to be covered with spray.

I held my breath and waited for the missile. There was an eruption from behind and below us, a water-spout spiralling up into the air. The missile had lost its lock and impacted with the sea a bare 400 yards away. I exhaled with relief and eased the stick back a touch, lifting us a few more feet above the waves.

'Target twenty-five miles. In your eleven. Locking it up.'

I nudged the stick left a little. Jane's voice sounded cool and assured, as if the water-splash had been no more than a whale sounding.

The dawn had crept steadily around the horizon. Even due west, the lowering sky was now brighter, flecked with long streaks of cloud reddening in the sunlight.

'Twenty miles, on your nose.'

I stared ahead, through the green target box, straining my eyes. Through the curtain of sea-spray, I glimpsed the dark shapes of the two Tempests weaving over the wave tops. I could see nothing beyond them but empty sea and sky.

I glanced at the tactical display. Our aircraft symbols began to diverge as we split for the attack, approaching the target from different directions in the hope of confusing the defenders. Our attack runs would be separated by thirty seconds, the minimum time to allow the shrapnel from the previous jet's bombs to disperse before the next one overflew the target. Any closer and we would be flying through an airborne cloud of razor-edged metal fragments.

'Fifteen miles.'

I strained my eyes again. We were less than ninety seconds flying time from it. Then I saw a smudge of smoke, a darker streak against the grey of the sky. 'Yes! Visual.' The green target symbols glowed in the Head-up Display in front of me. They danced before my eyes as the jet bucked and tossed in the turbulence of the gusting winds.

'Range ten miles, speed 600 knots, height fifty feet. Time to target sixty seconds.'

Two miles ahead, Noel was already rising from the surface to 150 feet, skimming the superstructure of the guardship, his finger poised on the bomb release. The sky ahead of us lit up. Missiles, tracer and a barrage of Triple-A flashed upwards.

Then there was a brighter flash and a cloud of smoke and steam. It was impossible to tell what caused it.

A few seconds later, I saw the dark shape of Shark's jet streaking over the ship. A tiny black oval detached itself from the jet, arcing down towards the sea. In its path I could see the superstructure of the guardship, stark against the sky. There were more missile streaks and a barrage of Triple-A, then a blast and gouts of belching black smoke.

'Strike one! Shark's hit it,' Jane yelled.

His jet was now almost invisible, hidden by the barrage of anti-aircraft fire. I watched it sweeping towards me over the surface of the sea, a typhoon of fire and smoke. It seemed impossible that anything could fly through it unscathed. I focused my gaze on the HUD, trying to blank my mind to what was waiting ahead.

'Range coming down.'

'Stick top's live, speed's good, timing's good, height's good.'

'Target's slightly left,' Jane said. 'Got it?'

'Locked on, looking good, looking good.'

The green symbol in the HUD crept towards the target mark. I hauled back on the stick, the throttles jammed against the stops. 'Committing, committing . . .' The green symbols merged into one and I stabbed the firing button.

There was a momentary delay – although I committed the weapon to fire, the computer chose the perfect moment to launch the bomb – then the jet lurched as 1,000 pounds of high explosive came off the rail, backed by all the velocity that our 600-knot speed could provide.

As we flew through the barrage of flak, I threw us into a screaming dive, away from danger. The horizon disappeared for a moment and my head was locked against the side of the canopy by the G-force. I eased the pressure on the stick a fraction and craned my neck to look back towards the target. Then the whole world seemed to erupt in a blizzard of fire.

'Chaff! Flares!' I banked hard left and forced the nose down again, gaining speed and bringing me closer to the safety of the sea. Torrents of fire followed me as I jinked and swerved, hurling the jet around.

There was a crack and a hole the size of a telephone directory was punched in the wing. I felt the drag and the vibration as the jet wallowed, then flew on as the fly-by-wire system corrected the instability.

'Missile launch!'

'Chaff. Flares. Chaff. Break left.' I hauled the jet into a screaming turn so close to the waves I could see the thin sheen of oil glistening on the surface.

'Break right. Chaff. Flares.' I hurled the jet the other way. The groan from Jane, the thud of her helmet against the side of the canopy and the sound of flares punching out from the rack came simultaneously. There was a flash of grey-white and a missile streaked towards us, so close it seemed impossible that its proximity fuse wouldn't detonate. Then it had flashed past, disappearing towards the horizon. There was no time for thought, every move was an instinctive, animal reaction to danger.

'Spike! Spike! Bogie, two o'clock high. On you! On you!'

'Where is he?' I cranked my head round, searching the sky.

'Coming down on you. In your two. On you!'

The Migs were returning to the attack. I took a deep breath and held the jet in straight and level flight.

'What the fuck are you doing?' Jane said. 'Let's get out of here.'

'It's too late to evade, we're too low and slow. I'm going to try to make him think we haven't seen him.'

'You're what? Shit. Three miles.'

I armed the Sidewinder, its familiar growling almost drowned in the shriek of the radar warner. I pushed the seeker-head as far right as it would go and then held my breath. I kept my head rigid, tracking the enemy jets with my eyes, as if even the faintest movement of my head in the cockpit would alert them.

The Mig pilot would want to make sure of his kill, holding his own heat-seeking missile shot until . . .

'Chaff, flares.' I ripped the throttles back, trying to mask the heat-source of our engines from the enemy's missile, and swung the jet hard right to face up to him, fighting the encroaching grey-out. I counted to three, then pushed the throttles forward again, against the stops.

The Mig loomed in the canopy, screeching towards us. I saw a missile leap from it and thrash across the sky, but the bone-crushing break, the chaff and flares had done enough. It slid past our nose, then the dark batwing shape of the Mig itself was upon us, so close its shadow darkened the canopy. The Tempest bucked in its jetwash, then it was past.

As the Mig hit our wake, it suddenly slipped sideways and nose-dived as the pilot lost control. At low-level, there was no escape. It hit the sea, exploding in a ball of flame and spray.

Chapter 15

There was no time to spare the pilot a thought. 'Where's the other Mig?' For a moment I saw nothing, then I glimpsed a silver chevron against the dark grey of the sea. Two objects cartwheeled away in the wake of the jet, sparkling in the light.

'He's bugging out, heading for home,' Jane said. 'He's probably out of gas.'

I glanced down at our own fuel gauge. We were guzzling our spare fuel and could only spend a few more minutes in the area. I craned my neck round. 'Did we hit the target?'

'Yes. He's making a lot of smoke and losing speed.'

I risked pulling up a little higher above the surface to look back. Clouds of black smoke were billowing from the port side of the guardship forward of the bridge. 'We haven't sunk the bastard though—'

'Missile launch!'

A column of fire rose vertically from the destroyer, looped like a giant question mark and then arrowed away.

'Chaff. Flares. Break right.' I cursed myself for my stupidity. My curiosity to see the effects of my handiwork could have got us killed. As I swung the jet left and right, I forced my head round trying to locate the missile. I could see no trace of it. 'Where is it? Where the hell is it?'

'I don't know, I've lost it.'

The sweat was cold on my forehead as the seconds crawled by. There was a sudden blast in the sky ahead and to my right. One of the other Tempests disintegrated in a spray of fragments.

I felt sick as I thumbed the radio. 'Falcon One? Two?'

Infinitely weary, Noel's voice came up through the static. 'Shark's gone. He did his job though. The guardship's finished.'

I swung my head to look back at the ship. Black smoke was still billowing from it and it was now motionless in the water and listing heavily to port. Its last defiant shot had been the one that killed Shark.

The *Eva Peron* was already visible on the horizon. 'Let's get that cruiser.'

'What if they try to pick up survivors from the guardship?'

Noel's voice hardened. 'Then it'll be an easier target.'

I cut the radio connection. 'He won't be that, whatever happens.' The cruiser, like the guardship, was a former Royal Navy ship. In theory it was less well defended against air attack. It had no fixed surface-to-air missiles but it had a dozen Bofors guns and if the ship's armoury did not already include hand-held SAMs, the troops embarked on it were certain to have them. In any event, the sheer volume of fire that those troops could generate simply by standing on deck and firing into the air was enough to deter all but the bravest pilot. I had my doubts how well that description fitted me.

'Screen clear,' Jane said. 'At least their Air Force seems to be staying at home now.'

'I don't think they'd be so cautious if they knew that all we had left was two aircraft.'

We dropped back into low-level, flying line astern behind Noel and Rees, and again began the countdown, arming the weapons and checking off the height, speed and range as we closed with the target.

The *Eva Peron* was an intimidating sight, twice the length of its guardship, its profile bristling with gun turrets. As Rees set his jet rising from low-level to begin its attack run, smoke-bursts immediately dotted the sky ahead of us. Sparse at first, they increased until it seemed that the whole sky was filled with fire. I gulped a mouthful of air, swallowed, then eased the stick back to begin our own run.

'Eight seconds from target.'

I had been scared by the blizzards of fire above the guardship. What I now saw rising from the cruiser froze the pit of my stomach. The ship's five-inch guns opened up, pouring out a torrent of rounds at one second intervals, as precise as the ticking of a clock. Each one detonated in a clump of grey-black smoke. Around them were sparkling chains of flak-bursts and the blue, white, yellow and green of tracer.

Smoke from the bursts of Triple-A hung like a fog over the ship, but through the wraiths I could see the decks black with men, all of them firing upwards, creating a curtain of lead through which we would have to fly.

As the other jet disappeared into the heart of the inferno, I saw the SAM launches: one, two, three, half a dozen, maybe more, streaked upwards. 'Commit—' I could hear the fear in Rees' voice. 'Abort! Abort! Abort!'

Before he had finished speaking, I had jammed back the stick, pressing it flat against my stomach as I pulled the jet up and over, away from the danger. I was flying almost inverted, the canopy no more than fifty feet above the sea. I held combat power for a few more seconds, until the last bursts of Triple-A had faded behind us, then eased back the throttles.

'Falcon One?'

There was silence.

'He's still on the screen,' Jane said.

'Noel? Rees? Are you okay?'

For a moment there was only the hiss of static in reply, then I heard Rees' voice, slow and weak. 'I'm hit, Sean, my shoulder. But I'm okay, I think. Wait.'

I counted the seconds of silence until his voice came through again. 'We're going back in.'

'Let me lead it—'

He cut me off. 'Beginning attack run.'

Once more as his jet lifted from the surface in the climb to launch the attack, the sky erupted with bursts of Triple-A and small-arms fire. Two more SAMs were launched at him and he threw the jet left and right, dodging and weaving towards the target. Then he was through, banking steeply away as the bomb detonated. There was a vivid orange flash, a cloud of grey smoke and a huge waterspout erupted thirty yards from the side of the ship. A shock wave sped outwards through the sea.

I swore and thumped the side of the cockpit in my frustration. 'He's missed.'

'He had big balls even to try it with a wounded shoulder,' Jane said. 'Let's just make sure we make our own shot count.'

I lowered my gaze, peering into the HUD and began the attack run.

'Six seconds.'

The sky ahead erupted with smoke and fire.

'Height's good, speed's good.'

The green symbols on the screen moved together as slowly as grains of sand trickling down the face of a dune.

'Four seconds.'

Lines of tracer groped their way towards the jet.

'Looking good. Bringing the height up now.'

As we climbed from thirty to ninety feet to deliver the bomb, a SAM was launched, a black stove-pipe blasting upwards, trailing its guidance wire.

'Chaff. Flares.' The symbols blurred in the HUD as I threw the jet from side to side. 'Pod's active,' Jane called. The jamming system began an electronic battle with the missile's guidance. It slid towards us, then jerked away, blasting past the wingtip.

The HUD symbols cleared and coalesced. 'Committing.' I jabbed the button and the jet bucked immediately as the bomb came free. I pressed the Tempest down as the superstructure of the ship flashed beneath us, trying to ignore the hail of fire still thrashing the air around us. I craned my neck to stare down at the ship. I could see their soldiers staring upwards and I looked directly into the faces of the men I was trying to kill.

There was a pause, then the foredeck of the cruiser crumpled. There was a flash of red and yellow fire, a gout of black smoke and then a deafening roar.

I stilled Jane's whoop of triumph. 'It's not finished. We've done some damage but it's still making headway.' I pulled us up and away from the last pursuing bursts of Triple-A.

'What can we do? We can't sink it with Sidewinders.'

'We'll have to reload, refuel and come back.'

'Have we got time?'

'We don't have a choice.' I thumbed the radio. 'Returning to base.'

'Keep formation with me.' Rees' voice sounded even weaker.

Noel took over. 'We've got some damage. We're losing power and fuel and part of the wing's been shot away.' A moment later I heard him put out a Mayday call to base.

We sped away from the cruiser and out of immediate danger. I formated with the other jet and flew around it, assessing the damage. It was a frightening sight. The end of one wing had been ripped away like a shark bite out of a surfboard. The tail was also damaged and a thin plume of vapour – leaking fuel – was streaming from the wing. Lines of holes up the fuselage and through the canopy showed the track of the gunfire that had wounded Rees.

'What's your situation?'

There was a pause before he replied. 'We're fuel critical and it's a pig to keep straight and level. It would be a struggle even without the shoulder.'

'How bad is it?'

'Bad enough. I've staunched it as best as I can, but I'm still losing blood.'

'Hang in there. We'll be down in less than ten minutes.'

It was clear from his voice that he was already badly weakened by loss of blood, but there was nothing we could do to help him except to fly alongside, talking, cajoling and encouraging him.

As we crossed the coast of West Falkland we were rocked by the turbulence from the air rising up its sheer cliffs. I saw Rees' jet yaw dangerously and pulled a few more yards away from him to give him – and us – a bigger margin of safety.

Flying the crippled Tempest one-handed would be taking every ounce of strength he had. I offered a silent prayer that he would make it.

The Rapier site on Byron Heights swivelled to track us as we passed. At that moment I would have swapped every Rapier missile on the Falklands for one Sea Eagle.

The flight back to Mount Pleasant seemed to take for ever. Rees' jet constantly lurched and dipped, stumbling through the air like a drunk, while his voice grew fainter and weaker.

'Come on. Just two more minutes, we're over the Sound.'

'Yeah, s'all right,' he said, his words slow and slurred.

'Descend 500. Keep under the cloud layer ... Rees!'

'Yes ... Descending.'

At last I could see the runway ahead of us in the distance. 'We're on finals now.'

I saw the flaps inching out of his wings. There was an agonising pause before the landing-gear came down. Closer to the base, I could see the emergency vehicles lining the runway. I flew in with him, wing to wing. As we crossed the perimeter, his damaged wing dipped and almost clipped the fence. He levelled, over-corrected, and then levelled again.

The jet crossed the apron. It seemed to hover and then dropped like a brick, clouds of blue smoke bursting from the tyres. It bounced back into the air, then touched down once more. The thrust buckets deployed and I saw the nose dip as the brakes started to bite. Then we were past him.

I pulled a long left turn to bring us back to the start of the runway for our own approach. As soon as we ground to a halt on the apron outside the Tempest shack I hit the canopy release button. I scrambled out of the cockpit and ran towards the other jet, with Jane a half-pace behind me.

Rees was being lifted from the cockpit, his head slumped

forwards onto his chest. A dark stain had spread from his right shoulder down to his waist and his face was as grey as the sky. Noel remained in the back seat, his normally ruddy face pale.

The Boss stood nearby, watching Rees being carried to the ambulance. He went across and put an arm around Noel's shoulders as he finally made it down the ladder. Then he walked across to speak to the ground crew already clustered around our aircraft, and finally turned to us. 'An hour, Sean and Jane. Then we'll have you airborne again.'

The ambulance revved up and drove slowly away. He glanced at it, then back at us. 'I've been watching the whole thing on datalink. You've done brilliantly already, but ...' He paused, 'I don't need to tell you this, but you're the last chance we've got. It's up to you now.' He turned away.

I watched Noel for a minute, then walked over to him. 'Rees will be okay, Noel.'

He nodded. 'I know. It's the risk we take. But all the way back I've been wondering if he got hit because I fucked up somewhere along the line.'

'He got hit because he happened to be in the wrong place and copped a round or a piece of shrapnel, but your navigation didn't put him there. It's just the luck of the game.' I pointed to our wing. 'A few feet left and I'd have been the one bleeding ... or worse.' I paused, checking his expression. 'Noel? Are you fit to go back up?'

He turned to look at me, puzzled. 'You mean if the jet wasn't knackered and there was a pilot available? Why?'

I hesitated, then blurted it out. 'I want you in the back seat with me for this mission.'

He was silent for a moment, staring at me. 'I'm not stupid, Sean. I know what this is about. It's a very flattering vote of confidence but it would be a mistake.' His voice was sympathetic, but firm. 'This isn't about wanting me in the back seat, it's about wanting to keep Jane safe, isn't it?'

I looked away, but he'd already read the answer in my eyes. 'I'm sorry, Sean, but she has to go with you. She's a good nav, better than I am, and right now, that's the only thing that counts.'

I hesitated for a second, but I knew he was right.

He forced a smile.

'What was that about?' Jane said, as I walked back to her.

'Just making sure he's all right.'

'He's better than Shark and Jimmy, that's for sure.' She gave a slow shake of her head. 'Poor Shark. His premonition was right, wasn't it?'

We stood close together, not speaking, staring at the ground. I was bone-weary and soaked with sweat, and I shivered as the wind gusted around us. The Boss called us into the shelter of the Tempest shack as a Land Rover screeched to a halt and one of the cooks ran in with a Thermos of tea and some sandwiches. I sipped the scalding liquid and tried to eat one of the sandwiches, but it felt as dry as chalk in my mouth and I laid it aside.

The ground crew were swarming over the jet, pumping in fuel and opening the engine covers. I heard one curse as he fumbled with the oil filler cap and burned his arm on hot metal. Two more stripped the damaged panel from our wing and began replacing it with one from the unmarked left wing of Rees' jet. They sprinted to and fro between the Tempests, shouting to each other, cannibalising whatever parts they needed, or searching through the mounds of spares cluttering the sides of the shack. As they worked, the armourers hauled two iron bombs from the dump and loaded them into position under the wings. Finally, the ground-crew leader shouted and waved his hand towards the cockpit.

The Boss tapped his fingers against his leg and glanced at us once or twice, as if he had something to say, but was not sure how. His gaze flickered away again before it came to rest on us. 'I've no words left. You know what has to be done and how much we're counting on you. Good luck.' He turned aside and rubbed at his eyes, then walked away without looking back.

I put my arm round Jane's shoulders. 'Do you know what my mother said to me, when she saw me off at Brize? "Be careful, Sean, I've lost one son out there. I don't want to lose another." I'm not making a very good job of following her advice, am I?'

We walked over to the jet. She turned to face me at the foot of the steel ladder. 'Last time pays for all.'

I nodded. 'Crazy, isn't it? All those millions of pounds, all those troops and all that equipment, and in the end it comes down to just one jet and two people.'

Her wan, tired face creased in a smile. 'It'll be okay,' she said. 'I've been waiting for you too long to lose you now.' She touched my cheek with her gloved hand, then clambered up the ladder and began strapping in.

As soon as we were airborne again, Fortress flashed us an update on the cruiser's course and speed. The first bomb strike had slowed the ship a fraction, no more. It was still making eighteen knots. It would be in a position to start landing its troops inside four hours, long before Cobra Force could get here.

We flew north-west over the mountains and out over the sea. The cloud was now broken and patches of sunlight struck the water, turning from pewter to jade. Jane and I barely spoke, lost in our thoughts.

No serviceman or woman would willingly return to the scene of an earlier firefight; to do so was to push your luck one notch too far. Now we were doing it, heading back to where the wounded but still potent enemy lay in wait for us.

'Okay, Sean,' Jane said. 'Contact fifty miles, locked up. It's down to us.'

Even without the patches of sunlight throwing the cruiser into sharp relief, the black smoke still coiling upwards from its bomb wound was an unmistakable signpost.

'If the guys with the SAMs react like they did last time, they'll probably blast every missile they have on the first pass.' I could hear my voice shake as I said it.

'Sean? We'll do it. They can't stop us.'

Jane began calling the range, speed and bearings, as I pushed the throttles forward into combat power. The Tempest leapt forward, pinning me back into my seat. The attack sequence began again, like a recurring nightmare. The green symbols marched across the HUD, the sky above the ship erupted with Triple-A and small-arms fire and the flash of SAMs pierced the fog of smoke.

I kept the jet ducking and weaving in evasion, but returned again and again to the attack line. As we neared the ship, I fired the cannons. The jet shuddered and slowed a fraction. Plumes of water rose into the air as the first shells hit the sea. I held the button as the twin lines of fire bit through the waves, climbed the side of the ship and raked the deck.

It sent a few of the enemy troops scattering for cover, but the volume of return fire barely slackened. Rounds stitched lines across the wing and there was a rattle from the rear of the fuselage as shrapnel smacked into it. A caption lit up on the panel.

'Radar warner's gone,' Jane yelled.

The warning was almost lost among the cacophony. Then the symbols intersected in the HUD and I hit the bomb release.

There was the familiar heartstopping pause before it came off the pylon. The jet bucked up and away and I banked hard left, forcing my head round to watch for the impact. There was another crack and a round ripped into the bottom of the cockpit, tearing a hole through which cold air rushed in a torrent.

Then the bomb detonated. The cruiser's deck just aft of the bridge lifted then fell back. A cloud of smoke and steam poured from the gaping hole. I watched and waited, holding the turn as the seconds ticked by. Incredibly the ship seemed to have lost no headway at all. The wake stretching out behind it barely deviated from the straight track towards the Falklands.

'What the hell does it take to sink that thing!'

'Shit, shit, shit.'

'What is it?'

'The radar's out. That Triple-A must have punched a hole straight through it.'

I gave a weary shake of my head. When we trained on the ranges, we progressively degraded our equipment, one stage at a time, until we were left to drop bombs like a Second World War pilot, lining it up by eye and pressing the trigger. It was not a scenario I had ever envisaged having to use in combat.

I scanned the warning panel, thought for a moment, then hauled back on the stick, pulling the jet into a steep, climbing turn. We spiralled upwards, the rush of the clouds across the nose visibly slowing as we washed off speed and energy.

'What's the story?' Jane said.

'We're going to do this as a dive and put the next bomb straight into the same spot as the last one. If that doesn't stop it, nothing will.'

'It's a hell of a shot to take. We'll be sitting ducks up here.'

'Maybe, but I can't think of a better option, can you?'

There was no answer for a moment, then Jane yelled a warning. 'Two bogies, two o'clock high, descending.'

I cast a despairing glance towards the sky, then hauled the jet back and left, flicked back the safety cover and stabbed the firing button twice, sending the last two Sidewinders off the rails. Without a lock they were all but useless, but I hoped the launch would at least force the Argentine jets to manoeuvre and buy us a few more precious seconds.

I put the nose of the jet into a dive and jammed the throttles forward. 'We'll have to chance it. Commencing attack run. Chaff. Flares.'

The airspeed bulleted upwards as the altimeter unwound faster and faster. I could hear Jane punching out the chaff and flares as swiftly as her fingers could hit the buttons. My flesh crept. Without the radar warner the first sign of a missile launch against us might be the flash as it destroyed us.

The deadly blossoms of Triple-A began to open again ahead of us and the cruiser zoomed into focus, seeming to leap to meet us as we accelerated downwards in a screaming dive. Vibrations rocked and shook the jet.

'Bogies in your four ... In your five.'

'Arming stick top.' My right index finger rested lightly on the firing button. I tried to blank my mind to everything but the cross-hairs of my sights and the root of the column of steam and grey smoke rising from a jagged black hole just behind the bridge of the cruiser.

Ground fire and tracer ripped the air around us, and again

I heard the crack as rounds or shrapnel pierced the Tempest's thin skin. The airspeed was close to maximum, the altitude dropping like a stone.

'Five thousand feet ... four ... Bogies in your six. In your six!'

The cross-hairs met at last on the edge of the jagged hole. I squeezed the trigger and felt the lurch of the jet as the bomb came off, 1,000 pounds of high explosive, falling towards the cruiser at close to the speed of sound.

I heaved back on the stick and jerked hard right.

'Three thousand ... two ... one ...'

For a moment the blurring motion seemed to slow. I even had time to look into the eyes of the gunners on the deck. Then the whole world erupted in flame. There was a single massive explosion from the cruiser, then a series of blasts, one after another, ripping it apart. The port side of the ship blew open, the thick steel curling back like burnt paper. The doomed cruiser wallowed, its wake turning back on itself as it circled, helpless. Then a massive cloud of steam engulfed the whole superstructure, as seawater poured in through the rent in the side.

The bridge began to rise into the air. The steel prow sliced through one wave, buried itself in the next and never rose again. The whole forepart of the cruiser disappeared, plunging beneath the water as the ship broke its spine.

The stern section remained afloat a few seconds longer, then it turned turtle and slowly slipped beneath the waves. A vast bubble of air broke surface a few moments later, then there was nothing but a steadily widening circle of thick, black, viscous oil.

A heartbeat later I heard Jane's warning cry. 'Missile lau—'
There was a blinding flash and a roar. I grabbed for the handle
beneath my seat and heaved. I felt the straps lashing tight around
me and then the blast and the headlong surge. A sharp edge
slashed my cheek and I felt a burning pain as the ejector seat
was hurled up into the air.

Chapter 16

I hit the water with a jolt that felt like solid ground. Then I plunged under, fumbling with the chute release on my chest as I sank lower and lower. There was a roaring in my ears. I looked up towards the pale green light of the surface in despair, then there was a crack as my lifejacket inflated. The yellow collar swelled around me and I felt myself propelled upwards.

I burst above the surface gasping for breath. I swivelled my head from side to side, but could see nothing for a moment as I lay in the trough of a wave. Then the swell pushed me upwards and I saw the yellow life-raft a few yards away. I hauled on the cord attached to my lifejacket and pulled myself over to it.

I hung panting from the side of the raft for a moment, salt water stinging the gash in my cheek, then I dragged myself over the side. I got to my knees and began searching frantically for Jane. She was floating, half-submerged, in the water twenty yards away, tangled in her chute.

I dug the paddle into the water, battling against the waves. It took an age to cover the few yards to her, my muscles screaming with the effort. I leaned over the side, grasped her hand and began to pull her upwards. She was banging at the chute release on her chest as water slopped over her face.

She choked and spat. 'The chute. I can't get it free.'

Still holding her with one hand, I reached for the button and pressed and twisted it, my fingers clumsy in the icy cold, but it was jammed solid.

'It'll be all right, Jane.' I tried to keep the panic from my voice, but felt the strain on my arm increase as seawater flooded the billowing chute and pushed it beneath the waves.

The weight of it dragged at Jane and I saw the terror in her eyes. I ripped my right glove off with my teeth and again tore at the harness, my fingers starting to bleed, while still holding her grimly with my other hand. She sank lower in the water, more and more waves breaking over her head.

I dragged her back towards the raft. 'Hold on.'

She spat the water from her mouth and shook her head. 'Let me go, Sean. You've got to let me go ...'

'NO!' I pulled the survival knife from my jacket and began slashing at her harness straps, struggling desperately to keep a grip on her arm as I did so. Then the harness twisted as another wave slapped against the raft. The knife slipped from my frozen fingers and disappeared into the depths, glittering mockingly as it dropped from sight.

Her words echoed in my head: 'I've been waiting for you too long to lose you now ...'

I swung back, seized the harness again and hauled on it with my last reserves of strength. Jane's face came clear of the water again, but her lips were already turning blue. She gave me a look of infinite sadness. 'My suit's split, Sean, it's leaking. You can't save me. Let me go.'

I made a final convulsive attempt to drag her into the boat, but raised her barely six inches from the water. I slumped back across the side of the raft, almost falling into the sea myself. My left hand lost its grip on the harness, but I still held Jane's hand with my right.

She gazed into my eyes as I felt her fingers slipping from mine.

I made a last despairing grab to try and hold her, but my fingers closed around nothing. She was already gone, sinking beneath the waves, the parachute wrapping itself around her like a shroud.

I stared into the green water, as if expecting her to rise back from the depths, but I was alone with the wind and the sea. I fell back and lay in the bottom of the raft, not caring where the sea took me or whether I lived or died.

The last hope of rescue faded with the light. I could feel the cold creeping up on me, and weakened by two days on the run I knew that I would not last the night.

I almost welcomed the weariness that crept over me. I no longer felt the cold. I smiled to myself and almost laughed. I recognised the euphoria for what it was, the onset of the hypothermia that would kill me, but I no longer cared. I lay back and closed my eyes, my consciousness fading in time with the rhythmic slap of the waves against the raft.

I was back on the hilltop as the same faceless, predatory figures advanced through the darkness towards me. I looked down the slope. The others – Mike, Geoff, Rose and Jane – had left me now. I had to stand against the advancing figures alone.

They came closer and closer. Their faces were still hidden by the black shadows of their steel helmets, but I knew who they were. The wind around them carried the stench of death. I gagged and choked. They stopped and stood in a half-circle, facing me. Then they raised their rifles and pointed them at my heart.

There was a movement at the periphery of my vision. Mike was walking towards me, the wind ruffling his fair hair. He was wearing his Para uniform and red beret. He stopped next to me and gave me a quizzical look, his head angled slightly to one side and the smile I remembered so well playing around his lips.

I reached out a hand towards him. He looked at the dark figures, then back at me and shook his head. He took my arm and pushed me gently behind him. Then I heard gunfire and saw his body crumple and fall.

The figures had disappeared. I stood alone on the hilltop, with the body of my brother lying at my feet. The smile was still on his face. I stared down at him, still hearing the fading echoes of their gunshots.

Then I heard another sound, faint at first, a rough chopping noise just audible above the relentless cry of the wind. A glow lit the night sky and the noise grew louder. Fierce, brilliant light beat down on the raft as the helicopter's rotors thrashed the surface of the ocean into spray.

A shadow blotted out the light. There was a thump as a pair of boots kicked at the raft and then dropped inside. I raised my head wearily and peered into the blinding light. 'English air crew. Aviatores Ingles.'

'Yeah, we fucking know that,' a Cockney voice said. 'That's why we're here.'

Epilogue

As I walked out towards the Tristar, I glanced around me. Everywhere I looked there were scorched and damaged buildings. At the far end of the runway I could see the tangled wreckage of several Tempests, bulldozed to one side to clear the area for the Cobra Force squadrons. Most of the jets were drawn up in the open and would remain there until the shacks had been repaired.

There was a movement to my right and I saw a tall, slim figure in the viewing area next to the tower. We stood for a moment in silence, studying each other. The wind and the cold had brought the faintest touch of colour to her pale cheeks, but the eyes remained shadowed and tired.

I walked over to her. 'Rose, how are you?'

'I'm fine.'

She reached out a hand and traced the line of the scar

on my cheek. 'Two heroes in one family. There'll be quite a celebration for you back home.'

'I hope not. I don't feel there's too much to celebrate.'

'I – I was sorry to hear about Jane.'

I nodded, not trusting my voice.

We both fell silent again.

'Will you come back?' she said suddenly, keeping her eyes fixed on the ground.

'I don't know. One day, perhaps.'

She gave a brief, sad smile. 'That means no.'

'It means, I don't know. If I stay in the Air Force, the decision may be made for me.' I paused. 'How's Bernard?'

'He's fine. Busy. Did you know we were buying George and Agnes's place?'

'No, I didn't. That's good, they would have liked that.'

'We'll keep our own land too. It'll be a fair-sized farm, though a lot more work as well.' A shadow crossed her face, then her expression brightened. 'I'm going to England myself next year – part of the famous social ventilation programme.'

'That's great. Will Bernard go too?'

'If he can tear himself away.' She gave a shy smile. 'Can I come and visit you in England?'

'Of course. It would be great to see you. Both of you.' I looked around. The last of the other passengers had disappeared up the steps of the Tristar. 'I have to go.'

She nodded, then leaned forward to kiss me. Her arms tightened around my neck for a moment, then she stood back, a tear shining in her eye. 'Goodbye, Sean.'

I felt her eyes still on me as I walked across the runway, its surface marked by fresh repairs. At the top of the aircraft steps I glanced back. She raised her hand to wave, but then her face crumpled and she turned away to hide her tears.

I looked out of the window as the Tristar taxied out towards the end of the runway. The long dark lines of the hills were mottled with purple and grey, and to the south the flatlands shone silver as sunlight sparkled on the water of a thousand tarns and streams. Tendrils of morning mist still clung to the hillsides like wraiths.

A moment later, the sun was gone and cloud was streaming in on the wind from the west. The sky darkened and the plane rocked and shuddered as a sudden squall blew through the airfield and hail rattled against the fuselage. The engines wound up to a scream and the Tristar began to rumble down the runway.

I stared out at the new white-fenced enclosure on the hillside, glistening in the rain. The Falklands had a few more graves, a couple more memorials. I'd shed one of the ghosts from my past, only to come under the spell of another. I knew this one would haunt me forever.